...verp ... Septe...ber 1943. Her ... Day when Lyn was just nine months old. ...er ...s three her mother Monica married Frank Moore, who be... 'Dad' to the little girl. Lyn was brought up in Liverpool and became a secretary before marrying policeman Bob Andrews. In 1970 Lyn gave birth to triplets – two sons and a daughter – who kept her busy for the next few years. Once they'd gone to school Lyn began writing, and her first novel was quickly accepted for publication.

Lyn lived for eleven years in Ireland and is now resident on the Isle of Man, but spends as much time as possible back on Merseyside, seeing her children and four grandchildren.

Praise for Lyn Andrews' dramatic Merseyside novels:

'An outstanding storyteller' *Woman's Weekly*

'The Catherine Cookson of Liverpool' *Northern Echo*

'Gutsy ... A vivid picture of a hard-up, hard-working community ... will keep the pages turning' *Daily Express*

'A vivid portrayal of life' *Best*

'An indisputably gifted storyteller ... warm-hearted and poignant' *Historical Novels Review*

'A compelling read' *Woman's Own*

'Plenty of realism and if you enjoy wartime sagas this one will please' *Nottingham Evening Post*

'A page-turning and beautifully written novel' *Irish World*

Lyn Andrews

Liverpool Sisters

HEADLINE

First published in Great Britain in 2016 by
HEADLINE PUBLISHING GROUP

First published in paperback in Great Britain in 2017 by
HEADLINE PUBLISHING GROUP

1

Cataloguing in Publication Data is available from the British Library

ISBN 978 1 4722 2869 7

Typeset in Janson by Avon DataSet Ltd, Bidford-on-Avon, Warwickshire

Printed and bound in Great Britain by Clays Ltd, St Ives plc

MIX
Paper from
responsible sources
FSC
www.fsc.org   FSC® C104740

Headline's policy is to use papers that are natural, renewable and recyclable
products and made from wood grown in well-managed forests and other
controlled sources. The logging and manufacturing processes are expected to
conform to the environmental regulations of the country of origin.

HEADLINE PUBLISHING GROUP
An Hachette UK Company
Carmelite House
50 Victoria Embankment
London EC4Y 0DZ

www.headline.co.uk
www.hachette.co.uk

Author's Note

Although the Goodwin family is fictitious, Olivia was inspired by my great-aunt Rose Gorry, who was a suffragette. This is in part her story and that of her family: William and Mary Gorry, her parents; Mary (née O'Donnell), her stepmother; and Ellen, her younger sister and my grandmother. It's a story of courage, determination, tragedy, ruthless ambition, callousness, love and hope, which I hope you will enjoy.

I would like to dedicate *Liverpool Sisters* to Margaret McMahon, who has possibly the most optimistic outlook on life of anyone I have ever known and whose cheerfulness and encouragement I value greatly. Thank you Margaret for your friendship, you are a joy to know.

Acknowledgements

There are many wonderful people who contribute to the success of a novel, sharing their years of experience and sound advice with the author, and I would like to thank them all. Particularly Jane Morpeth, Headline's truly amazing Chair; Anne Williams, my agent; Marion Donaldson, my editor; Richenda Todd, my copy-editor; Jo Liddiard and Caitlin Raynor in Marketing and Publicity and their teams; and those who work so hard in Sales; and also to Hannah Wann, Marion's Editorial Assistant, for her patience with my IT 'blips'!

Lyn Andrews
2016

Part One

Part One

Chapter One

1907

'It's like closing the door on our old life, isn't it, Mam?' Olivia Goodwin remarked, smiling at her mother as they stood on the worn stone doorstep of their terraced house. There was a note of wistfulness in her voice, however, for it was no longer *their* house.

Edith smiled back ruefully at her eldest daughter, thinking how at sixteen Livvie – as she'd been called from babyhood – resembled herself at that age. The same thick, light chestnut hair which waved naturally, the clear grey eyes and fair complexion, the same slender build – although her height she'd inherited from her father. And Livvie was right; they *were* closing the door on their old life. Number 11 Minerva Street off Everton Brow had been her home for most of her married life. The houses were old, early-Victorian terraced villas with a yard at the back and were far from what could be termed spacious, having only a kitchen, scullery and a parlour

3

downstairs and two bedrooms upstairs. They were not the easiest to keep clean either for they opened directly on to the street, but it had been 'home'.

She reached up to the brass door knocker, highly polished as usual, and gave it a slight push to ensure the door was firmly shut, before turning away. A frisson of regret washed over her at this final moment of departure. When they'd first come to live here they hadn't had much, just the very basic necessities really, but gradually over the years they'd acquired more and better quality furniture for her husband Thomas's efforts to raise their standard of living had been nothing short of superhuman. Now he'd decreed that this house – and indeed this area – was no longer at all suitable for their status and income and she'd been given little choice but to agree, but she was sad to leave this house behind for another family to move into for she was leaving so many memories behind too.

Both Livvie and her younger sister Amy had been born here, and here too she'd suffered the loss of her baby boys, both stillborn. Two boys whose tragic loss Thomas had bitterly regretted and railed against, while she had mourned them silently and stoically, knowing these things all too often happened.

'I suppose it *is* like leaving our old life, Livvie, but we should look on it as a new beginning – a blessing, in fact. Your pa's worked so hard so that we can all enjoy a better, a more comfortable life.' Her gaze took in the smartly tailored pale grey three-quarter-length coat edged with black braid that Livvie wore over a matching skirt that reached to her ankles, revealing black leather buttoned boots, and the large-brimmed, elegant hat that covered her daughter's upswept hair. At sixteen Livvie was classed as 'grown up' and was now dressed accordingly, but she, Edith, had never had such clothes at her daughter's age; she'd possessed a jacket for Sunday best but she'd had to make do with a shawl for everyday use. Yes, thanks to Tom's efforts they'd definitely come up in the world.

Livvie took her mother's arm as they stepped on to the pavement, slowly nodding her agreement. She knew she should be delighted, excited even – after all, they were moving to a much nicer area and a much bigger and grander house – but she wasn't. She felt very apprehensive. She knew all their neighbours here and she'd grown up with all of the kids; would they fit in in the new neighbourhood? Would they be welcomed and accepted or would they be looked down on and shunned? Despite her mother's optimistic cheerfulness she knew that Edith was feeling apprehensive too and was also suffering the wrench of having to leave friends and neighbours of many years standing.

She glanced down the street for the last time, seeing a couple of women standing on their doorsteps despite the raw cold of the October morning. Most of their farewells had taken place yesterday but those few stalwarts were watching the proceedings with avid curiosity for the Goodwins' furniture and possessions had all been loaded into the removal van her father had hired at some expense. He'd said it wouldn't be at all seemly or dignified for them to arrive in the new neighbourhood with everything piled haphazardly on to the back of a horse-drawn cart. These days her pa seemed to set great store on what he considered 'dignified', she thought. In the past when people had come into or left Minerva Street their possessions had been transported on a cart or, if they had virtually nothing, moved on a hand cart.

Her father was urging her mother and sister into the hired hackney which was to transport them to their new home.

'Livvie, stop dawdling! We don't have all day!' Thomas Goodwin's tone had a sharp note of irritability.

'Coming, Pa,' Livvie replied, casting a last glance over her former home and raising a hand to wave goodbye to the watching neighbours, before hurrying across to the hackney and climbing in, settling herself beside her sister, who appeared to be quite excited.

'Well, that's goodbye to Everton Brow and I can't say I'm sorry to be leaving all those narrow, dirty old streets behind,' Thomas stated with some satisfaction as the vehicle moved slowly off.

Edith managed a smile. 'Oh, I wouldn't say that, Tom. We had some happy times there.'

'And some that were not so happy either, Edith. No, life for us all will be far better from now on.' He brushed an imaginary speck of dust from the sleeve of his coat. 'I've achieved what I set out to do, what I always *intended* to do. Make my way in the world – in society – have my own business and a home in a respectable, affluent area.'

Edith nodded slowly. Yes, that had always been his ambition in life; he'd grasped every opportunity that had presented itself and had worked long hours, never sparing himself in his efforts to achieve that goal. Middle-aged though he now undoubtedly was, he was still what she considered to be a handsome man. He'd not put on weight, his bearing was still upright and almost military and even the fact that his once dark hair was now turning grey suited him. It made him look distinguished, she thought. His suit was of a good quality woollen cloth and his dark overcoat well cut, his bowler hat brushed to sleekness. In all he was the picture of a successful man, she mused with some pride. Oh, he wasn't the easiest of men to live with these days; she had to admit that. As he'd grown older he'd been spurred on by ambition and he'd become acutely aware of his shortcomings and strove to overcome them, developing a profound sense of 'decorum' which she thought sometimes bordered on the obsessional. At times he could be dictatorial and overbearing and he'd never been a very demonstrative man but she'd learned to accept all that. He was a good husband and father.

As the hackney made its way along the main thoroughfare out of Everton and towards the quieter, leafier suburbs of the city, Edith shifted her position slightly to try to ease the ache in her back. Thomas was now the successful businessman he'd striven so hard to be. He owned and operated a small factory situated on the Dock Road which made cakes of cattle food and next year he hoped to expand. A little smile hovered around the corners of her mouth. Well, cattle and what they consumed was something he had experience of for when she'd met him he was newly come to Liverpool from a small farm on the lower slopes of Pendle Hill in east Lancashire. His father had only been a tenant farmer and Tom had been one of six children, three of them boys. So, with no hope of ever owning any land of his own, he'd come seeking his fortune in Liverpool. Basically he'd just been a poor agricultural labourer, he'd told her, but he intended to change all that. He wasn't going to remain poor all his life and by dint of sheer hard work, thrift, some instances of good luck, a few risks and an inborn shrewdness and determination he'd done what he set out to do. Oh, there had been times when she'd barely seen him for he'd worked such long hours; times when she'd had to keep the home going and bring up the children virtually by herself, but she hadn't minded that for when the dilapidated building on the Dock Estate had become vacant he'd had enough money to rent it, do some renovations and start producing the oil-based cattle cake that his grandfather had first devised but never had the time or money to develop. In time he'd managed to buy the building at a nominal cost and to employ more workers. How could she demand that he spend more time with them when all his hard work was for their benefit? She shifted her position again, frowning a little at the discomfort.

'Mam, are you all right?' Livvie asked, having been watching her mother closely and thinking she looked a bit pale and tired. Both Amy and her father seemed more interested in watching the activities taking place on the city streets they were passing through.

'Yes. Just a little . . . discomfort, that's all. It's nothing to worry about. It's only to be expected. '

Livvie nodded although she wasn't totally convinced. There were times lately when she worried about her mam. At thirty-nine Edith Goodwin was too old to be expecting another child, according to Mrs Agnew from next door in Minerva Street. Everyone knew it could cause all kinds of complications for a woman of her age, so their neighbour had said, and her daughter Peggy – being the same age as Livvie – had repeated her mother's remarks. They had all been very surprised to learn of Mam's condition but she hadn't been worried until Mrs Agnew's pronouncement. Of course Mam still had four more months to go and she'd been fine so far but Livvie intended to make sure that she didn't over-exert herself with this move – and Amy could just do more to help as well, she vowed.

'Well, you'll have to rest and not go pulling and dragging things . . .'

'Olivia, there will be absolutely no necessity for your mother to "pull and drag" anything. Haven't I instructed two of my labourers to be on hand for such heavy tasks?' her father stated sharply, annoyed by his daughter's remark. Did Livvie have no sense of respect and decorum? She was only sixteen and should know better than to be issuing instructions to her mother. He frowned. He was determined that Edith should not exert herself during this pregnancy. He had been astounded, almost stunned when she'd told him the news, but as soon as he'd realised that there was still a chance that he could have a son to inherit the business he'd built up, he'd vowed that she would have the best care and attention he could afford.

He looked closely at his daughters; they were attractive girls, both with their mother's looks, although Amy at thirteen would never be as tall or as slim as Livvie and was inclined to pettishness if she didn't get her own way. Livvie he had to admit had inherited his stubborn determination, which he did not view as an asset in a girl, but he hoped to find suitable husbands for them both when the time came for he could never envisage either of them being capable of running a business. Indeed 'commerce' could not remotely be considered women's work. However, with a son . . . that would be a very different matter. A sense of satisfaction crept over him the closer to their new home they drew. If Edith presented him with a healthy boy he would indeed be a contented man.

Livvie had said nothing in reply to her father's rebuke but, like her sister, resorted to gazing out of the window and wondering just what the coming weeks and months held in store for them all. After Mam had had the baby Livvie knew she would be required to help more but she didn't mind that. Amy would continue attending school, something Pa had insisted upon. Her sister could leave at fourteen but as it appeared Pa did not intend either of them to have to work for a living, Amy would stay on until she was fifteen. That suited Livvie, she thought, for her sister could be lazy and resorted to sulking if she didn't get her own way. Mam said, regretfully, that she'd tended to spoil Amy, she having been born after the two poor little boys. Livvie smiled to herself. She was looking forward to having a new sister or brother and wondered what it would be like having a baby in the house after all this time?

Edith touched her husband's arm. 'How much further is it?'

He smiled at her and patted her hand. 'About five minutes, that's all.'

Edith smiled back; she would be relieved to get out of the vehicle for the cobbled roads did not make for a smooth journey. Of course she'd seen the house that was to be their new home, Tom had taken her on two occasions, but she wished she'd spent longer there for she couldn't remember the exact layout. Of course it had been big, much bigger than their old home, and it had a garden both at the front and the rear and there were steps leading up to the front door, but she frowned as she tried to remember where the dining room and parlour were in relation to the kitchen, scullery and larder. Of course there would be plenty to do when they arrived, even though two of Tom's men would be on hand to deal with the heavy furniture and carpets, but the girls would help her unpack and she hoped that by this evening the beds would at least be up and made and that there would be a hot meal of some description on the table.

As both the removal van and the hackney drew up outside the imposing house in the aptly named Poplar Avenue, a wide quiet road lined with trees, both girls got out and looked around while Thomas helped Edith to alight. They'd not been here before but their mother had described it to them.

'It looks very big and . . . posh!' Amy muttered to her sister as she stared at the house, beginning to feel rather out of her depth.

'It's certainly a lot bigger than our old house but while it seems a nice street, I wouldn't really call it "posh", Amy. I mean it's not Rodney Street or Abercrombie Square or anywhere like that; they really *are* posh.'

'Oh, you know what I mean, Livvie. I wonder are there any girls of our ages living nearby?'

'I expect so but if not then at least you're bound to make new friends at school.'

Amy didn't look convinced. She wasn't looking forward to starting a new school, not at her age. In fact she couldn't see why she had to go to school at all after her next birthday; surely she'd be better off at home, helping Mam, like Livvie? It was something she had more than once mentioned to her father but it had been dismissed out of hand and even sulking about

11

it for days had availed her nothing. Pa had stated firmly that she would finish her education like other well-brought-up girls did.

Thomas became businesslike. 'Right, let's go inside. There is no sense us all standing out here on the pavement,' he urged. After paying the driver of the hackney, he shepherded them up the long path and towards the steps that led up to the ornate front door with the elaborate brass knocker in the shape of a lion's head.

The van driver and his mate began to prepare to unload their furniture as two of Thomas's burly labourers emerged from the back of the house to help.

As they entered the wide hallway with the ornate – but empty – plate rack which ran around the walls a foot below the coved ceiling, Livvie shivered. 'It's so cold in here!' she exclaimed, rubbing her hands together. A pervasive heavy chill seemed to hang over the room.

'Of course it's cold, it's been empty for over a month!' her father remarked brusquely.

'It won't take long to get the fires going and then it will soon warm up,' Edith added firmly, although she realised that Livvie was right. It *was* cold and the air felt damp, something she hadn't noticed on her previous visits, but then that had been at the end of summer and now it was well into autumn. Determined not to show any sign of dismay she purposefully crossed the hall and opened the door to the parlour. 'Isn't this a lovely big, light and airy room? Won't it be just great for us all to be able to sit in here after supper and not feel as though we're crowded on top of each other? Now, first things first. Tom, if you'd ask the men to bring in some wood and coal we'll get the fires lit and then if they take the beds upstairs and assemble them we'll start to bring in the smaller boxes and unpack them.'

Livvie glanced surreptitiously at Amy; there was an awful lot to do before any of them could hope to feel as comfortable in this house as they had in their old one and she wasn't going to let her sister shirk her share of the work.

'I'm not sure if I'm going to like it here, Livvie,' Amy confided as they followed Edith back outside. Initially she had been excited but now she wasn't so sure – and there did seem to be a lot of work involved in moving house.

'Oh, don't go saying things like that or you'll upset Mam!' Livvie hissed. 'Besides, we've got no choice in the matter. This is our home now and we've got to give it a fair chance.'

'It might be bigger and grander but it's not as warm and welcoming. In fact that hall feels cold and . . . creepy!' Amy persisted sulkily.

Livvie gripped her arm. 'Stop that! There's nothing creepy about it. It's just cold. It'll be fine once we've got it warmed up and have all our own things around us.' They'd reached the pile of boxes being stacked on the front lawn. 'Now, you take one of those and I'll take another. Mam's marked them "Kitchen", so they're probably pans and stuff. It's going to be a long day, Amy, but we've got to help Mam as much as we can.'

Amy sniffed. 'I wish Pa had accepted Mrs Agnew and their Peggy's offer to help us out today.'

'So do I but he didn't so we'll just have to get on with it ourselves,' Livvie replied firmly.

Amy said nothing but she still felt there was something

disturbing about this house and began to wish they'd stayed in number 11 Minerva Street.

Livvie shrugged, determined not to be dismayed by her sister's pessimistic mood. After all, this was their new home, their new life and, only seven years into the new century, they were living in a modern era. Things couldn't just stay the same for ever, could they?

Chapter Two

———◆———

Those first few days had been chaotic despite all their efforts, Livvie thought at the end of the week as she sat on the edge of her bed staring aimlessly out of the window overlooking the garden at the back of the house. The lawn, the empty flower beds and the bare, skeletal branches of the trees and shrubs were shrouded by the deepening gloom of early evening but even in daylight she thought they looked dismal and forlorn. Still, no doubt in summer she would view the garden in a different light and it would be pleasant to sit out there in the evenings. They'd only had a small yard in their old house, enclosed by soot-blackened walls, definitely not conducive to sitting in.

To the delight and satisfaction of her father they had been invited for supper this evening to the Mayhews' house next door but neither she nor Amy were really looking forward to it for they had not met their neighbours in person yet.

Her mother had been somewhat surprised when the hand-written invitation had arrived. 'I wonder why Mrs Mayhew didn't just call to invite us? It would have been easier – it would have broken the ice so to speak. This is all a bit . . . formal.'

Her father had peered over his newspaper. 'Obviously that's not the way things are done here, Edith. I doubt there will be all the running in and out of people's houses by the minutes as there was in Everton. People here seem to respect each other's privacy more. You'd better reply in writing too. Tell her we'll be delighted,' he'd instructed before returning to his reading. Her mother had nodded and replied, smiling a little ruefully and thinking that at least it would be a nice change to enjoy a meal in a comfortable and well-ordered house.

By their second day in number 7 Poplar Avenue they'd all realised that their furniture and possessions, which had seemed considerable in Minerva Street, looked rather sparse in this much larger house and her father had stated that they would have to remedy that in the very near future.

Of course both Livvie and Amy were delighted that they now had a bedroom of their own instead of having to share one, although like the rest of the house the rooms appeared only half furnished. There were in fact four bedrooms and it had been decided that the fourth and smallest one would become the nursery. In addition there were two decent-sized rooms in the attic. At least the place was now warmer than when they'd first arrived, although Livvie felt that the hall still maintained its cold and rather gloomy atmosphere. Her mam had professed that she was delighted with the large and well-equipped kitchen, the practical scullery and spacious pantry. There was even a separate wash house with a copper boiler so there would be no need to boil and carry water out to the yard to fill the dolly tub, although Mam would be sending many items to the laundry now on her father's instructions. The house boasted both hot and cold water and that ultimate in luxury: a bathroom.

Livvie got to her feet. She'd better make an effort to get dressed; Pa would be furious if they were not punctual. She switched on the electric light, another of the house's modern features – no more spluttering and smelly gas jets – and drew the heavy curtains, shutting out what little remained of the view of the garden. She hoped it would be a pleasant evening for her mam's sake, because all the extra work had taken its toll on Edith; she was looking pale and exhausted but had refused all exhortations to rest more often. Livvie also sincerely hoped that in Mrs Mayhew her mother would find a friendly neighbour to chat with and introduce her to the other wives and mothers in Poplar Avenue. So far they'd only caught glimpses of the people who lived in the nearby houses. They'd all appeared to be well dressed and she'd seen them exchange greetings but none of them had stopped to gossip as they did in Minerva Street, nor had anyone called to welcome them or offer help as was always the case in the steep narrow streets of Everton Brow.

She carefully selected her newest dress from the wardrobe. It was of a cornflower-blue fine wool crêpe with the fashionable leg-o'-mutton sleeves, tight bodice and full skirt. The edges of the high collar, sleeve cuffs and seams of the bodice were decorated with rows of navy blue braid and she had a silver filigree fob watch – a sixteenth birthday gift from her parents – which she would wear pinned to the bodice. She was too young to wear a low-cut evening dress, even had she wanted to and had she possessed one, but was certain that the high neck and long sleeves would be more practical and suited to supper in what would probably be a large and maybe not very warm dining room. She would of course need help with the row of tiny buttons that fastened the back of the bodice and her boned corset would have to be laced a little more tightly. That was one thing she felt she would never really get used to about being grown up. She hated wearing the thing; it was so restrictive and she often felt she couldn't really breathe properly.

Thankfully, before she had to seek out her sister, Amy put her head around the bedroom door.

'Livvie, can you do something with my hair, please? Mam said it's got to look tidy but I honestly don't know what to do with it other than plait it and that looks so childish!'

Livvie smiled sympathetically. Amy was at an awkward age, too young to wear her hair up and her skirts longer but not wanting to appear still a child in pinafores and plaits either. 'If you'll help me with this awful corset and fasten up these buttons, I'll see what I can do,' she offered.

'I don't see why we have to go next door for supper as well,' Amy grumbled as she pulled the laces of Livvie's corset tighter. 'Why couldn't they just ask Mam and Pa? It will be a deadly dull evening with us having to be on our best behaviour and listen to their boring conversations.'

'Oh, it might not be so bad.'

'Maybe not for you, at least you'll be allowed to talk. I won't! You know what Pa's like when we're in what he calls "company".' She grimaced. '"Children should be seen and not heard",' she mimicked. 'And he still considers me a child. I'd sooner stay here in the parlour and read.'

Livvie gasped. 'That's tight *enough*, Amy! You'll have me passing out! You should thank your lucky stars you don't have to suffer this torture yet.'

'I suppose at least that's one good thing about being my age,' Amy replied, somewhat mollified, as she helped Livvie on with the dress and deftly began to fasten up the row of buttons.

'I did ask Mam if they had children of our age but she didn't know. Let's hope they have.'

'If they have let's just hope they're not *boys*! That would ruin the evening entirely!' came the curt reply.

Livvie sighed. 'You'll change your mind about boys too before long, Amy. Now sit down and let's see what we can do with your hair,' she instructed and her sister sat down obediently at the dressing table.

She brushed Amy's light chestnut hair until it shone and fell in waves over her shoulders and then took the sides back and secured them with two of her own silver slides embellished with tiny butterflies. 'There, now you look very presentable and not at all childish,' she announced.

Amy smiled and nodded, thinking her hair did look much better than usual and her rose-coloured dress with its trimming of brown velvet ribbon looked nice – even if it wasn't long enough to cover her ankles. Thankfully, neither her mam nor Livvie had suggested she wear the much hated ribbons in her hair. She sighed heavily as she got to her feet. 'Come on, we'd better go down and get this awful, boring visit over with. I hope we get something decent to eat, I'm starving!'

Livvie grinned at her. Amy was always starving.

* * *

The first thing that struck Livvie as they entered the house next door was the fact that the hall was warm and welcoming. It was carpeted and there were fine china plates adorning the rack and a polished table bearing a display of autumn leaves and flowers. The Mayhews were obviously not short of money for the door had been opened by a girl of Livvie's age in the black dress and white apron and cap of a maid, who took their hats and jackets while Livvie exchanged a surprised glance with her sister.

Mrs Mayhew greeted them all, smiling and holding out her hand. 'It's so nice to meet you, Thomas and Edith. And you are very welcome, Olivia and Amy. Please do come on into the parlour,' she urged.

Thomas thanked her formally and Edith smiled, thinking she seemed pleasant enough.

As the girls followed their parents and hostess Amy mouthed the word 'posh' to her sister. Livvie gave her a disapproving glance for like her mother she thought Mrs Mayhew didn't appear at all stand-offish. She looked to be about the same age as her mam but there were no threads of grey in her dark auburn hair and no lines of fatigue around her eyes.

As the introductions were made Livvie was pleased to find that they did in fact have children. There were three of them: Edward, who she surmised was a couple of years older than herself and who appeared very self-assured, Selina who smiled engagingly at her, and John – Jonty as he was known – who looked to be younger than Amy and who was obviously wishing he was somewhere else. Their father,

Charles Mayhew, was not quite as tall as her father, his hair was grey and receding and he wore spectacles but he had a friendly smile as he heartily shook her pa's hand.

'Thomas, I'm pleased to meet you. From what I've heard I'm sure we're going to get on very well. I'm a businessman myself – I'm in haulage.'

Livvie saw her father relax a little but she wondered idly what Mr Mayhew had heard about them and from whom?

'Really? I'm in manufacturing – in a small way as yet, cattle food, but I'm looking to expand the factory next year.'

'Then perhaps later on we can discuss whether or not we can be useful to each other?'

'It's very kind of you to invite us for supper, er . . . Maud,' Edith thanked their hostess as she settled herself in the comfortable armchair Maud indicated.

'Not at all, Edith, isn't it the neighbourly thing to do? But I said to Charles that we must give you time to settle in first, which is why I haven't called. Everything must have been so hectic for you. It's all such an upheaval at the best of times, so . . . how are you coping?'

'Oh, not too badly,' Edith replied. Her condition was obviously apparent despite the fine Paisley shawl she wore draped loosely over her dress.

'Well, if there is anything – anything at all – I can do to help, you only have to ask. Do you have any help in the house, Edith?'

'I have the girls. Amy is still at school but they are both very willing and capable,' Edith replied.

'I'm sure they are, as is Selina – after all they'll have their own households one day – but I meant hired help. I couldn't manage these days without Bessie and it's not hard to find a suitable girl – a maid of all work – and they don't demand a high wage.'

Edith was lost for words. It was something she had never contemplated doing, engaging a maid. She'd never considered herself the type of person to *employ* help in the house. It was usually her class of person who was the *employee*. She managed a smile. 'I . . . I'll have to think about it, Maud.'

There was no time to discuss anything further for Maud ushered them into the dining room and the girl, Bessie, served what everyone proclaimed an excellent meal, both Thomas and Edith complimenting their hostess on her culinary skills. After they'd finished, Maud offered to take Edith on a tour of the house, if she felt up to it and would be interested to see the improvements she'd made, while Charles Mayhew directed Thomas to his study so they could discuss business matters without boring the ladies, and Edward Mayhew was invited to join them as he was already working for his father. This left Livvie and Amy and Selina and Jonty to congregate in the parlour.

'Do you think you'll like living here?' Selina asked Livvie directly, plumping herself down on the sofa next to her.

'Well, I hope so. It's a much bigger house than our old one.' Livvie liked the girl, who seemed open and easy to talk to.

'So, do you think your mother will get someone like Bessie to help in the house?'

Livvie frowned. 'I don't know. We've never had anyone before. Amy and I help as much as we can.' She'd noticed how perturbed her mam had been when the subject had been brought up. 'Does Bessie live in?'

Selina shook her head. 'No. There are rooms in the attic if she wanted to but she doesn't. She'd sooner live at home.'

'I could help even more if they'd let me leave school when I'm fourteen, but Pa won't hear of it,' Amy put in.

Livvie laughed. 'Don't mind Amy, she doesn't particularly like school.'

'She's not the only one!' Jonty muttered and received a sympathetic look from Amy.

'Are you pleased that you're going to have a brother or sister? Although if it were me, I'd hope for a sister – brothers can be really awful at times,' Selina stated, looking pointedly at Jonty, who scowled back at her.

'Yes, and I don't think either Mam or Amy or me will mind, just as long as everything goes well.' She decided to change the subject. 'Do you go out much, Selina? What is there to do around here?'

'Not a great deal. There's the library and the park. It's nice to walk there in summer and there are some shops on the main road and of course I sometimes go into town with Mother. There really aren't many girls of my age who live nearby, most are either older or much younger, so I'm glad you've come to live next door.'

Livvie nodded. 'Amy and I were hoping we would make new friends.'

Selina smiled at her. 'It will be great to have someone to chat with, go shopping with – someone my own age.'

'They might not stay long, the last lot didn't or the lot before them or the lot before them either!' Jonty added, raising his eyes to the ceiling.

Selina shot him a look of exasperation. 'The last lot didn't have children of our age.'

Amy was intrigued. 'Why do people keep moving out then?'

Selina shrugged. 'Oh, people often move for all kinds of reasons.'

'Not every couple of months they don't,' Jonty muttered ominously.

Livvie looked at him thoughtfully. 'Why do you think they move?'

The lad shrugged. 'Can't settle or don't like the place. Maybe there's something . . . odd about it.'

Livvie turned to her new friend. 'It's strange he should say that, Selina. When we first moved in the house felt so cold. I mean really, really cold, especially the hall.'

'It still does,' Amy put in. 'In fact I think there's something creepy about that hall.'

Livvie laughed. 'Oh, for heaven's sake, Amy, don't start on that again.'

'Well, you've got to admit, Livvie, that it's not like the hall here.' Amy turned to Jonty. 'Our hall is *always* cold and it does feel sort of . . . odd. Yours isn't like that.'

The boy looked at his sister enquiringly. 'Shall we tell them?'

'Tell us what?' Livvie demanded, looking at them both in some concern.

'Oh, I'll tell them. You'll make a huge mystery of it and it's nothing really. Two years ago the woman who lived there then died. She wasn't old, not even as old as my mother. One night she fell down the stairs and, well, she broke her neck, poor thing. That's all.'

'It's not all, Selina, and you know it,' Jonty said indignantly. 'There was talk that it wasn't an accident. People said that she and her husband were always arguing and fighting. That she was pushed,' he added darkly.

'That was just gossip,' Selina shot back.

'The police came though, didn't they? They spoke to the husband,' Jonty continued.

'But they didn't come back and they didn't arrest him or anything.'

'What happened to him?' Amy asked.

Again Selina shrugged. 'He just moved away. That's all there is to it. It was terrible, of course, for poor Mrs Chadwick.'

'But ever since no one has stayed longer than three months in that house,' Jonty finished triumphantly.

'Oh, take no notice of him, Livvie! He just loves making a drama out of it all.'

Livvie managed a smile. Selina was probably right; it had been a tragic accident. These things happened. And lots of people did die in their homes, usually peacefully in their beds, so what was there to get upset about?

'It's haunted. That's what it is. That's why people don't stay,' Jonty persisted; loath to give up on his theory which he could see had alarmed Amy at least.

'Jonty, if you don't stop that I'm going to tell Pa that you're frightening our new neighbours!' Selina cried angrily. 'Take no notice of him, Livvie. Of course it's not haunted.'

'I won't. It was just a terrible accident,' Livvie said firmly although she could see the boy's words had upset Amy and she had no intention of repeating them to her mam. She'd have to make her sister swear she wouldn't either. She certainly didn't want her mother upset or worried. But it was unsettling to know that that poor woman had died at the foot of the stairs in what was now their house.

Both girls were silent as they returned home and despite her resolution Livvie shivered involuntarily as they crossed the hall before going upstairs to their bedrooms.

As Amy helped her to undress, Livvie made her sister swear she would say nothing of poor Mrs Chadwick's demise to their mother.

'But surely she *should* know?' Amy demanded.

'And perhaps Mrs Mayhew has told her but, Amy, you're *not* to repeat that nonsense Jonty told us. Promise? Mam's not to be upset.'

Reluctantly Amy promised but as Livvie crossed the landing to the bathroom she heard her mother's raised voice from behind her parents' bedroom door and stopped to listen, fearful that Mrs Mayhew had indeed reiterated her youngest son's observations.

'I'll hear no more on the matter, Tom! It's not often that I argue with you about anything, but this is just too much!'

Livvie bit her lip; Mam was really upset about something.

'But it would be to your advantage, Edith! What's wrong with getting a girl in to help? We can afford it.'

Her pa sounded aggrieved but she was relieved that the argument was obviously over them employing a maid and not about whether they should remain in this house or not.

'Because . . . because I wouldn't feel happy about it, Tom. We're not the sort of people to have staff to wait on us.'

'We are now!'

26

'No, neither of us was brought up like that! I'll manage as I've always done, with the help of the girls. And there's an end to it.'

'Edith, I was only thinking of your health.'

Livvie smiled as she moved away. Now Pa sounded contrite but she knew he probably still had his heart set on their having what her mam had termed 'staff', particularly as the Mayhews did, and maybe – for all she knew – the rest of the neighbours too. He was very anxious to fit into this society.

Chapter Three

Livvie soon forgot all about the tragic demise of Mrs Chadwick as Edith's pregnancy progressed and Christmas approached. She and Amy had to virtually take over the running of the household while Edith had to be content with supervising from the sofa where she rested as much as possible, for she remained adamant about not employing staff.

True to her word Maud Mayhew called often to see if there was anything she could do to help and to chat with Edith, something which Edith enjoyed. She soon found that she could talk to Maud about almost anything and that did help.

'You know I was rather anxious about this move, Maud,' she confided one afternoon when Livvie had gone Christmas shopping with Selina and Maud had come to keep her company.

'I can understand that but you seem to have settled well, Edith, and don't forget in your condition it was a huge upheaval.'

'I know but I worried that we wouldn't be accepted, coming from a much less wealthy area.'

'Good grief, Edith! Did you think we would all be terrible snobs and be looking down our noses at you all because you'd lived in Everton?'

Edith smiled ruefully.

'Charles and I didn't always live here, you know. Oh, no, we started married life in Anfield, in a small terraced house, but when times got better we moved here, just as you did. We're self-made and proud of it, Edith. And I can tell you that not all the other neighbours were born into affluent families either.' She smiled. 'But we've not forgotten our roots and neither will you. Were you quite happy when you found yourself in the family way again?' she asked to change the subject.

Edith thought for a few seconds and then she nodded. 'Yes. You see Tom wants a son so much, someone to pass the business on to, and I can't blame him for that. Isn't it what every man wants? But I admit, Maud, I was very, very surprised. I mean at my age and . . . well, I did worry. You see I lost two babies before I had Amy, both boys. They were stillborn.'

Maud nodded sadly. 'I'm so sorry to hear that, Edith. It must have been terribly hard for you.'

'It was and Tom took it very badly too. So when I found out I began to worry. I couldn't help thinking about the two other poor little mites.'

'That's only natural but you had Amy and she's fine so I'd try not to worry too much.'

'And Tom is determined that I'm going to have the best medical care he can afford.' She laughed. 'And look at me,

Maud, sitting here all day with my feet up – a proper "lady of leisure".'

'Make the most of it, Edith, for you know as well as I do that everything goes to pot after the birth, until you get into a routine.'

'It does indeed but I really do feel that these last weeks are so *tedious* and it's frustrating not to be able to do more physically, especially with Christmas nearly upon us. I'll be glad when I've been delivered.'

Maud concurred and they turned their attention to local gossip, of which Maud always seemed to have a plentiful supply.

They'd decided to position the Christmas tree in the corner of the parlour. It was a magnificent specimen – far bigger than anything they'd previously had – which Thomas had had delivered.

'Wouldn't it look better in the hall?' he suggested. That was where he'd had in mind when he'd bought it. 'It will make the entrance to our home look grand and very festive when people call.' They were on friendly terms with a few of the neighbours now and he didn't want them to think the Goodwins' home lacked style.

'There won't be many people visiting, Pa. Mam's not really up to entertaining, is she, and besides we wouldn't get the full benefit of it if it was out there,' Livvie replied. 'It looks much nicer in here.'

'I think Livvie's right, Tom. I'd hardly see it at all if it was out there: I spend so much time in here,' Edith concurred, smiling at her husband. 'Even though I really *would* like to have people in for drinks, I don't think I can do so much. But it's a beautiful tree – just right for the first Christmas in our new home.' She did wish they could entertain their new friends for she realised how much it meant to Tom. Perhaps next year they would be able to hold a party to really celebrate and no doubt by then they'd know more people too.

'And it's going to be great, Mam. A bit quiet but great just the same,' Livvie replied, thinking back to her shopping trip with Selina Mayhew. She enjoyed Selina's company and they'd spent hours deciding what gifts to purchase for their respective family members and friends, and buying cards, baubles for the tree, holly and mistletoe. Mam had written out the lists for the butcher, grocer and greengrocer and she'd taken them into the appropriate shops and sorted out delivery dates. Under Edith's supervision she and Amy had made the Christmas pudding, the mince pies and the Christmas cake.

'Maud, Charles and the family will of course be coming in on Christmas Eve for a drink. It's the least we can do as she's been such a help, and a confidante too.'

Tom nodded. 'Charles and I have worked out a very good deal in respect of transport costs; he's saved me quite a bit already and even young Teddy's come up with a couple of good ideas.' He turned to his eldest daughter. 'How do you get on with Teddy, Livvie? He's a bright lad.'

Livvie shrugged, concentrating on fastening the silver star securely to the top of the Christmas tree. 'He's all right, Pa. I don't see all that much of him. He's at work all day and when I go over he doesn't really have much to say to me.' She smiled a little ruefully. 'I think he looks on both Selina and me as a bit . . . young and frivolous.'

Edith shot her husband a surreptitious glance. She could see how his mind was working. He was thinking that Edward Mayhew would be a very suitable husband for Livvie. He was only two years older than her, seemed a steady and reliable young man, came from a respectable family and also had excellent prospects. Well, maybe he was right, she mused, and maybe in the future they might consider the matter more seriously, but Livvie was far too young for them to be contemplating a marriage for her yet. She just wanted them all to enjoy this first Christmas in their new home. Who knew what the future held? Her daughter might reject any plans for an 'arranged' marriage; she might consider it old-fashioned. Indeed Livvie might fall in love with someone else. She herself had married for love and she secretly hoped her daughter would too, despite any ideas Tom might have to the contrary. Yes, she was looking forward to the holiday.

It had been a quiet but very enjoyable Christmas, Livvie mused as she trudged through the snow on her way home from the library one afternoon towards the end of January. Mam said she had thoroughly enjoyed it and appreciated everything both she and Amy had done and even Pa had complimented her on the Christmas lunch. She'd been delighted with the beautiful gold bracelet set with garnets that her parents had given her and Amy had also been very pleased with the engraved silver locket on a chain that had been her gift.

She shivered as the icy wind stung her cheeks and pulled her scarf higher around her neck. It had turned really cold just before Christmas with heavy frosts at night but the snow had only arrived two days ago, which had delighted Jonty Mayhew and Amy, who was still young enough to enjoy a snowball fight with their neighbour's youngest son. The Mayhew family had called on Christmas Eve, bringing with them a bottle of fine brandy for her pa, a bottle of Madeira wine for her mam and chocolates for herself and Amy. They hadn't stayed long; Maud Mayhew had been firm about the length of the visit so as not to tire Edith, but it had been a really very pleasant couple of hours.

Livvie looked up as she approached the house, thinking how the snow, faintly sparkling now in the pale sunlight, made everything look so pristine and picturesque. The branches of the shrubs that bordered the lawn were like a tracery of white lace and the icicles hanging from the guttering resembled slender crystal droplets. It all looked very pretty, she thought. Of course there were the drawbacks too: steps and pavements that had become slippery and potentially dangerous, disruption to traffic – something both her pa and Mr Mayhew bemoaned – but she hoped it wouldn't all turn to grey slush for at least another few days.

After she'd taken off her coat, hat, scarf and gloves she went thankfully into the parlour where a fire glowed in the hearth. She poked at the embers and put more coal on and watched as it burned brightly; glancing quickly at the mantel clock she surmised that she had about half an hour to sit and start her new book before Amy arrived home and she would go up and wake Edith from her nap.

Mam really did get very tired now and her ankles swelled up, she thought as she settled comfortably on the sofa. It required a huge effort for Edith to get up, supervise the morning chores and the preparation of lunch before wearily climbing the stairs to the bedroom for her nap. Still, there wasn't long for Mam to go now and the midwife, a very capable woman called Mrs Forrest, had years of experience and called twice a week and of course the doctor also paid his routine visits. Pa was sparing no expense and she was glad of it.

Everything was ready; the small nursery had been decorated and furnished although her new brother or sister wouldn't sleep in there for a while. There was a beautiful crib, swathed in white lawn edged with lace, ready to be placed beside the bed in her parents' room although her mam had said that neither she nor Amy had been afforded such luxury. The new little layette and the dozens of terry-towelling nappies had all been washed and were now in the drawers of the chest in the nursery, plus all the numerous other items that a small baby seemed to need – most of which were a mystery to both herself and Amy. Selina had cooed over everything, saying she almost wished for a baby sibling herself until her mother reminded her that small babies tended to cry a lot, keep everyone awake and throw previously well-ordered households into chaos.

As the daylight began to fade Livvie got up to switch on the elegant standard lamp and draw the curtains. She spotted her sister making her way up the road. She'd take Mam up a cup of tea and then she and Amy would start to prepare the supper for Pa didn't stay late at the factory these evenings. He'd recently taken on a manager to oversee both the factory and some of the paperwork and had declared himself well pleased with Francis – Frank – Hadley, even though he was younger than Thomas had really wanted for such a responsible position.

The light was on in her parents' bedroom, which perturbed

her a little, and when she entered it was to find Edith sitting on the edge of the bed.

'Mam, you're awake. I'm sorry I'm a bit late. I got engrossed in my book. I've brought you a cup of tea and our Amy's coming up the path so we'll make a start on the vegetables.' She placed the tea on the bedside table but as she turned she realised that Edith's face was contorted with pain. 'Oh, Mam! Has it . . . has it . . . started?'

Biting her lip to stifle a cry Edith nodded. She'd been having pains on and off all afternoon. It was two weeks early but she really didn't view that as alarming for both the doctor and the midwife had reassured her that sometimes ladies got the dates confused, especially when they had never expected to become pregnant again.

'I'll send Amy for Mrs Forrest. You just stay there, lie back and try to . . . rest!' Livvie urged, feeling flustered, not really knowing what to do or what to expect.

Edith nodded. 'Livvie, would you ask her to call and tell Maud that . . . that it's started?'

Livvie fled downstairs, finding her sister in the hallway, about to remove her hat and coat. 'Amy, Mam's pains have started early! Go and fetch Mrs Forrest, you know where she lives, but call in to tell Mrs Mayhew on the way. I'll stay here with Mam. I think I have to boil water or something . . .'

Amy looked alarmed as she clapped her hat back on her head. She'd sooner go and fetch Maud and the midwife than stay here for she had no idea either of what the next hours would bring.

To Livvie's relief Maud Mayhew arrived within a few minutes and immediately took control.

'Livvie, I'll go up to her, dear. I know where everything she'll need is kept. You stay down here and start to prepare supper as usual. Upstairs is no place for a girl of your age to be now and Mrs Forrest will be here soon, I'm sure.'

'Oh, can you stay? Can you stay until she arrives? You see I really don't know what to do.'

Maud patted her arm reassuringly. 'Of course I'll stay and no one expects you to know what to do, Livvie. Mrs Forrest is very experienced so you just continue preparing your father's supper. It could all take a long time, you know. These things often do.'

Livvie nodded thankfully and went through to the kitchen. She was anxious for her mother but she was reassured that Edith was in good hands with Mrs Forrest and Maud Mayhew.

Amy was out of breath and flushed when she returned but was as relieved as her sister to know that Maud was with Mam. 'And I left a message for Mrs Forrest to come as quickly as she can. The girl who opened the door told me she'd just popped out. What do we do now, Livvie?'

'We wait. Mrs Mayhew said it could take a long time. She said we have to carry on as normal. Pa will want his supper when he gets home.'

'I don't think I can eat anything,' Amy confided.

Livvie shrugged. 'You not eating isn't going to help Mam much, is it? But suit yourself. I'll make a start on the potatoes if you'll do the carrots,' she said firmly.

The midwife arrived about half an hour later and after another half-hour Maud Mayhew came downstairs.

Both girls looked at her anxiously.

'Don't look so worried, everything is going well so far.

Now, Mrs Forrest would be very grateful if you could make her a pot of tea. I'll take it up to her. Then when your father arrives home, I'll go over to supervise our supper, then I'll be back to give Mrs Forrest a little break.'

'You don't think it will all be over by then?' Livvie asked.

Maud smiled kindly. 'Good heavens no! I'll be very surprised if baby Goodwin puts in an appearance before midnight and I'm sure Mrs Forrest would agree.'

Livvie managed a weak smile as she put the kettle on.

Thomas was very surprised and perturbed to find that his wife had gone into labour but he was reassured by both Maud and the midwife that all was well and that after he'd been up to see Edith he should have his supper with the girls and then retire to the parlour, for his presence upstairs would not be appreciated and that he should be prepared for it to be a long night.

'But I'm sure you'll be aware of that, Tom, and if it helps, I'll send Charles over to keep you company,' Maud offered.

'That would be appreciated, Maud. As you say, it could be a long night,' Tom replied.

As they sat in the dining room for supper Edith's cries could be heard more clearly for the bedroom was directly above it. Both girls looked anxiously at each other, Livvie biting her lip. Oh, poor Mam sounded as if she was having a terrible time but glancing at her pa she thought he didn't seem unduly concerned, but then he'd gone through all this when both she and Amy and her two stillborn brothers had been born so she took some comfort from that. Neither she nor her sister had any experience of this, after all.

'Is . . . is it always like this, Pa?' Amy asked tentatively as she pushed the food around on her plate. Mam was never ill but now she sounded as if she was in terrible agony and that scared her.

Thomas nodded. 'I'm afraid it is. But it's all worthwhile in the end. When it's over your mother will be exhausted but very happy. So stop looking so terrified, Amy, and eat your supper.'

'Did you finally decide on names?' Livvie asked, trying to divert their thoughts from their mother's suffering. There had been great discussions about names. Her pa naturally wanted Thomas but her mother favoured Martin. She didn't think her pa was very interested in girls' names but she, Amy and Edith all thought that Caroline was pretty.

'We did. "Thomas George Henry Goodwin". "George" after your mother's father and "Henry" after mine,' Tom replied with satisfaction. 'It sounded . . . impressive.'

'And we all like "Caroline" – if it's a girl,' Amy added.

Her father nodded although he didn't comment and Livvie rose to clear the table.

Thomas rose too. 'I'll take my newspaper into the parlour as Maud suggested. Amy, kindly open the door to Mrs Mayhew or Mr Mayhew when they call. If it's Mr Mayhew, show him into the parlour. No doubt Mrs Mayhew will go up to your mother.'

Amy nodded. He really didn't seem concerned at all but maybe that's how men always reacted at times like this. 'I'll be so glad when "baby Goodwin", as Mrs Mayhew calls it, finally arrives,' she confided as she helped Livvie to carry the dirty dishes into the scullery.

'So will I and I'm certain poor Mam will be too. I'll be glad when Selina's mother comes back; I'll feel much . . . easier. Now, let's get this lot washed and put away. At least it gives us something useful to do.'

Amy nodded. 'But what will we do for the rest of the time? What if . . . what if nothing's happened by the time we're going to bed?'

'Then we'll just have to try and get some sleep, which is more than poor Mam will be able to do,' Livvie replied grimly.

Chapter Four

———◆———

By the following morning it was obvious to the midwife and Maud Mayhew that something was wrong and the doctor had been summoned.

'She's completely exhausted, Doctor, and labour isn't . . . well, it isn't progressing as it should. In fact nothing is happening at all!' Mrs Forrest informed him.

He examined Edith and concurred, shaking his head and looking concerned. 'She's going to have to be taken to hospital and I'm afraid that an emergency caesarean section will probably have to be performed. They will do everything they can but I'm afraid . . . her age is against her. While I phone for an ambulance, would you kindly inform Mr Goodwin of how matters stand,' he instructed.

The midwife nodded and left the room while Maud Mayhew held Edith's hand and tried to look calm and composed although she was seriously worried about her friend.

Edith gazed fearfully up at Maud through a haze of pain and exhaustion. The doctor's words had made her realise that she might lose this child too. Oh, after all these terrible long hours of labour – she wasn't even sure now just how long she had endured the agony; maybe it was even days – there was the possibility that it had all been in vain. She was so, so tired. She had no strength left. And she was afraid too: she'd never had to have an operation before. Now she feared for both herself and her baby; all she could do was hope and pray that when she got to the hospital the doctors and nurses there would save her child.

Thomas was sitting in the parlour with Livvie and both were looking strained, anxious and tired. He'd not gone into work, saying that Frank Hadley could cope for today, and Livvie was glad he'd remained at home. She'd never been so worried in her life before. None of them had had much sleep but it had been decided that it would be best if Amy went to school as usual. Livvie had thought her sister would protest but after a night of tossing and turning, her hands over her ears to try to block out her mother's agonised cries, Amy had seemed relieved.

They both listened in silence as Mrs Forrest told them of the doctor's decision. 'He's phoning for an ambulance now,' she finished.

Thomas nodded, looking very anxious. 'Thank God we have a telephone and that Walton hospital isn't too far away.'

'Mrs Forrest, will Mam . . . will she be . . . all right?' Livvie asked, fear obvious in her voice. What had gone so wrong that Mam was going to be rushed in for an emergency operation?

'They will do everything possible, child. Your mother is exhausted and she's not a young woman, so they will have to . . . er . . . "remove" the baby surgically, but believe me she

41

will be in the best hands possible,' the woman replied with a confidence she wasn't feeling. These operations were not always successful and she held out little hope for the poor unborn child.

'Of course she is,' Thomas agreed confidently. 'But what of the . . . child?' he added, praying that this longed-for son – he was certain it was a boy – would not suffer the same fate as the other two. He doubted he could bear such bitter disappointment again.

'Everything is in the hands of the Almighty now, Mr Goodwin, but as I've just said, she'll be getting the best of medical care – they both will.'

He sat down and ran his hands distractedly through his hair. He had to find confidence in her assurances. Medical science and procedures had moved on a great deal since Amy had been born. He could only hope she was right. 'I'll go to the hospital with her,' he announced firmly, getting to his feet.

The woman nodded. 'Of course, but you'll have to wait outside, you realise that? They won't let you into either a ward or an operating theatre.'

'I do,' he replied but he felt he couldn't just sit here and wait for news.

'What about me?' Livvie asked with a quiver in her voice. Her heart was hammering against her ribs as anxiety overwhelmed her.

'No, luv, they'd not let you in at all, not at your age. You'd best stay here,' Mrs Forrest replied kindly. She could see how upset the poor girl was.

'I'm sure Mrs Mayhew will stay with you, Livvie,' Thomas added. Then they all heard the clanging of the ambulance bell as the vehicle approached and he went to get his coat and hat.

Livvie stood almost rigid with fear as her mother, pale as a marble statue, was taken out on a stretcher to the ambulance, accompanied by both the doctor and her father.

Maud Mayhew, emerging from the house where she'd been trying to set Edith's room to rights, put her arm around the girl's shoulders. She could feel her trembling.

'It's going to be all right, Livvie. She . . . They'll both get the best attention now,' she comforted, thinking that perhaps they should have called Dr Sumner earlier. But she'd had to rely on the midwife's knowledge and experience; after all it was eleven years since she'd had her last child – Jonty – and that had been a straightforward birth whereas Edith had had two stillbirths in the past. She prayed fervently that there wouldn't be a third, for her poor friend had already suffered so much.

'Perhaps it would be best if you came home with me, Livvie. I'm sure sitting here fretting won't help you. You'll have Selina for company and I'm sure Bessie can find you both something to do to occupy you and take your mind off things,' Maud suggested after the ambulance had departed. 'Your pa will let us know when there is any news. He'll probably telephone, he knows our number.'

Livvie nodded. She didn't want to just stay here alone agonising.

Maud managed a tired smile for she too was exhausted with worry and lack of sleep. 'No doubt by the time Amy comes home from school it will all be over and everyone will be fine.'

'I hope so. Oh, Mrs Mayhew, I just want Mam to come home strong and well.'

'We all do but she'll have to stay in the hospital for a while, dear, to recover from the operation. Don't fret now – the doctors are marvellous these days,' she said firmly as she ushered Livvie towards the door.

Somehow Livvie got through the day with the help of both Selina and Bessie, a sensible, cheerful girl who decided that it would be a good opportunity for all three of them to clean the family silver before lunch while the mistress went for a nap. 'She's worn out, poor woman. Stayin' up all night like that. It was very good of her you know, miss, to stay, like.'

Livvie managed a smile as she nodded. 'I'm so thankful she did. I . . . I just wouldn't have known what to do without her.'

'An' why should you? I mean you probably don't even remember your Amy bein' born, do you?' Bessie asked, lining up all the various items and handing out the polishing cloths.

'Not really. I was only three and I was taken into one of the neighbours' houses and when I got back she'd arrived and Mam was sitting up in bed, looking tired but happy.'

Bessie nodded. 'It was like that in our house too, except when our Stanley was born – he's the youngest. Oh, a right palaver that was: he arrived about two in the mornin' an' none of us got any sleep after that what with the neighbours in an' out and me da *celebratin'*!' She sniffed. 'I seem to remember that we none of us got much sleep for months afterwards either. He could certainly bawl, could our Stanley.'

'How old is he now?' Livvie asked, polishing the silver sugar sifter rather half-heartedly.

Bessie smiled at her. 'Oh, he's nearly nine but he's still a right little hooligan! He has me poor mam demented with his

44

antics. I tell you, Miss Selina, compared to our Stanley your Jonty is an angel.'

Selina grimaced. 'I'd certainly not call Jonty angelic,' she replied darkly.

Bessie did manage to keep their spirits up and after lunch suggested that both girls walk to the shops with her for she had to pass the mistress's list to the grocer. 'I know it's not a very interestin' thing to do but a bit of fresh air might help an' we could take a turn around the park too, even though the snow is turnin' to slush now,' she'd urged. And so they'd gone out for a couple of hours and Bessie had kept up a lively conversation about her siblings and their antics.

It was after three when they returned and Livvie hoped that there would be some news from her father for Amy would be home in an hour and she would have to return to their house, something she wasn't looking forward to.

'I can see that the fresh air has put some colour in your cheeks,' Maud greeted them, smiling.

'Should I make some tea, ma'am?' Bessie enquired.

'That would be lovely, Bessie. Now come and warm yourselves by the fire,' Maud urged.

'Has . . . has Pa telephoned?' Livvie asked.

Maud shook her head; she too had thought there would have been a phone call by now. 'I'm afraid not but I'm sure he will let us know when there is news and I always think that "no news is good news".'

'I'll have to go back next door after tea, Mrs Mayhew. Amy will be home.'

'Of course, dear. Would you like Selina to go with you?' she asked, looking enquiringly at her daughter.

'If you don't mind, Selina.'

'Of course not! What are friends for, Livvie? I'll stay until your pa gets back if you like,' Selina offered.

Livvie nodded her thanks. 'Oh, all this waiting is awful!'

'I know but I'm sure it won't be for much longer now,' Maud replied firmly.

When Amy arrived home she was surprised to find Selina Mayhew sitting with her sister in the parlour. 'How is Mam? Do you know?'

Livvie shook her head. 'Pa hasn't phoned yet. Mrs Mayhew is waiting for his call so Selina came back with me. I didn't want you coming home to an empty house and being worried.'

'But she *is* all right? I mean . . . ?'

'I don't know, Amy, and that's the truth. All we can do is wait. Are you hungry?' she asked as an afterthought. Her sister usually was.

Amy shook her head.

'Have you any homework?' Livvie asked, casting around for something that would keep Amy occupied.

'Yes, but how can I concentrate on stupid capital cities of Europe?'

Livvie sighed; her sister had a point.

They were all restless but hadn't even switched on the light or drawn the curtains before, to Livvie's infinite relief, a little while later she saw her father coming up the front path.

'Oh, here's Pa at last!' she cried, jumping to her feet and rushing out into the hall, followed by Amy and Selina.

The initial relief she felt as he came into the hallway quickly drained away as she took in his grey, haggard features and slumped shoulders. 'Pa! Pa, why didn't you phone? What . . . what is it? Mam . . . ? The . . . baby?'

In a daze Thomas took in the three girls standing huddled together and slowly shook his head but he said nothing. The words stuck in his throat. He just walked past them and up the stairs.

Livvie looked in horror at Selina as a terrible fear began to envelop her.

'I . . . I'll run and get my mother!' Selina cried, rushing to the door.

Amy clutched her sister's arm. 'Oh, Livvie, what's happened? Do . . . do you think the baby . . . ?'

'I don't know! He looked so . . . awful that it must be something terrible.' He'd wanted a son so much, she thought distractedly. It must be bad news.

'Do you think we should go up to him or wait for Selina's mother?'

Livvie was so confused she didn't know what to do. In truth she didn't want to hear what he would tell her – and what could she possibly say to him? How could she find the words to comfort him? Nothing had prepared her for this but she knew she *had* to go to him. 'I . . . I'll go up. You wait for Mrs Mayhew.'

Her hand was trembling on the banister rail as she quickly went upstairs and without knocking entered her parents' bedroom. Her father was sitting on the bed, his head in his hands, and she swallowed hard as she caught sight of the lawn-draped crib on the other side of the bed.

'Pa. Pa . . . please tell me what . . . what's happened?' she begged, a catch in her voice and tears not far away. She'd never seen her confident, self-assured father look so . . . broken.

He still didn't speak; he just shook his head.

She was becoming frantic, wondering if he had lost his voice or even his senses. 'Pa, please tell me? Please? We must know!'

At last he struggled to compose himself although he still didn't look up at her. 'They . . . they did everything they could, but . . . but it was . . . too late.'

Livvie gave a little cry of distress. 'Oh, Pa! The poor . . . baby!'

He brushed away the tears on his cheek. 'And it was a boy.' The words were uttered in anguish.

'Oh, the poor little thing! I'm so, so sorry, Pa. I . . . I can't tell you how sorry. And Mam? How is Mam?'

He looked up at her and at the expression in his eyes sheer terror gripped her.

'She was too . . . weak, lost too much blood. They . . . they couldn't do . . . anything. She . . . she just . . . slipped away.' His voice was harsh with grief and shock.

Livvie stared at him in disbelief. NO! It couldn't be true! It just *couldn't*! He was telling her that her mother too was dead! She shook her head, the tears welling up and sliding down her cheeks as she struggled to understand. Her Mam couldn't be *dead*! How could it have happened? They'd all said she would have the best care! She couldn't speak – it was as if her throat had closed over – and she was finding it hard to breathe. She felt sick and dizzy and so . . . cold! Then she felt strong arms around her and she collapsed against Maud Mayhew, sobbing uncontrollably.

'My God! Tom! What's happened?' Maud cried, holding the weeping girl close and taking in the slumped posture and haggard features of the man sitting on the bed.

'Both . . . both . . . gone, Maud. It was . . . too late.'

Her eyes widened and she uttered a cry of disbelief. What had gone wrong? They'd probably never know. But she realised that she would have to remain calm and in control and somehow help them all to cope with this terrible tragedy.

Chapter Five

———◆———

Livvie sat huddled in a corner of the sofa in the parlour. She could not stop crying. Nothing seemed *real*. In just a few minutes her world had come crashing down around her and she couldn't believe what had happened. Only this morning – a few short hours ago – Mam had been here in this house with them and now . . . now they'd never see her again, never hear her voice again, see her smile, hear her laugh. There was a huge void in Livvie's heart – in her life. She was so consumed by distress that she couldn't even think about her father or her sister, let alone about the poor little baby brother she'd lost that day too. All she could think about was how was she going to cope? How was she going to get through each day and night without Mam?

Time seemed to have no meaning. Her head was aching, her eyes swollen and burning, her throat felt raw and dimly she realised that she was cold. With an effort she pulled herself up into a sitting position and realised that the room was dark and growing chilly. The fire had burned low. She slid off the sofa and kneeling before the hearth piled more coal on and watched dejectedly as the flames grew brighter. She had no heart to switch on a light; she preferred the darkness.

She glanced around the room. They'd all had such hopes and dreams when they first came here, she thought dully. Mam had said they should look on the move as a new beginning, a blessing, but it hadn't proved to be for they'd had so little time here together. Despite the increasing heat from the fire she shivered, wishing they'd stayed in Minerva Street. Vaguely she remembered what Jonty Mayhew had said about this house, about the woman who had died here. She didn't believe that it was haunted but it hadn't proved to be a lucky house for them either for now there had been two more deaths. She shivered again. She would never now look on this house as the haven of comfort, happiness and security that their old home had been. Mam was gone and this house would never feel like home again.

She still felt numb and she didn't stir when Maud, accompanied by a quietly sobbing Amy, entered the room and switched on the standard lamp.

Maud sat down on the sofa with Amy beside her. 'Livvie, dear, I'm going to stay. I can't leave you all alone, not tonight. It's been such a . . . tragic and shocking day.'

Livvie sat back on her heels and nodded silently, grateful for Maud's words although she wondered how she would get through the night, let alone face tomorrow.

Maud patted Amy's hand comfortingly. The poor child had taken it badly but wasn't that only to be expected? Maud was still trying to accept the events of the day herself. There were formalities that had to be undertaken in the next few days and she wondered how Tom would deal with them all. How on earth they were all going to get through the funerals she didn't know but she would do everything she could to help ease their grief. She shook her head. Both girls were so young and to Livvie would fall the entire running of the house and the care of her sister. It didn't bear thinking about. Slowly she got to her feet. 'I'll make us all some tea and perhaps I can persuade your father to take a drop of brandy.' She also decided to send word to Bessie, asking the girl to come over and change the bedding after Edith's long labour.

'I . . . I'm glad she's staying, Livvie,' Amy said when Maud had left the room.

Livvie nodded. 'I still can't believe it all,' she said with a sob in her voice.

Amy began to cry softly. 'Oh, I wish we'd never come here!'

Livvie gathered her into her arms. 'So do I, Amy, and I . . . I don't know how we are going to cope tomorrow, but we'll just have to *try*.'

The days that followed seemed long, dark and utterly miserable to Livvie. She couldn't bring herself to go into her parents' bedroom even though her father seemed to have pulled himself together enough to pay a brief visit to the factory after he'd been to the Register Office. The bed remained unmade after her father left in the morning, something she knew would have horrified her mother, but she couldn't bear to see the empty side or remember how Edith had suffered those long hours of agony. And then there would be all Mam's things on the dressing table. Her hairbrushes and combs, the tortoiseshell-backed hand mirror, the trinket box and the box that held her hair pins, the little stand for her hat pins. No, she couldn't face that at all.

She knew her father had been to see the funeral director but she couldn't bring herself to ask him about the arrangements and he had barely spoken to her, shutting himself away from them in his loss. Without Maud Mayhew she wondered how they would have managed. It was Maud who impressed upon them that they must eat, and try to keep themselves occupied for Edith wouldn't have wanted them to fall ill with grief. It was Maud who had firmly locked the door to what was to have been the nursery after moving the crib into it.

Livvie had forced herself to go through both her own and Amy's wardrobe for clothes suitable for mourning. There had been very few for Edith had not approved of dark colours for her children. Livvie took out her grey coat and skirt. She would have to sew some more black braid around the collar and cuffs and a black band around one sleeve. Amy had a blue coat that she would get dyed black for the weather was still cold and they needed coats. Livvie knew she would, at a later date, have to go into town to buy more suitable clothes for the period of mourning would last at least a year. In her heart it would last a lifetime, she thought sadly.

The evening before the funeral Livvie made sure all her father's clothes were laid out and urged Amy to try on the coat that Maud had collected from the dyer's.

'I don't want to! It's bad enough that I'm going to have to wear it tomorrow, Livvie,' Amy protested unhappily.

'Please? I know how you feel, but I have to make sure it hasn't shrunk.'

Reluctantly Amy shrugged on the coat and buttoned it up. 'There! It's all right.'

Livvie nodded thankfully. 'It is.'

Amy bit her lip and tears sprang to her eyes. 'Oh, I wish we'd stayed in our old house. I've never really felt at home in this place!'

Livvie put her arms around her. 'I know, Amy, but even if we hadn't moved here Mam would still have . . . died. Nothing could have changed that and we have got good neighbours here too. I don't know what we'd have done without Mrs Mayhew.'

'I know but I just don't feel as if this is our *home*, Livvie. Not now.'

Livvie nodded her understanding. 'I've felt like that too but we . . . we've got to make the best of it. Mam was happy here and she would want us to be too. We can't go back; Pa wouldn't let us. I know how you feel but this *is* home now.'

The snow had virtually gone, leaving just slivers of grey slush in the churchyard where all the trees looked black and gaunt against the grey winter sky. It was still bitterly cold though and the two girls huddled together beside the newly dug grave. Livvie was surprised and quietly comforted that so many of their new neighbours had attended and even more surprised to see Mrs Agnew and three other women from Minerva Street. How good of them to come to remember Mam, she thought tearfully, oblivious to the fact that they looked so out of place amongst the other mourners, who were all far more expensively dressed.

Maud Mayhew stood with her husband and her daughter

and her heart went out to both girls: they were shivering with cold and the ordeal of burying their mother. Livvie looked suddenly very grown up in the sombre grey coat and black, heavily veiled hat and she could see the girl was desperately trying not to break down for Amy's sake. Amy was clinging tightly to her sister's arm, her face pale and pinched, and Thomas stood as though carved from stone, his face set in an expressionless mask as he strove to hide his feelings.

Livvie was indeed fighting back the sobs as she held Amy's hand. She'd never felt so bereft and lost in her life before. Oh, it was utterly inconceivable that her precious mam was being lowered into the cold, dark earth with the baby who had cost her her life and that soon they'd all leave this place and it would be . . . over. Mam would really and truly have gone from them and they would go home alone. Then she would have to try to face life without her and it would be a life where all her mother's duties and responsibilities would fall upon her. She would have to be more than a sister to Amy; she would have to run her father's home as smoothly and efficiently as her mother would have done and she would have to try to make a new life for herself. It was all too much for her to contend with and so soon, but it had to be done.

She felt Maud's hand on her shoulder and, squeezing Amy's hand in a gesture of comfort, she turned away from the graveside.

As her father shook hands with the vicar and thanked him, her gaze settled on his squared shoulders and straight back. He'd held up well, she thought. He'd lost his wife and helpmate of eighteen years and he'd lost another son too and she knew how bitterly disappointed he was at that loss. But slowly the realisation began to dawn on her. If Mam hadn't become pregnant she wouldn't have died. They wouldn't all be here today, bowed down with sorrow and pain. Life wouldn't have taken on the dark and depressing mantle that now enveloped it. Edith had known how much her husband had wanted a son and heir and she'd put her life at risk to provide him with his heart's desire. She'd ultimately sacrificed herself to try to give him what he wanted. For the first time Livvie thought how utterly selfish and irresponsible her father had been. He'd known Edith had lost two babies; he was aware that she was – as Mrs Agnew had remarked – old to risk having another child, that there could be complications and indeed there had been, yet . . . yet . . . had he given no thought to any of those things? Had his desire for a son been so important to him? More important than her mam's health? More important than her life? It was clear to her now that it had been. With that realisation something seemed to wither in her heart and she knew that from now on she would always blame him for her mother's death. As she followed him towards the waiting carriage she pursed her lips. It was a man's world and often women paid the price for men's ambitions – and paid dearly, she thought bitterly.

Chapter Six

———◆———

1909

'Miss, I'm sorry to interrupt you but . . .'

Livvie looked up from the grocery list she was compiling and smiled at the girl standing before her. Emily had been with them now for nine months and she was a willing and hard-working girl. Livvie'd struggled in the months after Edith's death, not only with her loss but with the running of the household, for she'd come to realise that her pa was something of a martinet where the timing of meals and adherence to her budget expenses were concerned. There had been a couple of unfortunate incidents concerning both: two suppers that were late and almost inedible and a serious overspend on provisions. At first she, like her mother, had resisted having paid help but her pa had insisted, stating firmly that they could well afford it and he didn't want either her or Amy to become slaves to housework and have no social life. She'd refrained from reminding him that her mother's life had revolved almost totally around her family and the house. Nor had she said that she didn't consider herself a 'slave' to housework at all, for her mother would have wanted her to take care of Amy and her father. She hadn't known how to go about finding a maid of all work but of course Maud Mayhew had come to the rescue and they'd engaged Emily Hudson, who was a year older than Amy and proving to be very satisfactory.

'You're not interrupting anything important, Emily. What is it?'

'Mrs Mayhew would like to see you, miss, when it's convenient, like. She sent Bessie over.'

Livvie frowned, wondering what had prompted this summons. After Mam's death, as a family they'd grown closer to their neighbours. Mr Mayhew had persuaded her pa to join the gentleman's club he frequented and often, when he was absent, she and Amy spent the evening with Selina and her siblings. Of course quite often Amy and Jonty squabbled, although of late that seemed to have become a less frequent occurrence as her sister was growing up, but she'd found Teddy Mayhew to be a lot friendlier towards her. She did wonder if that was because he felt sorry for her.

'Tell Bessie to say I'll be over in about five minutes. I don't want to be out when Amy gets home,' she replied. Since the day Edith died she'd not once let her sister come back to an empty house. Of course now Emily would be here but it wasn't the same. Amy had really struggled with her grief and loss. She'd pleaded to be allowed to leave school, to stay at home and not have to face the pity of her classmates. Not have to listen to them talking of their families, especially their mothers. Her pleas had fallen on deaf ears for Pa had flatly refused and so she'd had to continue her education although Livvie knew that her work had suffered in those first months. She always made time to sit with her sister when she got home and ask about her day, the way Edith had done.

'I'll just finish this, Emily. Then I'd be grateful if you would take it down to the Home and Colonial Stores and ask them to deliver it on Friday, please.'

Emily nodded. 'Will it be all right if I wait until the laundry's been delivered, miss?'

Livvie nodded. 'Oh, I'd forgotten about that and Pa's in need of clean shirts. Yes, take it down later on, please.'

The girl smiled, thinking there would be hell to pay if the master didn't have a clean shirt tomorrow morning. Miss Livvie would never hear the end of it. 'I will. They don't close until six, miss.'

'Amy and I will make a start on the vegetables for supper, so there's no need for you to be racing down there and back.'

The girl disappeared and Livvie finished off the list. It had all been a bit of trial and error managing the shopping, paying the household bills and making sure the laundry was collected and delivered on time, doing the housework and finding time to do the mending jobs too, but at least now she had Emily, although she refused to let her father know how much she depended on the girl.

She got up from the writing bureau that was set in a corner of the parlour and caught sight of herself in the mirror on the wall. Had she changed? she wondered. She certainly didn't *look* any different, she thought, although Selina said she was more serious and had definitely lost some weight. She peered at her image intently. Did she look older? Was that a frown line developing between her brows? Well, of course she *was* older; she was eighteen and she really must try not to frown when she was concentrating or that line would deepen.

Her attitude towards her father had changed; she was aware of that. She still blamed him for her mother's death, that hadn't changed, but she'd become more confident and self-reliant so she didn't always meekly agree with everything he said. Now, she would question his decisions if she didn't agree. She would never be rude or impertinent, that wasn't how Edith had brought her up, but she'd put her point of view quietly and politely and even if they couldn't agree, she at least felt she had made her opinions known. She was growing from a girl to a young woman and one who knew her own mind.

She made up the fire and glanced around the room to see that everything was in order before she left. It was very comfortably furnished now, she mused, and many of the pieces of furniture she had helped her pa choose. The fine china ornaments, cushion covers, lace arm caps on the chairs and sofa she had chosen herself, something that gave her a deal of satisfaction. She was sure Mam would have approved of her taste and the way she had tried to make the house look more like the affluent, comfortable home Edith would have wanted.

Taking her jacket from the cloakroom in the hall for the November afternoon was raw, she hurried next door to see what Maud wanted.

'She's in the parlour, miss,' Bessie informed her with a grin, taking her jacket.

Livvie found Maud sitting in a chair beside the roaring fire, gazing thoughtfully into the flames.

'Is something wrong?' Livvie asked as the older woman indicated that she should sit in the chair facing her.

Maud sat up straighter and collected her thoughts. 'No, dear. I just wanted to talk to you, to suggest something.'

Livvie waited in silence although she was curious.

'I've been thinking, Livvie, that as your poor mother has been . . . gone for nearly two years and we've all become closer and with Christmas approaching again . . . Well, have you ever heard the term "aunt by respect"?'

Livvie shook her head, wondering what on earth Maud had in mind.

'It's used as a term of respect and affection for someone who although isn't related is . . . close.'

'I see,' Livvie replied, although she didn't. She was still mystified.

Maud smiled ruefully. 'Oh, I'm not making a very good job of this, am I? What I am trying to say, Livvie, is that I would be very pleased if both you and Amy would call me "Aunt Maud". After all, dear, it seems absurd for you girls to call me "Mrs Mayhew" as if I am a perfect stranger.'

Livvie didn't know what to say. There had been times when it had seemed rather formal to call someone who had helped so much since Mam had died by her correct title. She thought for a moment and then smiled. 'I . . . We'd like that.' A thought occurred to her. 'Are we to call Mr Mayhew "Uncle Charles"?' she asked, thinking that perhaps her father might not approve, considering this 'not the done thing'.

Maud pondered this. 'I don't see why not.'

'I've a feeling that Pa might say it's . . . disrespectful.'

Maud nodded. Yes, Tom Goodwin just might say that. He

was overly conscious of what he considered 'proper', in her opinion. 'Well, there's no reason why you shouldn't refer to Charles as "Uncle" and I'll tell your father so myself.'

Livvie's smile had a hint of mischief in it. 'What about Selina, Teddy and Jonty? Do we call them "cousin"?'

Maud laughed. 'That I think would be taking it a bit far!'

Livvie laughed too. 'I can't see Amy being very happy calling Jonty her cousin.'

'Nor Jonty either!' Maud replied. 'Well, now that that's settled, let's have some tea and you can tell me what plans you have for the festive season. I've a few of my own.'

Livvie became thoughtful again. 'Only that like last year I'll try to make it as happy as I can.'

Maud nodded sympathetically, remembering how last year the poor girl had tried so hard but it had been an uphill task and not helped by the fact that all the extra work had fallen to her.

'At least this year, Livvie, you'll have Emily to help and of course we'd like you all to come here for lunch and to spend the afternoon and evening with us too – if you'd like to.'

Livvie nodded her agreement. She fervently prayed that this year Christmas would indeed be happier. They'd all been miserable last year, despite the fact that they'd come here for lunch and the Mayhews had done their best to raise their spirits, but it had been the first one without Mam and they'd all felt her loss deeply. 'Yes, thank you. Amy and I would like that and I'm sure Pa will too. Better than him sitting brooding.'

'Good, that's settled. We'll get together tomorrow morning with Bessie and Emily and sort everything out. You and Emily come over here when Amy's gone to school. She hasn't got much longer there now, has she?'

Livvie shook her head. 'No, and she'll be very relieved to leave. She hasn't been happy, she didn't want to have to go in the first place when we moved here and it's only in the last nine months that her work has improved. She really does miss Mam and is still struggling to come to terms with it all.'

Maud nodded. She was aware that Amy bitterly resented having to go to school and she was sure that in time the girl would feel the loss of her mother less. 'But don't let her mope around the house, Livvie, after she's left. That won't help her at all.'

'I won't. I'll find plenty of things to keep her occupied. She's going to have to learn to run a house, the way I have, because one day I'm sure she'll want to get married.'

'As she's only fifteen that's a long way off but I do agree.' Maud paused and looked intently at Livvie. 'And what about you? You should get out more often and meet . . . people. The last thing your poor mother would have wanted was for you to spend your life looking after your father. She would have wanted you to get married and have a family of your own.'

'I know, but I've got plenty of time yet to meet . . . someone.'

'Not if you don't go anywhere,' Maud reminded her succinctly. She'd been toying with the idea of having a small party for New Year. Charles had associates who had sons and daughters and she could ask Teddy to invite some of his friends too. Livvie was a very attractive girl and it wouldn't be at all fair if she just devoted her life to looking after Tom. The girl deserved a better future than that. And Maud had Selina to think about too; both girls had reached an age where an engagement could be considered. Idly, she wondered had Tom even thought about finding a suitable husband for Livvie? She doubted it, for he seemed too wrapped up in his business; but perhaps he was devoting all his energies to that to filling the gap Edith must have left in his life. She made up her mind. Yes, she'd have a party.

'I've had an idea. I think I'll host a small party to usher in the New Year. We haven't had one for years,' she announced.

Livvie looked surprised. 'I've never been to a real grown-up party before!'

Maud beamed happily. 'Then that's even more of a reason for me to host one.'

Bessie entered with the tea tray and Maud busied herself with the teapot. Livvie's visit had proved to be very satisfactory indeed, she thought.

'Shall I mention both Christmas and New Year to Pa . . . er . . . Aunt Maud?' she asked, hesitating a little over this new form of address.

'Just Christmas for now, dear. Give me a chance to let Uncle Charles get used to the idea of a New Year party,' she finished, handing Livvie a bone-china cup and saucer.

'What about Amy? Is she to come too?' Livvie asked, unsure if her sister was to be included.

'Of course. I think it's time she was allowed to put her hair up and lengthen her skirts. She's no longer a child, Livvie, she has to learn to be a young lady and to behave accordingly,' Maud replied firmly.

Livvie nodded, thinking her sister would be delighted to be invited and to have her first grown-up party dress. Aunt Maud was right, Amy wasn't a child. The realisation made her feel a little sad that Mam wasn't here to see Amy's transition.

'The Lord alone knows what I am going to do with Jonty! He's definitely not old enough for purely adult company; heaven knows what he'd go saying to people. I suspect I'm going to have to bribe him to keep a low profile,' Maud said with a rueful little smile as Livvie sipped her tea.

Amy was indeed excited at the imminent prospect of being invited to an adult party and having her first grown-up dress.

'You really mean it, Livvie? You're sure she said I was to go too?'

'Of course, Amy! We'll go into town at the weekend and do some shopping.'

Amy suddenly looked downcast. 'What if Pa won't let me go? What if he says I'm still too young?'

'Then I'll remind him that I was your age when Mam decided my childhood days were over, just as Aunt Maud has decided that yours are too,' Livvie replied firmly. Even if she had to stand up to her father over this she would do so. Amy wasn't going to be disappointed by some misplaced sense of what he considered 'proper'. 'You do realise, Amy, that you're going to have to be initiated into the wearing of the dreaded corset? It's one of the drawbacks of being grown up!' She grimaced. 'Someone, somewhere decided that all women should appear to have a tiny waist so we have to suffer for the sake of fashion.'

'Oh, I won't mind that,' Amy replied happily, thinking excitedly about the new dress and just how she would wear her hair.

Livvie grimaced again. 'Oh, you will, just wait and see.'

Thankfully Thomas put up no opposition when Livvie informed him of Maud's plans for a New Year's Eve party and the fact that Amy was invited and would therefore have to be attired accordingly. He just sighed and nodded.

'Just make sure she doesn't choose something inappropriate for her age.'

'Of course, Pa,' she replied and although relieved there had been no argument she thought that he really didn't seem very interested. He seemed more impressed by the fact that Charles Mayhew's friends and associates had been invited too.

The shopping trip was everything Amy had anticipated. Selina insisted on accompanying them and they window shopped to start with.

'Just to give you some idea of what's in fashion,' Livvie remarked as they gazed into the windows of some of Liverpool's bigger shops.

Amy was quite happy to do that and then they decided to settle for Cripps in Bold Street, which seemed to be displaying some very elegant clothes.

Livvie explained to the sales assistant what her sister required for the occasion and also confided that it was Amy's first foray into adult society. Three dresses were brought for Amy to try on as well as the necessary undergarments. One was pale blue moiré silk; one apple-green taffeta and the third lilac silk. All had short puffed sleeves, scooped necklines, tight bodices and full skirts and Livvie and Selina sat in the small, gilt-framed chairs provided and watched approvingly as each was fitted. Livvie and Selina exchanged sympathetic smiles as

Amy caught her breath, her eyes widening in shock as the corset lacings were pulled ever tighter.

'Oh, Amy, you look lovely in that apple green,' Selina enthused as the assistant carefully spread the wide skirts of the dress around the girl's feet. 'Your waist is just so tiny!'

Amy smiled her thanks, feeling as if her breath had been cut off completely, making speech impossible. Oh, Livvie was right! This felt like torture and how on earth was she supposed to eat?

'Which do you prefer, Amy?' Livvie asked after the others had been tried on.

'I . . . I . . . think the . . . green one,' Amy managed to get out.

Livvie nodded. 'We'll take that one then please,' she informed the assistant.

'A very good choice, miss,' the woman replied, nodding.

'Livvie, are you not going to buy one too?' Selina enquired. She herself had already seen a gorgeous cobalt-blue velvet trimmed with silver lace that she'd fallen in love with.

'I'd not thought, but I suppose I should have one. It's my first adult party too,' she agreed.

'And there will be quite a few rather nice young fellows attending, according to Mother,' Selina confided, arching her eyebrows.

Livvie settled on the lilac silk, feeling that she couldn't quite bring herself to wear very bright colours in public yet. Of course she wouldn't say that to Amy for her sister was obviously delighted with her dress and it really did suit her. Perhaps they would look for a fancy diamanté clip for Amy's hair too – that would set the dress off to perfection.

'And you'll need evening shoes, Amy, and a bag,' Selina urged.

'But nothing with too high a heel,' Livvie cautioned, wondering how her pa was going to react to all the expense.

With their purchases all boxed and wrapped they decided that refreshments were called for before making the journey home and, throwing caution to the winds, they headed for the Adelphi Hotel, Liverpool's grandest, for afternoon tea. It would round off the day and mark Amy's entry into the adult world of polite society, Livvie remarked.

Amy was of course delighted at the suggestion yet a little daunted by the prospect for neither of them had ever set foot inside such a palatial building before; but then she told herself she'd better get used to such places if she was now considered grown up. She knew that both Livvie and Selina were really looking forward to this party and she hoped she wouldn't make a fool of herself. At least Jonty wouldn't be around making fatuous or embarrassing remarks, she thought thankfully, since Aunt Maud was sending him to stay with a school friend for the night. As she sat down in the sumptuous surroundings of the grand lobby she glanced around. It certainly did live up to its reputation, she thought with a little thrill of excitement. She wasn't disappointed in any way.

Chapter Seven

———

Christmas had indeed been a much more joyful occasion than last year, Livvie thought as on New Year's Eve both she and Amy got ready for the Mayhews' party. She'd found Emily a huge help both with the shopping, baking and decorating the house. Pa had seemed in much better spirits and she had to admit that although she had missed Mam terribly, the pain hadn't been as raw as last year. Spending most of the day next door really had helped. Over the huge lunch, served by both Bessie and Emily – both of whom, when they'd finished, had gone to their respective homes – there had been so much light-hearted chatter that there had been little time to dwell on their sadness. She, her pa, Uncle Charles and Aunt Maud had played cards in the evening, which she'd enjoyed, even though she wasn't really very proficient and hadn't managed to win very often. Selina and Amy had spent the time leafing through magazines and discussing the merits of the hairstyles favoured by the ladies of the royal family. She thought Teddy had shown infinite patience with Jonty, although she suspected the half-tumbler of whiskey had contributed to that. Jonty was much taken with Kipling's *Jungle Book*; it had been one of his gifts, inspired by his enthusiasm for Baden-Powell's Boy Scout movement, which he intended to join, boring his elder brother with how it was all based on the characters in Kipling's book, something she was sure Teddy already knew. Yes, she had to admit that they had passed the day in a far happier mood than last year.

Sitting at the dressing table she clipped on her silver and amethyst drop earrings and patted her hair, pleased with her handiwork. She favoured the upswept style known as the 'cottage loaf', which she hoped suited her and looked elegant too. She'd spent a long time doing Amy's hair and it had taken a bit of persuasion to get her sister to agree that the style favoured by both Queen Alexandra and Princess May was rather too old for her and that a much looser, less rigidly curled and waved style would be better. The addition of the sparkly clip had added a touch of sophistication, she'd assured Amy, and her sister had happily gone to fetch her dress.

She stood up and looked at her own lilac silk laid carefully across the bed. She and Amy would help each other dress for it was virtually impossible to do up the tiny buttons that fastened the bodice back unaided. Sharing getting dressed was something she enjoyed but oh, how much easier it would be if they didn't have to wear such restricting and complicated clothes, she thought. Still, tonight promised to be worth it.

They were to be ready and downstairs in the hall by eight sharp, her father had instructed, and so with a last glance at their appearances in the long cheval mirror they went down.

As they descended the staircase, long skirts held up carefully to avoid tripping and with Amy clinging tightly to the banister rail in case she wobbled and fell in her newly acquired heeled slippers, Livvie thought how splendid her father looked in his new evening suit – a fairly recent fashion for men made popular by King Edward when he'd been Prince of Wales. Suddenly she wished Mam were here to see them all in their finery, particularly Amy, who did look lovely on this her first 'big' occasion.

'Well, I have to say it was money well spent. You both look very . . . presentable,' Thomas said, nodding approvingly. No one could say his daughters were not the equal of the girls and women who would be at the party tonight.

'Thank you, Pa, I'm glad you approve of our choices. You look very smart too,' Livvie replied as he ushered them towards the door, a little disappointed that all he had been able to come up with was 'presentable'.

'You both look the bees' knees!' Emily whispered enthusiastically as she opened the door for them.

Livvie smiled back. 'Thank you.' No doubt Emily would be glad to get off home now though, she mused, but there would be no time off for poor Bessie until much later tonight.

The Mayhews' house blazed with lights and Bessie ushered them into the hall where quite a few people lingered.

'Goodness, how many people were invited?' Livvie whispered to the girl.

Bessie raised her eyes to the ceiling. 'More than I thought there would be! It's quite crowded in the parlour too, but that's where the young ones mostly are, so I'd go in there.

There's food laid out in the dinin' room,' she informed them in a low voice.

They were greeted by Maud and Charles; Thomas was quickly introduced to Charles's friends and associates and drawn into their circle while Maud introduced their wives to Livvie and Amy.

Selina, looking stunning in the blue velvet, quickly drew both girls into the group of young men and girls who had congregated in the bay window.

'Amy, you look wonderful! I love what Livvie has done with your hair,' she enthused.

Amy smiled happily, although she felt rather shy.

'I hardly recognised you, Amy. You look so grown up – and quite stunning, I might add,' Teddy commented, smiling and thinking that both sisters were very attractive. He had to admit that Amy had definitely blossomed.

Amy blushed and managed another smile as he turned to Livvie.

'And you look very elegant, Livvie.'

'Thank you, Teddy,' she replied. She liked Teddy but had no romantic inclinations towards him.

'You look so elegant, Selina. That colour really does suit you,' Livvie complimented her friend.

Selina smiled back. 'Now, let me introduce you to everyone.'

Livvie soon found that most of their new acquaintances were pleasant and lively company and of a similar age to herself. She noted that Amy appeared to be a little out of her depth and stayed firmly by Selina's side, saying very little. Light-hearted topics of general interest were discussed until the older sister of one of Teddy's friends brought up the subject of women's suffrage and the fact that thankfully there was to be an official investigation into the treatment of women prisoners in Winson Green Prison in Birmingham.

'It's an absolute disgrace the way that poor Mrs Ainsworth was treated!' Millicent Parker said forcefully.

Some of the other girls nodded but Livvie noticed that all the young men remained silent. Of course she knew of the suffragettes and their demands – that every woman be given the right to vote – for they had been enduring prison sentences for four years. She thought they were all rather brave but she didn't have any strongly held opinions on women's rights. Naturally her pa had been very vocal in his opinion of Eleanor Rathbone, who had founded the Liverpool Women's Suffrage Society earlier in the year. He was profoundly shocked to say the least, he'd declared, that a woman of her standing in society, the daughter of a prominent Liverpool family, indeed herself an elected member of the city council, would initiate such a society. Livvie didn't think it was as awful as he made it out to be. Eleanor Rathbone was the very first woman member of the council so didn't that say something about women being capable enough to play a part in politics? She didn't see why she shouldn't have her say, just like the men. Of course she hadn't voiced such comments. Then just before Christmas her father'd been utterly incensed by the incident outside the Reform Club in Dale Street and had gone on about it for hours. Hundreds of women had gathered to demonstrate and two of them, dressed as orange-sellers, had thrown bottles, one of which had broken the window of Mr Asquith's car. The Prime Minister hadn't been injured but it was considered an outrage. They'd been arrested and sent to Walton Jail of course.

'How was she treated? What did they do to her?' she asked the girl. She hadn't heard of this Mrs Ainsworth.

'You mean you don't know? Surely you must have read about it in the newspapers?' was the incredulous reply.

'I'm afraid not. I don't have much time to read newspapers. You see my mother died nearly two years ago and I . . . well, I have to keep house.'

The girl nodded. 'Oh, I see. Well, she was given fourteen days in jail for her part in some incident in Birmingham to do with the Prime Minister's visit, although she didn't throw empty ginger beer bottles at him like those brave women in Dale Street. So of course she went on hunger strike in protest. The poor woman was force-fed by the prison doctor. She was held down by wardresses and treated abominably; she's now an invalid in a nursing home. What they did to her was quite horrible in fact—'

'I really don't think that this is the time or the place to be discussing this, Millicent!' her brother interrupted firmly.

'And I'm inclined to agree. I'm afraid I don't hold with their views and we're supposed to be enjoying the evening,' Teddy added and the conversation was abruptly terminated, quite obviously to the annoyance of Millicent Parker, who, muttering 'Men! Just typical!' went to find more congenial company.

'Have you an opinion on the matter, Miss Goodwin? Personally, I agree with Miss Parker.'

Livvie turned to the young man beside her who had asked her the question. So far he'd not contributed to the conversation at all and had seemed to be on the fringe of the group. He was obviously a bit older than the others and she noted that his suit was not quite as well cut but he seemed pleasant enough and he had kind dark brown eyes. 'I'd not heard of Mrs Ainsworth or the incident but, well, I don't think it's right that *anyone* should be subjected to such cruelty and humiliation. Of course I know what the suffragettes are demanding, but I wonder are they really going about it in the right way, Mr . . . ?'

'Francis – Frank – Hadley. I work for your father. I'm his factory manager and he very kindly obtained an invitation for me as I don't have any family. I would have spent the evening on my own, otherwise.'

Livvie smiled. She'd heard her pa talk about him approvingly but hadn't known he'd been invited tonight. 'Then I'm so glad he did. He speaks very highly of you so it's lovely to meet you.'

He smiled at her again. 'Thank you, Miss Goodwin. It's a pleasure to meet you too.'

'Please, call me Livvie. Everyone else does.'

'I think your father might view that as presumptuous, but may I call you Olivia?'

She laughed, thinking he knew her pa's ways well. 'If you must.'

He became serious. 'Most men don't approve of the tactics Mrs Pankhurst and her daughters and followers are using but I fear they have no other way of getting people – the people who matter and can change the laws – to take them seriously. They have exhausted all other avenues, so now it's "deeds not words" they are advocating.'

'So, you think women should be able to vote?'

He nodded slowly. 'Why not? Why shouldn't they have a

say in matters that affect their lives as much as those of their fathers and husbands? I also believe that all workers should be treated and paid fairly although I don't belong to an official trade union.' He smiled. 'But I have to say your father is one of the better employers. Now, shall we move on to something a little less political? I'm sure I'm boring you.'

'Not at all . . . Frank. In fact you've given me something to think about,' she replied truthfully as Charles Mayhew announced that the buffet was being served in the dining room. Frank Hadley courteously ushered her towards the door and Teddy gallantly offered Amy his arm, which brought a flush of pleasure to her sister's cheeks. She hadn't really given much thought to the suffragettes and their demands but she would now. He was right, why shouldn't women have some say in what governed their lives? Both Mrs Pankhurst and Eleanor Rathbone were educated women, as were many of their adherents, but these days many, many more women were better educated and even those who were not were far from stupid or vapid. She'd found Frank Hadley's opinions honest and informed and she liked him.

Chapter Eight

———◆———

She had gleaned a little information about Frank from her father. He was twenty-nine, orphaned at a young age but brought up by an elderly spinster aunt who had paid for him to be well educated. She had died five years ago, leaving him the small house she'd lived in all her life. He'd finished his education at Byrom Street Technical College, before gaining the experience Thomas required and excellent references. Thomas was impressed by Frank's knowledge, the way he worked and how he handled the men.

'He has a way of getting the best out of them without being overly heavy-handed. Strict but fair in all his dealings,' he'd stated. 'You seem very interested in him, Livvie?'

'Oh, I just thought he was very . . . pleasant and well mannered, Pa,' she'd replied, not wishing him to guess how much she'd thought about Frank Hadley since the party.

She'd also read everything she could find on the women's suffrage movement and was deeply disturbed to learn that many had been jailed and that the horrible practice of 'force-feeding' was indeed widespread. She'd read in her pa's newspaper that the two women who had posed as orange-sellers outside the Reform Club had both been sent to Walton Jail and had gone on hunger strike. Both had been subjected to force-feeding and she felt both pity and admiration for Selina Martin and Leslie Hall but thought, with growing resentment, that their sufferings seemed to be in vain. The government simply wouldn't listen to their demands. In fact Mr Asquith flatly refused to speak to any of them.

It came as a surprise therefore when she found out that both Emily and Bessie were keen supporters of Mrs Pankhurst. In fact it was Emily, asking if she could leave earlier the following evening, who revealed this information.

'Of course you can go early, Emily,' she replied to the request. 'Are you going somewhere special? To meet a young man, maybe?' She smiled. Why not? Emily was a rather pretty girl.

'Oh, no, miss! I . . . I'm going to a meeting with Bessie,' Emily informed her.

'A meeting?'

'Yes, miss. It's at the David Lewis Theatre. We've both been before.'

'I see. What is the meeting for?' she enquired, intrigued.

The girl looked a little uneasy. 'It's the suffragettes, miss. I . . . I hope you don't mind? Don't disapprove, like?'

Livvie shook her head. 'No, Emily, I don't disapprove although I'm certain my father does, so we'll not mention it. If he comments then I'll just say you are required at home.'

Emily nodded with some relief.

'I wouldn't have thought either you or Bessie would be interested in politics?'

'I suppose it is "politics" but we don't look at it like that, Miss Livvie. It's about getting a fairer deal for women – all women. Girls like us too, girls in service and working in factories. There's women in this city that have awful lives. I could name a couple in our street.'

Livvie was even more intrigued by this statement. 'Do you go to these demonstrations they have?'

'Bessie's been to one but . . . but . . . well, miss, my da would kill me! He holds the same views as the master.'

'She wasn't at that one before Christmas, was she? The one at which Miss Hall and Miss Martin were arrested?'

'No, miss. She couldn't get the time off. It was a busy time next door, if you remember? But we know that both those poor ladies are having a terrible time in Walton. It's cruel what they are doing to them! Really *cruel*!'

Livvie nodded. 'I know. I've been reading about it and it's shocking!' She looked thoughtful. 'Emily, would you and Bessie mind if I came with you to one of these meetings? I'd like to learn more about it all. I've only read things up to now.'

The girl was taken aback. 'You, miss? Well, I suppose it would be all right with Bessie and me. But what about your pa?' She could well imagine what he'd say.

'I won't tell him,' Livvie stated firmly.

'But what if he finds out, miss?'

Livvie realised that the girl was fearful of being blamed and losing her job. She smiled reassuringly. 'He won't, Emily. I won't tell anyone about it, not even Amy or Selina. I'll think up some plausible excuse, don't worry.'

Emily was still uncertain but at last nodded. 'I don't know when the next one will be after tomorrow night, but I can find out.'

'I'd be glad if you could, Emily,' she urged.

She racked her brains for an excuse but as she seldom went out alone in the evenings it wasn't easy. It had to be something that would satisfy not only her father but her sister and her friend as well and so she was relieved when Emily informed her that there wouldn't be another meeting until Selina Martin and Leslie Hall had been released from prison and would have recovered enough from their ordeal to address them all about their experiences.

A few days later she went into town after lunch to pick up the shirts her father had ordered and to do some shopping. She had intended to be back before the winter afternoon grew dark but, to her consternation, as she came out of the Bon Marché she realised that not only had she lingered too long admiring their display of hats in the millinery department and it was dark but that a thick fog was descending.

Pulling the collar of her coat higher about her ears she set off for the nearest tram stop, shivering as the cold, damp air enveloped her. Oh, this looked as if it was going to be a real pea-souper, she thought anxiously. She waited for what seemed like an age at the stop but no vehicle appeared; in fact there seemed to be very little in the way of traffic altogether and a few of the other people who'd been waiting too had walked away into the gloom.

'If I were you, miss, I'd start walking,' a man who was passing urged her and she realised that she would have to walk the long miles home. She stood hesitating for a few seconds and then decided she would walk to her father's factory. It wasn't that far, she'd been a few times in the past, and at least Pa had his car so maybe they wouldn't have to walk at all. If he drove very, very slowly they would get home – eventually.

By the time she reached the building her eyes were stinging, her throat felt raw and she could taste the soot that impregnated the swirling fog, the result of the smoke from thousands of domestic and industrial chimneys.

'Miss Goodwin – Olivia! What are you doing here? You look frozen!' Frank Hadley greeted her in concern as he ushered her into the office where a fire burned in the small hearth.

'Oh, Frank, I'm so relieved to have reached here! It's awful; you can barely see a hand in front of you!' She *was* relieved and she was indeed cold.

'Come and sit by the fire,' he urged.

'I was shopping so I didn't notice it coming down. There are no trams running, in fact nothing is moving, so I thought it best to make my way here and go home with Pa.'

He frowned. 'I'm afraid you've missed him, Olivia. Seeing how the weather was turning he decided to leave early. I said I'd stay on as it's not far for me to walk home and I let the men go about twenty minutes ago. I was about to lock up.'

'Oh!' she exclaimed, beginning to wonder what she should do now.

Frank came to an instant decision. He couldn't leave her here and he couldn't let her walk home on her own. 'Well, you sit there while I finish securing the place and then I'll walk you home. It's going to be a long, cold trek, I'm afraid.'

'Oh, Frank, I can't let you go all that way with me!' she protested.

'Nonsense! I wouldn't dream of letting you wander around the city in this and what do you think your father would think of me if I did? Totally irresponsible and ill mannered – and he'd be right. No, I'll take you home, Olivia.'

After half an hour she was very grateful to have him beside her and, as he'd suggested, she held tightly on to his arm. She knew both her father and sister would be worried about her but there was nothing she could do about that. To pass the time they talked about their lives and their childhoods. He was very easy to talk to, she thought as she told him about Emily and Bessie both belonging to the suffrage movement and confided that she intended to join them at the next meeting.

'But what I'm going to tell Pa, Amy and even Selina I don't know. And I don't suppose you approve?'

'You have a mind of your own, Olivia. It doesn't matter whether I approve or not: it's your decision. But perhaps you won't need to tell your father anything at all. He often goes to his club with Mr Mayhew, I understand?'

'That's a possibility, I agree, but what if he doesn't go that particular night? And what do I tell the other two?'

'Could you perhaps say I'd asked you to accompany me to a concert? There's bound to be one on at the Philharmonic Hall. A very respectable venue.'

She nodded although she doubted her pa would be very happy about her being seen in public in the company of his factory manager, no matter how 'respectable' the place. 'Yes, I could tell the girls that but . . .' She didn't want to hurt his feelings by implying that her father probably wouldn't approve.

'Then that's settled. You don't have to tell your father anything if he's at his club, you'll be home well before him.' He was well aware of what she was thinking. 'But, just to be on the safe side, I think when the meeting ends I'll be waiting for you. Sometimes there are groups of unsavoury characters just loitering outside to shout and jeer at the ladies – they look on it as a form of entertainment, and I'm afraid that the police do little to restrain them. At least I can see you safely on the tram.'

'Thank you, Frank. That's very kind of you,' she agreed. That was something she hadn't known. Hopefully she wouldn't have to tell Pa but if she did . . . well, she would say it would have been churlish to refuse his invitation but she didn't intend to make it a regular occurrence. She'd say the same thing to Amy and Selina.

It seemed as if they had been walking for hours and hours before they reached Poplar Avenue and she was exhausted and chilled to the bone by the time she climbed the front steps. She had no idea what time it was.

'Oh, miss! We've been so worried about you!' Emily cried as she let them in and Thomas appeared from the parlour.

'Livvie! Frank! Surely to God you've not walked all the way from the Dock Estate?'

'I'm sorry, Pa, for worrying you all. But when the fog came down I walked to the factory thinking I'd come home with you, but . . .'

'Come on over to the fire. You must both be exhausted and frozen,' Thomas urged.

'The men had gone and I was locking up when she arrived but I couldn't let her try to walk all the way on her own, Mr Goodwin.'

'Thank you, Frank. You'd better stay here tonight. You can't possibly walk all that way back,' Thomas announced, pouring two glasses of whiskey from the decanter that stood on the sideboard and handing his young manager one.

'Oh, I don't mind. I've not come . . . prepared, and I didn't intend to . . . impose,' Frank said. He hadn't expected this.

'You're not imposing. Emily will make up the bed in the spare room, and don't worry, we'll sort out the other things. Now, drink that down. You must need it,' he instructed firmly. 'Amy, ask Emily if she can prepare something for them both to eat, please,' he added.

'We had supper ages ago,' Amy informed her sister.

Livvie smiled tiredly at her. All she wanted now was a cup of tea, a hot meal and her bed. She'd never been so glad to get home and she was very, very grateful to Frank for his consideration, his company and his offer to help her find a way to attend the suffrage meeting. She got to her feet wearily to make a pot of tea but before doing so she turned to Frank. 'I'm really sorry that I dragged you all this way, Frank, but thank you.'

He smiled at her, admitting to himself that his liking for her was growing. In fact he felt strongly attracted to her.

'Well, perhaps next time, Livvie, you'll think about getting home earlier but I have to say I, too, am very grateful to you, Frank,' Thomas said somewhat dourly.

'It was the least I could do,' Frank replied, wondering if Thomas Goodwin would object strongly now should Livvie have to use an evening out with him as her excuse to attend a suffrage meeting. He was acutely aware that there was a vast difference in their social status, which made him feel slightly depressed. Thomas Goodwin would be almost as unhappy about his daughter walking out with him as he would about her going to a suffrage meeting. He had to keep his feet on the ground, he told himself, and not allow himself any delusions about the part he might play in Livvie Goodwin's life.

Chapter Nine

Livvie didn't have to inform her father of where she was going when the next suffrage meeting was held. He'd told her that he wouldn't be in for supper on Tuesday; he would have dinner at his club with Richard Fitzgerald, one of his associates, as he had something rather important to discuss with him. She'd been very relieved, preferring not to have to lie to him about her outing or risk revealing Frank Hadley's part in the subterfuge.

She'd already told both Amy and Selina that she was going to the Philharmonic Hall with him and the news had been met with some surprise by Selina at least.

'I think he's sweet on you, Livvie. After all, he walked all the way home with you that night in the fog and now he's taking you to a concert,' Selina had said archly.

'I don't know, Selina. I . . . I don't think so,' she'd replied, feeling guilty that she couldn't explain to her friend exactly why she would be seeing Frank.

'Do you . . . like him?' Selina wasn't going to be fobbed off.

After all, Henry Woodford, one of Teddy's friends, had asked her pa if he could call on her and she was delighted, so why shouldn't Livvie have a young man too? Granted, Frank Hadley was really quite old and only a factory manager whereas Henry was a cotton broker in Exchange Flags, but Frank was handsome enough and pleasant and it wasn't as if her friend was getting engaged to him or anything.

'Yes, I do like him. What is there not to like about him?'

Selina had tutted impatiently; Livvie was being hard to pin down. 'I mean do you think it could develop into something more? Affection, maybe?'

Livvie had laughed. 'You're beginning to sound like your mother, Selina Mayhew! I'm not thinking of settling down just yet! It's just an evening at the Philharmonic Hall, that's all.'

Selina had had to be content with that answer.

Amy had been more concerned and had asked different questions. 'Do you think you should tell Pa?'

Livvie had shaken her head. 'No. What if he forbids me to go? You know what he's like when he gets something into his head: there's no moving him. What if he says it's not "fitting"? What could I say to Frank even though it's just a concert? How could I hurt his feelings?'

Amy had slowly nodded her agreement.

'And it would be very churlish of me to refuse Frank after he's bought tickets and was so good making sure I got home safely in the fog.'

Amy had thought about that. 'Couldn't you say that to Pa?'

'I could but would it make any difference? No, Amy, I'll just not tell him. I'll be home before he is; you know he's often late back from his club and he says he's got something important to discuss with this Mr Fitzgerald.'

Amy had still been apprehensive. 'But what if you're not back? I'll have to tell him where you've gone and then he'll probably be furious you didn't mention it to him, let alone ask him first!' Amy certainly didn't want to face that prospect.

Livvie had smiled at her. 'You won't. Just go to bed a bit earlier; then you won't have to say anything to anyone. Leave me to deal with it – if it happens,' she'd said firmly. She really didn't want to embroil her sister in all this deception any more than was necessary and had begun to wonder if it was all worth it – until she remembered those two poor girls who had been sent to Walton Jail. They'd stood up for what they believed in so surely she could find the courage to face her father if need be? If he weren't so inflexible and old-fashioned there would be no need for her to think up excuses. She was eighteen years old; surely it wasn't inconceivable that she should want to go out in the evenings? Surely she had the right to attend this meeting without having to tell lies? She'd sighed, knowing her father would indeed be furious if he knew that she was interested in the suffragettes. If he found out where she'd gone there would be a huge argument and she'd probably not get out again, so what alternative did she have?

Thankfully the evenings were still dark so no one saw her as she walked to the tram stop where Bessie and Emily were waiting for her and they travelled into the city centre together. When they alighted she was surprised to see that there were crowds of women and girls entering the theatre – she hadn't expected there to be such interest.

'Are these events always this well attended?'

Bessie nodded enthusiastically. 'They are, miss. An' as you can see there are quite a few girls like us here too. It's not just for ladies an' the well-off; all women are welcome. As Miss Wilkinson says, "We're all sisters in this fight."'

She realised Bessie was right as they made their way inside the building. The majority of the women were well dressed but there were indeed many girls from the working classes. She was given a green, white and purple rosette to pin to the lapel of her coat although she informed the young woman who took her name that this was her first meeting and that she'd really come to learn more, not to join – just yet.

The woman smiled. 'That's quite all right, Miss Goodwin, you are still very welcome and we hope that you might join us – in time.'

The theatre, which wasn't one of the city's largest, being only a third of the size of the Empire on Lime Street, was already quite full but Bessie found them seats at the end of a row quite near to the front and Livvie settled down to listen to the speakers. There was huge applause when Miss Martin and Miss Hall were introduced, followed by some murmurings of sympathy for both looked pale and rather nervous.

'You can see they've still not fully recovered. Shockin', it was, the way they were treated,' Bessie whispered loudly and Livvie nodded.

As she listened to the two quietly spoken and indeed rather demurely mannered girls speak of the treatment they had suffered at the hands of the prison authorities Livvie felt anger rising, mingled with both pity and admiration. These were ordinary, usually law-abiding and hard-working young women from respectable backgrounds who had been humiliated and subjected to the abominably cruel procedures of force-feeding. Held down by wardresses, their mouths forced and kept open by a metal brace and a tube inserted down their throats and a thin gruel poured down it. It just didn't bear even thinking about, she thought, shuddering. But, as the rather formidable lady who had introduced the two young women had said, for years they had tried to reason, to negotiate, to put their demands calmly and concisely to the politicians and all to no avail. Now they were left with civil disobedience as their only weapon. They had no burning desire to break the law, they were not criminals, but they had reached the point of desperation. They were only demanding what was right and fair and look at the way they were being treated.

Incensed by the savage treatment Selina Martin and Leslie Hall had suffered, Livvie began to realise that sometimes in this life you had to stand up for what you believed in. But she really wasn't sure if she would have the moral, physical and indeed mental strength to endure what they had been subjected to.

By the time the meeting had drawn to a close she was thinking more deeply about women's rights. She felt certain that her mother would have approved. Although her mother had been of a different generation she was sure she would have had sympathy for the fairness under the law they were demanding and disapproved of the treatment they were receiving from the authorities. She would give the whole matter a great deal of thought regardless of what her father thought or said.

As they made their way towards the exits she sought out the woman who had given her the rosette. 'I very much enjoyed the meeting and would like to come again.'

Miss Wilkinson smiled. 'I'm glad you found it enlightening and we'd be happy to see you here for the next one.'

'Thank you and I intend to give some serious thought to what has been spoken about tonight. I don't know if I've got as much courage as those two young ladies, but I do admire and respect them,' she informed Sarah Wilkinson, who had shaken her hand. Afterwards Livvie had accompanied Bessie and Emily towards the doors.

'Will you tell your pa, miss? That you intend to come to the next meeting?' Emily asked.

Livvie shrugged reluctantly. 'Well, if I decide to attend on a regular basis I suppose I'll have to at some stage, Emily. I don't intend to go on telling him I'm going to fictitious concerts and the like, but don't worry, I won't involve either you or Bessie.'

Emily was relieved to hear that. 'He won't like it, miss. I know my da was livid when I told him. It was only because of my mam that I didn't get a hiding but he made me swear I wouldn't go on these demonstrations or go throwing stones or chaining myself to railings and the like.'

'Mine is none too happy either but I told him I don't care. I'm twenty-one, I work hard, I've a mind of my own an' if I want to "demonstrate" I will!' Bessie declared with spirit as they emerged into the street.

'Oh, look at this lot!' Emily cried, a little alarmed by the crowd of jeering men and boys who had congregated in the road outside the theatre.

'Take no notice of them, Em! They're just drunks and hooligans. I'll sort them out if they start on us! We'll all stick together, Miss Livvie, we'll be all right,' Bessie promised grimly, roughly shoving aside two scruffy-looking lads who stank of ale.

'Olivia! Olivia!'

Hearing her name Livvie peered through the crowd and relief washed over her as she saw Frank Hadley shouldering his way determinedly towards them. 'Oh, Frank! I'm so glad you came to meet us!' she called, glancing back at the jeering men.

With some authority and not a little force he shepherded the three girls away from the mêlée and towards the end of the road.

'Thanks very much for your help, sir, but I'm sure we would have managed, not that that flamin' copper standin' on the corner just watchin' would have shifted himself to do anythin' to help! They're just drunken bullies and I'm well able to deal with the likes of them. Goodnight,' Bessie said, urging Emily to walk ahead with her.

'That's a very strong-minded young lady,' Frank commented, offering Livvie his arm as he watched the two women walk briskly down the road.

'She is,' Livvie replied. 'I wish I was more like her. She told her father she's twenty-one, she's a mind of her own and she'll do as she pleases whether he likes it or not.'

Frank grinned. 'And what did you tell *your* father?'

She looked up at him and smiled. 'Nothing. He did go to his club, so there was no need to say anything, although I told Amy and Selina I was going out with you.'

He nodded. 'And did you find this evening . . . enlightening?'

'I did indeed. I was deeply touched, Frank, by what every-one had to say, especially Miss Martin and Miss Hall. Their treatment was brutal! Violent and horribly painful. I learned things I'd had no idea about before and I intend to go to the next meeting.'

'Then that's promising, Olivia. Times are moving forward. Will you tell your father of your decision?'

Livvie hesitated. 'I'm not sure yet. I'll have to think about it. But I know what he'll say and that he'll forbid me to have anything more to do with them,' she said flatly.

Frank nodded. 'I know. He thinks their demands are ludicrous and their behaviour outrageous. Perhaps it might be as well not to say anything – yet.'

Livvie sighed. 'I'll just have to hope that he's always out when there are meetings.'

'You know you can always count on me if you need an excuse,' he offered.

'That's really good of you, Frank, but I can't drag you into any arguments that might – *will* – occur when he finds out. It's not fair on you and I won't jeopardise your position or your standing in Pa's eyes.'

'And you think he wouldn't like his daughter to appear to be walking out with his lowly working-class factory manager?'

She stopped and looked up at him. 'I wouldn't care what he would think about that, Frank! You are far from "lowly", as you put it; you are well educated and have a responsible position and I don't have Pa's misguided sense of class. For heaven's sake, he started out as a farm labourer and you can't get much more "working class" than that! No, leave Pa to me. If I am to attend meetings regularly then I have to be able to stand up to *anyone* for what I believe in and I'm coming to the conclusion that I fully believe in what they are demanding.'

They had reached the tram stop and a tram was approaching. 'Then I have to say good luck, Olivia, I can see you're every bit as strong-minded as Bessie and you have my admiration.'

Before she could reply the tram rattled to a stop and he handed her on to the platform, waved and turned away. She felt her cheeks redden with pleasure at his compliment and suddenly she thought she really wouldn't mind walking out with him in reality. In fact she'd quite like it.

Chapter Ten

———◆———

She had no need to resort to more subterfuge to attend the next meeting for her father was once more going out, and again Frank met her and walked the three girls to the tram stop, Bessie and Emily tactfully walking on a little ahead.

'How did you know I would be here? It's almost impossible for me to let you know,' she asked as she held on to his arm and walked beside him.

'I made it my business to find out – the meetings are well advertised, and I knew your father wouldn't be at home tonight,' he informed her. 'But perhaps in future you could send a note in the post? I'll give you my home address. That way I'll know definitely if you will be attending.' He glanced back at the raucous crowd that had gathered to taunt the women as they left – he was no less concerned for her safety now than he had been last time he'd met her.

She nodded, wondering how, if she should need to say she was out with him, they could get their stories straight. Oh, she wished she could just put on her coat and hat and say she was going out and no awkward questions would be asked but she might as well wish that pigs would fly.

'Who is this Mr Fitzgerald Pa seems to be seeing so much of?' she asked to change the subject.

'One of his associates, I presume. Someone he met at his club but I've not come across him in the course of business. I didn't realise he saw that much of him.'

Livvie frowned. 'He's had dinner with him numerous times and has even been to see him in his home the last few Sunday afternoons. I asked Aunt Maud about him but she didn't know any more than me. Like you, she thinks he's just a business acquaintance but if you've not come across him . . .' She shrugged and then smiled up at him. 'Long may it continue if it means I don't have to tell him a pack of lies.'

He smiled at her. She was an open, honest girl and he knew it sat ill with her that she had to resort to such behaviour. 'But don't forget you'll have to keep up the pretence with Amy and Selina Mayhew,' he reminded her.

'I suppose so and soon I'll have Selina asking me if I'm walking out with you, although she's so taken up with Henry Woodford at the moment that my outings are not of much interest to her.'

'And what will you say, if she does ask?' he queried gently, hoping against hope that she had meant what she'd said about the difference in their class not mattering.

Livvie felt herself beginning to blush. The fact was that she really *did* like him and she felt safe with him. 'If she asks I'll say I am. Would you mind?' It did seem rather forward, she thought.

'Of course not but I know I'm not exactly who your father would choose . . .'

'I dread to think of the type of man he would choose and anyway it's nineteen hundred and ten, not *eighteen* hundred and ten! He chose Mam, so why shouldn't I choose whom I walk out with?'

He smiled down at her, wishing that all this talk about her walking out with him was based on reality, not just an excuse to her friends for her attendance at the suffrage meetings. 'Perhaps it might be wise not to mention anything to your father, even if you feel you should be able to choose whom you see?' he suggested.

Livvie smiled and nodded. 'Then let's hope he continues to see more of this Mr Fitzgerald, and then I can attend my meetings and see you afterwards.'

Before she boarded the tram he surprised himself by his boldness as impulsively he bent and kissed her gently on the cheek. Then he stood and waved as the vehicle pulled away.

Livvie sat down beside Emily and Bessie, her cheeks flushed and her eyes sparkling with happiness. He must *really* like her to have kissed her goodbye. 'If either of you say a single word to *anyone* I'll kill you both!' she hissed.

'Us, miss? We didn't see nothin', did we, Em?' Bessie replied in mock surprise and all three of them laughed.

Livvie thought about Frank a great deal the following day and she admitted to herself that she was really looking forward to seeing him again. She wondered if she should try to find out if her father would be out on the evening of the next meeting but she was really beginning to resent the way his ideas and opinions were restricting her life and her choices. Maybe she should just tell him the truth. She didn't want to have a full-blown argument with him but she would if necessary; she couldn't go on telling lies indefinitely. And maybe she should tell him that Frank Hadley met her afterwards and escorted her safely to the tram stop. He knew how trustworthy, loyal and conscientious Frank was; after all he'd been very concerned for her safety the night they'd walked home in the fog. She wanted the opportunity to get to know Frank better, she really liked him and she was sure he was attracted to her too. After all, he'd kissed her goodnight – and was that such a terrible thing? Would it really be the end of the world if in future Frank asked her out and she said yes? She'd told him she didn't agree with her pa's ideas on class but did Frank? She hoped not. She decided that she would pluck up courage and broach the subject of the suffrage meetings after supper that evening. At least her pa wouldn't be out tonight.

She was a little surprised therefore when Emily came into the dining room where she and Amy were just finishing setting the table to say that Mr Goodwin was home and that he wanted to see Livvie in the parlour.

'Did he say why and why he's home this early?' she asked.

Emily shook her head. 'No, and it's not my place to ask, Miss Livvie.'

'Of course. Well, I'd better go and see what he wants.' She sounded far more confident than she felt, wondering if he had somehow found out about Frank or the suffrage meetings. One thing was certain; it must be of some importance for him to come home early.

She found him standing in front of the fireplace, gazing intently into the flames.

'You wanted to see me, Pa?' she stated calmly. He turned to face her and she thought, with relief, that he didn't look annoyed. In fact he looked rather pleased with himself.

'I did, Livvie. I've something important to tell you. It concerns both you and Amy but I felt it best if I tell you first – on your own. I'll inform Amy later.' He smiled and sat down in an armchair and indicated that she should also sit.

Thoroughly mystified she sat on the sofa.

'It's good news. I want to tell you that I'm . . . getting married again.'

She stared at him, unable to believe what he'd just said. '*Married!* Who . . . when . . . ?' she stammered.

'To Miss Mary Fitzgerald. She's the sister of my good friend and associate Richard Fitzgerald.'

Livvie felt as if all the breath had been knocked out of her. So that's why he'd been seeing so much of this Richard Fitzgerald, why he'd visited him in his home. Obviously his interest had been in this woman! Slowly her shock began to dissipate to be replaced by a growing sense of outrage. Her mam had only been dead two years! Oh, she was aware that widowers quite often remarried after a relatively short period of time, but this woman was replacing her *mam*! But no! No one could replace her *mam*! The anger bubbled up inside and she jumped to her feet, clenching her fists tightly as she faced him, white-faced. He'd been responsible for her mother's death. His selfish desire for a son had cost Edith her life and now he was calmly announcing that he was getting married again – and very probably it was that same obsessive desire for a son that was at the bottom of it! Did he care nothing for how she and Amy would feel about this . . . this Mary Fitzgerald coming in to take their mother's place? About how they would feel about *any* woman he'd marry?

'Well, Livvie? Have you nothing to say?' he demanded; by her demeanour he could tell that she was far from happy.

'I . . . I don't know *what* to say except . . . how could you? How *could* you? Have you no . . . respect for Mam, for her memory, for all she sacrificed for you that you can even *think* of bringing another woman into this house as your wife!' she cried, beside herself with indignation.

His expression changed as he too got to his feet. 'Olivia! That's enough! Miss Fitzgerald – Mary – is not just *another* woman, she's—'

'I don't want to know what kind of a woman she is, Pa!' she interrupted, beyond caring if she angered him. 'She could be Princess May herself and I wouldn't care! No one will ever replace Mam and don't think that I will ever accept her.'

He glared at her, momentarily silenced. Although he'd realised that she would find it a shock he'd certainly not expected this furious reaction. He had no intention of trying to justify himself to her: she was his daughter and she would be dutiful. He'd not try to explain that he found Mary attractive and that a man had desires, or that he desperately wanted a son and he hoped Mary would provide him with one. She was young enough, being only twelve years older than Livvie herself, and was from a very respectable background. He knew her brother had been rather relieved to find a suitable husband for his sister, who was now of an age considered by many to be rather 'past her best' where marriage was concerned, and Mary had been gratifyingly pleased to accept his proposal.

'I certainly didn't expect you to be delighted by the prospect, Olivia, but I had hoped that you would understand and accept Mary, even welcome her . . .'

'No!' Livvie was adamant. Could he really not see how hurt she was?

'She has consented to be my wife and I expect you to at least be civil to her!'

'And just *what* am I to call her, Pa? Mam? Mother? Never!'

Thomas was losing his temper. How dare she be so openly scornful and impudent? 'I'll leave that for you, Amy and Mary to decide,' he snapped.

'And what about Amy? How are you going to tell her that this Mary Fitzgerald is supposed to replace Mam? It will break her heart; you know how she's struggled to cope since Mam died. Or are you expecting me to tell her?' She felt even more incensed when she thought about how her sister would take the news.

'My decision should not concern your sister unduly and I will tell her,' he stated firmly although he *had* been hoping Livvie would break the news to Amy. However, he considered Amy still to be a child despite her recent transition; her opinion or feelings on the matter were of little consequence to him. Amy would do as she was told.

Livvie felt she could endure his company no longer. She was deeply hurt and all she wanted to do was be alone and cry out her anger. 'Then I'll send her in to you now. Emily will serve your supper. I'm . . . I'm going out!'

He didn't reply or try to stop her as she stormed out of the room. She'd just have to get used to the idea of having a stepmother and so would Amy. No doubt in time things would settle down. At least he hoped they would for his own and Mary's sake. Livvie was being rather short-sighted too, as well as unreasonably emotional. Surely she must realise that Mary would take over the running of the household, relieving her of the responsibility she currently bore. Both she and Amy would marry in time and he had no wish to face a solitary old age. Perhaps by the time they did marry they would have younger siblings too. He certainly wasn't past his prime. No, he stood by his decision. It was for the best, he assured himself firmly, for everyone.

Livvie snatched her coat from the cloakroom and shrugged it on as she left the house, leaving a startled Emily, who had come into the hall staring after her. She ran down the steps and towards the front gate but as she pulled it open she stopped. Where was she going? Where *could* she go? All she'd wanted was to get out of that house. A house that held bittersweet memories for her but which she'd tried so hard to make into a comfortable, happy home for them all. But obviously her efforts hadn't been satisfactory and now he was going to bring in this Mary Fitzgerald who would want to change things, have things done *her* way.

She glanced across at the Mayhews' home. She couldn't burst in on them with this news, let them see how utterly abhorrent she found it. For an instant she wondered had Maud and Charles known? But no, she was certain that Maud would have at least hinted at something if only to prepare her for this shock.

She began to walk slowly along the road, her hands thrust into the pockets of her coat, heedless that she wore no hat or gloves. Oh, why did he have to do this? Couldn't he be satisfied with the way things were? His business was successful and they were comfortably off, and he had friends. Indeed, this woman was the sister of one of them. How was she to face her? How could she accept her into their home, see her in Mam's kitchen? What was worse – far worse – was the fact that she would be sleeping in Mam's bed, the bed where Edith had endured those long hours of an agonising labour. And she would share that bed with her father! Oh, it was . . . *horrible*! Surely he couldn't *love* this Mary Fitzgerald? How could he when he hadn't known her for very long? He'd loved Mam . . . or had he, really? Did he just want a son now, as he had all along?

As she walked on, tears falling slowly down her cheeks, she was oblivious to the fact that it had started to rain. All she knew was that she didn't want to go back home. She didn't want to have to comfort her sister, who would be as shocked and distressed as she was, and she certainly didn't want to see her pa. She felt she was looking at a future with no glimmer of happiness. But then through the gloom of despair she suddenly remembered Frank Hadley and the fact that she would be seeing him again soon. She dashed her tears away with the back of her hand. Well, if Pa was so consumed by his own selfish desires then maybe she would take her own path in life. She would join the suffragettes, regardless of what her pa thought. And she hoped she would see more of Frank and that they would become . . . closer.

Chapter Eleven

———◆———

Eventually Livvie realised that she couldn't walk the streets all night, she would have to go back no matter how repugnant the thought was for she had nowhere else to go and she was cold and wet. Slowly she retraced her steps but when she reached the house she decided to go in through the back door, not wishing to take the chance of encountering her father. She wondered if Emily had gone home, but even if she had it was still too early for Pa to have locked up for the night.

The girl was just finishing putting away the supper dishes. 'Miss! I was getting worried about you! You seemed so upset! Miss Amy's been asking for you. Oh, you're soaking wet! Here, at least dry your hair and sit by the range for a bit,' she instructed, handing Livvie a towel which she pulled down from the rack suspended from the kitchen ceiling.

Gratefully Livvie sat down and began to dry her hair. 'I'm sorry, Emily. I *was* upset and . . . and I felt I just needed time alone. Is Amy all right?'

Emily looked a little perturbed; she knew that something

serious must have happened for she'd never known Livvie to run out like that. She'd assumed that Livvie had gone next door but obviously not. It looked as if she'd just stayed out in the cold and rain. She'd been very annoyed about whatever her pa had said, which obviously concerned Miss Amy too. 'I think so, miss. She looked a bit peaky, if you know what I mean, but not what I'd call upset. The master called her into the parlour just after you'd . . . gone out.'

That surprised Livvie. 'And she wasn't upset? Where is she? And where is Pa?'

'He's gone next door to see Mr Mayhew and Miss Amy is in the parlour,' Emily informed her.

Obviously he'd gone to break the news to Aunt Maud and Uncle Charles, Livvie mused, and she wondered how they would react. She handed the towel back to the girl and reluctantly got to her feet. 'Thank you, Emily. I'll go and see her.'

She found Amy sitting reading, looking a bit pale but outwardly calm and composed.

'Livvie, where have you been? Emily said you'd gone out in a hurry but where did you go? To see Selina?'

Livvie shook her head and sat down beside her sister. 'No. I . . . needed some time on my own. I just walked. What did Pa say to you? Did he mention anything about his plans?' she asked tentatively, searching the girl's face for any sign of distress.

Amy put the book aside and nodded. 'He was very . . . nice with me, Livvie. He told me that he's getting married again and he hoped I would be happy for him and not be upset. We're to have a stepmother and it will all be for the best. I wasn't to think that she would be replacing Mam at all. He told me all about her and she will just be someone I . . . we can rely on and who will take over running the household, which will make life easier for us. He's bringing her to tea on Sunday so we can meet her and he hopes we'll like her and get on well together.'

Livvie just stared at her, completely taken aback by her attitude. She'd expected floods of tears and some of the anger she felt but obviously Pa had chosen his words carefully and with some consideration when informing her sister of his decision. She frowned; she certainly had no intention of playing 'happy families' with Mary Fitzgerald on Sunday afternoon. 'And . . . and what did you say? What do you think about him getting married again, Amy, and so soon after . . . Mam?'

Amy looked at her candidly. 'I didn't say anything. I don't suppose there's much we can do about it anyway. He's made up his mind and he's already asked her. Is that why you went out?' For the first time Amy seemed to notice her sister's damp and dishevelled appearance. 'Livvie, you're soaking wet! Where have you been?'

Livvie shrugged. 'I was so shocked and upset when he told me that we had a huge row about it and I just ran out. I've been walking for ages in the drizzle. I . . . I told him that I thought he was being disrespectful to Mam's memory. I think he's been very callous towards us, not to even mention this before now. I told him I'd never accept her. That she will never replace Mam . . .'

Amy was perturbed. 'But she's not going to replace Mam, Livvie. He said so. I think he is thinking of our future too and, well, she might be nice. He said she is a quiet, kind person.' Amy had had time to digest her father's news. Of course she had been a bit taken aback at first but then when she'd thought about it she didn't think she really minded the idea of a stepmother. She would relieve them of the running of the household, which certainly suited Amy, and it would be someone older, hopefully wiser and reliable to take her anxieties and her hopes to. She missed her mam and supposed she always would but she realised too that she missed the sense of security and stability that her mother's presence had always provided. Livvie did try but it wasn't the same.

Livvie said nothing. Amy was taking this far better than she had envisaged and seemed to have already accepted that Mary Fitzgerald was to be their stepmother. Was it fair of her to voice her outrage and disgust and so put the seeds of doubt and upset in her sister's mind? She pursed her lips as she stood up. Her pa had certainly said nothing to her about Mary Fitzgerald being a 'kind person' and she had no intention of changing her opinion of his actions.

'I think I'll go and have a bath and then go to bed, Amy. I'm cold and wet and I've walked so far that I'm quite worn out. If Pa asks you can tell him I'm back, that's if you are still up,' were her rather curt parting words.

She said very little to her father over breakfast the following morning although he greeted them both affably and informed them he would be home at his usual time that evening, and after she'd helped Emily to clear away she went over to see Maud Mayhew.

Maud took one look at her strained expression and put down the morning's post, indicating that she sit down, and asked Bessie to bring some tea.

'I can see by the look on your face, Livvie, that he's told you of his intentions. He came over last night to inform us. And I can also see that you are far from happy about this turn of events.'

Livvie nodded. Maud had put the matter very succinctly. 'He did and I . . . I was never more shocked and horrified in my life! Mam's only been gone two years, Aunt Maud!'

Maud looked sympathetic. 'I know, dear, and I have to admit I was very taken aback myself. I wondered if he would marry again, and I assumed that if he did it would be at some time in the future, but . . . well, I suppose he thinks it best for you girls to have someone to guide you, give you maternal support when you need it.'

'I don't *need* this Mary Fitzgerald to guide or support me! If I'm troubled about something I come to you, just as I am now,' Livvie interrupted firmly.

Maud sighed. 'And you can still do that if you feel so strongly, dear. But you have to agree she *will* be . . . helpful. And what about Amy? How has she taken the news?'

'Amy seems to have accepted it all without any fuss. I really can't understand her. I thought she would have been as upset as I am.'

Maud looked thoughtful. 'Maybe that's for the best, Livvie, and it really isn't fair that you should have to take the responsibility for her; she's growing up and needs someone older to depend on and advise her.' She paused. 'I know Amy misses your mother – as I know you do too, Livvie, and indeed I do myself – but I wonder if it's more than that. I wonder does Amy miss being "mothered"? It's not quite the same thing.'

That had never occurred to Livvie and her brow creased in a frown.

'Apparently he's invited her for tea on Sunday, so you can meet her,' Maud continued.

Before Livvie could reply Bessie appeared with the tea tray and shot an enquiring glance at Livvie. It was very unusual for her to come over this early in the day and she wondered what was wrong next door. Had Mr Goodwin found out about Livvie's attendance at the meetings? If he had she hoped that he didn't know that it was with herself and Emily.

'Well, if he thinks that I'm going to welcome her with open arms he's very much mistaken. I intend going out!' Livvie stated curtly, not caring if Bessie heard.

Maud said nothing until Bessie had left the room. 'I would really think hard about that, Livvie. Oh, I understand how you are feeling, it's been a shock and you feel it is . . . disrespectful to your mother's memory, but he's determined to marry her and maybe it would at least be wise to actually meet her. After all, she might be very apprehensive about meeting you girls. I know I certainly would be; she's taking on a family, not just a new husband.'

'Do you know anything about her? What did Pa say?' Livvie asked, digesting Maud's advice.

'Not much. He said she's the sister of his friend and associate Richard. He's known her a few months and she's quiet, kind, well mannered and considerate – quite a paragon in fact. Oh, and she's thirty years old, which made me wonder why she isn't already married.'

Livvie's eyes widened. 'Oh, Aunt Maud, that's even worse! Pa's years older than her!'

'I worked that out myself, but you know that might be an advantage, Livvie. Maybe she has a younger outlook on life than your father,' Maud remarked in an attempt to alleviate the girl's distress. Privately, however, she doubted the truth of what she'd just said. A spinster of thirty was more likely to be set in her ways, particularly as she appeared to have lived quietly with her brother and sister-in-law since her parents' deaths.

Livvie didn't reply; Mary Fitzgerald didn't seem at all likely to hold modern views as far as she could see. Not if she was happy to marry someone as middle-aged, old-fashioned and unbending in his opinions as her father. She sipped her tea and wondered if she should take Maud's advice and at least meet the woman who was to be her stepmother. If she refused and deliberately went out on Sunday her pa would be furious and if she was going to tell him that she was joining the suffrage movement she really didn't need to alienate him still further. She'd have to think about it more carefully. Maybe Aunt Maud was right.

Bessie handed Livvie her jacket as she was leaving, her curiosity getting the better of her. 'Is everythin' all right, miss?' she hissed.

Livvie nodded. 'Sort of. I'll be coming with you and Emily on Thursday and I'm going to join, Bessie. I've made up my mind.'

Bessie beamed at her. 'Good for you, miss!'

'And what's more I'm going to tell my pa too.'

'Really?' Bessie was impressed but she knew that there would definitely be more fireworks in the house next door before long.

'Well, if he can land us with a stepmother without so much as a by your leave, then I don't see why I have to ask his permission to join the suffragettes!' Livvie hissed.

Bessie's eyes widened. 'Is he gettin' married again?'

Livvie nodded.

As she watched Livvie walk down the path Bessie wondered if Emily knew anything about this; she'd certainly ask her. Judging by Livvie's words and attitude she was far from happy about it all and she really didn't blame her.

As soon as they entered the theatre on Thursday evening Livvie went straight to where Sarah Wilkinson was sitting. 'Miss Wilkinson, I've come to a decision and I would very much like to join the movement,' she stated firmly, proud of how prominently the green, white and purple rosette was pinned to the lapel of her coat.

'It's Miss Goodwin, isn't it? And I'm so pleased about your decision.'

'Do I need to sign anything?' Livvie enquired.

'Not at all. Your decision and your commitment are all we need. I hope you will find this evening's meeting instructive and informative.' She leaned forward. 'We are very honoured to have Lady Constance Lytton here tonight,' she informed Livvie.

'That's wonderful,' Livvie replied, before she rejoined Emily and Bessie. She'd read about Lady Constance, the daughter and sister of an earl, who was one of the staunchest supporters of women's rights and who had gone to prison disguised as a working-class woman to find out for herself just how they were treated, which turned out to be very badly indeed. On discovering who she was her treatment by the prison authorities had improved considerably, something she then brought to the attention of the press and thereby the general public. It had caused something of an outcry.

As she sat with Emily and Bessie and listened to the speakers, including Lady Constance, Livvie felt even more convinced that she had done the right thing. On their way here Bessie, with her usual forthrightness, had asked her if she was joining the movement just to annoy her pa but she'd said firmly she wasn't and in truth she meant it. His decision to marry again had brought the matter to a head in her mind but she had been feeling very resentful about his attitude for a while before he'd sprung that on her. She was a grown woman and, like Bessie, she had a mind of her own. And no matter what the future brought, she had resolved to follow her own path in life.

Chapter Twelve

───•>◦<•───

Frank was waiting for them when the meeting ended, as was the usual crowd of jeering men and boys, and he steered all three safely away from them. When Bessie and Emily walked on ahead, Livvie was thankful for she had so much to tell him.

Frank smiled down at her and offered his arm. 'Well, yet again you're fortunate your father isn't at home this evening.'

'I now know why. And he's not at his club,' she replied rather grimly.

'I can see something's upset you?'

It all came out in a rush. 'He informed me – us – completely out of the blue that he's getting married again! We're to have a stepmother. Can you believe it? Mary Fitzgerald, she's the sister of his "associate" Richard Fitzgerald. That's why he's been spending so much time away from home in the evenings!'

Frank was taken aback. 'I had no idea! I can see that must have come as a shock, Olivia.'

All the feelings that had overwhelmed her over the past few

days and which she'd tried to suppress in front of her sister burst forth. 'That's an understatement, Frank. I was outraged, horrified, furious! I still am! Mam's hardly cold and he . . . he's off paying court to her! And what's more she's thirty, Frank!'

He could feel her shaking with the force of her emotions. A serious expression settled on his face. He'd had no idea Thomas Goodwin intended to marry again and by many people's standards it was indeed very soon after Edith's death. He was beginning to understand how Livvie felt. 'Olivia, I had no idea. What can I say?'

'What *is* there to say? You would at least have thought he would have mentioned *something*! Sounded Amy and me out about how we would feel about it, but no! He just goes ahead and asks her as if we are of no importance, that our opinion – our feelings about it are of no consequence at all. And then he expects us to welcome her with open arms. It's beyond belief!'

'And what does Amy think?' he asked gently, thinking that his employer had indeed been insensitive, even crass in his handling of such an important and life-changing matter.

'She seems to have accepted it quite well. Which I suppose is something to be thankful for, but I . . . I just . . . can't! Not when I think of Mam. He's bringing this woman to tea on Sunday and I have no desire to meet her at all. I wish I could just go out but Aunt Maud doesn't think that's a good idea and, on reflection, I agree. If I do that he'll be livid and . . . and, well, I intend to tell him where I've been tonight. I've joined the suffrage movement, Frank, and I'm not going to hide that from him – or anyone else.'

He frowned. 'He won't be at all happy about that.'

'I know but I don't care! If he can make decisions that affect us all without consulting anyone, then so can I. I have a future of my own, a mind of my own, and I won't be dictated to on this matter.'

He nodded slowly. 'And I applaud you for that, but I hate to say this, Olivia, there is one big difference. He is your father, he is entitled to take decisions without consultation – indeed is accustomed to doing so – and he's your legal guardian until you become of age.'

Livvie frowned, feeling a little deflated at his words. 'I know that, but . . .'

'He could forbid you to attend another meeting, and he'd be within his rights to do so,' he reminded her gently.

She raised her chin determinedly. 'I don't care! I still intend to support the movement. He can't make me change my views and I'll tell him that if I have to. I'm determined to have this out with him, Frank, once and for all.'

He patted her hand encouragingly. 'Good luck then. You know you have my support and if you ever need to talk, I'm here for you. You have my address.'

She nodded. 'Thank you. I'm grateful for that.' And she was. Having his support felt all the more important to her now.

They parted company at the tram stop and again he kissed her goodnight, wondering what the outcome of this decision would be for her and wishing he could be of more help to her. Her emotions were clearly in turmoil and he hated to see her in distress.

'He's really nice, miss,' Emily commented as the tram trundled on its way.

Livvie nodded. 'I know, Emily, and I like him a great deal.'

Bessie looked thoughtful. 'Well, I think that's great, miss, but I don't think I'd mention to your pa that he comes to meet you, not if you intend to tell him you've joined. That might be a step too far.'

'Oh, miss. He won't blame us, will he?' Emily asked fearfully. She was a little afraid of the master and she certainly didn't want to lose her job.

'Of course not, Emily. There's no need for me to mention either you or Bessie. If he asks I'll tell him I just saw an advertisement for the meeting and decided to go along,' she assured the girl. But she could see Bessie's point about Frank. 'I think you're right, Bessie. He's going to be angry enough when I tell him what I've done but I'm not backing down. I don't care how much he carries on.'

Bessie pursed her lips. 'Well, miss, in my opinion, if you're not goin' to be at one another's throats morning, noon an' night, I think there's goin' to have to be a bit of give an' take between the pair of you or life in your house is not goin' to be worth thinking about.'

Livvie looked slightly chastened by Bessie's statement but she was also puzzled. 'What do you mean, "give and take"?'

'Well, for instance, if he agrees not to hit the roof an' forbid you to be a suffragette, then you'll agree not to make a song an' dance over his gettin' married again.'

Livvie stared at her, thinking that Bessie had a great deal of sense, even though her suggestion smacked a little of emotional blackmail. But Bessie's prediction of how life at home would change – and not for the better – made her think carefully. She'd just have to make sure when she spoke to him that she didn't put it quite as bluntly and she would have to try to at least be civil to Mary Fitzgerald. She smiled at the older girl. 'I think you've hit the nail on the head, Bessie.'

Bessie looked pleased. 'Well, you don't want to be livin' in a house where you can cut the atmosphere with a knife, now do you, miss? That wouldn't make anyone any better off, would it?'

Amy had gone to bed when she arrived home but there was no sign of her pa, so Livvie decided to wait up for him in the parlour. She was on edge, restless and couldn't sit still, wishing this interview was over and done with, so she paced the floor in front of the fireplace and rehearsed in her mind how she would broach the subject and what she would say to her father. She'd have to choose her words carefully if things were to go well and she'd have to be more . . . temperate in her views on Miss Fitzgerald.

At last she heard him come into the hall and took a deep breath, clenching her hands tightly together.

Thomas had seen the light on in the parlour as he'd come up the front steps and went to check that no one had forgotten to switch it off. When he opened the door he was surprised to see Livvie standing with her back to the fireplace, looking rather serious. He frowned, hoping there wasn't going to be a repeat of the events of the other evening. She'd barely exchanged more than a few words with him since then and he very much hoped that this state of affairs wasn't going to continue, especially when he brought Mary here on Sunday. Amy had seemed happy enough; there had been no tears or tantrums from her so why couldn't Livvie just accept the fact that poor Edith was dead and that nothing could bring her back? He had a future – they all did – and he'd chosen to spend his with Mary as his wife.

'You're up late, Livvie,' he remarked, sitting down in a chair.

'I waited up for you, Pa.'

'I can see that. Is there something you wish to discuss?' he asked, scrutinising her face for signs of anger. Thankfully there were none so maybe she had decided to accept the status quo.

Livvie sat down opposite him and vowed not to raise her voice or let her feelings get the better of her. 'There is, Pa. I . . . I've been out myself this evening.'

He raised one eyebrow, surprised. She was not in the habit of going out in the evenings. 'Indeed. Where to, may I ask? Or perhaps it should be "who with"?'

'No, I was on my own. Well, that's not strictly true. I was with other people, other girls and women.'

He wondered where this was leading.

Livvie took a deep breath. 'I know your feelings on the question of women's suffrage. I . . . I understand but I'm afraid I don't agree with them, Pa. I'm eighteen, I'm far from stupid or uneducated and I've read a great deal and listened to the arguments and I *do* support women's rights. That's where I've been, to a suffrage meeting in town. In fact it's not the first time.'

Thomas's brows had rushed together and she could see the hard set of his lips but she continued. 'Tonight, I came to a decision. I've joined the movement.'

He got to his feet, his cheeks flushed with anger. 'You've been going behind my back, sneaking out to these "*meetings*"

118

as you call them? They are nothing more than *gatherings* of women who are intent upon undermining and overturning decent society! Their demands are preposterous. Their actions are nothing short of disgraceful. No decent, respectable woman would entertain the idea of being seen as one of them. They're even prepared to suffer the degradations of prison, for God's sake! And you, Olivia, have taken it into your head to become one of . . . *them*!'

She held her nerve before this onslaught, determined not to lose her temper. 'I have, Pa. You can call them whatever you like, but I believe in what they are demanding and many of them are "decent women". I heard Lady Constance Lytton speak tonight and she made a lot of sense. They're not trying to overturn or undermine society! It's nineteen hundred and ten, Pa. Times are changing, and attitudes are changing too. I'm convinced they are right and I . . . I'm asking you not to forbid me to continue attending the meetings—'

'And if I do? What then, Olivia?' he interrupted, furious that she should be defending them.

'Then I'll be very, very disappointed. You can forbid me to go, Pa, but you can't and *won't* change my mind or my convictions. May I ask if Miss Fitzgerald has any views on the subject?' she added quickly.

That threw him. 'Mary? Why on earth should she?' he blustered.

'I know she's thirty so I was wondering if she has a more "modern" approach to . . . things?'

Thomas stared at her hard. What was she implying? he wondered. That he was marrying a woman far too young for him? Someone who would have more in common with herself than him? Her calmness both surprised him and made him suspicious. 'I doubt that Mary has any such notions! She's far too well bred.'

'And I'm not?' Livvie shot back. 'Perhaps I might find out if she has any views on the subject on Sunday?' she added quickly.

He bristled dangerously. 'I forbid you to mention the subject, Olivia!'

She got to her feet and faced him. 'Then of course I won't, Pa,' she replied calmly. 'And I've been giving the situation some thought and I'll be ready to meet her on Sunday.' She had been determined not to say 'happy' because she wasn't. 'After all, none of us want to live in an atmosphere of anger, resentment and hostility, do we?'

Slowly he nodded. 'No, that would be unbearable for . . . everyone and not at all what I had envisaged.'

'Then if we want to avoid that we'll both have to make compromises, Pa.'

He looked at her suspiciously. 'What kind of "compromises"?'

'If you will allow me to continue to attend the meetings, I will try my best to make Miss Fitzgerald welcome, for your sake, Pa, and so that life can be . . . normal and amicable.' Slowly she let out her breath.

He stared at her hard and then passed his hand over his eyes. As a businessman he was astute enough to know when a compromise had to be made but he deeply resented her for putting him in this position and undermining his authority over her.

He didn't speak for a few seconds as he thought about it

and Livvie wondered if she had gone too far.

'You will promise me that you will not attend any of these disgraceful demonstrations or get involved in any of their acts of civil disobedience? I won't stand for behaviour like that, Olivia! I won't have you bringing disgrace, condemnation and humiliation on this family. Not after I've worked so hard and for so long to improve our standard of living and our position in society, do you understand?'

Livvie felt relief flood through her. 'I understand, Pa. And I'll respect your wishes.'

'Then let that be an end to it. Nor do I want you to fill Amy's mind with all this "rights" nonsense; she's still an impressionable child and I won't have her indoctrinated. I'll allow you to attend these meetings but I don't wish to hear any details or talk about them and do not burden Mary with your views, either.'

Livvie nodded. She had no intention of 'burdening' Mary Fitzgerald with anything. She would be civil to her, that's all, until she had formed an opinion of her future stepmother. But at least she could continue to attend the meetings and give the women her support without having to tell lies. And of course she would also be able to see Frank. She'd certainly have plenty to tell him when she saw him next, she thought, feeling happier than she had done all week.

Chapter Thirteen

———◆———

Next morning Livvie was aware that she would have to tell her sister and the Mayhews what had happened last night for over breakfast her father had commented that he expected the house to be 'shipshape' and an exceptional tea provided on Sunday afternoon. Livvie, Amy and Emily would have to spend today and tomorrow making sure his wishes were carried out.

'Amy, I'm going across to see Aunt Maud and Selina. Will you come too? Emily can finish these dishes – we won't be long.'

'Are we going to ask Aunt Maud what she thinks would be best for tea on Sunday?'

'That amongst other things,' Livvie replied, thinking she might as well kill two birds with one stone and Maud was sure to have a good idea of just what would constitute an 'exceptional' tea.

She smiled and nodded confidently to Bessie as the girl opened the door to them. 'This is a quick visit – nothing to worry about, Bessie. We've just come to see what we can give Miss Fitzgerald for tea,' she announced.

'Oh, I see, miss,' Bessie replied, returning Livvie's smile and thinking that things must have gone well last night.

'I thought you two girls would have been up to your eyes baking for Sunday,' Maud greeted them.

Selina looked up from the magazine she had been leafing through. 'What's so special about Sunday?'

Maud cast her eyes to the ceiling. 'Honestly, Selina, is your head so full of Henry and what you will wear this evening that you've forgotten that I told you Livvie and Amy's future stepmother is visiting on Sunday?'

'That's part of the reason why we've come, Aunt Maud. What do you suggest we give her to eat? Pa wants something "exceptional".'

Maud nodded thoughtfully, glad that at least Livvie seemed to have taken her advice about not going out or making a fuss. 'You can't go wrong with cucumber sandwiches, ham sandwiches and perhaps smoked salmon, if you can get some. And remember to cut the crusts off. A Victoria sponge, some small fancy cakes – I'd get those from Lunt's Bakery: they do excellent ones; you would swear they were homemade and it will save you the trouble. And scones with jam and whipped cream. That should be enough. Provide both Indian and China tea, milk and lemon slices, just in case. I doubt she will be able to find fault with any of that.'

Livvie made a mental note of everything. 'I'll use the best china and table linen too,' she said, thinking how painful it would be to get out Mam's treasured Royal Doulton and embroidered Irish linen for the woman who would be taking her place. 'While I'm here, there is something else I wanted to tell all of you,' she announced tentatively.

'You and Frank Hadley are officially walking out!' Selina cried delightedly.

Maud shot her a sharp look. This was the first she'd heard of any kind of a liaison between Livvie and her father's young factory manager, even though they had seemed to get on well at that New Year's party.

Livvie laughed. 'No, Selina! We're not!' She became sober. 'I had a serious talk last night with Pa. You see, well, I've been attending the women's suffrage meetings. He didn't know; he was either at his club or at the Fitzgeralds'. But yesterday I decided to join them, become a suffragette, so I had to tell him.' Her announcement was met by three silent and astonished expressions but she managed a smile.

Selina recovered her composure first. 'Why on earth did you do that, Livvie? I thought you were out with Frank Hadley. I didn't know you were interested in things like . . . like politics! It's all so boring! Oh, Livvie, please don't say you are going to get all serious and dull like Millicent Parker!'

'For heaven's sake, Selina, Livvie is nothing like Millie Parker!' Maud retorted, although she viewed Livvie's statement with some concern. Like Thomas, Charles had no patience with the suffragettes and even she had her doubts about their demands, never mind their campaign of civil disobedience. 'What did your father say, Livvie? He can't have been best pleased.'

'He wasn't, Aunt Maud.'

'Oh, Livvie, you didn't have another row, did you?' Amy put in.

Livvie shook her head. 'No, Amy. I told him very calmly but firmly that I agree with them, I will support them and that nothing he could say or do would make me change that.'

Maud frowned. She had never seen the girl so determined in her views and she listened carefully as Livvie informed her of what her father had said to her on the subject.

'So, you'll go on going?' Selina was mystified as to why Livvie felt so strongly about women's rights. She'd never mentioned any of this before; Selina had thought her evening excursions were to see Frank – and she knew that neither her parents nor Teddy viewed the suffragettes favourably. To an extent she understood why. At least she *thought* she did.

'I certainly will be going,' Livvie replied firmly.

'At least your father's trying to make sure that you don't get into trouble. I have to say that their behaviour is getting more and more extreme,' Maud commented. 'But I don't suppose he wanted any kind of enmity between you when Miss Fitzgerald visits. Things will be tense enough without an atmosphere of simmering anger and resentment between you adding to it.'

'I expect you're right, Aunt Maud,' Livvie replied.

'Well, dear, I can't say I totally approve but I admire your spirit in standing up for what you believe in. I just hope you are not being misled,' Maud said seriously.

'I'm not, Aunt Maud. I believe that one day women will have the right to vote and hopefully it will be soon. Now, we'd better get back and help Emily, we've a lot to do before Sunday.'

As the two girls left Maud wondered if Livvie was using her newly found beliefs as some form of protest against Thomas remarrying. But then the girl had said she'd been attending the meetings before his announcement. Sadly she wondered would Livvie have even considered embracing the suffrage movement had Edith been alive? She and Edith had discussed the movement, of course, and her friend had been of a similar mind to herself, but with some reservations, although Edith had not broached the matter with Livvie, not wanting to put ideas into the girl's head. Judging by Selina's attitude she had little to fear of her own daughter becoming a suffragette. For that she was profoundly grateful.

By Sunday everything in the parlour, hall and dining room had been polished to within an inch of its life. A vase of early spring flowers graced the half-moon table in the hall, which Emily had remarked brightened the place up no end and looked properly welcoming. The circular, drop-leaf tea table in the parlour was covered with a pristine white linen cloth and Edith's rose-strewn china tea service took pride of place. Livvie surveyed their handiwork with satisfaction; both she and Amy were wearing their newest dresses and both felt they looked tidy yet smart. Her dress, tightly fitted at the waist with a high collar and leg-o'-mutton sleeves, was of a shade of misty heather while Amy's, identical in style, was cream, trimmed with russet velvet ribbon, and Livvie had assured her it made her look more grown up than her fifteen years.

'Are you nervous, Livvie?' she asked, patting her hair and scrutinising her appearance in the mirror on the wall.

'Not really,' Livvie answered. 'Are you? *She's* the stranger coming into *our* home,' she reminded her sister.

Amy nodded. She did feel apprehensive; she sincerely hoped that she would like Mary Fitzgerald, but what if she didn't? 'What are we to call her, do you think?'

Livvie rearranged the sugar bowl for the third time and gave a dismissive little shrug. '"Miss Fitzgerald", I suppose. Surely Pa won't expect us to call her "Stepmother" yet.'

'Emily's very curious to see what she's like,' Amy confided, glancing again through the window to see if there was any sign of her father's car yet.

'Well, she's not the only one. Bessie, Aunt Maud and Selina can't wait to hear all about her.'

'Oh, I do hope she's as nice as Pa said she is,' Amy mused aloud.

'Amy, I'm sure she can't be too bad, otherwise Pa wouldn't have decided to marry her,' Livvie said firmly but she wasn't convinced by her words. She had begun to wonder if Mary Fitzgerald was in fact very attractive; maybe that was what had drawn her father's attention to her. She was after all still young compared to him.

Before Amy could reply the car drew up at the gate and both girls instinctively smoothed down their skirts. 'Well, here they are. We'll soon find out what she's like,' Livvie stated flatly. She shared none of her sister's interested anticipation. They'd have to accept this woman into their home whatever she was like.

Emily, looking quite pretty in her best black dress, white frilly apron and cap, showed her employer and his fiancée in.

Livvie clasped her hands tightly together, still unable to stem the resentment she felt but determined to appear unconcerned. To her surprise Mary Fitzgerald was rather a plain young woman with light brown hair, dressed in a slightly severe fashion which did nothing to flatter her features. She was small and slim with a pale complexion but her dark brown eyes did look kind. Her dress too was plain with no braid or ribbon trimmings, and was of a dark grey and black plaid. She wore pearl drop earrings but Livvie did not notice any other jewellery.

Thomas beamed at his daughters, thinking they both looked well and had clearly worked hard and he sincerely hoped that they would behave correctly, especially Livvie. The last thing he wanted was for Mary to be upset for he was indeed very fond of her. It wasn't the same depth of emotion he'd felt for Edith – he'd loved his first wife deeply – but Mary's quiet, gentle and rather self-effacing manner was what had first attracted him to her. He now thought of her as a 'restful' person and he'd gone to some lengths on the occasions when he'd taken her out to draw her out. 'Olivia, Amy, this is Miss Mary Fitzgerald who has done me the honour of agreeing to become my wife and, of course, your stepmother.'

Livvie forced herself to smile but Amy's smile was one of genuine pleasure and relief. 'We're very pleased to meet you, Miss Fitzgerald,' she said.

Livvie gave a little nod of assent. 'You're welcome, please do sit down.' She hoped she sounded calm and in control of her emotions. She could see that the older woman looked a little disconcerted but was trying to overcome it. Was she indeed apprehensive about meeting them, as Aunt Maud had suggested?

'The flowers in the hall are beautiful; did you arrange them, Olivia?' Mary asked.

'Yes. I thought they brightened the hall up, it's a rather dark space,' she replied, thinking fleetingly of how they'd viewed it when they'd first come here and of the unfortunate Mrs Chadwick.

'Do you like flowers, Miss Fitzgerald?' Amy asked.

'I do, Amy. Your father tells me there is a lovely garden at the back of the house.'

Thomas took over the conversation, informing his daughters that Mary loved gardens and hoped that in the summer they could all spend more time enjoying theirs and that with Mary's guidance he intended to have more flowers and bulbs planted.

Livvie sat and listened, watching both her father and Mary intently. Her pa seemed delighted with his future wife and Amy too seemed to have taken to her. She noticed that Mary didn't seem to hold any strong opinions on anything; she was as he'd said: quiet, gentle and well mannered, but that didn't make all this any easier for her. She got to her feet. 'If you'll excuse me, I'll go and help Emily with the tea. Amy, you stay and keep Pa and Miss Fitzgerald company,' she instructed, smiling at her sister before departing for the kitchen.

'Well, what's she like, miss?' Emily asked, pouring the boiling water from the kettle into the teapot. 'She looked . . . all right, from what little I saw of her.'

'Pleasant enough, I suppose, Emily, but we don't know her yet,' Livvie replied, pouring the milk into the little gilt-edged jug.

'I somehow thought she'd be, well, a bit more "stylish", if you know what I mean, she being only thirty.'

Livvie nodded. No doubt Bessie had instructed Emily to take in every detail of Mary's appearance. 'She's a bit old-fashioned, I have to agree. Is that everything? You take the tray and I'll carry the cake stand and open the doors,' she stated, bringing the conversation to a close. The sooner they got tea over with and Pa took Mary Fitzgerald home the better she would feel.

Amy and Mary were in an animated conversation while her pa looked on happily, she saw as she re-entered the room. While she helped Emily transfer the contents of the tray to the table, she glanced surreptitiously at Mary Fitzgerald and was disconcerted to find that her speculative glance was met by Mary's brown eyes, and again she had the feeling that there was something Mary was holding back.

Forcing a smile she thanked Emily and then turned to her future stepmother. 'Would you like to pour, Miss Fitzgerald?' she asked. Well, it was only polite to ask, she thought grimly; the girl was going to take over the household soon enough.

Mary looked hesitantly at Thomas who nodded his approval.

'Thank you, Olivia. Isn't this a wonderful tea? You've gone to a lot of trouble I can see and I'm grateful.'

Livvie managed a more genuine smile. 'Well, it is something of an occasion after all.'

Mary was more relaxed now, she thought as her father outlined their plans. They were to be married in three weeks, in a very quiet ceremony. There would be Mary, her brother and sister-in-law, himself of course, Charles and Maud Mayhew – for Charles had agreed to stand for him – and naturally both girls. There would be a reception in a private room of the Imperial Hotel on Lime Street and then he and Mary would depart from the station next door to spend the weekend in Llandudno.

Livvie digested all this in silence. Of course she'd expected that she would have to attend the ceremony but hadn't known that Maud would be there too. This gave her some comfort, as did the news that he wouldn't be bringing Mary home that night as his wife. She didn't think she could have stood that; at least them being away for a few days would give her time to try to come to terms with the idea of them occupying the same bed. Glancing at her sister she thought Amy looked enthralled by it all, her pa looked very pleased and proud of himself and Mary . . . well, she too looked happy. It was only she who felt upset and miserable, wondering if wherever she was her mam could see them all and hear all their plans.

Oh, she had a great deal she needed to tell Frank and in that moment she wished he was here beside her, someone who understood how she really felt and whom she could rely on for some comfort and support.

Chapter Fourteen

———◆———

Livvie had quickly learned that Maud had been informed of all the plans for the wedding, which would take place the weekend after Easter. Both she and Amy were to have new outfits for the occasion. Maud suggested that they go into town to buy something suitable.

Livvie had also been very disappointed to learn from Emily that there wouldn't be another meeting for a while, which meant of course that she wouldn't be able to see Frank for some time. There would, however, be a rally in the centre of the city over the bank holiday.

'Well, I won't be able to attend that, Emily. I said I wouldn't go to such things,' she said bitterly.

'Neither will I, miss. My da would go mad! Bessie will be going though, wild horses wouldn't keep her away,' the girl had replied.

She had been so looking forward to seeing Frank; there was nothing else for it, she thought in desperation. She'd have to write to him and see what he could suggest. He'd promised he would be there if she wanted to talk and she *did*; she couldn't wait long.

She received a reply to her note by return of post and was both relieved and delighted when he suggested that he could meet her after she had finished her shopping on Saturday afternoon, for the factory closed down at noon. He suggested St John's Gardens at the back of St George's Hall at about four o'clock.

She hadn't put much thought into choosing her outfit for the wedding; after all she would only be a guest and a reluctant one at that, so what she wore wasn't very important. She'd opted for the first two-piece costume she'd been shown, a light sage-green jacket and skirt in summer-weight mohair with a very pale green chiffon blouse trimmed with lace to go under it. She'd also selected a wide-brimmed matching hat trimmed with ostrich feathers.

Amy, however, had other views and had insisted on trying no fewer than four outfits.

'Oh, for heaven's sake, choose one, Amy, or we'll be here for hours!' Livvie urged impatiently, glancing at the fob watch pinned to her jacket.

Finally Amy settled on a shell-pink wool crêpe costume, the lapels of the jacket and the cuffs edged in dove grey. A blouse, similar to the one Livvie had chosen but in dove-grey chiffon, would go under it and a hat of the same pink trimmed with grey ribbon and a very large bow was her final choice.

Livvie was very relieved as they left the Bon Marché and Amy left her to walk to Bold Street to look for a bag and high-button boots to match her outfit. She smiled to herself thankfully as she hastened her steps towards Whitechapel, which would lead her eventually to St John's Gardens; her sister had been so engrossed in her shopping that she'd made no comment when she'd told her she was meeting Frank Hadley. Her pa wouldn't be home until later that evening for he was having supper with Mary.

The gardens were not too crowded, she mused as she walked between the flower beds now full of colourful primulas and daffodils. There were buds on the trees and shrubs too, she noticed as she followed the pathway that skirted the statue of Father Nugent, his hand on the shoulder of a ragged street urchin. The statue was the city's tribute to the priest known for his compassion for the plight and welfare of the poor children of the slums in the last century.

Set against the ten-foot-high walls that backed the neo-classical St George's Hall were stone seats. She spotted Frank sitting on one and waved.

He got to his feet, smiling. 'Olivia! It's good to see you. Would you like to go for some tea?'

She smiled. 'Thank you, Frank, but there's no need. It's pleasant to sit here now that there are flowers in bloom and there's a bit of warmth in the sun.' She sat beside him on the bench; it seemed so long since she'd last seen him and she so wanted to confide her news. 'Well, I told Pa I'd joined the suffragettes.'

'And?'

Livvie informed him of what had occurred and Frank looked slightly amused as he digested this information. 'Ah, I see, you struck a bargain. That was enterprising of you, Olivia; you're your father's daughter all right. So, what's she like? Do you think you will be able to get on with her? Do you think you'll be able to . . . accept her, in time?'

Livvie shrugged. 'I don't know; accepting her will be hard, Frank. She'll effectively be taking Mam's place even if Pa denies it. She'll be presiding over the breakfast and supper table, and the kitchen, discussing meals with Emily, things like that. But she seemed quiet, no superior airs at all, which I'd half expected. In fact she appeared a bit, well, ill at ease.'

'I suppose that's only to be expected. It must have been rather daunting for her.'

Livvie nodded. 'Amy got on all right with her though so I suppose that's something to be grateful for. The wedding is the Friday after the Easter weekend, just a small family service followed by a private reception but I'm not looking forward to it, Frank. But at least then they are going away to Llandudno for a couple of days.' A thought suddenly occurred to her. 'Frank, I wonder if I asked Pa, would you like to attend? After all, he does think highly of you and relies on you a great deal.' It would make the ordeal so much more bearable if he could be there, she thought. It might help to take the edge off the sense of finality she felt the ceremony would bring to her.

Frank shook his head. 'I don't think that would be possible, Olivia. It's a Friday, a normal working day, and I'll be expected to keep the factory going in your father's absence.'

She looked dejected. 'Oh, I'd forgotten that.'

He wished he could have gone for her sake, but it was impossible. For a start he was aware that his employer wouldn't want his presence at such an intimate, private ceremony, no matter how highly he was regarded. But Olivia would be feeling upset and he very much wanted to try to cheer her up.

He'd missed seeing her too. Suddenly he had an idea which might appeal to her, if he had the courage to suggest it. 'But as they are going away, Olivia, I wonder, perhaps . . . perhaps you'd like to go out for the day on the Sunday? If the weather is fine we could even go for a sail, around the coast or across to the Isle of Man.'

She smiled at him. This was something he'd never suggested before and she was delighted by the prospect of spending a whole day with him. 'I'd really like that, Frank.'

He too was more than pleased at her decision. 'Then I'll find out about the times of the sailings and let you know and we'll make some definite arrangements.' He got to his feet. 'Now, I insist we go for some tea. It will be growing chilly soon if we continue to sit here and after that I'll walk you to your tram.'

Livvie tucked her arm through his as he picked up her parcels. She felt she could now manage to get through her father's wedding without feeling too distraught and resentful for she had the promise of a whole day out with Frank to sustain her and to look forward to.

They had driven with their father the short distance to the church with the Mayhews following in their own car. Maud, resplendent in a rich plum-coloured dress with a matching jacket and a large hat trimmed with birds of paradise plumes, had complimented both her and Amy on their appearance and given Livvie's hand a quick squeeze, whispering, 'Try not to get too upset,' before they'd left the house.

As they alighted and made their way into the building, Livvie felt her heart and spirits sink. They were not regular church-goers and the last time she'd come here had been for her mam's funeral service; her sadness mingled with the bitter wish that her pa had had more sensitivity and chosen somewhere else to remarry. As she sat down in the pew Maud, who was next to her, leaned towards her, patted her hand and whispered, 'I know, Livvie, but it *is* our parish church and Mary's too.'

Livvie nodded, trying to push away the memories. Fortunately they didn't have to wait long before the small bridal party arrived and as she glanced briefly at the bride she was surprised to see that Mary Fitzgerald wasn't wearing the traditional white as she'd expected; something she was entitled to do, it being the first time she was to be married. The russet silk dress and matching hat looked rather dull and drab for the occasion.

The thought occurred to Maud too as they all got to their feet and Thomas and Charles took their allotted places beside Mary and her brother, Richard. Was the young woman trying to appear older, more mature than her years? she wondered. Still, she looked happy enough, she mused. Then she noticed the expression on Mary's sister-in-law's face and pursed her lips: perhaps Mary was relieved to be getting married. Alice Fitzgerald was a small, stout woman who looked to Maud to be in her late thirties and she did not have the look of a contented person – far from it. As the service commenced she heard Livvie try to stifle a sniff and reached for the girl's hand.

Livvie was unable to hold back the tears. 'I'm . . . sorry, Aunt Maud,' she gasped, 'but . . . but I feel it's all so *final* for Mam!'

'I know, dear,' Maud whispered. 'There's no going back

once they've exchanged vows but try to think of the positive side of things. She might even prove to be a confidante for you – in time.'

Livvie nodded and dabbed at her eyes with her handkerchief. She just wished it was all over. It was as if her pa was erasing the memory of her mam altogether. He was promising to love, honour and cherish his new wife as he had once done her mam and he *hadn't* 'cherished' Mam at all. She could never forget that if it hadn't been for him Edith would still be alive and none of them would be here now.

She did feel better once she and Amy were being driven into town in Charles's car for Maud kept up a lively conversation all the way to the hotel. Amy seemed excited at the prospect of the small reception, for the Imperial was one of Liverpool's largest and most elegant hotels and neither of them had been there before. At least there would be Aunt Maud and Alice Fitzgerald to talk to, Livvie mused; it would relieve her of having to converse solely with her new stepmother, something she felt very loath to do at this precise time when her feelings were still so raw.

They were shown into a private room. It was very elegantly furnished in royal blue and gold and suspended from its ornate ceiling was a large crystal chandelier. The meal they were served she had to agree was excellent with smoked salmon for the first course, followed by rack of lamb and completed with crème caramel and petits fours. There was an iced wedding cake and even champagne; her pa had certainly spared no expense. He smiled proudly around at his guests as he proposed a toast to the new 'Mrs Thomas Goodwin' and Livvie forced herself to smile as she raised her glass whilst feeling it would take her a long time to get used to hearing Mary addressed by that title.

After the coffee had been served, she excused herself saying she had to find the powder room; she was disconcerted when Mary rose too and said she would accompany her.

Maud, half-heartedly listening to a tedious diatribe from Alice Fitzgerald about the impossibility of finding reliable and efficient staff, could only watch as they left the room, knowing Livvie wouldn't be at all comfortable alone with her new stepmother.

They were halfway across the ornate lobby when Mary spoke. 'Olivia, I know today has been . . . difficult for you.'

'It has, I don't deny it,' Livvie agreed, wondering what was coming next. 'To start with I don't know what I'm expected to call you. I . . . I can't call you—'

'Of course not!' Mary interrupted quickly. 'I wouldn't expect that. Has your father not suggested anything?'

Livvie shook her head.

'"Stepmother" sounds so . . . cold and formal, like something from Grimm's Fairy Tales. So, do you think you could call me "Mary"?'

'I don't think Pa would like that.'

To her consternation the young woman took her arm and guided her to one of the brocade-covered sofas scattered around the large room, all flanked by potted palms which afforded a degree of privacy.

'Olivia, I think if I explained to him that I'd be happy . . . that I'd prefer you to call me by my Christian name, he would agree.' Mary twisted the new gold band around on her finger before she continued. 'You see, I feel there is something I have to tell you. It was something of a . . . shock when I first met you,' she confided.

Livvie looked at her curiously. 'Why?'

'You see I was expecting to meet two young girls, girls very much younger than yourself and Amy in fact.'

Livvie remembered the look on Mary's face when they'd first been introduced. 'Didn't Pa tell you how old we were? Didn't you know?'

Mary shook her head. 'No. He always referred to you both as "my young daughters" and spoke as though you were indeed quite young. I . . . assumed – I had no idea . . .'

Livvie was taken aback. 'Didn't you ask him?'

Mary shook her head. 'It didn't seem relevant. I assumed I was going to be a stepmother to two little girls who had tragically lost their mother and I was happy with that.'

Livvie was shocked by this revelation. 'And then you found out that soon I'll be nineteen and Amy sixteen. You realised that in fact we were not "little" girls but two very grown-up girls. I can't believe it! What did you say to him?'

'Nothing. I'd already accepted his proposal, Olivia, I couldn't go back on that; nor did I want to. I . . . I'm very . . . fond of Thomas. And he hadn't deceived me in any way. I'd just reached the wrong conclusion.'

Slowly Livvie nodded; she could understand that and she began to think that her pa hadn't been very fair to Mary either. Livvie was sure he'd misled her stepmother; in fact it seemed to her that he'd deliberately kept their ages from Mary. Was he afraid Mary would turn him down? 'Had you known, would you still have accepted?' she asked bluntly.

'Probably I would. In fact yes I would, but I'd have liked to have given it more thought, to have had more time to get used to the fact.'

Livvie began to feel increasingly annoyed by her father's actions. 'I . . . We didn't know, er . . . Mary. In fact we knew nothing about you until he just announced that he was marrying you and bringing you to meet us.'

It was Mary's turn to look taken aback. 'He never mentioned . . . *anything*?'

'No. That's why it was such a shock and so hard for me to accept.'

'I can see that. Oh, Olivia, I'm so sorry. I thought he'd spoken of me, and the fact that he intended to propose.'

Livvie managed a wry smile, thinking Mary seemed sincere, and how shocking it must have been to find that there was little difference in her age and that of her two stepdaughters. Oh, her pa had acted true to form, she thought bitterly. He'd consulted no one and considered no one but himself.

'I'm sorry too, Mary. I'm afraid it's just typical of Pa. We've had time to get used to his rather high-handed ways; you're just finding out.'

Mary smiled. 'I'm sure he didn't mean to upset anyone. Do you think we . . . we can try to make the best of things?'

'I'll try, that's all I can promise.'

'That's all I ask, Olivia.'

For the first time that day Livvie felt happier and as she got to her feet she smiled. 'At least you won't have to try very hard with Amy. She's quite pleased to have a stepmother.'

Mary rose too. 'I'm glad and I hope we'll all get on well. That will please Thomas.'

As they reached the powder room Livvie began to think

that she had misjudged Mary but she couldn't help feeling that her young stepmother had been rather too trusting. She appeared to have accepted everything her father had told her. But maybe that was because she really did love her pa – and suddenly she thought of Frank. It would never enter her head to doubt anything he told her either and a warm glow of anticipation filled her. She was looking forward to Sunday and after Mary's revelations the future didn't look too fraught now. She actually felt she was beginning to warm to Mary.

Chapter Fifteen

<hr />

That Sunday morning dawned bright, sunny and quite mild and as she pinned her hat firmly on before the mirror in the hall, Livvie smiled to herself. She was to meet Frank at the top of the floating roadway which led down to the Landing Stage. Of course she'd asked her sister if she would like to join them on the outing; it wouldn't be fair to leave Amy on her own for the whole day. 'Would you like to come too? It would be a treat, Amy,' she'd asked.

Amy had thought about it. She was very, very tempted but then she'd realised that she'd just be in the way. Livvie and Frank wanted to spend the day together; they wouldn't want her tagging along. 'Thanks, Livvie, but I think I'll stay here. I don't mind – really. You go off and enjoy the day with Frank. I'm going to spend the day getting my scrapbook up to date. It's been a bit neglected lately and Aunt Maud has given me some lovely pictures and pieces of paper lace and I've got some pressed flowers too. When I've finished it I might even take it over to show Aunt Maud and Teddy. He's always saying that he thinks I'm quite . . . artistic.' She blushed as she spoke. He seemed far more interested in her these days and she was delighted by the fact. 'Will you bring me some postcards, Livvie?'

'I will and of as many different views as I can find,' she'd promised. Amy had enthusiastically embraced the very popular pastime of assembling a scrapbook and Livvie was delighted to support her.

When she alighted from the tram she was surprised to see that even though it was still early there were crowds of people thronging the Pier Head, obviously encouraged by the mild weather to venture forth on outings on both the Mersey ferries and the small steamers of the Coast Lines and the Isle of Man Steam Packet Company. She pushed her way through and caught sight of Frank waiting for her; she waved to attract his attention.

'Everyone seems to be going somewhere today,' she said, laughing, as she took his arm.

He grinned back at her. 'Can you blame them? It's a great day for a sail. There's very little wind and there's sunshine too. I've got the tickets so we'll head down to the *Ben-my-Chree*, get aboard and find a seat. I've a feeling it's going to be quite crowded,' Frank predicted.

They joined the passengers queuing at the gangway and once aboard decided to head for the open deck. It was too fine a day to be cooped up in the saloon, Frank declared happily as he led the way towards the bow to find seats.

'It shouldn't be too breezy here, there's a bit of protection from the superstructure but we'll still get a good view,' he promised as they settled themselves for the journey.

'How long does it take and how long will we have ashore?' Livvie asked, glancing around. She'd been across the Mersey on the ferry a couple of times of course but she'd never been on a ship that actually left the river and ventured into open waters.

'About three hours and we'll have four hours in Douglas before coming back.'

'Have you been there before?' Livvie asked.

'No, so it will be an adventure we can share together,' he replied, laughing. He was determined that they were going to enjoy the day.

The ship pulled away from the Landing Stage and steamed slowly towards the estuary and the open sea beyond and Livvie pushed a few wisps of hair that had escaped back under her hat. She'd chosen to wear a walking costume, an oatmeal-coloured loose jacket and a shorter skirt which made it easier to move freely, together with a light straw hat, trimmed with a plain band of brown grosgrain ribbon – far less elaborate and smaller than the hats she usually wore. She was glad of her choice, she mused, for there was quite a stiff breeze now the ship was moving.

Frank was watching a pair of gulls swooping and diving over the bows but wondering how she had coped with the wedding. She seemed cheerful enough this morning so perhaps it hadn't been too much of an ordeal. 'I chose the Isle of Man because I didn't think you'd want to go to the North Wales coast,' he said hesitantly. 'I know your father and stepmother are in Llandudno – that's one of the Coast Lines' more popular ports of call.'

She smiled ruefully. 'No, we certainly wouldn't want to

intrude on them! They'll be back tomorrow though.'

'I know. Your father informed me he would be resuming work on Tuesday morning. How was it? Did everything go to plan?'

Livvie nodded and proceeded to tell him about the day's events. As she finished she turned to look at him. 'And I had my first real conversation with Mary. She asked me to call her that, not "Stepmother". She thinks it sounds too formal and cold.'

'I see,' Frank replied, thinking that sounded promising.

'And she told me something that made me look at her position in a different light, Frank. When she met Amy and me she didn't know how old we were. She thought, from the way Pa always spoke of us, that we were very much younger. She was expecting us to be "two little girls who had tragically lost their mother" – her very words. I couldn't believe it! He'd kept our true ages from her! She'd no idea she is only twelve years older than me – it came as a shock to her. Nor did she know that he hadn't even mentioned her to us, that he'd just announced he was going to marry her. I can't understand him!'

Frank frowned. 'I can understand up to a point why he just announced his intentions, but . . . but why didn't he tell her how old you are?'

'Perhaps he thought that it might be easier for her to accept two very young girls, rather than older ones, or that she'd turn him down because he's too old for her, although she said she wouldn't have. I really believe that she does care for him even though he wasn't fair to her at all. But I think she's going to have to get used to his . . . ways and might find it difficult.'

'It doesn't sound as if she knows him very well at all, Olivia.'

She nodded. 'No, I don't think she does. She's really only known him for a couple of months and I suspect that her brother urged her to agree as I suppose it's quite a good match for her, Pa having a business and everything. But I think she's naïve and that she trusted him too much. She believed everything he told her but . . . but I can understand that too, in a way.' Frank had tipped his straw boater back from his forehead and the breeze was tugging at his hair and she thought how handsome he was and how much she trusted him. 'What I can't understand is why he has to be so *arrogant* all the time. No one else's feelings or opinions seem to matter. He does as he pleases and is always *right*!'

Frank nodded. 'What you have to remember is that he was brought up in the last century, Olivia, and those were the principles and attitudes that were deemed normal. It was not a woman's place to question anything. He has the same attitude towards his workers. It's *his* factory; he is providing them with employment and paying their wages, so he makes all the decisions. If he ever consults anyone it is usually his business associates. Or, very, very occasionally, me.'

She frowned, wondering how he could readily accept that. Still, her pa paid his wages too, she remembered.

'So you don't feel as unhappy about her being your stepmother now?' he probed gently.

'No. I realise that Pa treated both of us rather shabbily so we're going to try to get along. I know it will be difficult at first, for her as well as me – I'm going to have to get used to seeing her take over roles that were Mam's, and she's going to find the daily routine different with Amy and me there all day, and that Pa isn't the easiest person to get on with at times. But I'm not going to make life harder for her by being sullen and awkward.'

'I'm so pleased that you're trying to accept her now, Olivia. I . . . I hate to see you upset and unhappy.'

She smiled at him. 'You really are very considerate, Frank. Now, shall we forget all about Pa and Mary and enjoy our day?'

Livvie was surprised when they docked alongside the pier in Douglas to see that it was a rather smart resort. Flanking the wide promenade, which seemed to stretch for miles, on the landward side were rows of very elegant houses. Some were five and six storeys high; all were in pristine condition and painted either white or pale grey or cream. The sandy beach swept in a wide arc around the coastline and out in the bay, perched on its rock, was the Tower of Refuge, which they'd passed as they'd sailed in and which apparently had been built to aid shipwrecked mariners. Beyond the town were green hills and on their lower slopes were yet more elegant villas. It was not yet warm enough for people to be venturing into the sea but many were enjoying the mild weather walking on the beach or along the promenade with its painted and gilded lampposts.

They followed the crowds who had disembarked from the ship and at a kiosk Livvie bought half a dozen postcards for Amy's scrapbook. They then decided to take a trip on the horse-drawn tram along the promenade and back which Livvie found something of a novelty for the trams in Liverpool were operated by overhead wires connected to a trolley and travelled more quickly, although the brisk trot of the horse did give them more time to take in the sights.

'I think we'd better try and look for somewhere to have lunch,' Frank suggested as he helped her off the vehicle and Livvie realised that she was indeed hungry.

They walked into the town and along Strand Street with its array of shops, although most were closed, it being Sunday, and decided to try Crookhall's Imperial Restaurant, which looked inviting with its double-fronted windows, gilded lettering and array of attractive potted plants.

'I think they must get better weather here than in Liverpool. Did you notice all the palm trees growing along the promenade?' Frank remarked as they studied the menu.

'I did and I thought it was unusual for such exotic trees to be growing here out in the open. I've only ever seen them growing in the protection of the palm house in Sefton Park,' she replied, thinking she might try something described on the menu as 'queenies', which also sounded rather exotic.

'I feel as if I'm actually on a holiday in a different country!' she laughed when the waiter explained that they were queen scallops, a local delicacy.

'You are, miss, although we're part of the Empire too,' he informed her.

'It is a pity we're only here for a few hours. I'd have liked to see more of the island,' Frank mused.

'Well, maybe we'll come back one day,' Livvie replied hopefully as she sipped the lemonade the waiter had brought.

The time seemed to have flown by, she thought as they reluctantly made their way back to where the steamer was tied up. 'It's been a really lovely day, hasn't it, Frank?'

'And it's not over yet, Olivia. We've got three more hours' sailing before we get back to Liverpool.'

She nodded happily as they again made for the open deck to find a seat.

They didn't say a great deal as they watched the sun drop lower in the sky in a blaze of red and orange which turned the sea to molten gold and the bow wave to a ribbon of bronze and indigo. They didn't need to, Livvie thought. They had walked a great deal and so were tired; it was a companionable silence and she didn't want this magical day to end.

'It's a beautiful sunset, the perfect end to the day. Have you enjoyed yourself, Olivia?' Frank asked eventually. It was a long time since he'd felt so carefree or content and he hoped she felt the same.

'Oh, I have. I've loved every minute of it and thank you too; it was just what I needed.'

Frank took her hand and gently squeezed it. 'I was half afraid to ask you, Olivia, thinking you might refuse as your father wouldn't approve. But we seem to have so little time together that I wanted to spend . . . longer with you.'

His words made her heart beat faster and the gentle pressure and warmth of his hand reassured her. 'Oh, Frank, you're not still worrying about what he will say about me seeing you?'

'I do have to take that into consideration – we can't ignore it – but . . . but I've grown very . . . fond of you, Olivia, and want to see more of you. You do realise that?'

She smiled up happily at him, her heart beginning to race. 'I do and I've become fond of you too and I'm not at all concerned about Pa and his ideas of what's "proper"!'

Many people had now gone to sit in the more comfortable and warmer saloon and Frank was able to take her in his arms, overjoyed that his feelings were reciprocated. 'So you won't think it . . . forward or improper if I ask you to come out with me again?'

She was feeling a little dizzy at his closeness. 'No. I'd like to. Perhaps we could indeed go to a concert.'

He kissed her and she slid her arms around his neck and clung to him. She knew now that she was more than just fond of him. Was she falling in love with him? she dared to ask herself. She must be for she felt now that she never wanted to be apart from him. She never wanted this kiss to end but at last he drew away and she sat leaning her head on his shoulder, his arms still around her, feeling happy and content.

He, too, was beginning to realise that he loved her but she was young and he didn't want to put any pressure on her. He didn't want to suggest that they be seen as officially walking out. Not yet, at least. That commitment would present them both with a problem for he knew that Thomas Goodwin would not think he was nearly good enough for his daughter. No matter what Livvie said to the contrary that was a fact and he didn't want to cause any more upset or ill feeling in her life; she'd had enough these past months. No, the occasional concert or play and the walk to the tram after her meetings would have to suffice for a while.

Livvie watched the sun disappear and the sky grow dark and she shivered, feeling chilly and knowing this time in Frank's arms was coming to an end. Perhaps when she'd got to know Mary better, when her stepmother had settled in, she might ask her advice on whether she should tell her pa of her feelings for Frank. She wanted to be able to meet him openly and more often, as Selina and Henry Woodford did. She wanted everyone to know that they were serious about what they felt but she also had to think of Frank and his position. She sighed, knowing that soon the lights of Liverpool would become visible and they would be home.

Part Two

Part Two

Chapter Sixteen

1911

Somehow the months had slipped by and she hadn't yet found a way to ask Mary's advice about Frank, Livvie thought as she dressed for the party being held to celebrate both the coronation of the new King, George V, and Selina's engagement to Henry Woodford. Aunt Maud, in typical practical fashion, had decided kill two birds with one stone. Frank was still waiting for her after each suffrage meeting and they'd been to concerts and plays as well. Little had been said about these outings. She'd assumed that her father had been too busy with his business and wrapped up in his new wife to notice and that Mary didn't want to appear to be prying and so hadn't asked her any direct questions about her absences. The more she and Frank had seen of each other, the more their love for each other had blossomed. Livvie had confided in Selina and at her request Frank had been invited to her mother's party for her friend. The time was approaching,

Livvie realised, when she had to make a decision herself about telling her father about Frank – with or without her stepmother's advice – for Aunt Maud was no fool and Livvie suspected she knew she and Frank were walking out, although unofficially.

She paused and gazed at her reflection in the dressing-table mirror. She was twenty and this last year hadn't been easy, she thought. Both she and Mary had found the early days difficult to adjust to but at least there had been no cross words, just the occasional strained silences when they disagreed over something, usually household matters but occasionally something she termed 'political'. She'd become more and more involved with the suffragettes, but she'd refrained from attending the demonstrations – which were becoming more frequent, more widely attended and attracting more public attention and even some sympathy – although lately she had begun to feel that she really should stand up and be counted and show more support. However, she'd discovered women's rights were something Mary didn't agree with. It was an outlook she found hard to accept in someone so young but, as Frank had pointed out, her stepmother had been brought up very differently to herself. She had always had to defer to the men in her family, first her father and then her brother, and, never having lived in a poorer part of the city and seen a different side of life as Livvie once had, Mary's outlook was much narrower. And Livvie had to admit that her stepmother didn't seem to have either the same self-confidence or the courage of her convictions as Livvie herself did. So how would Mary view Livvie's feelings for her father's factory manager and the fact that they'd been seeing each other now for over a year, unbeknown to either Thomas or herself?

Livvie frowned as she struggled with the clasp on the silver filigree necklace that set off her pale peach taffeta and lace evening dress. She knew that she would need to sound Mary out before long for lately her father had taken to remarking how well Teddy Mayhew was doing and the fact that next year she would come of age and should really be thinking about her future, as Selina was doing. No doubt that subject would be brought up again before long. Picking up her long white gloves and her silver mesh purse, she went to see if her sister was ready.

Both her pa and Mary were waiting for them in the hall and Livvie thought that her stepmother looked rather pale and a little pinched, though it could just have been the deep magenta silk of her dress, which drained the colour from her cheeks and didn't suit her at all. It made Mary look much older than she was, but maybe that was the desired effect for this evening. This was the first time that Mary would be introduced to the Mayhews' circle of friends as Mrs Goodwin.

'Before we go next door to join the celebrations for Selina and Henry and King George and Queen Mary, there is something I wish to say,' Thomas said, glancing affectionately at his young wife and indicating they all go into the parlour. 'It doesn't affect you really, Amy, but you might as well be a party to it,' he added.

Mary smiled back at him apprehensively.

What now? Livvie wondered silently.

'Of course we are all going to wish Selina and Henry every happiness for the future; I know that both Charles and Maud are delighted. It's a very happy occasion and a very satisfactory arrangement.' Thomas paused, wondering whether to continue or not. He decided to press on. 'And when I first heard about their betrothal, it made me think. It made me realise that you and Selina are the same age, Livvie, and here she is with her future secured, no doubt to the relief of her parents.'

Livvie had a nasty feeling that she knew where this was leading. From the way Mary was darting pained glances at him, Livvie inferred that her pa had discussed whatever he was going to say with her stepmother.

'As your father I've been thinking about your future too, Livvie. Mary and I have talked it over and I've also had a quiet word with Charles, and I know that he at least would not be averse to Edward – Teddy – taking more of an interest in you.'

'Me!' Livvie blurted out, unable to stop herself and slightly annoyed by his actions. Yet again, he was making decisions that affected her without any prior consultation.

Amy raised her eyebrows in surprise. Livvie wasn't in the least interested in Teddy Mayhew; she was virtually walking out with Frank Hadley. She, on the other hand, was very taken with Teddy, even though he was quite a few years older than her. She didn't view that as an obstacle, however, given the age difference between Mary and Pa. Even Jonty knew how she felt, for he teased her about Teddy, although she hotly denied that she was 'sweet' on him.

'It would be a very good match for you,' Thomas continued hastily. As he'd said he had been giving the matter some thought lately, more so since Mary had imparted the more than pleasing news that she was going to have a child. He wanted no unpleasantness from Livvie about the forthcoming baby, however. So, if she had Teddy Mayhew to occupy her thoughts it would be an advantage and he was just the sort of young man Thomas expected her to marry. Nor did he want her remaining at home until she was much older, the way Mary had. It was high time she thought about her future. 'He's from a good family, has excellent prospects and is a thoroughly decent young man,' he went on determinedly.

Livvie was trying to regain her composure. Oh, he'd been hinting about what a good husband Teddy would make but she'd not expected this. Her pa must be deadly serious if he'd actually broached the subject with Charles Mayhew. 'But I had no idea that he had *any* interest in me, Pa! I like him, of course, but . . . but just as a friend. I've sort of grown up with him.'

'Well, isn't that all to the good? You know each other quite well by now and that always helps,' Thomas pronounced.

She had to put an end to this conversation, Livvie thought desperately. There was no way she would ever consider Teddy Mayhew as a husband! She didn't love him. She loved Frank. 'We do but . . . but there are some things we don't agree on, Pa. Quite serious and important things – well, they are to me at least.'

Thomas frowned; this wasn't going the way he had hoped. 'What "things"?'

'Like you and his father, Teddy doesn't agree with women's suffrage and you know that I do and that I feel very strongly about it too. There would inevitably be arguments about that for a start.'

'Oh, for heaven's sake, Olivia! Don't bring up that nonsense again!' Thomas cried, exasperated.

Seeing that this subject was bound to worsen the argument

between father and daughter, Mary decided to intervene. This party, she was certain, was going to be something of an ordeal for her; she knew very few of the people who'd been invited and was shy and ill at ease with strangers at the best of times. She was sure, too, that there would be speculation, especially amongst the women, about why she had married a man so much older than herself. In fact she wasn't much looking forward to the evening and, with the early symptoms of her pregnancy adding to her discomfort, she certainly didn't need ill feeling between Thomas and his daughter to mar it still further. 'Perhaps we should leave the subject for now? There's plenty of time in the future to discuss it and we don't want anything to spoil the celebrations, do we? I'm so looking forward to meeting everyone, Thomas,' she added, smiling at him and hoping she sounded sincere.

Thomas reluctantly decided she was right, and he didn't want anything to upset her either, he thought, remembering the two babies he and Edith had lost and then Edith herself and another unborn son. 'You're right, my dear. Perhaps I shouldn't have mentioned the subject this evening,' he conceded and, ignoring Livvie's obvious consternation, ushered them into the hall.

Livvie breathed a sigh of relief, silently grateful for Mary's tact. Trying to regain her composure, she determined that she would avoid Teddy's company if at all possible and that she would have to find a way to tell Frank of this completely unacceptable idea of her pa's.

Maud had surpassed herself, Livvie thought as Bessie showed them in. It was such a grand occasion that not only Emily had been drafted in to help but Maud had hired Bessie's younger sister Maggie for the evening too.

'Aren't the flowers just gorgeous, miss?' Emily whispered, looking quite overawed by the large arrangements of red tulips, white lilies and blue delphiniums which decorated all the rooms.

'They're exactly the same flowers they were having in the abbey for His Majesty's coronation,' Bessie informed them. 'An' they probably cost almost as much too!' she added sotto voce. 'I have to say they're very tasteful though. The mistress isn't one to go in for festoonin' red, white and blue buntin' all over the place.' She lowered her voice. 'Mr Hadley's in the drawing room, Miss Olivia.'

Livvie smiled and she and Amy went through to congratulate the happy couple while Aunt Maud introduced Mary to those in the company who had not yet met her.

Seeing that her father and stepmother were otherwise engaged, Livvie excused herself and, leaving Amy, with Teddy at her side, happily admiring the engagement ring, made her way to Frank's side.

'I have to say that Mrs Mayhew seems to give very lavish parties. You look especially lovely, Olivia,' Frank greeted her, taking a champagne flute from the tray Emily was carrying and handing it to her.

'Thank you. Yes, I suppose it's because it's a joint occasion she's rather pushed the boat out,' Livvie replied, sipping the sparkling wine and smiling at his compliment. He looked very handsome too, she thought: he'd invested in an evening suit for the occasion.

'There was a street party in full swing when I left home;

they were all having a whale of a time. Flags and bunting everywhere. Mrs Baldwin's piano had been dragged out into the street and Mr Baldwin was hammering out all the popular songs,' he informed her.

'It sounds great. There will be a lot of parties going on around the city, and bonfires too,' she added, thinking of her days in Minerva Street.

'Your stepmother is looking a little . . . overwhelmed,' he whispered and she looked across the room to where her pa and Mary were now surrounded by a group of people. Mary didn't look at all comfortable.

'She's quite shy when meeting new people,' Livvie explained. 'I must tell you that I'm very grateful to her, Frank, for quashing a conversation Pa started before we left home.'

He looked puzzled.

She took another sip and glanced around to make sure she wouldn't be overheard. 'He's got this mad idea about Teddy Mayhew taking an interest in me – as he put it. I don't want Teddy to be *interested* in the slightest! Oh, I like him well enough as a friend but nothing more, Frank! But Pa must be taking it seriously because he's even mentioned it to Charles Mayhew. I couldn't believe my ears when he told me that!'

'And is Teddy "interested" in you, Olivia?' Frank asked, feeling his heart sink. Teddy Mayhew was just the sort of person her father would approve of.

'I don't think so. I haven't a clue what Teddy Mayhew feels – we don't even see that much of each other. Actually, I think that Teddy is more interested in Amy than me and I know she's sweet on him.' She glanced over to where Teddy and her sister stood. Amy was smiling shyly up at him and he was obviously not bored in her company for he was chatting quite animatedly to her. 'It's Selina and Henry getting engaged that's put it into Pa's mind. I'm just going to have to tell him that the only person I'm "interested" in is you.'

Frank smiled at her but he was concerned. He could see her pa's point of view. Teddy Mayhew could offer her far more than he could and one day he'd inherit his father's business too. 'Will it cause problems, Olivia?'

'It very nearly caused a row before we came over – that's when Mary intervened. But he won't give up. I'll have to tell him to get the idea right out of his head. I have no intention of becoming involved in any way with Teddy Mayhew. I also told him that Teddy doesn't approve of the suffragettes, so for a start that doesn't make me look very favourably on him and no doubt we'd argue about it.'

Frank looked serious. 'So, I take it he wasn't very pleased?'

'That's when Mary stepped in but he's not going to dictate something as important as my future to me, Frank. He married for love – twice, if he really does love Mary. So why should I have to marry someone of *his* choosing that I don't love? And you know that I love you.'

Before Frank could reply Maud appeared, smiling. 'Now, what has the pair of you looking so serious? This is supposed to be a celebration! It's time for the buffet now and to toast the new King and Queen and Selina and Henry.' They had looked very solemn about whatever they were discussing and she'd noticed that they seemed quite intimate, as if they knew each other very well. Maybe Selina was right that there was indeed some affection between them.

'It was nothing much really, Aunt Maud. Frank was

commenting that Mary seems a bit overawed but I told him she's shy meeting new people. We don't have company very often, as you know.'

Maud nodded. 'I know that but she'll cope admirably, I'm sure. Now, let's move along to the dining room.'

After the buffet had been served her father, along with two of his associates, engaged Frank in a conversation concerning what impact the recent seamen's strike might have on business in the city. Disgruntled, Livvie went to seek out her stepmother.

'I think they are demanding rather too much for most employers to agree to,' Charles Mayhew said seriously. 'Five pounds, ten shillings a month for seamen and firemen on cargo ships, men without any skills.'

'But you have to agree, Mr Mayhew, that they do hard and dangerous jobs in poor conditions,' Frank put in.

Thomas nodded his agreement. 'The engine room of a steam-driven ship is a far from safe or pleasant place to work but what I think drew the most objection was their demand that some sort of employer–union conciliation board be formed. The unions are demanding too much say in what are basically employers' rights. If there's a disagreement then it should be left to the employer. I'm not in favour of any kind of union interference in *my* business and we've one or two agitators already, haven't we, Frank? Grey and Clayton.'

Frank looked thoughtful. 'I wouldn't call Billy Grey an "agitator"; he's a good worker who expects a fair deal – a staunch union man.'

Thomas frowned. 'Well, that Fred Clayton certainly has too much to say for himself and I believe he and Grey are "mates". I've heard Clayton and he's a follower of that Larkin fellow who's stirring up trouble in Ireland: I don't trust him at all.'

'There's always trouble of some kind in Ireland,' Charles added pointedly.

'Just as long as it stays there and doesn't spread over here. Larkin's views are too extreme by half, in my opinion,' Thomas stated. 'We've all worked too hard to see our businesses put in jeopardy by rabble-rousers and the like.'

'I think, gentlemen, that conditions in Ireland are not quite the same as here in Liverpool, but I believe in the principles of the unions, if not all the practices,' Frank stated. 'Change is in the air all around us; we are going to have to take more liberal views on quite a lot of things in the future, if I'm not mistaken. We can't stop the march of progress.' He received a suspicious stare from his employer and smiled. 'That's just my opinion, of course. I don't think the seamen's dispute will impact on us too badly,' he added, trying to lighten the conversation, wondering how he could extract himself from the group.

Livvie found Mary sitting on her own in a corner of the drawing room looking pale and tired. 'Are you all right? It's very warm in here. Have you had anything to eat?' she asked, sitting beside her.

'Yes, thank you, and I'm fine. It is warm and I'm just a bit tired, that's all.'

Livvie smiled at her. 'It is all a bit of a crush and some of Aunt Maud's friends are a bit, well, opinionated.'

Mary smiled back and nodded. 'I was finding some of them a bit wearing.'

'Shall I ask Pa to take you home? I'll say you have a

headache,' Livvie suggested, hoping to get Frank away from her father and his friends. It was a party, for heaven's sake, not at all the place for politics – local or national.

'No, no! If I can sit here I'll be fine, Olivia. I don't want to be a killjoy!'

A little disappointed, Livvie nodded her agreement but was relieved when she saw Maud approaching.

'Are you feeling all right, Mary? You look rather pale,' Maud enquired, ever the perfect hostess.

'I'm quite well, thank you,' Mary replied courteously. She was clearly a little in awe of Maud Mayhew.

'I see Thomas has abandoned you,' Maud stated, looking pointedly at the small group of men and thinking that the young woman didn't look well at all.

'That's typical of Pa,' Livvie commented acidly, still annoyed that she couldn't spend this time with Frank.

'That's typical of men in general, Livvie! Mary, would you like something to drink? Perhaps a cordial?'

Not wishing to appear ungracious Mary said that would be very welcome as the June evening was very warm.

'Good. Livvie, will you go and ask Bessie to bring a glass of elderflower cordial while I go and break up that "board meeting"!' Maud said purposefully. Really, Thomas should have more consideration for his young wife, she thought. She was convinced that Mary Goodwin was expecting. There was just something about her face, a pinched look around her nose and mouth: something Maud had seen often enough before to know what it foretold. If she was right, then it was something else that Livvie was going to have to come to terms with. She wondered how the girl would take it. And she was certain that there was something more than just friendship between Livvie and Frank Hadley so that rather ridiculous notion Charles had mentioned about Livvie and Teddy would have to be firmly quashed. Not that she would object, of course, but she didn't think Teddy had any particular feelings for Livvie and it was obviously not what either Livvie herself wanted or Edith would have wished for. Edith had always maintained that she wanted her girls to marry for love, not for wealth and a position in society.

Chapter Seventeen

———◆———

Livvie decided next morning that she would have to tell her stepmother about her feelings for Frank before her father could bring up the subject of Teddy Mayhew yet again. She found Mary sitting in the shade of the large elm tree that dominated a corner of the garden, leafing through a catalogue of flowering bulbs. She smiled to herself as she sat down beside her on the ornate bench; Mary did love the garden and now, in the middle of summer, it looked lovely with the roses Mary had had planted in full bloom, their perfume heavy on the warm June air.

'I've been trying to decide which bulbs should be planted for next spring and summer. I particularly like these lilies; they have a gorgeous perfume too.'

Livvie glanced at the picture Mary indicated and nodded her approval. 'Lovely. It's very warm already, don't you think?'

Mary nodded, fanning herself with the leaflet. She was feeling the heat and this morning she'd been sick. 'It is; I'll be exhausted by this afternoon.'

Livvie noticed that she did look rather wan. 'Did the party tire you? It was rather late when we got home.'

Mary smiled. Olivia was observant and her state of health wouldn't go unnoticed for long so maybe it would be best if she told her the news. 'Oh, I didn't mind that. You see, I have something to tell you, Olivia.' She took a deep breath; she really would have preferred Thomas to have imparted this news.

Livvie stared at her expectantly.

'I . . . I hope you will be happy for me . . . us, Olivia. You see, I'm going to have a baby.'

Livvie was stunned. A baby! She was to have a stepsister or -brother! Oh, she supposed she should have known this was inevitable, but a sharp pang of grief stabbed her as she thought of her mother and the baby brother she'd lost. 'I . . . I am . . . happy for you, Mary,' she managed to stammer, thinking that no matter how hard it would be she would have to come to terms with it. She was also realising that now wasn't the time to bring up the subject of her feelings for Frank. She couldn't burden her stepmother; she would have to seek Maud's advice.

Mary smiled shyly, relieved at how well Livvie seemed to have taken the news for Thomas had expressed some worries. 'Your father is delighted, of course. He is longing for a son.'

'I know,' Livvie answered grimly, again thinking of her mam. 'And up to now he's only had Amy and me and, as you are aware, we don't always see eye to eye.'

'Oh, he does love you both, Olivia!'

Livvie nodded. 'I suppose he does, in his own way.' Then

she grimaced. 'As long as we do as we're told. Now,' she continued, smiling resolutely, 'you are going to have to rest more. You can rely on Amy and me to help out.'

'That is kind of you, Olivia. I'm so pleased that you're not upset.'

Livvie got to her feet. 'Of course not,' she said firmly, thinking that first she must impart this news to her sister and then after lunch she'd go and see Aunt Maud.

Livvie found Maud too sitting in the garden in a shady arbour that protected her from the sun.

'It's too hot to sit inside; at least there is a bit of a breeze out here,' Maud pronounced. 'How is Mary this morning? She looked very tired last night but she did stay until everyone else went home.'

'It was late when we finally got to bed, but it was a great party. Everyone enjoyed it and Selina was so happy.' Livvie paused. 'Aunt Maud, Mary isn't feeling very well because . . .'

'She's expecting, isn't she?'

'How did you know that? She only told me this morning. Did Pa tell Uncle Charles?'

Maud shook her head. 'No, he said nothing but I suspected as much last night. It's a certain look about her face; you recognise it from experience, Livvie. How do you feel about it?' she queried gently.

'I was surprised and of course I . . . I can't help thinking about Mam.'

'But you're not upset or horrified or even . . . disgusted? It's usually the natural outcome of a marriage, you know.'

Livvie nodded. 'I know and I'm not upset. She is very happy about it, which is also natural, and I couldn't bring myself to say what I really thought.'

'Which is?' Maud asked.

'That I think Pa is so *selfish*! I can't forget that it was because he was so desperate to have a son that Mam risked her life to please him.'

'And paid the ultimate price for it,' Maud said sadly. She could understand how Livvie felt but the girl was young and things were not always so black and white in life or in relationships either: something she'd learn in time. 'Mary will have to take things easy, Livvie. She's thirty-one and it's her first child. Most women are much younger, still only girls really. I was when I had Teddy and so was your mother when she had you. Still, Mary appears healthy enough.' She patted Livvie's hand. 'I'm glad you are taking it so well, Livvie. You're growing up, becoming more mature.'

Livvie smiled at her. 'I suppose Pa will be relieved I'm not going to cause a fuss too. He's delighted of course.'

'As he should be. And what about Amy?'

'Oh, naturally she's thrilled.'

Maud nodded. Of course there would be a huge difference in the ages of Livvie and Amy and their brother or sister but she certainly hoped both Mary and the baby would be all right.

'There's something else I wanted to talk to you about, Aunt Maud. I was going to ask Mary's advice but . . . but now I don't feel as though I should burden her with it.'

Maud looked at her shrewdly. 'Your relationship with young Frank Hadley?'

Surprised yet again, Livvie nodded. 'We've been seeing each other for over a year now, Aunt Maud, and I . . . I love him.'

'I see. Does he love you?'

'Yes, but . . .'

'Your father doesn't know? And I suspect he won't approve. Has he mentioned this notion of his concerning you and Teddy?'

'He has but I look on Teddy as a friend, Aunt Maud. It's Frank I love and hope to marry – one day.'

Maud nodded. 'He's a very decent young man, Livvie. The only objection I can see from your father's point of view is that he hasn't the same expectations from life as some.'

'You mean Teddy?'

'Or someone of Teddy's ilk, but don't let that stop you, Livvie, not if you truly love each other. I'd advise you to have a quiet word with your father. He's got to know at some time so why not now? With the knowledge that he's to become a father again he might see things in a different light, and he obviously has been thinking about a marriage for you. You can also tell him that I've spoken to Charles and quashed that notion about Teddy very firmly. I want my son to choose his own wife, the way Selina has chosen Henry. Pick your words carefully, Livvie, don't argue with him.' Maud smiled. 'I know you can do that; you managed to get your own way over the suffragettes.'

Relieved, Livvie smiled back.

'And what does Frank think about your views on that?' Maud asked.

'He agrees with me. He can't see why women shouldn't

have the vote and he's always waiting for me after meetings – there's usually a crowd of hooligans congregated outside, jeering and shouting abuse, you see.'

Maud pursed her lips in disapproval at this although Frank Hadley rose higher in her estimation for taking care of Livvie.

'I haven't told Pa or Mary about Frank and me because I don't want to jeopardise Frank's position in any way. He has to work with Pa.'

'I see but I don't think you will. Yes, he's young for such a position but he's very efficient, your father relies on him a great deal and he trusts him too. Remind him of that, Livvie, and the fact that for the next six months at least, he's going to have to think of Mary and try to spend more time with her too.'

Livvie felt far more confident now as she thanked Maud and left to leave. She'd made the right decision in seeking Maud's advice; she doubted Mary would have been so decisive, and she was very glad that Aunt Maud had spoken to her husband about that mad idea of her pa's. It would certainly help if he realised that Maud wasn't in favour of it. She had plenty to think about now, she mused as she walked across the garden towards the house.

Bessie was carefully watering the huge flower arrangement in the hall. 'As if our Maggie an' me haven't got enough to do clearin' up without keepin' this lot fresh, but she expects them to last at least the week an' I can't say I blame her as she paid so much for them.'

'I wonder that she didn't ask Mrs Woodford if she would like to take some of them. I heard Henry's mother admiring them and they seemed to get on well together,' Livvie remarked.

'Oh, they do an' I liked her too. Miss Selina won't be warrin' with her ma-in-law the way me mam always was when we were kids. Granny Grey always called me mam "the Lady"! She thought Mam was stuck up. I ask you! If you knew me mam, Miss Olivia, you'd laugh at the thought of it. "Oh, it's the Lady come to visit us!" she always used to say; I can remember it well. It always narked me mam no end, which was why we didn't visit her very often. No, Miss Selina won't have to contend with anythin' like that.' Bessie lowered her voice. 'Did you an' Mr Hadley enjoy yourselves last night?'

Livvie nodded and smiled. 'Yes, and I've just been talking to Aunt Maud about him and she's advised me to tell Pa that we're walking out.'

Bessie nodded sagely; she was fully aware that Thomas Goodwin knew nothing about his daughter's feelings for Frank Hadley. 'At least then it will all be out in the open, miss.'

'It will and we'll be able to see more of each other too. There's something else "out in the open" now too, Bessie. My stepmother's expecting – she told me this morning – but keep it under your hat until the rest of the family know.'

Bessie leaned closer. 'Well, that should make him happy an' keep the pair of them occupied so they won't go on about you bein' a suffragette. By the way, there's goin' to be a big rally next month or maybe early August. Mrs Pankhurst is goin' to speak an' her daughter Christabel too. I'll be goin'.'

Livvie looked thoughtful. 'You know, Bessie, I just might come with you. I don't feel as though I'm doing nearly enough and I'd like to hear Mrs Pankhurst speak.'

'You'd be very welcome, miss. It's just a rally, I don't think there's any civil disobedience planned.'

Livvie nodded. Her pa would have got used to her walking out with Frank by then, she was sure. And Frank wouldn't object to her taking part in this rally, she knew that. She made up her mind. Yes, she'd definitely go.

Chapter Eighteen

———◆———

Mary blushed but smiled happily when Livvie congratulated her father that evening.

'I suppose it will take a bit of getting used to at first, having a baby in the house, but I'm sure we'll all enjoy it and Amy was thrilled when I told her,' she assured Mary.

Mary smiled at her, glad that Livvie had taken it on herself to impart the good news to her sister. She felt rather shy about telling people, even those closest to her.

Amy had found an excuse to go over to the Mayhews' house although Livvie suspected the real reasons were to see Teddy and remove herself from her father's presence in case there were cross words.

'I've already told Mary that both Amy and I will help as much as we can so she can rest over these next months,' Livvie told her father.

Thomas beamed at her. He hadn't expected this attitude at all. He'd expected her to purse her lips and look down her nose at best. 'That's very considerate of you, Livvie.'

She smiled back, remembering Maud's advice and knowing she still had to bring up the subject of herself and Frank. 'But you'll have to do your bit too, Pa. You'll have to try to get home earlier and spend more time with Mary. You'll need his support, won't you, Mary?'

Mary nodded, smiling. She would, for her emotions seemed to be all over the place and at times she was a little afraid of what the coming months held. Pregnancy and childbirth were not subjects that had ever been discussed by either her late mother or her sister-in-law. Quite often Thomas was late home from the factory, tired and preoccupied. He worked too hard in her opinion.

Thomas reached out and took her hand. 'And you'll have my support, my dear. From now on I'll leave at six sharp, I promise. Thank goodness I can safely leave Frank in charge of things.'

'He seems a very reliable and capable young man. You're fortunate to have found him,' Mary agreed.

Livvie took a deep breath. 'I've got something to confess to you both, concerning Frank. I should have told you months ago that Frank and I are walking out. I – We love each other. And his intentions are completely honourable, I can assure you.' She waited with bated breath for the explosion of wrath from her pa but it was Mary who spoke.

'Oh, Olivia, I'm so pleased for you! He's a very nice person. Although perhaps you should have told us earlier?'

Livvie silently blessed her for her tact and support. Surely now her pa wouldn't create a huge fuss and furiously demand that she never see Frank Hadley again?

'Indeed you should have told me, Livvie!' Thomas snapped,

trying to control his annoyance for this had certainly come as a bolt out of the blue. He'd wanted better for her. He'd wanted Teddy Mayhew not his factory manager – and she'd been seeing Frank Hadley behind his back. 'How long has this been going on?' he demanded.

'Over a year now, Pa,' Livvie replied, her voice steady.

His annoyance turned to anger. A year! And not one word had been mentioned – and what was worse she'd made him look a fool! She'd let him bring the matter up with Charles, when all the time . . .

'We didn't tell you, Pa, because I suspected you wouldn't approve and at first I wasn't sure exactly how I felt about Frank or he did about me. I didn't want to put Frank in an awkward position either,' Livvie explained hastily.

'And how did this relationship develop, may I ask?' Thomas asked curtly, ignoring the concerned look on Mary's face.

'After Frank walked me home in the fog, he insisted on waiting for me after I'd been to a suffragette meeting to escort me safely to the tram stop. He's continued to meet me ever since and then . . . then lately, after you married Mary, we've been to concerts and plays together,' Livvie explained. Before he could comment she rushed on. 'I know you wanted someone with a better position, Pa, but I . . . I love Frank and you have to agree that he's honest, sincere and hard-working.'

Thomas glared at her. 'He is but he is still my *employee*, Olivia! A working-class man, not a business or professional man. Teddy Mayhew would have been a far more suitable match!'

'I could never love Teddy, Pa. It wouldn't have worked and we'd both have ended up miserable. Aunt Maud didn't approve either; she wants Teddy to choose his own partner the way Selina has.'

'Does she? So you've spoken to her about this before you deigned to mention it to *me*! You've made me look a fool in Charles's eyes too!' Thomas couldn't keep the anger and disappointment out of his tone.

'I didn't intend to humiliate you, really I didn't. I asked her advice because I didn't want to burden Mary with it. Oh, Pa, please don't be angry!' Livvie begged. 'Surely you can understand how I feel about Frank?' She glanced pointedly at her stepmother, reminding him that he'd chosen both his wives, not had them foisted on him. 'I . . . I don't want us to fall out over it, Pa. Not now, when we should all be happy and looking forward to the baby,' she pleaded.

'Thomas, dear, we don't choose whom we fall in love with,' Mary gently reminded him. Yes, he'd wanted someone of Teddy's ilk, she knew that, but there was certainly nothing wrong with Frank Hadley that she could see and she didn't want there to be an atmosphere of animosity in the house for she hated discord of any kind.

Thomas could see her point. He certainly didn't want anything to upset his wife now and Livvie would have to marry someone – as would Amy – and next year she would come of age and wouldn't need his consent. All she had to do was wait; then she could and *would* marry whom she pleased. At last, and reluctantly, he nodded. She was proving to be a huge disappointment to him, he thought bitterly. Since Edith had died she'd become strong-willed, opinionated and stubborn. Why couldn't she be more like Amy, who was far more biddable and conservative in her manner and views?

'There will be no "falling out" as you put it, Olivia, but I have to say I am deeply, deeply disappointed in you. Everything I have worked and striven for you don't seem to consider at all important – and now this!'

Despite the relief she'd felt at his first words, Livvie bit her lip. 'I'm sorry you feel like that, Pa, but . . . but I can go on seeing Frank?'

'You can. I won't forbid it. But, Olivia, I don't approve and don't think you can invite him here socially.'

That hurt but Livvie nodded. At least he had given his consent – but only because he wanted nothing to upset Mary, not because he wanted her to be happy with the man she loved. He obviously had no intention of welcoming Frank into the family; she wasn't even being allowed to bring Frank home. Mentally she shrugged, telling herself that she didn't care. All that mattered was that he now knew and hadn't forbidden her to see Frank again. Neither had he threatened to give Frank notice, which was something she'd worried about. But she wondered how it would affect the working relationship between them. She hoped there would be no friction.

'And now I consider the matter closed,' Thomas stated firmly, although he fully intended to broach the subject with his factory manager and leave him in no doubt about how he felt about it all.

On Monday morning Frank knew immediately from his employer's attitude that Livvie had told him they were serious about each other. Thomas greeted him frostily and immediately demanded to see the work schedule for the week, without any pleasantries about their respective weekends.

'We're working at full capacity and the order to be shipped out on Friday will be ready on time,' Frank confirmed.

Thomas nodded curtly; however, he wanted that order ready by Thursday at the latest in case there were any delays caused by a strike by seamen, who were again threatening action. 'I need it to be ready before that.'

'I've heard the rumours concerning another strike, but we have other orders to complete and I doubt the men will be able to get everything processed a day early.'

Thomas handed him back the schedule and stood up. 'They'll have to or we will incur penalties. *I* will incur financial penalties and I will not have regular and important customers deeming Goodwin's Animal Feeds an unreliable supplier.'

'I'll inform them, Mr Goodwin,' Frank replied, knowing this wouldn't go down well at all; there were only so many working hours in the day.

'Before you go, Frank, there is something I wish to discuss with you.'

Frank nodded. 'I take it that Olivia has told you we are walking out.'

Thomas nodded.

'I would like to assure you, Mr Goodwin, that my intentions are honourable. I love Olivia and I wish to marry her. I haven't proposed yet but I'm sure she won't turn me down.'

'Indeed!' Thomas snapped. 'Well, you may as well know that I do not approve of this match at all and I wonder about your "honourable" intentions when you kept it from me for over a year! I don't consider that to be an honourable state of affairs at all!'

Frank flushed at his words. 'That was a decision we made

together. I'm not saying either of us was comfortable about it, sir, and it was wrong. But I will care and provide for her to the very best of my ability; you have my word on that.'

'You will have to wait until she is of age because I will not give my consent before and I have instructed Olivia not to invite you to the house. My wife is expecting and is not in any condition either to entertain company or endure any . . . unnecessary stress or ill feeling.'

Frank felt shaken by his employer's hostility and the revelation concerning Mrs Goodwin, but he assumed that Olivia knew her stepmother was pregnant. 'I understand. Please accept my congratulations,' he replied coldly.

At least now he knew where he stood. Thomas Goodwin would not willingly accept him as a son-in-law; to put it bluntly he did not want him to be part of the family, he did not even want him in his house. He would never be good enough for Olivia, he was not the right class, but he'd known that from the very beginning and it didn't impact on his feelings for her at all.

'Now, if you'll excuse me, sir, I'll go and have a word with the foreman about these orders,' he said formally.

'Impress upon him it is *imperative* that the order for shipping is ready by Thursday morning!' Thomas instructed grimly as Frank left the room.

To Thomas's annoyance Frank returned ten minutes later, accompanied by George Mercer, the foreman.

'I'm sorry to report, sir, that Mr Mercer says it can't be done,' Frank informed him.

'Not by Thursday morning, it can't, sir. Not unless we delay two other orders.'

Thomas's anger was increasing. The day hadn't started well with that strained interview with Frank and now this. He glared at the foreman. 'Have you told the men that we'll lose money and probably our reputation for reliability to boot?'

'I have, sir. Their reply was they can't do nothing about that unless you're prepared to pay them to work over,' George Mercer stated flatly, although he knew how this would go down. Thomas Goodwin wasn't a man to part readily with overtime pay. It ate into his profits.

'And who suggested that?' Thomas barked at the two men standing before his desk. 'No need to tell me, I have a damned good idea whose suggestion that was! Clayton and Grey?'

'Not Grey, sir,' Frank informed his increasingly irate employer, wondering if Goodwin's attitude was fuelled by his anger and resentment at the fact that he intended to marry Olivia.

'He's as bad as Clayton! They're in each other's pockets. I've seen them talking together. It can't be done unless they're paid extra, be damned! Of course it can; it's been done before on more than a few occasions when we've had a deadline and they've been happy to do it! They value their jobs; there are far worse employers in this city than me! I'll bet those two have urged everyone else to agree with them, too. Well, I'll not stand for it! Get them up here, Hadley, at once!'

Frank left with the foreman, leaving Thomas pacing the floor and fuming. It was all the fault of these agitators! How dare they tell him it couldn't be done on time! How dare they demand more money! How dare they threaten the good name of his business! Was everyone determined to thwart him from his own daughter down to his foreman and workers?

Frank ushered the two men in. Clayton was the younger of the two, being several years younger even than himself and Frank knew he was a single man, unlike Billy Grey who was middle-aged and had a family to support. Grey was respectable working-class; in fact the Mayhews' maid Bessie was his eldest daughter.

'Both Mr Mercer and Mr Hadley have informed me that you're refusing to get this order out without paid overtime?' Thomas fulminated.

'That's right, sir. Not if you want everything else out as well,' Clayton answered.

Thomas glared at him. The man's tone was far from respectful. 'And does everyone else agree with you?'

The younger man faced him squarely and nodded. 'The men are solidly behind the decision. It's only fair. It can't be done otherwise.'

Thomas felt the man was actually challenging him and anger suffused his cheeks. The impertinent young upstart! 'So, you're running this factory, this business now, are you, Clayton? You know what can and can't be done? How old are you?'

'Twenty-five, Mr Goodwin.'

'And you are refuting all my years of experience? How dare you, you arrogant young pup!'

'Sir! Mr Goodwin! It . . . it was only a . . . suggestion. Not everyone agrees,' Billy Grey put in. Of course it was only fair that they be paid to work overtime to get this order out but he felt Clayton wasn't going about it the right way. You couldn't threaten a man like Thomas Goodwin.

'I don't pay you to make suggestions, Grey!' Thomas snapped back.

'We only want what's right,' Clayton said doggedly.

'*I'll* be the one to decide what's right, not the likes of you! You're dismissed, both of you! Now get out.'

'Sir, please we didn't mean . . . Please reconsider . . .' Billy Grey begged. He needed this job; steady employment was hard to find in this city if you were an unskilled labourer and middle-aged to boot. But his plea fell on deaf ears.

As they both left, Frank could see how upset Billy was. He was a hard-working, reliable family man and Frank felt that he at least was being unfairly treated for he doubted Grey fully agreed with Clayton. Clayton, with his radical socialist ideas, had the arrogance of youth, with no thought or care for the consequences. Frank had little time for him for he was an agitator and obviously the instigator of this dispute.

'Mr Goodwin, please will you reconsider Billy Grey's position? This was all Clayton's doing, I'm certain of it. Grey has been with us for over ten years and has proved a good worker and never caused any trouble before. He's a family man too: he needs the job. Clayton is a single man with radical views. He has much less to lose.'

'Grey should have thought of all that, Frank, before he got involved with that . . . anarchist!'

'If I go and speak to the men, tell them what this . . . dispute has led to, and get them to agree to get the order out on time, will you reinstate Billy Grey?' Frank pleaded. He got on well with the workers and he was sure he could work out which orders could safely be left until later. Indeed this strike might never happen and all this would have been unnecessary. Billy would have lost his job for no good reason.

Thomas glared at him. His authority had been challenged

and he was in no mood to back down. 'I want them both off my premises. I'll not tolerate them a minute longer!'

Frank felt anger rising in him. The unfairness, the harshness of Thomas Goodwin's decision, the complete lack of consideration for the consequences for the Grey family, was something he felt he couldn't stomach. Clayton had gone too far in trying to undermine his employer's authority but not Billy.

'It's not fair that Billy Grey should suffer because of Clayton's behaviour. The man is *not* a troublemaker. It's utterly unjust that he should lose his job – and at his age he stands little chance of getting another, especially if he's tarred with the same brush as Clayton.'

Thomas got to his feet, anger making his blood boil. 'So now you think *you* have the right to criticise my decisions too! You've overstepped the mark, Hadley!'

'This need never have happened—' Frank started to reply, determined to do his best for Grey.

'You have the audacity to stand there and argue with me? Well, if you feel so strongly about the likes of those two, you'd better join them. I'm terminating your employment!'

Frank was shocked into silence. He'd not expected this but he was determined not to let Thomas Goodwin see his true feelings. Mustering what dignity he could and trying not to think of what he could do now and, worse, of how this would affect Olivia, he nodded curtly. 'So be it. I'll work the remainder of the week to see these orders out, if that's required.'

'It is,' Thomas barked, sitting down at his desk and drawing some papers towards him as Frank turned and left. Oh, this was all such a bloody mess, he fumed. But he wasn't going to be criticised or have his decisions questioned by his own factory manager. And this was the man who wanted to marry his daughter!

He dropped his head in his hands and groaned, some of his anger dissipating. What the hell was he going to do now? He'd have to try to find someone else, which wouldn't be easy, and in the meantime he'd have to shoulder the heavier workload himself. It would mean he'd have to work even longer hours and he'd promised Mary he would be home early every night – a promise he could no longer keep and which would no doubt distress her. That was the last thing he wanted. And when Livvie found out he'd dismissed Frank he could well foresee the tempestuous arguments that would follow, which definitely wouldn't be beneficial to Mary's health and wellbeing. Then he remembered how he'd felt the day he'd been told that both Edith and his son were dead. Was he prepared to face that again? Was he prepared to risk the welfare of the child Mary was carrying? he asked himself. He wondered, dejectedly, if he'd been too hasty dismissing Frank. Had he let his pride and his anger get the better of his judgement? The blame for all this could be laid at the feet of the Seamen's Union, he thought bitterly, but he'd have to think long and hard about how he'd handle the consequences of losing Frank Hadley, and the impact it would have on his life.

Chapter Nineteen

———◆———

Frank was still stunned as he went back out on to the factory floor. He couldn't believe he'd just been sacked and in such a callous, dictatorial way. He knew he'd never get another job as good as this – or at least the one he'd had up to five minutes ago. Dismissed and with no references, so despite his education and experience he'd find getting a similar position almost impossible. His future, which had seemed so secure, suddenly looked very bleak indeed. Should he have kept quiet? he wondered bitterly. He'd known Thomas Goodwin was already annoyed about him wanting to marry Livvie, so should he have stirred that annoyance into anger by his defence of a work mate? But it was done now and he just hadn't been able to stand by and see Billy Grey turned out like that for no good reason.

What future did he have now though? He had some savings but they wouldn't last long if he was forced to survive on them. He was going to have to face the problem and try to find a solution but at this precise moment he could barely think straight.

'Mr 'Adley, could I 'ave a word?' He was distracted by Billy Grey who'd collected his few belongings and was waiting by the doors to the loading bay, looking worried and dejected.

Frank nodded. 'Of course. I'm so sorry, Billy. I tried to get him to change his mind, but he's adamant.'

Billy shrugged. 'I'm very grateful for you tryin'. I don't suppose there's a chance of any kind of a reference? I'll stand no chance of gettin' work without one.'

'I'm afraid not, and there'll be no reference for me either.'

The older man looked puzzled.

'He's sacked me too,' Frank stated bluntly.

'Bloody 'ell! 'E never 'as? You're the best manager 'e's ever 'ad! George Mercer's always sayin' that. Why, Mr 'Adley?'

'Because I told him plainly that I didn't think his treatment of you was fair. He doesn't like his authority being questioned.'

Billy digested this and then nodded. 'I'm sorry you've lost your job too but . . . but thanks for tryin' to stand up for me, I appreciate it.'

Frank managed a wry smile. 'It hasn't done either of us much good, Billy, has it? At least I'll be staying until the end of the week. After that . . . God knows!' He held out his hand and the older man shook it. 'Good luck, Billy, and I'm very, very sorry.'

'It's life, Mr 'Adley. Gives you some 'ard knocks sometimes. We'll manage, we'll 'ave to, but the missus isn't goin' to be very 'appy. Well, good luck to you too,' Billy added before turning away.

Frank watched him walk slowly away. No, he didn't suppose

Mrs Grey would be happy but then neither would Olivia – and neither was he, but there was very little any of them could do.

As the day wore on Thomas became more and more agitated and convinced that he'd acted hastily. He realised just how much he depended upon Frank to keep things running smoothly. He was constantly hearing the complaints of his associates about unreliable, incompetent, untrustworthy employees and now he would be adding his voice to theirs. It would be very hard to replace Frank, to find a manager he could trust entirely and so relieve him of some of the stress of running a business like this. He was reminded of the saying 'cutting off your nose to spite your face'. The thought of going home and telling both Mary and Livvie of Frank's dismissal began to seriously trouble him. All the ramifications of his decision were beginning to dawn on him and he felt the weight of them becoming oppressive, making it impossible to concentrate. Yet he found it just as difficult to back down. He'd always stood by his decisions. But was this the most foolhardy one he'd ever made? It might very well prove to be costly in so many ways, he thought, unable to put the matter out of his mind.

By the end of the day, when Frank came to inform him that the day's production was on schedule and that, with some manipulation, the order for shipping would be ready on time and without the need for overtime, he'd reached a reluctant decision.

'That's very welcome news. And I . . . I've been thinking, Frank. Perhaps I was a little hasty this morning. Rather too harsh on you. I'd consider it very . . . satisfactory if you would stay on, bearing in mind the . . . er . . . circumstances at home.'

Astonished, Frank didn't reply for a few seconds. He hadn't expected Thomas Goodwin to capitulate in any way and realised how hard it was for his employer to admit he was wrong. Although he felt relief surge through him he was still determined to try to help Billy Grey's cause. 'Thank you, sir. I'll be very happy to stay on and hope to continue to give satisfaction.'

'Good, and I'm sure you'll continue to be your efficient self,' Thomas replied.

'But . . . but what about Grey? He asked for a reference, he knows he doesn't stand a chance without one, and I had to refuse him. He's not a young man, Mr Goodwin, and he has a responsibility to his family, as you do yourself. He's not a troublemaker and if you could see your way to reinstate him . . . ?'

Thomas set his lips in a tight line. Frank was driving a hard bargain but perhaps he was right in the matter of Grey. Thomas wanted no further disputes. 'Has he left the premises?'

Frank nodded.

'Then send word to him to recommence work tomorrow, but make it very clear, Frank, that I will have no further instances of insubordination or agitation. Do you understand?'

Frank felt another wave of relief wash over him. 'Understood, Mr Goodwin, and – on Grey's behalf – thank you. I'll go and see him myself.'

'And let that be an end to it all. Damn strikes! They'll ruin the country, you mark my words!' Thomas stated, determined to have the final word on the unfortunate matter but relieved that the problem had been solved and he could go home on time after what had been a fraught and exhausting day.

Denison Street was like all the streets that bordered the Dock Estate, Frank thought as he turned into it. Narrow, cobbled and flanked by rows of old, two-up two-down terraced houses whose brickwork had been blackened by decades of soot from the surrounding factory chimneys and the power station at the Clarence Dock.

It was Mrs Grey who opened the door to him, a middle-aged woman with fading hair, wiping her hands on her stained calico apron.

'Could I speak to your husband please, Mrs Grey? I'm Frank Hadley, factory manager at Goodwin's.'

'You could iffen 'e was 'ere! 'E was that upset about gettin' the push I sent 'im off to the pub. Go an' drown yer sorrows for an hour, I told 'im.'

Frank frowned. 'Oh, I see.'

'If it's important, like, I'll send our Stanley down to fetch 'im. An' it was very good of you to stand up for 'im, Mr 'Adley. Our Billy told me all about it.'

Frank smiled at her. 'There's no need to send for him. Just tell him he's got his job back – we both have. Tell him to report to George Mercer tomorrow morning at seven, as usual.'

'Oh, thanks be to God! I never expected this, Mr 'Adley! Thank you! You've no idea 'ow much worry's been lifted off me shoulders!' Hetty Grey cried, before turning around and shouting, 'Stanley! Stanley, lad, get yerself down to the Thornbush and tell yer da to get 'ome. 'E's got 'is job back!'

'I won't keep you from your family any longer. Good evening, Mrs Grey.' Frank raised his hat in farewell.

As Frank turned away he smiled to himself; no doubt Billy would be just as delighted as his wife. What had started out as a day of dire actions and worse consequences had ended in a return to the status quo to everyone's relief – although perhaps Thomas Goodwin wouldn't view it in quite that manner. As Frank quickened his steps towards the nearest tram stop he pondered whether or not he should tell Olivia of the day's events. There really was no need to now, he finally decided. No, it was better to let sleeping dogs lie; it wouldn't help to antagonise Thomas further. He chuckled inwardly. Although she would certainly deny it, Livvie was very like her father in some ways. But at least now they could go openly to places and see each other more frequently.

Livvie was surprised when Emily informed her next day that Bessie had called in and wanted a 'quick word' if possible. Her first thought was that Bessie had some new information on the planned suffrage rally.

She was hovering by the open kitchen door expectantly. 'I can't stay, Miss Olivia, but I just wanted to come an' ask you to thank Mr Hadley for me, when you see him next, like. Me mam's so relieved! We all are!'

Livvie's forehead creased in a puzzled frown. 'Thank Frank for what, Bessie?'

'Me da's job, miss. Mr Goodwin sacked him yesterday and Mr Hadley stood up for him and got him his job back. Your pa sacked Mr Hadley too, but changed his mind, didn't you know?' Seeing Livvie's shocked expression she hastened on.

'Oh, Lord! Me an' me big mouth! It's all right now though, miss. It's all blown over an' Mr Hadley is still the manager.'

Livvie couldn't believe what she had just heard. Why on earth would her pa dismiss Frank? Was it because she'd told him about being in love with Frank? No, it couldn't be if Mr Grey had been involved. 'What was it all about, Bessie?'

'Something to do with being paid overtime, me da said. I didn't understand it all but the upshot was Mr Goodwin sacked Fred Clayton and me da, but Mr Hadley stood up for me da. Perhaps I shouldn't have mentioned it, miss, I don't want to cause any trouble but . . .'

'No, you did right, Bessie. I'll pass on your thanks to Frank when I see him on Friday evening,' Livvie assured her.

After the girl had left Livvie was thoughtful. Not a word of this had been mentioned by her pa; in fact he'd been in quite a good humour yesterday evening. He'd come home on time, and after a pleasant supper he'd sat in the garden with her and Mary and she'd taken that as a sign he was coming to terms with her relationship with Frank for it hadn't been mentioned at all. Obviously the whole matter of this dispute didn't have anything to do with that but there must have been some very heated words for her father to sack Frank, albeit briefly. She supposed she shouldn't worry about it too much. She'd not mention it to her pa – she had no wish to alienate him in any way – but should she ask Frank what had happened to cause her father to take such a drastic and unexpected decision? She'd have to think about that but he'd probably tell her anyway, she guessed – if he wanted her to know of course. As it was work-related he might not, for he didn't discuss what went on at the factory a great deal and she seldom asked. They produced cattle cake. What was remotely interesting about that?

She felt shaken, though. Although it appeared to have all been sorted out it made her realise how much influence her father still had on her future, on Frank's too and even that of Bessie and her family. But to have stood up for Bessie's father at obviously great risk to his own position made her feel very proud of Frank.

She met Frank on the Friday evening after the incident at the factory in the gardens of St Nicholas's Church at the Pier Head. She loved the gardens for they were a haven of peace and tranquillity amidst the bustle of the riverfront and the breeze coming off the river was cool and pleasant. The church was centuries old and known as the 'sailors' church' because of its position adjacent to the waterfront and the old George's Dock – long since filled in, the space now occupied by the three new and magnificent buildings known as the Three Graces.

He was waiting for her, sitting on one of the benches dotted around the gardens. At that time of day – early evening – the gardens were virtually deserted.

'Have you been waiting long?' she asked as he kissed her cheek in greeting and she sat down beside him.

'Not really, it was easier for me to come here straight from work rather than go home and it's a pleasant place to sit and . . . think.'

'I told Pa about us, Frank.'

He nodded. 'I know and he was quick to tell me he doesn't approve.'

'I don't care! It's my life, Frank, and I love you! I told him that too, but he didn't forbid me to see you. There was no argument – you see Mary is expecting and he doesn't want to upset her in any way. He doesn't seem to mind my being upset by his attitude though.'

'He told me that too and I congratulated him. I'm sorry it has to be this way, Livvie, really I am. I'd hoped that he would accept me and be happy for me to become part of the family, but . . .'

'So am I but that's Pa – and it's his loss.'

'I told him my intentions are honourable and that I want to marry you and I do.' He kissed the tip of her nose. 'Will you have me, Livvie? I can't offer you very much, nothing on the scale of what you're used to. All I can give is my love and devotion and I'll cherish you . . .'

Her heart was bursting with happiness and she threw her arms around him. 'Oh, of course I will! There's never been anyone else for me, Frank. There never will be and I'll be happy to start out like Mam did with very few material things – they don't matter! We love each other, we'll be together and happy, and that's enough.'

There hadn't been much else said after that for a while and she was grateful for the seclusion that surrounded them. It was the perfect place for a proposal.

Later they'd strolled along the waterfront.

'I intend to buy you a ring, Livvie.'

'Oh, Frank, that's not necessary. I'm just happy to know that we can get married when I come of age.'

'It *is* necessary, Livvie,' Frank insisted. 'It's what your father will expect.'

'Mam never had an engagement ring – at least not before

she was married. She didn't mind, she always said her wedding ring was all she needed and that's all I'll need too,' she stated firmly.

Frank shook his head. 'No, you'll have an engagement ring and a decent one too. I insist.'

She laughed. 'Well, if you *insist*.'

'I do and we'll go tomorrow afternoon to buy one, Livvie,' he promised.

Chapter Twenty

———◆———

As the long and increasingly hot days of summer passed Livvie felt that things were progressing quite well on all fronts. Her pa was in a better humour most of the time, although Frank was barely mentioned, which she often found hurtful; however, she hoped that after the baby was born his attitude would soften. Mary was blooming although she did tire easily and the heat didn't help, making her ankles swell, and she was prone to headaches. Selina was planning her wedding with Maud and had asked both Livvie and Amy to be bridesmaids. Amy was thrilled and was also delighted that Teddy Mayhew seemed to be paying her more attention, which was gratifying, something she'd confided to Livvie.

Livvie smiled to herself. Amy was indeed growing up and turning into something of a beauty and she doubted there would be any opposition from her father if that interest developed into something more serious.

She was getting ready to meet Frank, who had insisted on accompanying her to the rally that was being held that afternoon on St George's plateau, the wide-open expanse in front of the neo-classical St George's Hall in Lime Street. She'd chosen to wear a white voile blouse and a pale blue linen skirt, both of which were suited to the warmth of the day, and a large white hat trimmed with a big blue bow which would shade her face from the sun. This blouse was one of her favourites with its intricate pintucking and delicate pale blue embroidery for she'd been wearing it when Frank had proposed. She glanced down at the square sapphire surrounded by tiny diamonds that adorned her left hand. She was very proud of it. Of course her pa hadn't remarked upon it at all, but both Mary and Amy had admired it.

She was meeting Bessie at the tram stop and they'd travel into town together, but Frank would be waiting for her when she alighted in Lime Street.

'There's no need for me to stick to you like glue, miss, and play gooseberry. It's a rally; there'll be no trouble,' Bessie had assured her.

Before she left the house she looked into the parlour where Mary was resting with her feet up. She hadn't told either her father or stepmother where she was going.

'I'm going out now – is there anything you need, Mary? Emily's off for the afternoon but we'll both be back later.'

Mary smiled but shook her head. 'No, thank you, Olivia, and if I do Amy will no doubt be back from Maud's house soon. Enjoy your afternoon. I take it you are spending it with your fiancé?'

Livvie nodded and smiled, ignoring the glance her father cast in her direction over the top of his lowered newspaper.

The tram was crowded and the afternoon was very hot and

by the time they alighted beside the Steble fountain at the top of William Brown Street there were beads of perspiration on both their foreheads.

'It doesn't exactly help that we were packed into that tram like sardines in a tin – not in this heat!' Bessie grumbled, dabbing her cheeks and forehead with a handkerchief she'd dipped into the waters of the fountain. 'I'll make me own way home, miss,' she added as Frank came towards them.

'I didn't expect there to be so many people here,' he said as he greeted Livvie. He took her arm and they followed the crowds along the road towards the plateau, flanked by its huge bronze crouching lions and the mounted statues of Queen Victoria and Prince Albert.

'Everyone wants to hear Mrs Pankhurst,' Livvie reminded him, beginning to feel quite excited at the prospect of seeing and hearing this redoubtable lady. 'Though no doubt Her Majesty up there wouldn't approve,' she added, indicating the statue.

'I don't think we stand much of a chance of getting anywhere near the front, so we might not hear very much,' Frank warned her.

'Just being able to be a part of it all is enough. This is the first time I've ever been to a rally, Frank – I'm breaking my promise to Pa,' she added, giving him a wry little smile.

'Does that bother you, Livvie?' Frank asked seriously. Deep down he didn't agree with her decision to flout her father, but he understood her commitment to the cause and how frustrated she felt that she had been forbidden to attend such gatherings.

'I suppose it should, but, well, surely he can't object to me just *listening* to speeches? And there won't be any trouble.'

Frank nodded, although he intended to keep a sharp eye out for any sign of rowdiness and get her away in case they got caught up in it. He was aware that at these rallies it wasn't always the suffragettes and their supporters who instigated the trouble and unless there was a real danger of the whole thing turning into a full-scale riot, the police would not intervene. It was the reason he'd insisted he accompany her.

As they joined the ever-increasing crowd on the plateau he noticed that there were significant numbers of policemen standing in groups on the opposite side of the road as well as those who were directing the traffic along the busy thoroughfare and he wondered if they were expecting disorder. He was thankful therefore that they could only find a place towards the back of the crowd.

Livvie was disappointed that she couldn't hear everything Mrs Pankhurst was saying but she got the gist of it and she felt a surge of pride that at last she was here and openly showing her support. Everyone around her was wearing a green, white and purple rosette and some of the ladies were wearing sashes too. She'd pinned her own rosette on as she'd travelled on the tram. She soon forgot the stifling heat and the crush as she strained her ears to catch Mrs Pankhurst's words.

It was Frank who noticed the scuffle that had broken out on the very edge of the crowd to his left. This was just what he'd feared and he tightened his grip on Livvie's arm. There were numerous pubs along the length of Lime Street and no doubt some form of counter-protest had been dreamed up by their customers after a bellyful of ale.

'Livvie, I think it's time we left,' he urged.

'But, Frank, it's not over yet! Christabel Pankhurst's going to speak next!'

'There's some sort of trouble brewing over there and I think we'd better go before it gets out of hand, Livvie. Remember you're not supposed to be here and if it gets worse and is reported in the newspapers or on the wireless . . .'

She peered in the direction he was looking in and frowned. 'Oh, there're always drunken hooligans hanging around, they think it's free entertainment!'

'I know but there're also large numbers of police officers outside the Empire and that doesn't bode well, Livvie. I'm not going to have you exposed to any kind of danger and it's very easy for the innocent to be caught up with the guilty. The police already take a dim view of these rallies,' Frank replied firmly.

She nodded, bitterly disappointed but knowing he was right. If she wanted to attend future demonstrations then she had to stay out of trouble, so she wouldn't argue or risk her pa's anger if he found out.

As they extricated themselves from the crowd and retraced their steps, skirting the scuffling and jostling that seemed to be involving more and more people, he squeezed her hand. 'I'm sorry for dragging you away, Livvie, but remember the old saying "those who fight and run away, live to fight another day". It won't always be like this. More and more people are beginning to agree with Mrs Pankhurst.'

She nodded. 'But how long will it take to convince those drunken idiots?'

'There are some diehards who will never change their minds, I have to admit,' he agreed.

And her pa was one of them, she thought bitterly. What could the suffrage movement achieve if men like her father would only support them? She hoped Bessie would be all right, but was then comforted by the thought that she was more than a match for most rabble-rousers.

When she arrived home she was greeted by a white-faced and anxious Amy.

'Oh, Livvie, I'm so glad you're home!'

Livvie grasped her sister's hand and found Amy was trembling. 'What's wrong?' she asked. Surely her pa hadn't found out where she'd gone? She hadn't even told Amy.

'It's Mary!'

'What's happened?'

'She . . . she's miscarried!' Tears slid down Amy's cheeks as Livvie uttered a cry, then drew her sister into the dining room.

'Tell me what happened.'

'When I got in she . . . she said she didn't feel well, so Pa suggested she go and lie down. I went up after about half an hour, just to see . . . if she was all right, and . . . and . . . Oh, Livvie, she was in agony and there was . . . blood . . .'

'Poor Mary!' Livvie cried, distressed for both her stepmother and her sister who had witnessed Mary's suffering.

'I . . . I ran back down and told Pa and then I went for Aunt Maud and Pa went for Mrs Forrester . . .' Amy began to sob.

Livvie put her arm around her. Oh, this was all so terribly familiar, she thought. All the memories of the day when her mam had gone into labour came flooding back and tears pricked her eyes. 'Amy, is . . . is Mary all right? She's not . . .'

'She's very weak but Mrs Forrester says she'll recover. She's sleeping now.'

'Oh, thank God for that! And the baby?'

Amy shook her head. 'Mrs Forrester said he . . . he was too small.' Amy dashed away her tears with the back of her hand.

So, she had lost a little stepbrother, Livvie thought sadly. It was as if her pa was destined to be denied a son. 'Where's Aunt Maud? Is she still here?'

Amy nodded. 'Yes, she's with Pa. They're in the parlour. He . . . he's . . . devastated.'

He would be, Livvie thought, remembering how he'd looked the day he'd told her Mam was dead. But at least Mary had survived. 'I . . . I'll go and see them.'

As soon as she opened the door Maud rose and took her arm, drawing her out of the room. 'He's not himself, Livvie. He's shocked and very upset. He's saying he's cursed, which is nonsense. These things happen, sadly; I've tried to tell him that. Mary isn't a young girl, she has a delicate constitution and this oppressive heat hasn't helped.'

Livvie nodded. 'But she *is* going to be all right, Aunt Maud?'

'As long as she rests and takes things easy, according to Mrs Forrester, but we've sent for the doctor just to be on the safe side.' Maud too was remembering the day Edith had died. 'And I intend to have a word with the doctor before he leaves too.'

Livvie looked at her quizzically. 'What for?'

Maud lowered her voice. 'I don't think it will be wise for Mary to become pregnant again for a while and I'm hoping he will agree and have a word with your father about it. It's not my place to bring the matter up with your father, Livvie, but I – we don't want another tragedy.'

Livvie understood. 'No, we don't want to have to go through that again, Aunt Maud! This is bad enough.'

'Then let's hope your father will accept what the doctor tells him,' Maud said firmly.

Livvie nodded. She too hoped he would, rather than selfishly pursuing his obsession for a son and heir. It wouldn't be fair to Mary or indeed any of them to put them through all the worry and anguish of that.

Suddenly she felt very weary; the day hadn't worked out as she'd planned. Aunt Maud was right; this heat didn't help. It was to blame for a lot of unpleasant things.

Chapter Twenty-One

—◦——

The heatwave continued on through August with temperatures of ninety-seven degrees recorded regularly. People were horrified by the number of children who had died, particularly in London where the figure was approaching nine hundred. In the slums of Liverpool the numbers were creeping steadily up too as disease, malnutrition and poor sanitation took their toll.

Mary slowly recovered, but her condition was not helped by the stiflingly hot days and oppressive, sultry nights when everyone found it difficult to sleep. She was subdued and listless, her condition bordering on the depressed, Livvie thought. She had to be coaxed to eat and, when pressed, confided to Livvie that she felt she had let Thomas down very badly and that Dr Sumner had advised that they should not try for another baby until she had fully recovered her health and strength, for she was no longer a young woman.

'He spoke very sternly to both me and your father, Livvie. It was quite embarrassing for me and hard for him to understand,' she confided.

Livvie nodded. 'I can see that but he was only giving you sound medical advice.'

'I know but it . . . it's my . . . duty to have children and I want them too.'

Livvie wanted to retort that it was her health – maybe her life – that the doctor was concerned about, not her 'duty' but she said nothing.

The effect it had on her father was predictable, she soon came to realise. He seemed bitter and began to distance himself from them all, spending more and more time at the factory although conditions there in the heat were far from ideal. Frank told her that being on the factory floor was like working in a furnace; he didn't know how the men bore it and everyone was praying it would soon become cooler. If she'd had any hope that her father's attitude towards herself and Frank would soften, it disappeared completely after Mary's miscarriage.

Thankfully when August passed into September the weather became seasonably cooler and Mary seemed to be improving, although as there was still a great deal of labour unrest across the city her father's disposition and temper did not. Livvie continued to attend the suffrage meetings and even went with Bessie to a very much smaller rally at the Pier Head towards the end of the month. This time she firmly declined Frank's offer to accompany her, saying that she would be perfectly fine with Bessie and that she would have to learn to take care of herself: she wasn't a child. He wasn't happy about her decision but she felt he had enough to contend with having to work with her increasingly irascible father without having to worry about her too. To everyone's relief the rally passed off without trouble.

She and Amy were summoned to Maud's house one afternoon in October to discuss their bridesmaids' dresses, for preparations for Selina's wedding were well under way. It was one of those beautiful autumn days when the morning mists clear to leave the sky shining and pale blue. The leaves on the trees had started to turn the vibrant shades of gold and orange, and chrysanthemums and Michaelmas daisies filled the flower beds, Livvie noticed as they walked to their neighbours'. She knew her sister was excited at the prospect of becoming involved in the preparations but she had other things on her mind. She needed to talk to Bessie about the next demonstration that was being planned – news of the venue had spread, but she didn't yet know precise details.

They found Maud and her daughter sitting at the dining-room table surrounded by the swatches of material Selina had acquired from various establishments in the city. They both duly seated themselves.

'As it's going to be a spring wedding, I thought these would look lovely. Which do you like best?' Selina asked, spreading out four swatches of silk which varied in tone from baby blue to vibrant cobalt. 'Don't they remind you of the colours of bluebells?'

'Oh, I do like the pale blue, Selina,' Amy enthused, fingering the delicate material.

Maud looked rather sceptical. 'As it's to be an April wedding and could be still quite chilly, I think that perhaps something a bit more substantial than silk might prove a better choice.

Perhaps a nice heavy taffeta? You'd still have the choice of colour, Selina.'

Selina considered this. 'You might be right, Mother. It can be cold in April.'

Livvie said she really didn't mind which shade of blue they settled on, after all it was Selina's wedding, although Amy said she still preferred the pale blue and both Maud and her daughter agreed.

Selina then produced various pictures of dresses which she'd cut from magazines and after some discussion they opted for a style with long sleeves but with a lower neckline and a short train, all of which would be trimmed with matching lace; small wreaths of silk flowers in the same shade of blue were suggested for their hair, rather than hats. When at length the pictures and swatches were put aside, Amy and Selina began happily discussing what the bride intended to wear.

Maud turned to Livvie. 'How is Mary?'

'She seems a little better, Aunt Maud. She's started eating again and I hope she's going to regain some of the weight she's lost.'

Maud nodded. 'That's good news. She is very thin. At least she seems to have lost that "haunted" look though. Sometimes it can take a while to get over something like that. It doesn't just affect the body but the mind and the spirits too.'

Livvie agreed. 'She was very dejected after it happened. I only wish Pa would spend more time with her. It would help to cheer her up, I'm sure.'

Maud sighed. She knew how bitterly disappointed Thomas was. 'Maybe he will once all this unrest is settled. I don't know what things are coming to – there seems to be strike after strike. I couldn't believe there were actually riots in Wales in the summer. I know it's worrying Charles too; he seems to think that the country is going to hell in a hand cart! But I try not to take too much notice and to assure him it will all settle down soon. How is Frank?'

'Fine, although I think he has to cope with far more than he tells me,' Livvie replied, casting her eyes to the ceiling.

'And do you two have any plans?' Maud probed, moving away from the grim, unsettling subject of labour unrest. Livvie would be twenty-one next May and would then not need her father's permission to marry Frank Hadley.

Livvie smiled. 'No definite date, but we hope to get married in June next year. I'd like a summer wedding, even though it will be a very small and quiet one compared to Selina's. And of course Frank does have a house already so I'll just move in. I'll have a ready-made home, you could say.'

'But you'll want to put your stamp on things, I'm sure. I imagine, being a bachelor's home, it will be rather plain and old-fashioned.' Maud smiled, wondering if Thomas would unbend enough to give his daughter away or indeed attend the ceremony at all. 'If Selina had her way we'd be inviting half of Liverpool. As it is it's going to be a much larger affair than either Charles or I had anticipated.' She leaned closer to Livvie and dropped her voice, glancing quickly at the two girls who were engrossed in a conversation about a new magazine for women that had just been published called *Woman's Weekly*. 'I think that actually Teddy is going to ask your father's permission to take Amy out in the very near future.'

'Really? Oh, she'll be thrilled, Aunt Maud. She's been longing for him to ask,' Livvie whispered back.

Maud tapped the side of her nose with her forefinger. 'That's just between us for the moment.'

Livvie grinned. 'Of course. At least Pa won't object to that!'

Maud laughed. 'No, he won't and neither will I. She's a lovely girl.'

Before they left Livvie managed to get a few words with Bessie on the pretext of enquiring how her father was getting on and Amy left them to talk, her head full of brides' and bridesmaids' dresses.

'Have they decided when it's to be, Bessie? I know we're going to demonstrate outside the governor's house at Walton Jail.' Livvie kept her voice low.

'This Sunday afternoon, miss. We're to assemble at three o'clock sharp; it's known that he'll definitely be at home then. Miss Wilkinson an' some of the others are bringin' placards. "Women against Force-Feeding in Walton" they'll have on them.'

Livvie nodded, thinking of the treatment of Miss Martin and Miss Hall. The horrible practice hadn't been suspended, not in Walton Jail at least. 'I'll meet you there, Bessie, at about five to three. It's not that far from here on the tram.'

'It's a bit further for me, miss, so I'll set out earlier. I'll wait for you at the top of Hornby Road an' we'll walk down to the prison together.'

Livvie nodded as she left. She wasn't going to tell Frank about this outing for she knew he'd arranged to meet David Benson who was an old friend and she didn't want to spoil his afternoon's enjoyment. She'd meet him later that evening as they were going to the Philharmonic Hall and then she could tell him all about the demonstration.

* * *

Bessie was already waiting on the corner of Hornby Road and Rice Lane when Livvie arrived. She could see groups of women and girls walking down the road ahead of them to where the massive grim walls of the Victorian prison dominated the skyline. Flanking this side of the road were the small, neatly kept houses occupied exclusively by the prison officers and their families and at the end of the block, set slightly apart, was the much larger house of the prison governor. It was encircled by wrought-iron railings around which the suffragettes were gathering and some were indeed holding up large placards declaring 'Women Against Force-Feeding in Walton' and 'Shame on you, Governor'.

Livvie nodded and exchanged greetings with the women she was acquainted with and she perceived there was an excited, yet grimly determined mood about them all. After about ten minutes Sarah Wilkinson positioned herself at the front of the crowd by the railings and with the aid of a loudhailer began to speak, demanding that the cruel treatment of women imprisoned for their beliefs cease at once and that the governor come out and address them. Her words were met with cries of agreement to which both Livvie and Bessie joined in. She could see no sign of any movement in the house and wondered were they wasting their time?

'Is he even in there, Bessie?' she shouted over the noise.

'Oh, aye, miss! He's just keepin' well out of sight, that's all. Ashamed to show his face let alone come out an' speak to us! The coward!' was the dismissive reply.

As Sarah Wilkinson stepped down a cheer erupted, then there followed the distinctive sound of breaking glass and

Livvie gasped. Someone must have thrown a stone, which had obviously broken a window. It was followed by another and yet another and then she was propelled forward by the crowd behind her and she got separated from Bessie. She tried desperately to turn around and push her way out of the mêlée but it was almost impossible, and as she continued to struggle she heard the sound of thudding feet and the shrill blasts of police whistles.

Everything then happened so quickly. One minute she was fighting her way through the crowd, the next she was seized by both arms and dragged unceremoniously away, losing her hat in the process. She began to struggle frantically but the grip on her arms was like a vice and she cried out in pain and terror. The next minute she was lifted off her feet and thrown bodily into a police van, landing in a sprawling heap on the floor. Gingerly she hauled herself up; her shoulder was throbbing for she'd fallen heavily on it. She looked around dazedly and realised she wasn't alone; there were eleven other women already in the van sitting on the floor around her. All were dishevelled, some were obviously as terrified as she was, but there was no sign of Bessie. One girl had a trickle of blood oozing from the corner of her mouth and she was crying as an older woman tried to calm her.

'He had no right to strike you! No right at all – you weren't struggling,' she was insisting angrily.

'I didn't do *anything*!' the girl sobbed.

Livvie was trembling violently from shock and she clutched at the arm of the nearest woman as panic rose in her. 'I didn't do anything either! I was just listening and then I heard glass breaking, then . . . then I was dragged off!'

'We all were. There wasn't supposed to be any violence. No one said windows were going to be broken,' the woman declared vehemently. She was about Maud's age and seemed more angry than afraid.

'What will happen to us now?' Livvie begged fearfully. Oh, she really was in trouble now! And what had happened to Bessie?

'They'll take us to the police station and charge us with . . . something! It won't matter what. Then we'll appear in court in the morning and no doubt find ourselves on the inside of that damned prison for fourteen days. That's what usually happens. Then the only way to protest at such outrageous treatment is to refuse food, to go on hunger strike.'

Livvie felt sick with fear at her words. Nothing like this had ever happened to her before. She'd have to spend the night in a police cell and then . . . Oh, her pa would be furious for she'd broken her promise and defied him. And what would Frank think? He didn't even know she'd come here and when she didn't turn up this evening he'd be frantic. She began to cry quietly; she didn't dare to dwell on what now faced her. It was all too terrifying and the worst of it all was that she was completely innocent.

Bessie, bruised and dishevelled, had fought her way out of the crowd and managed to evade being arrested but she'd seen with horror Livvie being dragged towards the Black Maria. She stopped running when she reached the junction with the main road, her breath coming in painful gasps as she leaned against a wall. Oh, God, what now? she thought in desperation. Who the hell had thrown those stones and how had the coppers managed to get there at just that moment? There'd been no sign of them before that. Had the governor been warned? Had the coppers been warned? Did one of *them* actually throw the stones? She wouldn't put it past them, she thought bitterly. But what would happen to Miss Olivia? She couldn't go to the police station and demand they release her, for Olivia had done nothing wrong: they wouldn't believe her. They wouldn't take any notice of her. They'd probably throw her in a cell too.

As she tried to tidy her appearance she wondered frantically if she should go and tell Mr Goodwin what had happened. No, she didn't dare do that, she couldn't face *him*, but she'd have to tell someone. Mrs Mayhew? she wondered. But she'd probably lose her job if she confided in her mistress. No, it would have to be Mr Hadley, she reasoned. Miss Olivia was engaged to him and he didn't disapprove of her being a suffragette. *He'd* believe that they were innocent, that they'd taken no part in the vandalism. She began to feel a little calmer. She'd go home first, tidy herself up and then go and see him; she knew where he lived. And he'd stood up for her da, hadn't he? So he'd certainly stand up for Miss Olivia. Squaring her shoulders she began to walk quickly and determinedly towards the tram stop. It had all gone so horribly wrong, she thought, wondering fearfully what the outcome of this afternoon's events would be for Olivia Goodwin.

Chapter Twenty-Two

She would be black and blue all over, Livvie thought bitterly as she was herded in through the back entrance of the police station with the eleven other women, but at least she'd managed to pull herself together a bit and she was no longer shaking. They'd all been thrown violently around as the van travelled through the cobbled streets towards the city centre, for there had been no seats and nothing to hang on to during that desperate journey. She realised that they hadn't been taken to the nearest station, which was in Rice Lane – that wouldn't have been big enough to accommodate them all – so this must be the Main Bridewell in Dale Street, she thought as she looked around.

The room was stark with limewashed walls, bare except for posters of desperate-looking individuals and lists of Rules and Regulations and Fines. Against one wall were set rough wooden benches and on another there was a small fireplace but no fire burned cheerfully in it: it was littered with cinders, cigarette ends and spent matches. There were two heavy doors leading off the room and ahead was a long wooden counter behind which stood a huge, burly officer making notes in a ledger.

'This is the lot who were causing mayhem outside the governor's house at Walton, Sergeant. Smashing windows and causing an affray, resisting arrest – the usual,' the policeman who had pushed her inside curtly informed his superior.

The sergeant included them all in his disapproving glare. 'A nice carry-on, ladies, I must say! Right, well, let's have your particulars. One at a time, if you please,' he commanded.

'This is a disgrace! An outright disgrace. Just what are we going to be charged with, may I ask?' the oldest woman in the group demanded angrily.

The custody sergeant glared at her. 'Criminal damage, causing an affray, breach of the peace – amongst other things, madam!' He turned to Livvie. 'Name, address and date of birth!' he snapped.

'Miss Olivia Alice Goodwin, number seven Poplar Avenue, Aintree. I was born on the sixth of May, eighteen ninety-one and I didn't do any of those things you mentioned! I was attending a peaceful demonstration; you've no right to arrest me!'

He looked up and gave her a hard stare and the burst of courage she'd mustered instantly faded.

'That's for the prosecution and the court to decide but it didn't sound very "peaceful" to me. Name of legal guardian, miss, seeing as you're under twenty-one.'

'My father, Thomas Goodwin, of the same address,' she replied, trying not to think of her pa's reaction to all this.

It was all written down and then he paused and leaned

towards her. 'Is that the same Goodwin who owns the cattle feed factory on the Dock Estate?'

She nodded.

'Well, I dare say he's not going to be very pleased about your antics this afternoon, is he? Go and sit over there. Next!'

Livvie was ushered to one of the benches set against the wall where she waited, under the grim gaze of the other officers standing around, until everyone's details had been recorded. Most of the other women were subdued and frightened although trying not to show it, but Sarah Wilkinson and another woman, a Mrs Nora Frodsham, seemed not to be distressed at all. In fact Sarah Wilkinson had confessed that she had indeed thrown the stones which had smashed the windows and appeared to be proud of the fact, something which shocked Livvie for she'd always seemed so quiet. But then she remembered that Sarah Wilkinson had been at the very front of the crowd, the nearest to the railings, and now she knew why.

They were all escorted through one of the doors, which led into a dimly lit, narrow corridor, and then down some steep stone steps to an even darker and narrower passageway where heavy iron doors were set into the thick walls. Some of the doors were closed, others open. She shuddered involuntarily as she realised that these were the cells. She and three others were pushed roughly inside one of them and the door slammed shut and locked from the outside. She sank down on the edge of the narrow bed and gazed around. Oh, it was horrible, she thought. It was small with bare brick walls; it was lit by one spluttering gas jet on the wall and smelled of damp, disinfectant and something even less pleasant. There were no windows and she realised they must be under the main building. In one corner stood a battered and rusting enamelled bucket and on the bed was one threadbare, greasy, grey blanket. She shuddered, beginning to tremble again from fear and the cold dampness in the air. No doubt there would be bugs and vermin in here too. They were all going to have to spend the night here and she felt utterly mortified as she realised what purpose the bucket served. She'd never been so humiliated in her life. Would they get anything to eat? she wondered vaguely, although at this precise moment felt she couldn't face food of any kind – and she'd have to refuse to eat it anyway; it was what was expected of suffragettes. Then in the morning they would all go before the court and, dirty and dishevelled as they would be then, they would look like common miscreants. She'd be charged with at least affray or breach of the peace and then . . . then sentenced to . . . what? Despite the presence of her companions, she felt utterly alone and afraid. She'd wondered when she joined the suffragettes if she'd have the moral courage and stamina to face what Selina Martin and Leslie Hall had endured; now she was about to find out, she thought in despair.

Bessie had told no one at home about the events of the afternoon but had got changed and taken a tram to where Frank Hadley lived. To her consternation there was no response to her insistent knocking on his front door – he was obviously out. Oh, what now? she thought frantically. Well, there was nothing for it but to wait, she decided. She couldn't abandon Miss Olivia. She noticed a little café around the corner; she'd go there and wait and have a cup of tea. It might steady her nerves, she hoped.

She had two cups of tea but at last she decided that she would have to go back to see if he was in. It was getting late; she couldn't hang around much longer for she was due back at the Mayhews' before suppertime.

As she turned into the road she was very relieved to see him walking towards her from the opposite direction.

'Miss Grey! Bessie! What brings you here?' Frank greeted her, noticing with some concern that she looked upset. He'd spent a very pleasant afternoon with David Benson, an old school friend whom he kept in regular touch with. 'What's wrong?'

'It's Miss Olivia, Mr Hadley. Oh, I don't know how to tell you, but she . . . she's been arrested!'

'My God! What for, Bessie?' Frank cried, horrified.

In a rush, her words tumbling over each other, Bessie relayed the events of the afternoon as Frank's expression grew more and more serious.

'Where did they take them, Bessie?' he asked when she finally paused for breath.

'I don't know, Mr Hadley, I swear. I didn't stop runnin' until I got to Rice Lane.'

'Isn't there a police station there?'

Bessie nodded. 'But it's only a small one.'

Frank frowned. If they'd arrested a significant number of the suffragettes they'd have taken them to the main station, Hatton Garden in Dale Street. 'Bessie, thank you for coming to tell me and I'm sorry I was out. You get off home now, I'll go into town and see what – if anything – I can find out,' he urged.

She nodded. 'Should I tell Mrs Mayhew? Won't her pa an' stepmother be worried when she doesn't come home?'

Frank was thinking quickly. 'Say nothing to Mrs Mayhew for now, Bessie. We were supposed to be going to a concert this evening, so Mr Goodwin won't worry – yet.'

Bessie felt very relieved that she could now leave it to him to try to help Miss Olivia.

'I'll walk to the tram stop with you; then I'll go to Dale Street to enquire if she's there,' he informed her.

'Oh, nothing like this was supposed to happen, I swear it! It was just a demonstration!'

'The best-made plans, Bessie. Well, let's hope it's not too late to do something about it,' Frank said grimly. Oh, poor Livvie, she must be distraught, he thought as they walked back down the road.

The Main Bridewell was deserted except for the desk sergeant and a woman sitting on a bench, her shawl pulled tightly around her, looking very ill at ease. It was early evening, obviously a fairly quiet time. No doubt later when the pubs closed it would be busier, Frank thought. It was the first time he'd ever been inside this grim building and he shuddered as he approached the desk.

'Can I help you, sir?'

He nodded. 'I hope so, Sergeant. There was a disturbance this afternoon, I believe, outside the governor's house in Walton.'

The man's polite expression changed. 'It was more than a "disturbance". Those damned women were demonstrating again but this time they took to smashing windows.'

'I know. Were the ladies concerned brought here?'

The man nodded curtly. 'All duly charged and now in the cells downstairs. They'll go before the magistrate in the morning.'

'Is there a Miss Olivia Goodwin amongst them?'

The sergeant scanned the ledger in front of him. 'There is, sir.'

Frank felt some small sense of relief that at least he'd found her; he wouldn't have to visit every police station in the city. 'I'm her fiancé, Sergeant, Frank Hadley, and I'm also the manager of her father's factory. Goodwin's Animal Feeds.'

'Then I pity you both! It's nothing short of a disgrace the way these women carry on and it's a pity that neither you nor her father are able to keep her under control. I can tell you no daughter of mine would be allowed to behave like that.'

Frank could see he'd get no help here. 'What is she charged with, please?' he demanded curtly.

'Breach of the peace, sir.'

'I see,' Frank replied, thankful she'd not been accused of the more serious charge of criminal damage. 'I . . . I don't suppose there is any chance that I could see her?' He didn't hold out much hope.

'Sorry. Not a chance in hell, sir!'

'And none of her being released on bail?'

'No, she's been remanded in custody,' was the blunt reply.

Frank nodded and turned away. There was no point staying any longer. He knew what he had to do now and he wasn't looking forward to it at all. He would have to go and tell Thomas Goodwin that his daughter had been arrested and would be tried in the morning. But at least it would stop her father from worrying when she didn't come home, he thought ruefully. Oh, Mr Goodwin would be furious and Frank understood why, but maybe . . . maybe Thomas just might be able to use his influence to find some way out of all this for Livvie. Surely she needn't have to go to prison? It was a minor offence and her first; could she not pay a fine and be bound over to keep the peace? He wished she'd told him that she had planned to attend this demonstration; he would have done his utmost to persuade her against it, although he knew she wouldn't have deliberately courted trouble. But the damage had been done now. No doubt she'd just unwittingly become embroiled in it and had, in his opinion and judging by what Bessie had told him, been wrongfully arrested as he suspected many of the others had been too. All that would do nothing to assuage her father's fury though, but when he thought of her incarcerated in a cramped, dark and no doubt unsavoury cell, distraught, afraid and expecting the worst tomorrow in the form of a prison sentence, he resolved to do all in his power to get Thomas Goodwin not to abandon her to that terrible fate. She didn't deserve it.

Chapter Twenty-Three

It was Emily who opened the door to him. She looked both concerned and afraid. 'Bessie told me on our way to work what happened.'

Frank smiled at her. 'Don't worry, Emily; you won't be dragged into this. Will you tell Mr Goodwin I'd like to see him, please? And that it's very important.'

When Thomas emerged and Emily had hastily scurried back to the kitchen Frank took a deep breath, having rehearsed what he intended to say. However, Thomas forestalled him.

'Has something happened at the factory?' he demanded.

Frank shook his head. 'No, sir.'

'Then what is so *important* that it brings you here on a Sunday evening? Is Livvie not with you? My wife seemed to think she was.'

'No, she's not, Mr Goodwin. If I might suggest that we talk somewhere . . . else.' He looked pointedly at the parlour door. 'I wouldn't want Mrs Goodwin to be disturbed.'

Thomas nodded and ushered him into the dining room.

'Now what's all this about, Frank?'

'We were supposed to be going to the Philharmonic Hall but . . .'

Thomas frowned. 'But what?'

'Livvie didn't turn up. She—'

'Then where is she?' Thomas demanded.

'I'm afraid she's at Hatton Garden, sir. She's been arrested and charged with breach of the peace.'

'WHAT!'

Frank thought the man was going to have an apoplectic fit. His face went puce, his eyes bulged and a vein in his neck throbbed visibly. 'Calm down, sir, I beg you! She's been wrongfully arrested, I'm certain of it. There was a demonstration outside the governor's house at Walton Jail this afternoon; there was some trouble and windows were smashed but she didn't have any part in that, believe me!'

Thomas sat down heavily, seething with fury. Damn her! Damn her to hell and back! She'd promised she'd take no part in such demonstrations and now not only had she broken that promise but she'd been *arrested*! She'd defied him openly and done the very thing he'd warned her he would not stand for. Oh, she'd tested his patience to the limit recently in supporting and joining those damned women and then becoming engaged to Frank Hadley, but this was just beyond belief. His patience had run out. How could she deliberately bring such shame and humiliation on them all? The utter disgrace! How was he now to face his family, his friends, his associates – even his workers – who would all soon learn that his daughter . . . his *daughter* had been locked up like a common criminal! Despite his outrage he realised that he would have to do something to limit the disgrace she'd brought on them all. Afterwards he would decide what he was finally going to do about *her*! 'This . . . this is the . . . *end*!' he spluttered, almost speechless with rage.

'Sir, can we not think of something we can do to help matters?' Frank urged. 'It's a minor offence and it's her first; surely there must be some way of avoiding a prison sentence and maybe even being force-fed? As I said, I'm certain she's innocent. I know she shouldn't have been there but I'm sure she just got caught up in a situation that got out of hand. Livvie just wouldn't do something like that, you *know* she wouldn't.'

Thomas glared up at him. 'I don't *know* anything about her any more, Frank! She's changed beyond all belief in this past year! And why didn't you do something to stop her going there this afternoon?'

'I didn't know she intended to, I swear! She didn't tell me and I'd arranged to meet an old school friend. As soon as I heard I went straight to Hatton Garden and spoke to the desk sergeant but they wouldn't let me see her. She . . . They'll all go before the magistrate in the morning.'

Thomas uttered an expletive and then got to his feet, trying to suppress the fury that consumed him, obliterating thoughts of his daughter's plight. 'Then there's nothing we can do tonight and a night in a cell might bring her to her senses – though I doubt it! I'll have to phone Edgar Illsworth, my solicitor, and ask what the hell we can do about this damnable mess! Come with me in case he wants to speak to you too,' he ordered.

Frank nodded as he followed Thomas into the hall; at least

Thomas was trying to do something positive even though he was clearly incandescent with rage.

After apologising for the lateness of the hour and the intrusion, in clipped, angry tones Thomas informed his solicitor what had occurred and then passed the phone to Frank.

Frank answered the questions put to him as concisely as he could and then handed the instrument back to his employer. At the end of the brief conversation Thomas hung up and turned to Frank. 'Both myself and Mr Illsworth will attend the hearing in the morning. You'll have to oversee things at the factory until I can get in.'

Frank nodded, relieved that at least Livvie would have some moral support.

'Edgar assures me that he is confident she will get off with a fine as there don't appear to have been any independent witnesses they can call on to substantiate a charge of breach of the peace.'

'Will he be representing her legally?' Frank asked.

The older man nodded. 'It's her right. From what you say, she's not been charged with criminal damage or aiding and abetting or resisting arrest and Edgar says that as far as he's aware it is not yet against the law in this country for someone to peaceably listen to speeches. If it was, half the population would be in jail along with most of our politicians.'

'Thank God for that,' Frank said fervently.

Thomas passed a hand over his eyes, silently cursing Livvie but clinging to Edgar Illsworth's advice for reassurance. 'What am I going to tell Mary? And Amy?'

'I'm so sorry, sir, but I'm sure Livvie never intended for them to be upset or for *anyone* to be distressed.'

Thomas glared at him. 'Then she should have thought more carefully about the consequences of her actions! She's pig-headed, wilful, disobedient, deceitful and selfish – and you want to marry her! Well, you're welcome to her for I wash my hands of her entirely. I just hope you can keep her under control, Frank! Now, I'll bid you goodnight. Mary will wonder what on earth is going on and I'm very loath to have to tell her.'

Frank didn't reply. What was there to say? He'd done his best to help Livvie and her plight did now at least look more hopeful but there was nothing he could do or say to change her father's opinions or stem his anger. As he walked down the path he wondered how Livvie was coping, knowing he most likely wouldn't have any news of her until this time tomorrow.

Livvie had spent a terrible night. It had been impossible to sleep as they were so cramped that even space to sit on the narrow bed was at a premium but she'd been too worried and anxious anyway. Nora Frodsham had tried her best to keep their spirits up but the cell was too cramped and eventually became very stuffy and they were all depressed thinking of the fate that awaited them the following day. They'd been brought a meal of sorts, in the form of a thin, greasy and unappetising stew and a slice of dry bread in a chipped enamel bowl. Even had she wanted to eat she couldn't and her stomach had revolted at the mere smell of the stew. Without her fob watch, which was still pinned to her jacket, she wouldn't have known what time it was and when the gas jet had been turned off, leaving them in complete darkness, even that small comfort was denied her.

When the door was flung open and an officer instructed them to 'stir yourselves' and to follow him, she realised, with both relief and apprehension, it was morning. Trying as best she could to tidy her hair and smooth her creased skirts, Livvie duly followed him into the passageway where they were joined by the other women who had been incarcerated in the cells next door.

'We all look terrible!' she said to Mrs Frodsham.

'Of course we do but try to hold your head up, Miss Goodwin. Show them they haven't cowed us by treating us like common felons,' she said firmly.

Livvie nodded but her heart was beating wildly as they were led back upstairs.

'What happens now?' she asked the older woman as they were ushered into a small room adjacent to the courtroom. During the hours of their imprisonment she'd learned that Nora Frodsham had been arrested on two other occasions.

'They'll call us one by one. The charge will be read and we'll be asked how we plead.'

'I see,' she replied. Somehow she'd have to try to appear calm and dignified and not break down no matter what sentence was passed on her but the thought that she might have to spend two whole weeks in a cell like that filled her with horror.

After fifteen minutes had elapsed her name was called but to her surprise when she stepped outside it was to find her father's solicitor Mr Illsworth waiting for her.

'Miss Goodwin, I'm here to represent you. Your father is in the main body of the court. He . . . We were informed by Mr Hadley last night of what had occurred,' he told her.

'What do I have to say or do?' she asked nervously, although she was very relieved to see him. Bessie must have told Frank, she realised, and he must have braved her father's wrath to give him the news.

'Just go over with me the sequence of events yesterday afternoon,' he instructed gravely.

Livvie told him exactly what had happened. He asked a few questions, made some notes and nodded.

'When asked how you plead, Miss Goodwin, you will reply, "Not guilty, sir." After that you will say nothing further unless specifically asked to. I will do the necessary talking and with any luck you will get off with a fine, which your father has agreed to pay. You will then have to swear to keep the peace in future and you'll be released.'

Livvie nodded her understanding. She felt infinitely calmer now, although it was still going to be an ordeal.

It went exactly as Edgar Illsworth had predicted although she quailed as she caught sight of her father's set features, knowing that she would still have to face him when this was over.

She was given a severe dressing-down by the thin-faced, dour magistrate at the end of which she agreed to be bound over. It was with a huge sense of relief that, escorted by Mr Illsworth, she made her way to the heavy courtroom door where her father was waiting.

When they reached the doors leading to the street Thomas shook the solicitor's hand. 'I'm in your debt, Edgar. We all are.'

The man smiled thinly.

'Thank you, Mr Illsworth,' Livvie added, holding out her

hand. So far her father had not addressed a word to her but she knew the storm would break once they were outside the building.

She shivered in the cold air of the autumn morning. At least it smelled fresh and clean, she thought thankfully. All she wanted to do now was to go home, have a bath, something to eat and then maybe sleep. She yearned to put the last twenty-four hours firmly behind her.

Thomas pointed to where the car was parked, indicating she follow him.

She took a deep breath, knowing she must try to apologise. 'Pa, I—' she started.

'I don't want to hear a single word from you, Olivia. Get in the car!' he snapped, cutting her off. 'I'll deal with you when we get home but you've gone too far this time. You've made a public spectacle of us already and I don't intend for it to continue on the street.'

She bit her lip as she slid into the seat beside him, feeling her heart sink. There was going to be serious trouble when she got home and there was no avoiding it.

Chapter Twenty-Four

———◆———

Mary greeted her in the hall. She looked anxious and as if she hadn't slept all night. 'Oh, Olivia, thank God they let you come home! Are you all right?' Her stepdaughter looked exhausted, grubby and dishevelled and she just couldn't begin to imagine what the girl had been through since she'd left home yesterday afternoon. She'd been terribly worried about her.

Livvie managed a smile. 'I . . . I think so.'

Before either of them had time to say another word Thomas intervened. 'Get upstairs and for God's sake make yourself look presentable! I'll speak to you in the parlour when you look less like a vagrant,' he snapped at his daughter, before turning to his wife. 'Mary, I'd like a word with you and with Amy, if you please.'

Livvie fled upstairs, wishing now she'd never broken her promise and gone to that demonstration. There was no time for the bath she longed for, but hastily she washed, changed her clothes and redid her hair. Then, mustering all the courage she could, she went down to face her father's wrath.

She entered the parlour to find him standing staring into the flames of the fire that burned in the hearth. She clasped her hands tightly together, trying to appear calm but contrite. 'Pa, I really am sorry. I never intended—' she began.

Thomas, glaring at her, cut her short. 'You are *not* sorry, Olivia! You are only sorry you got caught! It's not the same thing. And if you hadn't been caught you would have continued to attend these . . . these . . . displays of anarchy and vandalism. You defied me, deliberately defied me! I warned you I would not stand for such behaviour and by God I won't! I will not allow you to continue to bring humiliation and condemnation down on me – or on this family!'

'Pa, please . . . I truly *am* sorry! I'll never do it again, I promise!' Livvie begged; she'd never seen him so furious.

He slammed his fist hard against the mantelshelf, causing the china ornaments to move precariously towards its edge. 'You expect me to believe you? You promised once before, if you remember. I no longer have faith in *anything* you say. You have disgraced me, you have disgraced yourself and you have disgraced your mother's memory! Do you think she'd approve of the way you've behaved? Do you think she'd be proud of the way you've turned out? She didn't bring you up to be such a . . . hoyden!' he shouted at her. He'd been determined not raise his voice but his outrage and bitterness got the better of him.

At the mention of her mother Livvie began to cry quietly. No, Edith would not have been proud that she'd broken a promise and ended up in a cell.

'My patience has been sorely tested by your behaviour

of late and now it has finally given out. I'll stand for no more lies and disobedience from you. You are no daughter of mine, Olivia, and you will go upstairs and pack your things. I want you out of this house before I return from the factory this evening. I don't care where you go but you are NOT staying here. This is your home no longer, do you understand?'

She staggered back in horror, unable to believe his words. 'Pa! Pa! Don't say that! Please, don't say that! You . . . you can't do this. Where will I go? What . . . what will I do?' she begged, beginning to sob.

'I don't care, Olivia! The matter is at an end! It is the last time you will ever bring shame and distress into this house. I have instructed both Mary and your sister not to speak to you. You will go and pack your things – now!'

Livvie fled from the room, half blinded by tears and shaken to the core. Oh, she'd known he would be angry but she'd never expected *this*! She couldn't take it in. He was turning her out and he didn't care what happened to her. As she reached the landing she paused and clutched the banister rail tightly, feeling dizzy and sick. She couldn't go to Mary or Amy for help; he'd forbidden them to even speak to her! Her thoughts were whirring around in her head and she felt for a few seconds that she was on the brink of collapsing.

When she reached her bedroom she sank down on the bed shaking and sobbing. She glanced around; this would no longer be her room, or her home. Where could she go? What was she supposed to pack? she thought frantically. Oh, she'd been such a fool! Yes, she'd defied him and yes, she'd brought disgrace on him but surely . . . surely she didn't deserve to be turned out like this? Did he really not care about her? Were his pride and reputation more important to him? She got to her feet, desperately trying to gather her thoughts but it was so hard, especially after the ordeal of the last twenty-four hours: she felt punch-drunk. Her hands were shaking and she couldn't concentrate as she haphazardly pulled items from the wardrobe and drawers and stuffed them into a small case that was stored on top of the wardrobe.

She was still sobbing quietly as she stood in the hall, one hand on the door latch. This house had never been the happy home that the house in Minerva Street had been, she thought bitterly. Her mam hadn't lived long enough to enjoy their new affluence, she'd lost a baby brother and a stepbrother, but now that she was being forced to leave it for ever it was a terrible wrench.

Closing the door behind her, she dashed away her tears with the back of her hand and walked slowly down the path, wondering if her sister and stepmother were watching from one of the windows as no doubt her father was. Her life here was over, she thought leadenly as she turned towards the Mayhews' house. Maud was the only person she could turn to for help.

Mary stood slightly back from the drawing-room window, her arm around Amy's shoulders. The last hours had been some of the worst in her life, she thought, deeply distressed at what she was witnessing. She understood Thomas's anger but she'd never realised that he could be so cold-hearted and implacable. She'd begged him to reconsider but he'd been adamant and had in fact warned her not to interfere in matters that did not concern her. Olivia and Amy were his children, he'd harshly reminded her, and that had hurt for she'd become fond of both girls. Now she was desperately worried. What would become of her eldest stepdaughter?

Amy couldn't believe what was happening. Her secure and happy little world had been shattered. Whatever had possessed Livvie to behave the way she had? Amy would never have had the courage to defy her pa and make him so furious. It was utterly inconceivable that Livvie had been arrested, kept in a cell and taken before the court; nor could she believe that her pa had thrown Livvie out and had forbidden them even to speak to each other. He had upset both Mary and herself terribly and she too was wondering what would happen to her sister now. 'Oh, Mary, I wish . . . I wish things were the way they used to be. I wish Livvie had never become a suffragette,' she said with a sob in her voice.

Mary nodded sadly. 'So do I, Amy,' she replied as she watched Livvie disappear from sight.

Bessie took in her tear-stained face, the case, the utter shock and despair in her eyes and pulled her inside. 'Oh, Miss Olivia! What's happened?'

'I . . . I got off with a fine, but Pa's furious. He's thrown me out, Bessie. Is . . . is Aunt Maud . . .' Livvie could barely get the words out.

Horrified, Bessie put her arm around her and ushered her towards the parlour. 'She's in here.'

Maud too was clearly shocked to see Livvie in such a state and after Bessie informed her briefly of what had happened she sent the girl to make a pot of strong tea while between sobs

Livvie told her of yesterday's events and of Thomas's reaction. Maud was horrified and gravely concerned by both Livvie's ordeal and her father's treatment of her but she could understand to an extent his anger. Livvie had been a fool to provoke him, she thought, and over the months she seemed to have been oblivious to the fact that she was severely trying his patience. She did not approve of the girl's behaviour either. Oh, Livvie might believe very strongly in women's rights but that was no excuse for her to openly defy and deceive her father, not after she had promised. And to get *arrested*! It beggared belief. It was very unfortunate that she'd been caught up in trouble not of her making but it would not have happened had she stayed away.

'Oh, Livvie, why ever did you go? Why did you blatantly disobey him?' she said sadly. 'All you had to do was wait until you come of age, marry Frank and then if you still wished to attend these things . . .'

'Aunt Maud, I didn't think there would be trouble. What am I to do now? All I can think of is that I'll have to go to Frank for help but I don't want to get him more involved than he already is. What if Pa dismisses him because of me? Now particularly because of me?'

Maud shook her head firmly. 'Angry as he is with you, he'll not do that. He relies on him far too much and whatever else he is, your father is not a fool. But I don't know what Frank can do to help, Livvie?' Maud desperately wanted to help, to take Livvie in, but she simply could not risk causing dissent in her own household and the possibility of going against her husband's will for Charles Mayhew agreed with Livvie's father on the matter of the suffragettes and would be equally appalled by her arrest. Nor could she risk a subsequent serious rift between the two families. If that were to happen any hopes of a marriage between Teddy and Amy would be out of the question.

'Could I not stay in his house?' Livvie pleaded. It was the only thing she could think of.

'You can't possibly stay with Frank, Livvie! He would have to move out, find lodgings. You'd completely destroy your reputation and his by being seen to be living together without the sanctity of marriage. You would both be ostracised by . . . everyone and your father would indeed dismiss him then. No, Livvie, that is out of the question. Unless of course you were to get married,' she added hastily.

Livvie shook her head. 'Pa won't give his permission; you know he won't. And he'll go on refusing just to . . . spite me. Oh, Aunt Maud, I know I can't stay here. What am I going to do? I . . . I'll be on the streets and I know he'll stop my allowance!' She broke down again, sobbing in desperation.

Bessie, who had brought in the tea tray, looked distressed at having heard this last exchange. Maud had been too preoccupied to notice her. She was scandalised by Olivia's plight but angry too that Thomas Goodwin was treating his daughter so callously. Like Livvie she realised he was ruthless enough to stop her allowance and leave the girl penniless.

'Ma'am, I . . . I couldn't help but hear an' maybe I can help, like.'

Maud looked at her in some confusion. 'You, Bessie?'

Bessie nodded for she'd instantly thought of a solution to Olivia's predicament. 'She can come an' live with us, ma'am. If he really has thrown her out and she's nowhere else to go, I know me mam wouldn't see her penniless an' on the streets. We've not much room an' it's not what she's used to, but . . . but, well, it's better than nothin'.'

Maud was taken aback. 'But what will your parents say? They'll have to know why she's been turned out.'

Bessie looked grim. 'An' I'll tell them but I *know* they won't turn her away. I won't let them. After all, didn't Mr Hadley get me da his job back? As you said, ma'am, she can't live with Mr Hadley until they're wed an' her pa won't give his permission before she's of age, but one good turn deserves another an' I'm sure Mr Hadley will be grateful she's a roof over her head.'

Some of Livvie's despair began to ebb away and Maud too was beginning to feel a palpable sense of relief for things had been looking desperate. 'Are you sure, Bessie?' she questioned. It wasn't ideal but Thomas had left Livvie with no alternative.

'If I can have an hour off to go an' see me mam about it, Miss Olivia can come home with me this evening,' Bessie urged, pleased to see Olivia had calmed down a little.

Maud nodded decisively. 'Yes, take as much time as you need, Bessie. Livvie, you must stay here until this evening. You are very distressed; you must be hungry and utterly exhausted by the whole ordeal. I'll make sure you have every comfort and, Bessie, do you think you could get word to Mr Hadley? I'm sure he will want to see Olivia this evening. Do you think your parents would object to him calling? It won't inconvenience them at all?'

'I shouldn't think they'll mind. After all it's only natural he'll want to see her an' make sure she's all right after all that's happened. If you don't mind I'll get off now, Mrs Mayhew.'

Livvie wiped her eyes and slowly got to her feet. She grasped Bessie's hand tightly, relief flooding through her. 'Bessie, thank you. I didn't know what to do so I can't tell you how grateful I am. It . . . it's so generous of you. And I really do want to see Frank this evening. Thank your mam too for me, will you, please?'

Bessie smiled. 'I'll do that, miss,' she promised. Bessie had realised that, distraught as she was, Miss Olivia had said nothing about them being at the demonstration together; she'd been careful not to put Bessie's job in jeopardy. Well, if Miss Olivia's own family and the Mayhews wouldn't or couldn't help, *she* certainly wouldn't let her down, she thought grimly, just as Miss Olivia had not let *her* down. She'd ask her mam to go down to Goodwin's factory and have a quick word with her da and he could pass a message on to Mr Hadley. She didn't know how they were all going to fit into the one bedroom she already shared with her two sisters, and Miss Olivia wasn't used to being so overcrowded, but they'd manage and it would only be until Miss Olivia came of age. After that she'd marry Mr Hadley and then her pa would have no say in her future at all, the miserable, hard-hearted, bad-tempered, stuck-up old git that he was! she thought savagely. Oh, her family didn't have a fine house in a good area or as much money as the Goodwins but, as hard up as they were, she knew her da would never throw her out on the street just because she'd made a show of him. She was certain that if Miss Olivia's mam were alive she'd not have allowed it either. That Mary Goodwin was afraid of her own shadow, she concluded scornfully, but then in Bessie's opinion she was married to a monster!

Chapter Twenty-Five

Livvie had slept most of the day. Maud had insisted she eat the meal she herself had prepared, for Livvie had had nothing to eat since yesterday. Then she'd given her a very small dose of laudanum and settled her in Selina's bedroom, firmly drawing the curtains on the raw autumn day.

She explained to her worried daughter what had occurred and asked that Livvie now be allowed to sleep. 'She's been through a terrible ordeal, Selina, as a consequence of that demonstration, and now she has to face a life that will be very different to the one she's been used to. She'll be going home with Bessie later this evening but Livvie's going to have to make sacrifices, so I trust you will have some consideration for her even if it will inconvenience you somewhat.'

Selina had nodded her agreement. 'I don't mind that, it really is awful for Livvie, but what about . . . what about my wedding? Can she still be a bridesmaid?' she'd asked.

Maud had tutted exasperatedly. 'Oh, for heaven's sake, Selina, at this precise moment I can't even think about that.

We'll have to see how things progress,' had been her rather sharp reply.

When Livvie woke, it was dark and she reached for the bedside lamp and then lay looking at the pattern the light cast on the ceiling. She did feel better, less hurt, afraid and frantic, and the aching tiredness in her bones had gone. But as she lay there she reflected a little bitterly on the fact that neither her sister nor Mary had made an attempt to come to see her. Her pa might have forbidden them to speak to her but they could at least have tried to see her before she left this neighbourhood, probably for ever. She was sure Maud would have woken her if they'd come. She wondered if her father would tell Frank that he'd thrown her out and what Frank would say and do – at least she'd find that out later this evening. Oh, she was longing to see him, longing to find comfort and hope for the future in his arms, but then she realised that they wouldn't have the privacy for such gestures. There were six people living in that small house in Denison Street, soon to become seven.

She sat up, looked at the clock and realised she'd have to get dressed and be ready to go home with Bessie. She really was so grateful to the girl and her family and she knew Frank would be too.

In the kitchen Maud hugged Livvie as she prepared to leave with Bessie. How she wished things could have been different, Maud thought sadly. This would have broken poor Edith's heart but had her friend lived she was sure the situation would never have arisen. 'Make sure you keep in touch, Livvie.'

'I will, I promise, Aunt Maud. I'll let you know how I am getting on and thank you for . . . for letting me stay here and for looking after me,' Livvie replied, tears pricking her eyes. She'd seen nothing of Charles Mayhew, Teddy or Jonty although she was aware they were in the house.

Selina hugged her. 'I hope everything will turn out right for you, Livvie. I really mean that and I still want you to be my bridesmaid, no matter what anyone says.'

Livvie smiled at her. 'Thank you. I'd like that, Selina.'

Bessie gave an audible sniff and Maud became brisk. 'Right, we'd better not keep you, Bessie. You're sure your parents are quite happy about all this?'

'They are, ma'am, an' Mr Hadley will be callin' at about nine, so we'd best be off now.' She was impatient to get away; tearful farewells were the last thing Miss Olivia needed.

They walked to the tram stop in silence, both lost in their own thoughts, but Bessie had insisted she carry Livvie's case part of the way.

'It will be a bit of a crush, Miss Olivia, but Mam says not to worry, we'll manage,' she assured Livvie as they boarded the tram.

'I won't mind, Bessie, I'm just grateful to her. I used to share with Amy before we moved,' Livvie replied, smiling sadly as she thought of those happier days.

'Look on the bright side, miss. You'll definitely have more freedom now,' Bessie remarked cheerfully. 'Me mam and da won't be demandin' to know where you're goin' an' who with all the time. After all, you're not a child; you're a grown woman now.'

Livvie nodded as she considered this. She'd also been thinking about how she would manage financially. 'I'm going to have to get a job, Bessie. I've got a bit of money left from this month's allowance and I want your mam to have that, it's only fair. I can't ask her to keep me for nothing. But I'm certain Pa won't go on giving me an allowance so I'll have to earn my own living.'

'What kind of a job, miss?'

Livvie shrugged. 'I don't know. I'm not trained for anything, except housework. I wish now Pa had sent me to train as a nurse or a typist or a seamstress – something useful.'

'Oh, miss! You can't go into service!' Bessie cried, appalled at the thought of Olivia on her hands and knees scrubbing floors.

'I will if I have to, Bessie. But maybe I could get a job in a shop or an office. My maths and English are good, even if I've no actual experience.'

'Why don't you see what Mr Hadley can suggest, miss?'

'I will and, Bessie, will you please stop calling me "miss" or "Miss Olivia". You're my friend; you've shown me more kindness than anyone and I'll be working now, like you, so please call me "Livvie".'

Bessie frowned; it didn't seem right but then, well, she supposed they *were* friends and Olivia would now be living with them. 'It will seem a bit odd at first . . . Livvie.'

Livvie smiled at her. 'There you see, it's not hard.'

Bessie grinned back. 'No, it's not.'

Denison Street reminded Livvie of Minerva Street although it was not as steep as the streets on Everton Brow, she thought as they walked towards Bessie's home. She felt a little apprehensive for she'd never met her friend's family and everything would be unfamiliar and perhaps a little awkward at first.

'We're home, Mam!' Bessie shouted down the narrow and dimly lit lobby as she ushered Livvie into the house.

The kitchen door opened and Hetty Grey came towards them, smiling, her hand outstretched. 'You're very welcome, miss. Come on into the kitchen an' meet the rest of my lot,' she urged.

Livvie smiled at her, thinking she was probably the same age her mam would have been now. The first thing that struck her was how small and cramped the room was. The furnishings were well worn and shabby although everything was spotless. Four avidly curious pairs of eyes were fixed on her and she smiled again, this time hesitantly.

'This is Mr Grey – Billy – Maggie, Annie an' our Stanley,' Hetty reeled off.

Livvie shook hands with them all, even young Stanley, who was a thin lad with a shock of untidy hair, an infectious grin and short trousers and woollen socks that sagged around his ankles.

'Annie, luv, you take Miss Olivia's case up to the bedroom,' Hetty instructed briskly as she indicated that Livvie take off her coat and hat and sit down. 'She can unpack it later. 'Ave you 'ad yer tea, miss?' she asked, busying herself with the kettle and a large brown earthenware teapot.

'It's "supper", Mam. And yes, she had something before we left,' Bessie replied.

Hetty frowned at her eldest daughter. 'Well, I'm sure she'd love a cup of tea just the same.'

'I would, Mrs Grey, and I'm very, very grateful you've taken me in, I really don't know what I would have done otherwise. And please call me "Livvie". Everyone does.'

Bessie's mother nodded. 'Well, Livvie. I don't say I agree with our Bessie an' you goin' off to the likes of these demonstrations – look where it can lead – an' I can understand yer da gettin' mad over it, but I wouldn't see you without a roof over yer 'ead. I know it's not what you're used to, but—'

Livvie interrupted her. 'Mrs Grey, we lived in a house like this in Minerva Street on Everton Brow until I was sixteen.' She paused. 'And I wish we'd never left there, believe me. Mam said we should look on it as a new beginning but we were happy in that little place in Minerva Street. The house in Poplar Avenue only ever brought me heartbreak and unhappiness. Oh, it's very much bigger and grander but it never had the same feeling of . . . home. I'm glad to be here, glad to be part of your family and I'll help out as much as I can. I'm not afraid to get my hands dirty. Mam taught me how to do chores properly and to cook and I'll get a job as soon as I can too.' She withdrew an envelope from her bag and handed it to Bessie's mother. 'In the meantime, I insist you take this.' She turned to Bessie's father as Hetty took the envelope, nodding and placing it on the overmantel behind the spill holder. 'Mr Grey, thank you for letting Frank know where I am.'

Billy nodded. ''E was very put out, as yer'd expect, Livvie, but I told 'im not to worry. We'll look after yer.'

Livvie's eyes filled with tears as she took the mug of tea Hetty handed her. They were all going out of their way to make her feel welcome and no matter what deprivations lay ahead of her she wouldn't mind. They were good people and she was very grateful to them.

* * *

For the first time that day she actually laughed with Bessie and Maggie and Annie as they helped her unpack and tried to find enough space for her things in the cramped bedroom.

'I shouldn't have brought all this stuff, Bessie, but I wasn't thinking straight.'

'I don't suppose you were but somethin' a bit more practical might have served better.' Bessie laughed, holding up a cream lace blouse, the collar and cuffs of which were trimmed with tiny bows of pink ribbon.

'Oh, that's dead gorgeous, I ain't never seen anythin' like it,' eighteen-year-old Maggie breathed enviously.

'Well, I'm not going to get much wear out of it now. As Bessie says it's not at all "practical". So, would you like it, Maggie – for Sunday best? You're about the same size as me,' Livvie offered.

'Me?' Maggie cried, astounded. 'Oh, wouldn't I just! Thanks, Livvie!'

Bessie raised her eyes to the ceiling. 'We'll be able to do nothing with her now, Livvie. She'll stick her nose in the air an' go paradin' up an' down the street all Sunday even if she catches her death in the process!'

Livvie smiled at her, thinking that when she got a job she would have to get some clothes more in keeping with her lifestyle now. That's if she could afford to of course for she realised she wouldn't be paid much.

Frank arrived a few minutes early and as Hetty ushered him into the kitchen he threw all caution to the winds and took Livvie in his arms. 'Oh, Livvie, I've been so worried about you!'

She clung to him in relief. 'I'm all right, Frank. At least now I am.'

There was a snigger from young Stanley, which was quickly silenced by a cuff around the ears from his father.

Frank released her but kept hold of her hand. He'd never been so shocked in his life as when Thomas Goodwin had told him that he'd thrown her out. He'd been so stunned that he'd been lost for words although his employer had quickly followed that statement by informing him that he wanted to hear no recriminations or pleas from him on her behalf. In fact he never wished to hear her name spoken again.

'Mr 'Adley, I'm afraid I can't offer yer the use of the parlour for a bit of privacy, like, for we 'as to use it as a bedroom,' Billy explained ruefully.

Frank smiled at him. 'Please don't apologise, we understand.'

'But iffen yer like, Mr 'Adley, you could . . . talk in the lobby,' Hetty suggested.

Livvie smiled at her gratefully and drew Frank into the hallway.

'Oh, it's been terrible, Frank! Being arrested and charged and locked in a cell all night was bad enough and . . . and I expected Pa to be furious but . . .'

Frank held her tightly. 'I would never have expected him to be so cold and cruel, Livvie. You poor, poor girl!'

Her emotions overwhelmed her and she began to cry softly and he kissed the top of her head as he held her. 'We'll get married as soon as we possibly can, Livvie. In the meantime, don't worry about anything. I'll take care of you, you will want for nothing,' he promised.

She calmed down a little as she looked up at him. 'I'll have to get a job, Frank. He'll stop my allowance and I can't live here for free. If it hadn't been for Bessie I . . . I don't know what I'd have done. Aunt Maud couldn't help. She did what she could; it's very difficult for her and I do understand that. But he . . . he even forbade Mary and Amy to say goodbye!'

Frank felt his anger increasing. 'You know, Livvie, I think I'm going to have to look for another job,' he confided seriously. 'I don't think I'm going to be able to go on working for him – not after this. Oh, he was furious all right when I told him you'd been arrested. I thought he was going to have an apoplectic fit but he did seek Mr Illsworth's help. I knew that he'd give you a hard time but . . . but I never expected him to act like this! You'd been through enough without this!'

At his words her face crumpled. 'Frank, I'm so sorry! Oh, I've made such a terrible mess of things. I don't want you to have to get another job, one that won't be as well paid or as prestigious for you.'

Seeing she was becoming upset again, Frank nodded. 'Well, we'll see how things go, Livvie. The main thing is that you've got a home.'

She smiled up at him through her tears. 'I have and I'll get a job, Frank. I'll be all right and it's only for another few months.'

'You don't need to work, Livvie. I've promised to take care of you. I'll pay Mrs Grey for your keep,' he urged, knowing she was going to find it hard enough adjusting to life in this overcrowded, dilapidated house on the edge of the Dock Estate without having to face finding employment for which she had no training or experience.

Livvie shook her head, feeling far stronger and more confident than she'd felt all day. 'No, Frank. I'll work until we get married. He threw me out to fend for myself and I won't give him the satisfaction of thinking I can't cope. I'll show him that despite being used to the comfortable life he provided I'm not going to fall apart or go under now he's turned me out of it! Mam worked until she found she was expecting me and I'll work too. I won't let him think he has won, that he's ruined my future or my happiness.'

Frank kissed her, his pride in her rising. 'Livvie, my precious darling, you're worth ten of him. Now, I think we'd better go back into the kitchen as I haven't thanked Billy and Hetty yet for their kindness.'

She felt much happier now, she thought as she held on to his arm. The coming months wouldn't be easy but she didn't care for from now on she would be free of her father's dominance.

Chapter Twenty-Six

It was amazing how quickly you could adjust to circumstances when you were forced to, Livvie thought as she walked up Denison Street that bitterly cold December evening. Her head was bent against the wind which stung her cheeks and made her eyes water and she was sure there would be snow before long. She pulled her coat tightly to her with one hand as she struggled along the street clutching the parcels she carried in the other. She'd been Christmas shopping in her lunch break from the offices of the Palm Line Steamship Company where she worked as a clerk. It was a rather boring job and she was stuck in a dark pokey office on the third floor of the building in Water Street, but she was grateful for the work.

It hadn't been as easy to find employment as she'd envisaged, she thought as she trudged towards Billy and Hetty's house. Her lack of experience had cost her at least half a dozen positions and she'd begun to despair until finally she'd been offered this one. As she'd protested vehemently to Bessie, if no one would give her a chance, how on earth was she to gain any experience? She'd been very apprehensive when she'd climbed the narrow stairs that led up to the offices of the Palm Steamship Line, but at least she'd obtained an interview, something that hadn't happened before. Tentatively she'd knocked on the frosted glass of the door, which was embossed with the image of a palm tree and the name of the company, and had entered the small and dimly lit room. She'd given her name to the man sitting at a desk and been told to wait.

From behind another door she could hear the sound of a typewriter so obviously there were other offices, she mused.

'You're to go in, miss,' the clerk informed her as he reappeared.

It was another dingy little room dominated by a huge old-fashioned desk behind which a middle-aged man sat peering through heavy spectacles at what appeared to be a letter. She gripped her bag tightly; it was obviously her letter of application.

'Sit down, Miss . . . er . . . Goodwin,' he instructed.

'Thank you, sir,' she replied.

He put down the letter and pressed the fingertips of both hands together as he regarded her. 'So, I understand that you are looking for employment?'

She nodded. 'I am, sir. You see . . . recently my circumstances have changed and I desperately need to find gainful employment.'

She was well spoken and her clothes were of a quality not usually worn by a working-class girl. Obviously well educated too, he surmised. Her handwriting was neat, her spelling and grammar excellent, so quite possibly she was from a middle-class home but had fallen on hard times. It happened. 'I take it you have no experience of office work?'

Livvie bit her lip. 'I . . . I'm afraid not, but I am used to keeping simple accounts and attending to . . . correspondence and I'm very willing to learn. I'm reliable and completely trustworthy and I do really need this job, sir. I regret my lack of experience but I'm sure if you will give me a chance, you won't regret it.'

He regarded her thoughtfully for a few minutes. Even with her lack of experience she was an improvement on the applicants he'd seen so far. Finally he nodded. 'Yes, I think I can take that chance, Miss Goodwin. Now, I'd like you to start . . .'

Livvie hadn't really heard the rest of his words she was so overcome with relief but when she'd finally left the offices, happiness and a sense of satisfaction had filled her. She'd actually got a job, starting the following Monday on a two-week trial period, and she was going to be paid. For the first time in her life she would have money that was her own! It had been an exhilarating thought and a small triumph of independence.

Thankfully, she'd found she could cope quite well and had proved satisfactory. There were other girls employed there who were helpful and friendly, instructing her on how to use the filing system, sort invoices and cargo manifests and in fact two of them travelled to work on the same tram as her each day which seemed to make the journey more convivial. She didn't earn very much, less than the allowance her pa had once given her each month. She paid Hetty for her keep and the remainder went on her fares, lunches and other small expenses. She did try to save a little each week and so she'd managed to accumulate enough to buy inexpensive gifts for the family for Christmas. She felt it was the least she could do to repay their kindness. She and Frank had agreed they wouldn't buy each other anything expensive, just a token to celebrate the season. After all, they would have a wedding to pay for in six months' time. Very few of the clothes she'd brought from Poplar Avenue were suitable for her new, more austere lifestyle and so she'd had to purchase a serviceable dark two-piece costume and some plain blouses for work. She shivered as an icy blast buffeted her, grateful that at least she'd had enough sense to put on her decent winter coat the day she'd left Poplar Avenue for she couldn't have afforded to buy one of the same quality now.

When she reached the house her hands were so cold that she fumbled with the key to the front door, dropped it and finally resorted to hammering loudly on the door knocker.

'I'm sorry, I can barely feel my fingers and I've dropped my key,' she apologised to Hetty who opened the door to her.

'That's a right lazy wind; it goes straight through yer, instead of goin' round yer. Come on into the fire, luv. I'll get our Stanley to come out an' look for yer key,' Hetty urged.

Despite some early misgivings, Hetty felt Livvie had settled in well; she never complained and she did help with the chores for which Hetty was grateful. All three of her girls were now in service and not at home a great deal, so she was often thankful for Livvie's aid.

'What 'ave yer been buyin' now?' she asked as Livvie dumped the parcels down on the dresser, for the table was already set for the evening meal.

'Just some small gifts for Christmas,' Livvie replied, holding her hands out gratefully to the warmth of the fire in the range. A large pan of stew was simmering away and the savoury odour permeated the room; she realised she was hungry for she'd not had time for any lunch.

'Didn't I tell yer not to be spendin' money on us, Livvie! They only pay yer buttons in that place,' Hetty scolded.

'Oh, it's nothing much, but I had to get you all *something*,' she answered and leaned across to the older woman smiling as she lowered her voice. 'Stanley's set his heart on that box of lead soldiers he saw in Hardman's window so I couldn't disappoint him, could I? I'll have to give them to you to hide until Christmas morning.'

Hetty tutted and cast her eyes to the ceiling. 'You'll 'ave that lad spoiled rotten, Livvie!' she retorted but secretly she was pleased. Having no brothers or even stepbrothers, Livvie was fond of the boy – despite his antics – and Hetty suspected she missed her sister although she got on well with her girls. She knew that it hurt Livvie that she didn't hear from Amy very often. Oh, there were letters – or notes rather; Bessie brought them home – but they were all full of what Amy was doing, what Amy thought, what Amy felt. Nothing much about how Livvie was getting on, if she was happy or what plans she had, and the girl seldom mentioned her stepmother or her father either. In Hetty's opinion she was a spoiled little madam who was totally engrossed in herself and some lad called 'Teddy'. She also suspected that although hurt and annoyed with her father, Livvie still loved him and missed her home.

Livvie had divested herself of her coat and hat, tied an apron over her work clothes and begun to slice up the large loaf which would be served with the stew, thinking how happy she was here. Yes, they were rather overcrowded but there was always someone to talk to, laugh with, even bicker with occasionally and there was always merriment and a great deal of chat in the house when they were all in, which was a change from her old home. Billy was a quiet, placid man who did not attempt to dominate his mainly female family but liked nothing better than to sit in front of the fire with his newspaper after supper and at the end of the working week go to the pub for a couple of pints with his neighbours. He was occasionally called upon to chastise his errant son after some scrape or another, although usually it was Hetty who dealt out an instant punishment. Living with Bessie's family and in this neighbourhood reminded Livvie so much of the happy days of her childhood in Minerva Street. Many of Hetty's neighbours were friends too and called often, just as her mam's old neighbours had done, and everyone helped each other if they could. Joys and sorrows and worries were all shared and there was definitely more of a sense of friendship and community here.

Bessie had been right that she would have more freedom; there were no raised eyebrows or curt remarks or an inquisition every time she went out, but she found that her new lifestyle didn't lend itself to much leisure time. Of course she could no longer go to demonstrations, having sworn to keep the peace, and she would not risk the chance of again becoming caught up in trouble for that would indeed end in her being sent to prison, but she did go to the suffrage meetings with Bessie, Maggie and Emily and it was from Bessie and Emily that she learned most of what was happening in Poplar Avenue. The main topics of interest seemed to be the plans for Selina Mayhew's wedding and the development of Amy and Teddy Mayhew's relationship, at which her pa had expressed his delight and satisfaction, something Livvie had fully anticipated. She was of course delighted for her sister but the other, more worrying information was that her stepmother's health hadn't improved. In fact Emily had commented that she seemed to have got thinner and had developed quite a nasty cough, which Mary insisted was due to the cold weather and would no doubt disappear when the days became warmer. Livvie hoped she was right but there was nothing she could do to help so worrying about Mary was a rather futile exercise. At least her stepmother wasn't pregnant again, which in the circumstances was something of a relief.

'It was very good of you to ask Frank for Christmas lunch, Hetty, although it's going to be a bit of a squash getting us all around the table.' She laughed, glancing at the cramped room which the table and the dresser seemed to dominate.

'Oh, we'll manage. There'll only be the five of us to sit down, like. After all, the girls won't be 'ome until mid-afternoon; they've to serve the meal at work. They'll 'ave their dinner later,' Hetty replied laconically.

Livvie nodded. It was one of the drawbacks of being in service. Even for holidays like Christmas you didn't get the full day off; she was now far more appreciative of the assistance she'd had from Emily when she'd lived in Poplar Avenue.

'An' I couldn't leave Mr 'Adley to have 'is dinner on 'is own, now could I? Not on Christmas Day,' Hetty continued. 'What kind of a Christian woman would that make me? Not very Christian at all, in my book!' She paused in stirring the stew. 'Well, luv, just think. Yer'll be 'avin' yer Christmas dinner together in yer own 'ome next year.'

'We will, won't we?' Livvie agreed happily.

Hetty frowned as she replaced the pan lid. 'Will yer send them a Christmas card, Livvie? Yer stepmother an' yer pa, like?'

Livvie shrugged. 'I suppose I should. It is the season of "Goodwill to all men" but I really don't feel as if I want to.' She paused as she considered the matter. 'But Mary will be upset if I don't and I don't think she's very well.'

Hetty nodded although she could understand why the girl didn't want any contact with her father.

Privately Livvie didn't think for one moment she would receive anything from her pa. If she were to receive a card at all it would be from Mary, and she wondered just what kind of Christmas they would all have this year. As far as she was concerned she was looking forward to it but she doubted her family's Christmas would be as joyful, particularly if Mary was ill.

She sent word regularly to Maud, via Bessie, telling her how she was settling in, that she'd found work and was looking forward to next summer when she would be able to marry Frank. She smiled to herself, thinking ruefully that they had very little time alone together. Privacy was out of the question in this house, although when he called – and that was usually at least twice a week – Hetty always endeavoured to find things that needed doing in the scullery. She'd urge Billy to go for a pint and chase Stanley either off to bed or out to one of his mates' houses, but there was little she could do if her girls were home from work. Oh, yes, they were both counting the months now until she turned twenty-one.

The nearer the festive season drew the more frenetic things seemed to become in the small house in Denison Street. Everyone was excited but particularly young Stanley, who was trying Hetty's patience to the limit. When she'd finally got him to bed on Christmas Eve she sank down gratefully in the chair by the range. ''E's got me worn to a frazzle!'

Livvie, who was wrapping her gifts at the kitchen table, laughed. 'You can't blame him; Christmas is a time for children, after all. Amy and I used to fight to stay awake all night, just to try to get a glimpse of Santa, but we never did. We'd be up at the crack of dawn on Christmas morning to see what he'd left us though. When we were young it was just a cheap little toy, an orange and a new penny but we were thrilled just the same. It wasn't until we got older and Pa began to make more money that we got more expensive things.'

Hetty smiled at her. 'That's all my lot ever got too, an' sometimes when Billy didn't 'ave regular work there wasn't even enough for the penny toy.'

Livvie paused, staring into space, remembering the joy and wonder of those days that seemed so long ago now. 'You know, Christmas was never the same after we moved from Minerva Street. Oh, that first Christmas in the new house we had an enormous tree with brand-new decorations, Amy got an engraved silver locket and I got a gold bracelet set with garnets, we had a regular feast of a meal and Maud and her family called bringing us brandy, wine and chocolates.' She paused. 'It was the last Christmas we had with Mam, although thankfully we didn't know that.'

Hetty nodded sagely. 'You still miss 'er, Livvie, don't yer?'

'I do. I suppose I always will.'

'It's not until you have kids of yer own that yer realise just what it is to be a mam.' She paused as there was a thump from upstairs. 'An' sometimes yer wish you'd never bothered! If that lad is out of the bed again, I'll swing for 'im, I swear I will! An' he'll not get that box of soldiers you bought him either!'

Livvie laughed again. Yes, she was looking forward to tomorrow even though things wouldn't be nearly as lavish as they'd been in Christmases past.

They were all up early next morning for Bessie, Maggie and Annie had to go to work. Hetty had to get the goose into the oven and Stanley's excitement couldn't be contained. His eyes dancing, his cheeks flushed and his hair standing up in spikes he exclaimed in wonder over the contents of his stocking.

'Mam! A gun an' soldiers! A proper toy gun! An' the soldiers! I saw them in 'Ardman's, but I didn't think I'd get them! Just wait till I go an' show Charlie an' 'Arry!' he cried, delighted with the small replica gun and the box of painted soldiers.

'Well, you're not goin' annoyin' their mams just yet, lad!' Hetty instructed firmly, although she was just as excited and pleased as her son.

Before they left for work, Bessie, Maggie and Annie

exchanged small gifts with their parents and brother but decided they would wait until later that afternoon before giving each other and Livvie the things they'd bought.

After they'd gone and when Stanley had set off to see his mates and Billy was contentedly smoking his pipe, Livvie helped Hetty to set the table and prepare the meal. The kitchen was warm and smelled of the delicious odours of roasting goose and plum pudding. There wasn't room for even the smallest tree but Livvie had bought red and green crêpe paper and showed Stanley how to make paper chains which they'd hung across the ceiling, and Bessie had brought a big armful of holly from the Mayhews' garden to decorate the lobby and kitchen, although she'd had a bit of a time persuading the conductor to let her on the tram with it.

Bessie had reported the exchange with some indignation. 'Was I mad bringin' that on the tram an' did I intend to attack his passengers with it? he demanded. Right narky he was too. Well, I gave him a flea in his ear, I can tell you! "Where's your sense of the Christmas spirit? An' I'm not walkin' home either!" I told him,' she'd finished determinedly.

Frank arrived at one o'clock bearing more gifts. 'Happy Christmas, everyone! Happy Christmas, Livvie darling!' he greeted her with a kiss.

'Take yer coat an' 'at off, Mr 'Adley and sit by the fire. Dinner's almost ready,' Hetty instructed.

'It looks very festive in here, Billy, I have to say,' Frank said admiringly as he handed the older man a bottle of whiskey and a bottle of sherry. 'Something to celebrate with,' he explained before handing Hetty a box of crackers decorated with red ribbon and sprigs of artificial holly.

Billy was delighted for he could seldom afford spirits and Hetty thought how considerate and well mannered Frank was. The cost of what he'd brought with him was probably more than she'd paid for the goose – he'd even brought those fancy crackers which would no doubt delight young Stanley for he'd never had them before. The whiskey was a good brand and so was the sherry; it wasn't the usual cheap stuff that she said tasted like paint stripper. He and Livvie had certainly made their Christmas even cheerier than usual.

When they were all seated and the meal was served, Livvie smiled happily across at Frank. 'Isn't this just great?'

He smiled back. 'It certainly is, and it's the first time in years that I've haven't spent the day quietly on my own.'

Hetty thought how dreadfully sad that was but she smiled at him. 'Well, we're delighted to have yer, Mr 'Adley, an' from now on yer won't be spendin' it on yer own. Next year you and Livvie will be in yer own 'ome.'

'We will and I think after we've finished this marvellous meal, we'll sit down and set an actual date in June. That will be something to look forward to,' Frank suggested.

'Oh, it will, Frank,' Livvie replied delightedly. This was the first Christmas since her mam had died that she'd felt really happy. She didn't need opulent surroundings, fine china and crystal and expensive decorations and gifts, just Frank and people who cared about her.

Billy raised his glass of whiskey. ''Appy Christmas and good luck to yer both.'

'And to a June wedding,' Hetty added, beaming around at them all.

It sounded so wonderful, Livvie thought as she sipped

her sherry. June, when it would be warm and sunny, there would be new leaves on the trees and flowers in the parks and gardens and she'd happily become Mrs Frank Hadley. Things hadn't turned out too badly at all. What else could she ask for in life?

Chapter Twenty-Seven

———◆———

The warm sunny days of June still seemed so far away, Livvie thought as she set out for Maud's house that wet and windy Saturday afternoon in March. It would be the first time she'd been back to Poplar Avenue and but for the fact that she'd been required for a fitting of her bridesmaid's dress she wouldn't have gone at all. She hadn't been able to refuse for Selina's wedding was next month.

She glanced around as she walked up the tree-lined road, contrasting the quiet avenue with Denison Street; she really didn't miss it now, she told herself. The branches of the trees were still bare and were bending and twisting in the wind and there was no one about as it was a far from pleasant day. She determinedly kept her gaze averted as she passed her old home. It would be the first time she had seen her sister, Selina or Maud in months for none of them had come to visit her in Denison Street and nor had she expected or wanted them to. Hetty would have become flustered and embarrassed at having no parlour available in which to entertain them and what little leisure time she now had was spent with Frank or helping Hetty. But there were times when she had missed them, she thought as she went up Maud's path.

As usual it was Bessie who opened the door to her. She grimaced as Livvie shook her umbrella out before handing it to her. 'It's a shockin' day. You must be soaked, Livvie.'

'I'm not too bad, Bessie, your mam's brolly kept the worst off me, but it's not a bit like spring.'

'They're in the parlour with the dressmaker an' her apprentice an' I have to say the frocks look gorgeous, from what I've managed to see of them,' Bessie confided.

'Well, I just hope the weather gets better, Bessie, or they'll be ruined and we'll probably catch a cold into the bargain,' Livvie replied as Bessie took her coat and hat.

Maud's parlour seemed to be filled with swathes of material, half-finished dresses and all the other accoutrements of the dressmaker's profession, Livvie thought as she entered the room. Obviously all the men in the house had been barred from entering the parlour this afternoon.

'Livvie, come here and let me look at you!' Maud cried. She hugged her and then held her at arms' length. 'You do look well, I have to say! A more independent lifestyle seems to suit you!' She was relieved for she often wondered how the girl was faring. Despite the cheerful notes and messages delivered by Bessie, Livvie's life must have altered so much in these past months, but she appeared to have coped well with those changes.

Livvie smiled at her. 'I *am* well, Aunt Maud. I haven't wasted away.'

'Oh, Livvie, it's lovely to see you!' Amy greeted her and hugged her in turn.

Amy seemed to have become more grown up, more poised, even elegant, Livvie thought, taking in her sister's dress, which was the height of fashion. Livvie knew she was very much in love with Teddy Mayhew so maybe that had something to do with it. 'Amy, you look radiant! So grown up and I'm so happy about you and Teddy.'

'Oh, Livvie, I've got some wonderful news for you!' Amy confided excitedly, turning and smiling at Maud, who nodded encouragingly. 'Teddy has asked Pa if he can marry me!'

Livvie hugged her sister again, pleased by this news and knowing her pa would have given his consent. 'So, you're engaged?'

Amy nodded happily. 'Teddy asked me last night and we're going for the ring next weekend.'

'And of course we're delighted for them both,' Maud added.

'I'm really happy for you, Amy,' Livvie said sincerely. It was what Amy wanted; just as she wanted to marry Frank.

'Oh, from now on there will be so much to think about and do,' Amy enthused.

Maud took the situation in hand. 'There will. Right, well, I don't think we should waste any more of Mrs Sweetman's valuable time. Amy, if you'd like to try on your dress first I'll get Bessie to bring Livvie some tea – she looks decidedly cold. It's a miserable day for the time of year.'

'I just hope the weather improves! It will be just awful if it's like this,' Selina added, anxiously glancing towards the window against which the rain was lashing.

'I'm sure it will, dear. There's no need to get yourself into a state about it, we've got five weeks to go yet,' Maud said firmly. There were enough things for her to worry about without Selina getting into a state over something they had no control over at all, she thought. She was very relieved to see that Livvie did in fact look well and happy and that she seemed pleased at the news of Amy's engagement.

Bessie brought the tea and Livvie gratefully sipped it as she watched the dressmaker pinning and adjusting the pale blue taffeta and lace. The dresses were indeed beautiful and must be costing Charles and Maud quite a bit, she mused. She'd have no occasion to wear such a dress again once Selina's wedding was over, she realised, but then a thought struck her. Maybe she could wear it for her own wedding? She wouldn't have enough money to buy a wedding dress and even if she did it would be rather a waste. She hoped Frank would think she looked beautiful whatever she wore.

When at last both the pale blue dresses and the gorgeous confection of white silk and lace that was Selina's dress had been fitted and carefully packed and the dressmaker and her assistant had departed, Maud again summoned Bessie and asked that afternoon tea be brought.

'And how are you finding working, Livvie? Is it difficult, confusing, tiring?' Maud enquired as she handed her a slice of Victoria sponge on a china tea plate.

'No, not at all. It's rather . . . repetitious but as I had no experience I was fortunate to get the job at all. I actually enjoy earning my own money. It's very satisfying, although there's not a lot of it,' she laughed.

'But don't you find it tedious having to get up and go into town every morning on the tram, particularly if you don't feel like it and the weather is awful?' Amy asked, thinking it wasn't something she'd enjoy very much. 'What time do you have to get up?'

'About six o'clock but I don't really mind as everyone else is up too. We all have to go to work, you see, except Mrs Grey. And of course Stanley has to go to school,' Livvie replied.

Amy wondered how they all managed to get ready in such a small house for she was aware of Bessie's sisters and brother and the fact that those houses had no bathrooms. There wouldn't be much privacy at all and no time to get washed and dressed in a leisurely manner.

'Of course I help Mrs Grey – "Hetty" as she insists I call her – with the housework for all the girls are in service now,' Livvie informed them.

Amy nodded. It definitely didn't sound like the kind of life she would enjoy. Both she and Mary were glad of Emily and no doubt when she was married she would employ a maid too.

'And have you and Frank made any definite plans yet?' Maud asked.

Livvie nodded. 'We decided on Christmas Day that we'll get married on Saturday the eighth of June, in the late afternoon after the factory has closed. Hetty insisted on inviting Frank for Christmas lunch and we discussed it after the meal.'

Maud nodded and smiled. 'So, in three months' time you'll be Mrs Frank Hadley.'

'I will and I'm so looking forward to it. I've been to Frank's house. We went one Sunday afternoon, so I could see what my future home is like, and it's quite a pleasant little house. Of course it's not nearly as big as this one but it's a bit bigger than Hetty and Billy's and Frank does own it.'

'And will there be things you'd like to change?' Maud wondered.

Livvie laughed. 'Only the hall, it's very dark – all brown paint and varnish. I think we'll paint it a lighter colour. The furniture is a bit old-fashioned but we won't be able to afford to change that for a while. Still, it's comfortable and I think I'll be very happy there.'

'I'm sure you will be,' Maud agreed, wondering if Livvie intended to tell her father and Mary of her plans. She doubted it.

'And will we be invited to the wedding?' Amy asked tentatively.

'Of course! I'd like you to stand for me, Amy, you're my only sister.' Livvie smiled apologetically at Selina. 'I'm afraid I'm not having bridesmaids as such. It will only be a very quiet wedding.'

Amy nodded, thinking Livvie was right to keep the wedding a small affair and wondering if her father would in fact object to her standing for her sister. She hoped not but if it caused an almighty fuss then she'd just have to agree not to although she would hate to disappoint and upset Livvie. At least there wouldn't be any ill feeling at her wedding, she thought thankfully, and she knew her pa would be only too happy to pay for an event on the scale of Selina's. In fact there was a party planned for next weekend to celebrate her engagement to Teddy – it was all so very exciting.

After tea was over Livvie had to remember not to get to her feet and help Bessie clear away the dishes as she did at home and Maud sent Amy off to find Teddy. Realising that she would soon have to leave, Livvie began to make her excuses but Maud stopped her.

'I sent Amy off to find Teddy because I wanted to tell you, Livvie, that I'm hosting a small party for their engagement next Saturday. Your father wanted to have a lavish celebration next door but I managed to talk him out of it.'

'Why? Oh, I know we wouldn't have been invited, Aunt Maud, and we wouldn't have attended even so; I don't have any suitable clothes for things like that now.'

'That wasn't the reason, Livvie. Mary is not well, not well at all. She insists she is fine and won't have Dr Sumner to see her but . . . but she's just not up to organising parties and entertaining guests.'

'What's the matter with her?' Livvie asked anxiously for Maud's grave expression didn't bode well. 'Hasn't she got over the miscarriage properly? Is it something to do with that?'

Maud shook her head. 'That hasn't helped, I'm sure, but from what I've seen and heard from Emily over the past months I feared the . . . worst so I went to see Dr Sumner myself, seeing as Mary flatly refuses to do so. Of course he wouldn't discuss Mary's health – it's not ethical – but I assured him I just wanted advice as I was very concerned about her. I informed him of what symptoms I was sure Mary was suffering from and he said that it sounded very much like . . . consumption, but of course he couldn't be certain without seeing her. He emphasised that I wasn't to take it as an official diagnosis and he urged me to do everything I could to persuade her to allow him to visit her but . . .' Maud shrugged helplessly.

Livvie's eyes widened with shock. 'Oh, no! Emily told me

she's lost weight and she's got a bad cough but . . . What is Pa doing about it?' Livvie demanded. There was no cure for tuberculosis, or consumption as it was generally called. It was a disease of the lungs which resulted eventually in death – and it was not an easy death either, so she'd heard.

'I'm not even sure he's aware how badly her health has deteriorated, Livvie. She tries hard to hide it, resting when he's out, and he doesn't seem to spend much time at home these days at all. He's very involved in expanding the size and facilities of the factory to double the orders and output.'

This stunned Livvie, although she knew from Frank that when it was finished Goodwin's would be one of the largest factories on the Dock Estate. 'Oh, Aunt Maud, tell him to *make* Mary see the doctor. There might be *something* that can be done. It might not be consumption and if it is maybe she could go to a sanatorium or somewhere where the air is better. She . . . she's still so young!'

'Don't you think I've tried, Livvie?'

Livvie got to her feet. 'I'll go over and see her, Aunt Maud. Perhaps I can persuade her.'

'Livvie, your father is at home. I doubt he'll let you over the doorstep.'

She sat down again, knowing Maud was right. Oh, poor Mary. He was leaving her to face her illness and no doubt her fears alone. He was too engrossed in his expansion plans. Why did he need a bigger factory producing double the amount of cattle cake? And what was it all for anyway? she thought angrily. He still had no son and heir to leave it to and no doubt he blamed Mary for that fact. He'd not leave Livvie herself a single penny, she was sure of it, nor did she care for she wanted nothing from him. Did he intend to leave it all to Teddy and Amy? And what was wrong with Amy that she couldn't see how ill her stepmother was? she wondered bitterly. Was she too taken up with Teddy and her own plans for the future? Livvie had never wanted a stepmother but she'd accepted Mary and had even become fond of her and now . . . now she would be denied seeing her, denied the chance to try to help. Her father was treating Mary abominably! What was wrong with her family that they were so . . . so blind and selfish?

'I'll just have to write to her, Aunt Maud. It's all I can do, but will you let me know if she . . . she gets worse and I'll try and come to see her one evening before he gets home?'

Maud nodded as she clasped Livvie's hand. The coming months would be hectic for them all, mainly in a pleasant way, but they would also be tinged with worry and even sadness for she doubted poor Mary Goodwin would see another Christmas.

Chapter Twenty-Eight

<hr/>

After confiding in both Hetty and Bessie, Livvie decided not to wait weeks for Maud's summons. After Amy's engagement party was over she would go to see Mary.

'I'll go straight from work a week on Wednesday; apparently Pa doesn't get home until after eight most evenings according to Emily. That will give me about an hour to spend with Mary,' she announced.

Hetty nodded her agreement. 'God 'elp 'er, it's not an easy way ter go. I've seen enough of it in me time, it's rife around 'ere.'

'I'll try to persuade her to see the doctor – maybe he'll be able to do something to help her.'

'Perhaps he could get her into one of those places by the sea; I've heard that sometimes helps. The muck in the air in this city is enough to make anyone ill,' Bessie added.

Livvie nodded. There might still be something that could be done. 'I'll tell Frank I'm going, he'll have to know, and if Pa decides to leave early maybe he can delay him. The last thing

I want is a confrontation with Pa. There would be a huge row and that wouldn't help anyone,' Livvie said firmly.

She was lucky to catch a tram quickly that evening. Sometimes, as everyone finished work at the same time, she had to wait for ages and they were always crowded to capacity, which meant having to stand, and when the weather was warm that didn't make for a very pleasant journey.

It was still light as she walked quickly up Poplar Avenue and the wild weather of the weekend before last seemed to have at last passed. Emily knew of her plans and had said she would be on hand to let her in. Livvie had explained that she didn't want to ring the doorbell, alerting both Mary and her sister to her visit.

'She's resting upstairs, Livvie,' Emily informed her as she entered the house.

She nodded, barely glancing around the hall. She felt no sense of nostalgia, only concern. 'And Amy?' she enquired.

'Gone next door – as usual; all to do with Miss Selina's wedding. You wouldn't believe the fuss and palaver that's going on over there!'

Livvie smiled grimly. 'Oh, I would, Emily. I hear it all from Bessie.'

On reaching the landing she was very surprised when Emily indicated the door of what had been her bedroom but she said nothing and, knocking gently, went inside. She was truly shocked to see the change in her stepmother. Mary had never been robust but she'd lost a lot of weight and her eyes seemed to have sunk inwards, with dark circles beneath them. She was very pale except for two bright spots of colour on each cheek, highlighted by her pallor. She lay propped up on pillows but as she caught sight of Livvie she tried to raise herself. 'Oh, Olivia!'

Livvie instantly went and took her hand and eased her gently back on to the pillows. 'Mary, Aunt Maud told me you're not well so I decided to come to see you.'

'But your . . . your father, Olivia . . .'

'He doesn't know and I'll be gone before he gets home. Amy doesn't know I'm here either and there's no need to tell her, if you don't want to.'

Mary smiled gratefully. 'It's just a heavy cold that's gone to my chest, Olivia. I . . . I can't seem to shake it off at all and I feel so . . . tired too.'

Livvie shook her head. 'Mary, I think it's more than that and so does Aunt Maud. Please, please let Dr Sumner come to see you. I'm sure he will be able to give you some medicine or recommend . . . something,' she urged.

Mary shook her head. 'No. No, I don't want Thomas to worry. He's got so much on his plate just now with the expansion. When he gets home he's exhausted; that's why I moved into this room. My coughing was disturbing his sleep, you see.'

Livvie frowned. 'Do you cough much?'

'It comes and goes in . . . spasms and I often get very . . . warm during the night, so it's best for me to sleep in here.'

At her words Livvie's heart dropped. Hetty had told her that night sweats were a common symptom of the disease. 'When you have one of these "spasms", Mary, is . . . is there any . . . blood?'

Mary closed her eyes, her fears washing over her. Yes, there was blood and she knew what it meant but she hadn't admitted it to anyone. Now she was aware that Olivia possibly knew what was wrong with her. 'Only . . . occasionally and very little. Probably because the coughing can be quite . . . strong,' she finally answered.

'Then you *must* see the doctor, Mary. It will only get worse if you don't. Please, please say you will? I'm so worried about you and I'm sure if he realised Pa would be too,' she begged.

'If it gets any worse, Olivia, I . . . I'll think about it. But please don't say anything to Amy or Maud or anyone who might tell Thomas. I don't want him to worry until the expansion work is complete.'

Livvie knew that was all she was going to achieve and she bit her lip as she nodded her agreement. Mary wasn't going to help herself because of her misplaced loyalty for her pa. Her being so ill, so young, was a tragedy, Livvie thought; she was only thirty-two.

'Tell me about yourself, Olivia. How are you coping?' Mary asked to divert the conversation away from herself.

For the next half an hour Livvie told her all about her life, about what it was like to live in Denison Street, to go to work each day, what she did there and the plans she and Frank had for their June wedding. However, she could see her stepmother was tiring and so at last she said she had better be leaving.

'I'll try and come again, Mary,' she promised.

'I'd like that, but I don't want either you or Thomas to get . . . upset.'

Livvie smiled. 'I'll make sure he never knows. I'll tell Frank when I intend to come and he'll make sure Pa doesn't decide to come home early. Try and rest now, Mary,' she urged and, for the first time in her life, she bent and kissed her stepmother on the cheek. Closing the door quietly behind her she shivered, thinking this house seemed very unlucky for a great many of its occupants, herself included.

Emily emerged from the kitchen to let her out, looking anxious. 'How is she?'

'Not good, Em. I've tried to get her to agree to see the doctor but . . .' Livvie shrugged.

'Mrs Mayhew's tried and all.'

'Is she coughing blood, Em?' Livvie probed, knowing Emily would be aware of this for she attended to the items that were sent to the laundry.

The girl nodded sadly. 'But not very much.'

'Yet,' Livvie stated bluntly, feeling both helpless and angry that Mary seemed bent on both denying and trying to hide her illness and the fact that her father appeared to be oblivious to it.

Before either of them could speak the front door opened and Amy breezed in looking highly delighted about something and sporting a large diamond ring on her left hand. Her expression changed as she caught sight of her sister.

'Livvie! What on earth are you doing here? Pa's not home, is he?'

'No, he's not. I came to see Mary, Amy. She's ill, or hadn't you noticed?'

Amy looked perturbed. 'She's got a bad cough; I didn't think it was anything serious though. Not serious enough for you to come back here. I just hope Pa doesn't catch you. If he finds out I don't want anything to do with it.'

Emily glanced at Livvie and seeing her expression of outrage backed away towards the kitchen.

'Amy, how can you be so . . . blind? It is *serious*! It was Aunt Maud who told me just how serious she thinks it is. You *must* have noticed how thin she's got! She's coughing blood too, but she won't admit it as she doesn't want to worry Pa!'

'I didn't know that, Livvie. And anyway how could I be expected to know that?' Amy demanded rather irritably.

Livvie was upset about her stepmother's condition but at her sister's attitude she became angry. 'Amy, do you care nothing for her? You must have realised she's ill, an ordinary cough doesn't last this long and doesn't cause loss of weight. Didn't you even think to tell Pa that she should see a doctor?'

'I . . . I . . . He wouldn't have taken any notice of me,' Amy replied, feeling guilty for the first time, but annoyed with Livvie for seeming to put the blame on her. 'I didn't know about Mary; she's not said anything much about feeling ill.'

'You've got eyes in your head, Amy. You should have been able to see how weak she is!'

'So it's all my fault now? You're not even supposed to be here, Livvie, and you come back and start blaming me!' Amy cried pettishly.

Livvie lost her temper entirely. 'I don't believe you just said that! I came because I'm very concerned about her and if I'd still been living here I'd certainly have known she's ill and would have called the doctor myself long before this. Aunt Maud is almost certain that Mary's got consumption, Amy! Are you so completely self-obsessed that you think of no one but yourself?'

'I think you should go, Livvie! Now! I'm not going to listen to any more of your . . . your nasty remarks!' Amy cried, stung by her sister's words, which she knew deep down were true.

She had been too wrapped up in her romance to take much interest in her stepmother's health.

'I'll be glad to. Neither you nor Pa care anything for either Mary or me! You're callous, uncaring and selfish to the bone – both of you!' Livvie flung back at her before wrenching open the front door and storming out. She wished she never had to come back here but she couldn't abandon Mary – she'd have to try to find some way to visit. She just didn't understand Amy's attitude and now she really didn't want her sister at her wedding; she'd ask Bessie to stand for her. There was far more love, care and consideration in Hetty's family than there was in her own, she thought bitterly. Had her mother lived things would have been very different, but without her influence her father and sister had gone their own selfish way. She would have to call on Maud now and explain how things stood between Amy and herself.

'Don't ask, Bessie!' Livvie stated as the girl opened the door to her.

Bessie looked concerned. 'I'll tell her you're here, Livvie.'

Maud was surprised to see her. 'Livvie, I didn't know you were coming! Of course you're very welcome,' she greeted her.

'I decided to come to see Mary and' – Livvie shook her head sadly – 'I think you're right. She admitted she's coughing blood, though not much yet, and that she's having what Hetty called "night sweats". I couldn't persuade her to see Dr Sumner; she said she'll think about it if it gets worse. Oh, Aunt Maud, what can we do? Did you know she's moved into my old bedroom? She said the coughing disturbs Pa. She's determined not to worry him and she's desperately trying to hide her illness from him until this expansion work is finished!'

Maud sat down beside her on the sofa and took her hand; she could see how upset the girl was and she was very disturbed herself. It looked as if the disease had progressed even further than she had imagined and it was time to do something positive. 'I'm truly sorry to hear that, Livvie, and I think that it's high time your father was made aware of how serious Mary's condition is. She wasn't well enough to attend the engagement party; he came on his own.' She'd been tempted to tell him then but had deemed it not the right time for it would certainly have put a damper on the evening.

'And there's more, Aunt Maud. Just as I was leaving Amy came in and . . . and, well, we had a row because I told her a few home truths. I just can't believe that she didn't notice that Mary is ill. She seems completely self-centred and carried away with all the plans for her future.'

Maud nodded her agreement. 'She's still quite young, Livvie, and I think all this fuss over Selina's wedding and her own engagement has blinded her to reality. But she's going to have to know too.'

'She does. I told her. Oh, what's wrong with my family? They're so selfish and hard-hearted.' She chewed her lip anxiously. 'It's going to be very awkward now for me at Selina's wedding. I said some things to Amy that she won't easily forget but I'll just have to bite my tongue because I don't want to spoil Selina's day.'

Maud could see Livvie's point about the wedding; things could prove to be quite strained. 'Selina will understand, once I've explained. I doubt your father will be attending now, Livvie, if I can make him see the truth about Mary, and Mary herself certainly won't. Amy might well come to her senses . . .'

Livvie nodded; it would help if she didn't have to face her father. 'Maybe . . . maybe if I were just to attend the church service? I think I could be civil to Amy for that long,' she suggested.

Maud sighed heavily. 'I'll have a word with Selina and see what she thinks. Oh, believe me, this wedding is putting years on me. I'm getting to the stage where I will be glad when it's all over.'

Livvie managed a wry smile. 'Don't say that, Aunt Maud. Selina is your only daughter and you *will* enjoy it. But I can assure you that there won't be half as much drama around my wedding.'

Maud smiled back. 'No, I don't suppose there will!'

Livvie got to her feet. 'I'd better be going. I don't want to take a chance that Pa will see me leaving here. But tell Selina that she can be certain there will be no arguments between Amy and me on her big day.'

Maud showed her out, hoping that Livvie and Amy *would* settle their differences and thinking the sooner she sorted this mess out the better. She was not looking forward to telling Thomas that his young wife did not have much longer on this earth.

Chapter Twenty-Nine

◆━━◆

Maud left it until the Saturday afternoon when she knew Thomas would be home although she had already spoken to Amy. Her future daughter-in-law had come over the morning following Livvie's visit and she'd been both indignant and upset. 'It was a shock to find her standing in the hall and she was horrible to me, utterly nasty! She virtually blamed me for Mary's illness!' Amy had blurted out.

'That's ridiculous, Amy. Of course she doesn't blame you, but she finds it hard to believe that you hadn't even noticed how ill Mary is.'

Amy had started to protest but Maud silenced her with an impatient wave of her hand. 'You really are going to have to start growing up, Amy. Oh, I know everything seems so very exciting and enthralling at the moment – Teddy's proposal, your ring, the party and Selina's wedding – but there are other matters of importance to consider and there's more to a marriage than frivolous anticipation. There will be many, many years ahead of you as a wife, not just the one single day when you're the centre of attention as a bride. Livvie knew Mary was ill and came to see her and naturally she was upset to find she has such a serious condition. I'm sure there was no need for you both to quarrel, but it's done now. Livvie has promised to put aside your differences and I expect you both to behave and not spoil what should be the happiest day of Selina's life, and hopefully you can settle your differences. I hate to see this enmity between you and so would your poor mother. And from now on Mary deserves some consideration and a great deal of care.'

Amy's expression had changed at her words and Maud thought she looked so young, vulnerable and rather fearful. What the girl had needed as she was growing up was the advice and wisdom of her mother and she knew that Edith would have provided it unstintingly. Mary had been either unable or unwilling to do so and Thomas had never given his girls a great deal of his time or attention.

'Livvie said . . . she said Mary has consumption. Has she really? Will she . . . die?'

Maud had nodded sadly. 'It will need medical confirmation but I'm almost certain she has and you know there's no cure. It's about time your father realised it too. I'll tell him, Amy, although it's not a task I relish, and then we'll have to see about doing everything we can for poor Mary,' she'd concluded and Amy had left in a far more sombre and subdued mood.

Maud was thankful that Selina had taken the news in a far more mature way than she had anticipated: she'd half expected hysterics as her daughter's nerves were getting a little frayed to say the least. She had been upset and concerned when Maud told her of the rift between Amy and Livvie but she had agreed with her mother that if the girls at least made an effort to appear civil on her wedding day, as they'd both promised, then it would not mar the day. It was infinitely better than Livvie not attending at all.

Maud's heart was heavy as she knocked on the Goodwins' door at four o'clock on Saturday afternoon. As Emily let her in Maud asked if Mary was in the parlour with Thomas; if so she would have to ask him to come over to her house for she didn't want to distress Mary further by having this conversation in front of her.

'No, ma'am, she's resting upstairs. She was up this morning but then after lunch she had a bad fit of coughing and . . .'

'She's getting worse, Emily, isn't she?'

Emily nodded sadly before knocking on the parlour door.

Thomas got to his feet as Maud entered but she indicated that he remain seated.

'I'm sorry to disturb you, Thomas, I know you have little time for leisure these days, but it's not really a social call. I'm afraid there is something I should have told you before this.'

He frowned, wondering if it was to do with Amy's engagement. That all seemed to have gone very well.

Maud steeled herself. 'You must be aware that Mary isn't well. In fact she hasn't been well for some time now.'

He nodded his agreement. 'She didn't recover as I'd hoped after the miscarriage and she has a cough she can't seem to shake off.' He'd reluctantly accepted the doctor's advice about Mary not becoming pregnant again after she'd lost the child although it hadn't been easy, but of late the expansion of the factory had been taking up all his time and energy. He hoped that once it was completed things would return to normal.

Mary had seemed to accept the situation and had even moved into Livvie's old room so as not to disturb him. Sometimes he felt they were drifting further and further apart and were living almost separate lives, although he didn't dwell on it too much.

'I'm afraid, Tom, that it's not possible to "shake off" . . . consumption,' Maud informed him quietly.

He stared at her and then slowly started to shake his head in disbelief. 'No. It can't be . . . *that*! She would have seen the doctor if she'd thought . . .'

'She won't, so I did. I'm so very, very sorry but she has all the symptoms. Night sweats, weight loss and she's started coughing blood. I've begged her to see Dr Sumner – only he can confirm it, Tom – but she flatly refuses. She has tried to hide it from everyone, but most of all you. She didn't want to worry you. But now you must get the doctor to see her. We have to do everything possible to help.'

He dropped his head in his hands. He'd call Sumner straightaway but he knew that Maud was very likely right about his wife. Now she'd spelt it out, he could recognise all the signs for himself. And if she was right, this was the worst news possible, he thought, and something he'd never anticipated. It saddened him to think that he was going to lose his second wife; Mary had always tried her best to please him and make his life run smoothly and of course he'd be a widower – again. She would die; it was inevitable for there was no cure. Sometimes a stay in a sanatorium helped but there was never a full recovery, it just prolonged the suffering. Livvie would get married in a couple of months as soon as she was twenty-one, Amy was engaged and would marry and he'd be alone, he thought bitterly. He felt that he was now too old and too weary to contemplate yet another marriage. Everything he'd ever worked for seemed to be turning to dust. He'd have to get an official diagnosis and then . . . then he would have to think about Mary's care.

'Are you all right, Tom?' Maud enquired, for he'd not spoken.

At last he looked up and nodded. 'It . . . it's a shock, Maud. But thank you for telling me. I know you have so much to do these next few weeks – as I do myself. If the diagnosis is as you say, I'll arrange with Dr Sumner for someone to come in to nurse her. I can't expect a young girl like Amy to take on that responsibility.' He stood up. 'And now, I . . . I'll go up and see my wife.'

Maud too got to her feet, relieved the ordeal was over but slightly shocked that he seemed to be thinking only of the practicalities regarding the medical care of his wife. He'd said nothing about how he felt or how Mary must be feeling, nor had he expressed concern for her. He'd not regretted the fact that he'd been too preoccupied to even notice her decline and she was beginning to think that Livvie was right in her assertion that he was selfish and cold.

The following week Amy informed Maud with relief that Dr Sumner had been to see Mary and confirmed that sadly she had been right and that he was arranging for two nurses to be engaged to care for her stepmother. One would come during the day; the other would remain all night. Now that she could no longer deny it, Mary seemed to be resigned to her condition and no longer attempted to leave her bed. At least she would be getting the best care available, Maud had thought grimly, although it was far, far too late.

Livvie too was relieved when Bessie relayed the news to her. Both Bessie and Hetty had listened to Livvie's account of her visit home in shocked silence.

'And I want you to stand for me, Bessie, when I get married. I'm not having Amy – sister or no sister!' she'd finished.

Hetty had shaken her head, unable to believe the two girls could have fallen out so badly. But then they were completely different in character, like chalk and cheese. 'Well, yer'll 'ave ter be on yer best behaviour, the pair of you, for Miss Mayhew's weddin', like,' she said sternly. 'Can't ruin that, not after all the fuss an' expense.'

'Well, I will be. I've promised Aunt Maud. It's up to Amy how she behaves,' Livvie had reiterated grimly.

The nearer the day of the wedding drew the more apprehensive Livvie felt. Frank wouldn't be there for he'd be working that morning, nor would Mary, and of course her father wouldn't attend now in deference to his wife's condition. She'd gone to Maud's for the last fitting of her dress straight from work on the last Monday evening before the do, but had been unable to go to see her stepmother. Tactfully Maud had arranged for Amy's final fitting to be on the previous Friday.

The weather had improved greatly; the days were often sunny and mild now and the evenings although calm were still chilly. New foliage was appearing on the trees and shrubs; there were tulips and camellias flowering in the gardens: all of which pleased both the bride and her mother and made Livvie realise that her own wedding was now only two months away.

'Hopefully Saturday will be a gorgeous spring day with lots of sunshine and everything will be prefect, Aunt Maud,' Livvie had enthused as she'd taken her leave that Monday evening.

'I really do hope so. Try to be here for half past nine, will you, dear?' Maud pressed as she saw Livvie out. The wedding was at half past ten so by the time they'd got dressed and helped Selina into her bridal finery the two sisters wouldn't need to spend much time in close proximity, and of course there would be other people around too, herself included, but she did hope that they could use the occasion to try to patch things up between them.

As she alighted from the tram on the corner of Denison Street and King Edward Street Livvie caught sight of the old man who sold newspapers and strained to catch what he was shouting. A small crowd had gathered around him and so she went to investigate.

The crowd was strangely silent as if stunned by the news vendor's words and the bold black headlines on the copy of the *Echo* he was brandishing.

'What is it? What's happened?' she asked a man she knew vaguely as one of Billy's neighbours and drinking companions.

'Beyond belief, girl, it is! Just beyond belief,' he replied, shaking his head.

'What is?' she urged.

'That ship, the *Titanic* . . . it . . . it's sunk!'

Livvie just stood and stared at him. It was the newest, biggest liner afloat and the most luxurious, the flagship of the White Star Line, and there had been so much written about it in the papers. It had only sailed from Southampton on its maiden voyage five days ago and was said to be attempting the fastest crossing to New York, a record held at present by the Cunard Line.

'They said it was unsinkable! How? When? Where?' she exclaimed.

'Hit an iceberg they say, and it ripped a hole in her hull. There's thousands lost!'

Livvie handed over her coin and took a copy of the paper from the vendor as she struggled to believe the news. It was a tragedy of mammoth proportions, she began to realise as she read the shocking initial accounts. One thousand five hundred people were reported drowned in the freezing cold waters of the Atlantic. There were men from Southampton and Liverpool working in the stokehold, it was reported, and they'd have stood no chance at all as the water poured in through the gashed hull. She quickened her steps towards Hetty's house wondering if they'd heard about this terrible disaster.

As soon as she walked into the kitchen she realised they knew. Hetty was in tears and Billy looked both grim and shocked; even Stanley was pale and subdued. She handed the paper to Billy and sat down at the table, all thoughts of the forthcoming wedding forgotten.

'They said it was unsinkable! They said it *couldn't* sink! Oh, all those poor souls!' She was fighting back tears.

'No ship is unsinkable,' Billy remarked scathingly as he scanned the lines of newsprint.

'I just can't take it in. 'Er from Dublin Street must be in a right state. 'Er 'usband was one of the Black Gang – 'e was a stoker.' Hetty sniffed and wiped her eyes with a corner of her apron.

'It says 'ere that the survivors were picked up by Cunard's *Carpathia* – they'll be taken to New York,' Billy said. 'Then there'll be 'ell to pay for someone, you mark my words.'

'That won't bring those poor souls back, will it?' Hetty remarked sadly. 'Oh, it's a black, black day.'

Livvie silently nodded her agreement and then wondered what impact this appalling tragedy would have not only on the cities of Liverpool and Southampton but on Selina's wedding, which was less than a week away now.

Chapter Thirty

———◆———

As the sequence of events surrounding the tragedy became known the whole country reeled with shock and disbelief, the population of Liverpool especially so. Those initial feelings soon turned to outrage and anger and the answers to many questions began to be loudly and insistently demanded on both side of the Atlantic. Why were the numerous warnings of ice not heeded by Captain Brown? Why was the ship travelling at full speed through the dangerous waters of an ice field? Why had the watertight compartments buckled and been breached? Why were there not enough lifeboats? Why were some lifeboats found to be empty and others with only half a dozen survivors on board? Why were the large numbers of steerage-class passengers kept virtually – and fatefully – confined to the lower decks by barriers that had been locked? And why had the chairman of the White Star Line – Sir Bruce Ismay – been saved when so many others had been left to perish in the freezing water? Public inquiries were being demanded by the people of both

America and the British Empire.

Both Maud and Charles Mayhew had been as stunned and horrified as everyone else and quickly realised that the very lavish entertainment planned to celebrate their daughter's wedding would be neither appropriate nor sensitive.

'We can't cancel the entire ceremony, Charles. It would break her heart,' Maud said gravely when the subject had been broached.

'But how can we go ahead with it all, Maud? It would be an act of crass insensitivity to say the least if we do. So many people have been lost,' her husband reminded her.

Maud thought about it. 'In the circumstances I think we should just go ahead with the church ceremony followed by the wedding breakfast as planned. The evening reception, the musical entertainment and the dancing will have to be cancelled. I'm sure people will understand that in all decency there's nothing else we can do,' she suggested.

Charles nodded his approval. All the money he'd spent would be wasted but at a time like this that could not be helped, not when there were now so many widows and fatherless children in the two ports in the country that had suffered the greatest loss. 'I'm afraid you're going to have quite a lot of extra work, my dear, writing to those guests that will be affected.'

Maud smiled sadly. 'And so will Louise Woodford, but it can't be helped, Charles. I'm afraid that poor Selina and Henry's choice of date was . . . unfortunate. I do hope it won't affect how she feels on each wedding anniversary in the future.'

'I hope not too, but her choice wasn't nearly as "unfortunate" as that of those who booked their passage on that ship, God rest them,' he replied. No one could have foreseen this terrible tragedy, he thought.

Selina was disappointed but she too realised it would have been very inappropriate to have held what would have been tantamount to an evening soirée and ball a week after the disaster and during the remaining frenetic days accepted her parents' decision. There was too much raw suffering for her to put her feelings first.

It was a still apprehensive and saddened Livvie who duly made her way to Maud's house on a beautiful April morning. It was inconceivable that there was so much grief and pain in the world on such a day, she thought. Frank had brought the tragedy home to her personally, for he was mourning the loss of the school friend he'd spent the afternoon with the day she'd been arrested. David Benson had been going to start a new job as an engineering draughtsman and a new life in New York and had been amongst those drowned. It seemed everyone knew someone who had been affected.

As Livvie walked up Poplar Avenue she longed to call in to see her stepmother, but it was impossible. There wasn't sufficient time and she had no wish to antagonise her sister, who was certain to find out and report the visit to her father. Indeed, her father, if he'd been true to his promise to pay more attention to his sick wife, might well have been there.

When she arrived at the Mayhews' house Maud was ready: dressed not in the outfit she'd bought for the occasion, but in a grey dress trimmed with bands of purple which, though still elegant and becoming, she felt was more appropriate than the bright peony-pink dress and matching jacket she'd planned to wear. Her large grey hat, trimmed with feathers and bands of purple satin ribbon, reposed with her gloves on the table in the hall.

'We'll go on up to Selina's bedroom, Livvie. Amy has already arrived and is dressed. She's helping Selina and I'll assist you – you'll need to be laced a little tighter, I think. And I was sorry to hear about Frank's friend. It's tragic. So many young lives wasted.'

Livvie nodded. 'He's upset. They'd kept in touch for years and he'd only learned a few weeks ago that David intended to go America. He was looking forward to going so much – he'd even given Frank his new address. He would have been Frank's best man at our wedding but he'd already made the decision to go. No one can quite believe it.'

Maud patted her hand sympathetically. This wasn't the atmosphere she'd envisaged would surround Selina's wedding day.

When they entered the bedroom, Amy was fastening up the row of tiny buttons at the back of Selina's dress.

'Oh, you look absolutely gorgeous!' Livvie enthused. Indeed Selina looked stunning. Yards and yards of white silk embellished with lace seemed to cascade around her friend and as Amy placed the pearl circlet to which was attached the cloud of silk tulle veiling over Selina's carefully coiffured hair both she and Maud had tears in their eyes.

'Do I? Do I really? It . . . it's not all too much?' Selina wondered doubtfully.

'Of course it's not all "too much", Selina, and Livvie is right. You look gorgeous,' her mother said firmly as she turned to relace Livvie's corset and help her into the pale blue taffeta and lace. She'd noticed that the two sisters had not exchanged any kind of a greeting and she frowned as she fastened up Livvie's dress.

As soon as Livvie had fixed the circlet of blue flowers in her hair she stood back and smiled at the bride. 'Now we're all ready.'

Selina smiled back. 'I'm a bit nervous but I'm very happy – but do you know what would make me even happier?' She held out a hand to Amy and the other to Livvie. 'That both of you will forget your quarrel and not just for today.'

Livvie looked enquiringly at her sister, wondering what she was thinking.

Maud held her breath, hoping Selina was doing the right thing, wondering if either of them would make the first move towards reconciliation. If they didn't it could make matters so much worse.

Eventually it was Livvie who broke the silence. 'I think there's been enough sadness in the world lately, Amy. None of us know what tomorrow will bring and it . . . it's not how Mam would have wanted us to behave.'

Amy slowly nodded in acknowledgement. She too had been deeply saddened by the loss of the *Titanic* and the fact that Mary's condition seemed daily to be worsening. 'I . . . I'm sorry, Livvie. I was selfish and . . . inconsiderate. I realise that now.' She looked pleadingly at Maud as tears threatened.

'I'm so relieved that you're both willing to let bygones be bygones and you're right, Livvie. It's the last thing your mother would have wanted. Life is too short to spend it quarrelling. Now, we'd better go down and collect the flowers and await the cars,' Maud finished briskly, defusing some of the emotion.

Livvie smiled at her sister as they both took Selina's long train, thinking that now she would enjoy the day far more than she had anticipated. She would find an opportunity, later, to ask Amy how their stepmother was faring.

It was a beautiful service, Livvie thought. The church was full of spring flowers, candles and music and both Selina and Henry looked so happy. There had been a moment of sadness when the vicar had asked them all to join him in a prayer for all those who had perished so recently, and out of respect the hymn 'Eternal Father Strong to Save' had been sung. Silently, Livvie had prayed for their souls and that of Edith. After that the newlyweds, the bridesmaids, their parents and families and guests had had photographs taken and then been driven to the Imperial Hotel for the wedding breakfast.

When the meal and the toasts and speeches were over, under the buzz of conversation Livvie turned to her sister. 'Amy, I didn't want to mention it earlier, but how is Mary?'

'She seems to be failing more and more each day, Livvie. Oh, the nurses are very good and she is being brave about it but I often wake in the night hearing her terrible coughing. It's the most awful sound imaginable.'

Livvie looked concerned. 'And . . . Pa?'

'He . . . he's not home a great deal, Livvie.'

'That damned expansion work!' she exclaimed. 'But Frank thinks it will be completed in about a month. At least he hopes it's going to be finished before we get married.' She bit her lip, remembering that now she'd asked Bessie to stand for her.

'It will be your turn next, Livvie, and at least your day won't be overshadowed by tragedy.'

'At least I hope not,' she replied, thinking of her stepmother's health.

'Livvie, I . . . I'd like to attend your wedding but I don't think I should be the one to stand for you. Pa wouldn't be happy about it and I don't want to cause any upset, not while Mary is so ill,' Amy said tentatively. 'I hope you're not hurt and disappointed?'

'No, Amy. I think you're right,' Livvie agreed, thankful that Amy herself had solved the dilemma. Clearly her sister still shied away from antagonising their father and she could understand that; there was enough distress in that house at present without adding to it.

'I'm glad we've made up our quarrel, Livvie.'

'So am I. And, Amy, will you let me know how Mary is?'

'I will, I promise,' Amy vowed, thinking how much some contact with her sister would mean in the days ahead. 'Do you think I could meet you when you've finished work one evening and we could go to somewhere like a Lyons Corner House for something to eat? I could tell you how Mary is and you can tell me all your plans.'

Livvie reached out and took her hand and squeezed it. It couldn't be pleasant for her sister left to her own devices all day in that house with a nurse and her dying stepmother. 'Of course, Amy. We could make it a regular meeting,' she suggested. Amy would probably be very happy when the day arrived when she would marry Teddy Mayhew and she too could leave her father's house for a home of her own.

* * *

After the wedding breakfast Livvie went back to Maud's house to get changed and asked if she could leave her bridesmaid's dress there as they were so short of storage space at Hetty's. When she arrived back in Denison Street later that afternoon she was pleased to find Frank waiting for her, perusing Billy's copy of the *Daily Post* with a mug of tea at his side.

He laid it aside as he stood to greet her affectionately. 'I felt restless so thought I'd come and find out how it all went. It must have been quite a fraught few hours for you?'

She smiled as she kissed him. 'No, actually it wasn't.' She understood that he didn't want to spend the time alone in his house but as usual there was not much chance of privacy here. 'It's a gorgeous afternoon, why don't we get the tram to Stanley Park. It's a shame to stay stuck indoors,' she suggested.

Frank nodded. One of their favourite places for a stroll in fine weather was the waterfront but neither of them had any desire to go there today. Personally he didn't want to see a ship for a long time to come, regardless of its size.

There were still quite a lot of people in the park even though it was nearing five o'clock, Livvie realised as they walked along the path towards the lake and the glasshouses. The flower beds were a riot of colour and there was still some warmth in the sun.

'It was all very tastefully done, Frank, and Selina looked radiant,' she informed him.

'I'm sure she did and Mrs Mayhew always does things to a very high standard.'

'Cancelling the evening reception was the right thing too, but the best part is that Amy and I have made up our quarrel.

That was Selina's doing – we couldn't refuse her on her wedding day.'

He stopped, turned and smiled down at her, kissing her on the forehead. 'I'm so glad about that, Livvie. I know you wouldn't admit it but it was troubling you, wasn't it?'

She nodded. 'Yes, it would have upset Mam. I'm going to meet her on Tuesday after work in Lyons in Whitechapel. It was her suggestion. I think that despite everything she's rather lonely, Frank. Oh, I know she goes over to Maud's to spend most evenings with Teddy but she's stuck in that house all day with only Emily to talk to and poor Mary . . .'

'How is Mary?' Frank asked. Thomas Goodwin seldom spoke of his wife and Frank felt if he asked about her too often he was intruding.

Livvie shook her head. 'Amy says she's slowly getting worse, despite the nursing care, and Pa isn't home much.'

'Well, all the work at the factory should be finished in a few weeks – the new machinery is being installed this week – then maybe he'll have more time to spend at home. And as we're taking on more men he's even talking about employing an assistant for me as once we're in full production my workload will double too. Lately his time has mainly been occupied with obtaining new orders and he's been organising the extra haulage and transportation with Mr Mayhew. That will mean more profits for Mayhew and Son Haulage too.'

'Aunt Maud will be pleased. But I just hope Pa's extra time won't come too late for Mary.' She smiled at him. 'But it's great news that you're to have help, Frank. I thought he'd just expect you to go on coping with everything.'

He smiled back. 'It appears not, so I'll have more time to

spend with you, once we're married. It won't be long now, Livvie.'

'Oh, I know and I can't wait. Hetty's been very good to me but I want a home of my own with you.'

As there was no one in sight Frank took her in his arms. 'I'm finding it hard to wait too, Livvie, I want you so much. At least me having to work all the hours God sends does have an advantage,' he added wryly, thinking that he was so exhausted by the time he got home from work all he was fit for was sleep. But his dreams were full of her – he couldn't wait until they were finally man and wife.

Chapter Thirty-One

———❦———

Livvie's meetings with Amy did become a regular weekly event and she knew they both looked forward to it. In the time since they'd quarrelled she realised that Amy had grown up considerably, and as April turned to May and she finally turned twenty-one, she was surprised that, when they met as usual in Lyons, her sister had bought her a gift. It was a silver bangle engraved with her name and date of birth. Amy had gone to some trouble and Livvie was very touched. 'Amy, it's beautiful, thank you!' she said, turning it over in her hand.

Amy smiled. 'Well, it is a special birthday and one you'll always remember. Now you can finally marry Frank without Pa's say-so.'

Livvie became serious. 'And maybe in years to come I might even be able to vote.' She hadn't given up on the suffrage movement; she followed their activities closely and hoped that in the end they would win the right to vote. 'But talking of Pa, Frank was saying that work at the factory is almost complete and I was thinking, Amy, that I'd like to visit Mary before he starts to spend more time at home. What do you think?' she asked tentatively as she sipped her tea. She had no way of knowing how her sister would react to this request but she realised that she would have to visit her stepmother soon for Amy's reports were growing more worrying.

Amy wiped her fingers on her napkin as she considered Livvie's words. 'I think you should. For one thing I know she'd like to see you again and if shortly Pa's going to be home more, there'll be less chance to avoid him.'

Livvie nodded thankfully. 'When do you think I should come?'

'What about Thursday evening? He always supervises the making up of the wages then. Nurse Slattery will be on duty but she won't mind and I'll explain to her that there's no need to mention your visit to Pa.'

Livvie smiled at her. 'Thanks, Amy.'

'You'd best prepare yourself for the . . . change in Mary,' she warned.

Livvie bit her lip; she'd been shocked enough the last time she'd seen her stepmother and now she realised that this might be the last time she would ever see Mary in this life. It was a very sobering thought. 'Do you find it all . . . upsetting to cope with?'

Amy nodded. 'Sometimes I do, Livvie. The nurses take care of everything medical, and for her comfort, but I try to sit with her for a couple of hours each day, depending how she's feeling. Sometimes I read to her. I think it helps to take her mind off her condition.'

'That's good of you.' Livvie hadn't realised Amy spent so much time with their stepmother.

Amy's face fell. 'I . . . I wish I was getting married in just over four weeks, like you.'

Livvie reached across the table and took her hand. 'I can understand that. Have you and Teddy made any definite plans yet?'

Amy shook her head. 'Not yet. We decided to leave that until after Selina's wedding.' She smiled wryly. 'Give Aunt Maud time to catch her breath. But I'd really like to get married either before Christmas or early next year. After . . . after Mary's . . . gone I don't want to stay in that house, Livvie.'

'I can understand that too. You always said you felt there was something disturbing about it.'

'There is. I remember the day we moved in and I thought then it was creepy, even before Jonty told us about Mrs Chadwick. We were never as happy as we were in Minerva Street, were we?'

'No, but we'll both have homes of our own in the not-too-distant future. You've that to look forward to.'

Amy smiled as they both finished their tea. 'Yes, I have. So, I'll see you on Thursday evening.'

'It will be about a quarter to seven, depending on how quickly I can get a tram,' Livvie informed her as she gathered up her bag and gloves.

She'd steeled herself for her visit but when Amy showed her into Mary's sickroom she couldn't hide her distress and pressed her fist to her mouth to stifle her cry.

Nurse Slattery came over to her. 'She's sleeping, fitfully. You must see a great change in her, Miss Goodwin?'

Livvie nodded. Her stepmother had lost so much weight

she was skeletal and her skin looked almost transparent. The disease had aged her terribly. She no longer looked like a young woman of thirty-two, she looked like a ravaged sixty-year-old. 'I . . . I didn't realise. She . . . she's very ill, isn't she?'

Nurse Slattery nodded sadly. 'It would be a blessing if God took her but I don't think that is imminent. I've nursed too many cases like her to know she could linger on for weeks yet.'

'Can I sit with her?' Livvie asked, feeling a little calmer but wondering how Amy coped with this each day.

'Of course. She might wake, but she might not. I'll leave you but if you need me there's a little bell on the bedside table.'

When she'd gone Livvie gently took Mary's wasted hand; it felt hot and yet at the same time clammy. Poor Mary, how she must be suffering, she thought. How could her pa spend so much time at the factory? Him being there wasn't *that* important surely? It wasn't more important than being with his wife as she barely clung to life, or at least it shouldn't be. Her eyes met those of her sister who had taken her place on the opposite side of the bed and she realised that there were tears in Amy's eyes as there were in her own.

Mary stirred and caught sight of Livvie and attempted to smile.

Livvie gently patted her thin hand. 'I've come to see you, Mary. Amy tells me you are being very well looked after by the nurses. We meet for a bit of supper each week, so I get a regular progress report on you.' It was so difficult to know what to say, she thought. It would be futile and insensitive to ask Mary how she felt.

'I'm so glad, Olivia, and it . . . it's good of you to come.' The words were little more than a hoarse whisper.

Livvie managed a weak smile. 'You know I'd come more often, but . . .'

'I'm afraid I missed your birthday,' Mary said apologetically.

'Oh, I'm a grown-up woman now so don't you be worrying about things like that. I spent it with Frank, which was how I wanted it.'

'I expect you'll be getting married soon?'

Livvie nodded. 'In a little over four weeks' time, on the eighth of June to be exact. I . . . I wish you were well enough to be there.'

Mary shook her head sadly. 'Even if I were you know I . . . I couldn't . . .'

Livvie squeezed her hand again. Oh, yes, she knew all right. Her pa would not have allowed it.

'I wish you so much happiness for the future with Frank, Olivia,' Mary managed to get out before the dreadful coughing began. The harsh, rasping spasms increased and Mary fought for each breath until they finally overwhelmed her. Desperately she pressed a linen cloth to her lips as a horrible gurgling sound came from her throat.

Both Livvie and Amy got to their feet, Amy quickly ringing the little bell for the nurse knowing Livvie would not want to witness the pitiful sight of their young stepmother coughing up her life's blood.

Nurse Slattery took charge immediately and Amy drew Livvie out of the room.

'There's nothing we can do to help her, Livvie. It's best to leave it to Nurse Slattery; she knows exactly what to do.'

'Oh, Amy! I never even got the chance to thank her for her wishes for my happiness. Or to say goodbye!'

Amy shook her head sadly. 'I know, but she'll be so utterly exhausted when the spasm is over that I don't think Nurse will let either of us see her again tonight.'

'And of course Pa will be on his way home now, so I'll have to leave,' Livvie added bitterly. Mary had wished her happiness with Frank but she wondered had Mary ever known any happiness in her short life at all?

The day she had longed for had finally arrived, she thought as Bessie brought her up a mug of tea and drew back the bedroom curtains letting the warm June sunlight flood into the tiny room.

'Special treat for the bride,' Bessie announced. 'An' Mam says it's probably the last time you'll ever get a cup of tea in bed,' she added, pulling a comical face.

Livvie laughed. 'I don't think I've ever had tea in bed in my life, Bessie, except maybe when I was a child and was poorly.'

'At least you've plenty of time to get ready. There's definitely no rush and I'll be back after I've served the lunch.'

Livvie nodded. Aunt Maud had given Bessie the afternoon and evening off and Frank wouldn't finish until noon either. She'd sent a brief and rather formally worded note to her father, informing him that she would be getting married at the Register Office at three o'clock and that he was welcome to attend, if he so wished. She'd had no reply and nor had she really expected one, but at least he could never say he hadn't been invited. She was hurt though. Would it really have been so hard for him just to have replied, using Mary's illness as an excuse for his refusal? He was aware Amy would be attending and her sister had informed her that although he'd said nothing to her on the matter, she'd known from his attitude that he did not approve. She'd had a few moments when she felt saddened by how things had turned out, wishing that her pa had willingly accepted Frank and that her wedding could have been a much grander affair with Amy, Selina and Bessie as bridesmaids and with Mary in attendance, her pa proudly walking her up the aisle, instead of a very simple civil ceremony. But she'd pushed the thoughts determinedly from her mind. She would *not* think like that, she told herself. She regretted nothing, she loved Frank and it was her heart's desire to marry him. The loss would not be hers but her pa's.

She did spend a rather leisurely day, fussed over by Hetty and then Bessie when she arrived home from work. Reluctantly she'd decided against the pale blue bridesmaid's dress for, as she'd said to Bessie, they would be travelling to Brougham Terrace on the tram and she would look very incongruous, not to say ridiculous, dressed up to the nines in taffeta and lace.

'I think you'd look great an' people would be made up to see you an' congratulate you, I'm sure. Everyone loves a bride on her weddin' day. It's the custom round here for brides to walk to the church or wherever so all the neighbours can come out, admire your finery and wish you luck,' Bessie had urged.

Livvie had smiled, remembering that had been the custom in Minerva Street too, but she would feel far too self-conscious. So she'd bought a very pretty pink linen two-piece costume instead, under which she'd wear one of the fancy white blouses she'd brought from Poplar Avenue, and a large pink and white hat.

'It will be far more appropriate and more serviceable too. I can wear it on lots of occasions afterwards,' she'd told both Hetty and Bessie.

Hetty had nodded her agreement and Bessie had smiled. 'It's just as nice as the blue taffeta. You'll look gorgeous, Livvie!'

With the house only having the scullery for everyone to wash in, things got a bit hectic but at last they were all ready. Bessie wore her best dark blue skirt and an embroidered blouse, Hetty the only decent dress she possessed and a hat borrowed from a neighbour and Billy, who was giving her away, his only suit, which had been redeemed from 'Uncle's' pawnshop on Friday and sponged and pressed to within an inch of its life. He sported a white shirt with a starched winged collar and a tie for the occasion. Stanley was looking both mutinous and excited, his unruly hair plastered down with water, his boots polished and a stiff Eton collar adorning his jacket, all of which he hated wearing. He'd also been threatened with dire and dreadful punishments by both his parents if he misbehaved and made a show of them.

Amy, Selina and Maud would meet them at the Register Office – Charles Mayhew was driving them there but was not staying – and then Maud was treating them all to afternoon tea at the Stork Hotel, something to which Hetty was looking forward though with a certain amount of trepidation. She'd never been inside a hotel or had afternoon tea and Maud Mayhew was Bessie's employer and so much grander than they were. And then there was Stanley's presence in such a place and company to worry about.

The little group, which included Frank and his best man,

were waiting just inside the rather austere building when the wedding party arrived.

Livvie felt her heart beginning to race as she smiled at Frank, who wore his best suit and sported a white carnation as a buttonhole.

'You look lovely, Livvie,' he greeted her, thinking she in fact looked radiant.

'I feel lovely too,' she replied, suddenly a little shy now that the moment was imminent.

'This is Ernest McGibbon, my friend who's agreed to be my best man,' Frank introduced the young man at his side.

Livvie smiled at him, thinking fleetingly of tragic David Benson, as Maud passed her the posy of flowers she'd had delivered by the florist that morning. But even the thought of poor David couldn't dampen the happiness that was welling up inside her. She couldn't believe that in a matter of minutes she would be Frank's wife at last.

Maud handed Bessie her posy and introduced herself, her daughter and Amy to Bessie's parents. Then a clerk appeared to usher them into the office where the ceremony would take place. Livvie glanced around at the plainly furnished room. It was quite unlike a church, in fact it was very reminiscent of an office, but there was a vase of flowers set on the table behind which stood the middle-aged, morning-suited registrar.

As the registrar proceeded to introduce himself Maud thought despite the floral arrangement the place looked rather austere and she wished Livvie had chosen to get married in a church. She could have chosen the one local to Denison Street; Maud quite understood she would not have wanted to have the ceremony where Selina had been married for that church was where Edith had been laid to rest and also where Thomas Goodwin had married Mary Fitzgerald, not the happiest of occasions for the girl.

Livvie's hands trembled slightly as she made her vows but her voice was steady and clear and her heart felt as if it were going to burst when the registrar pronounced them man and wife and Frank bent to kiss her.

'I love you, Mrs Hadley,' he whispered.

'And I love you too, Mr Hadley, so, so much,' she whispered back, her eyes shining and the new gold band firmly on her finger.

It was all over very quickly and with very little sense of occasion was the thought that came simultaneously to the minds of Maud, Selina Woodford and Amy. The two girls were mentally contrasting it to Selina's wedding service. Feeling a little sad for her sister and determined that her own wedding would be in a church Amy smiled and kissed Livvie and then Frank, who she now realised was her brother-in-law.

Maud also kissed Livvie on the cheek and shook Frank's hand and Hetty and Billy followed her lead, offering their congratulations, and then Livvie found herself back outside surrounded by the smiling little group of her sister and friends. She could hardly believe it. She *was* Mrs Francis Hadley now! The only thing that would have added to her joy was if her mother could have lived to see it.

Maud, determined that Livvie would at least travel to the hotel in a dignified fashion, had ordered three hackneys, which delighted both Livvie and Frank and was viewed with relief by Amy and Selina and with something akin to awe by Bessie, her parents and especially her brother.

'She's certainly givin' yer a great send-off, Livvie,' Hetty hissed before Maud ushered them towards the second cab.

'An' aren't we goin' to the hotel in style, too, Mam?' Bessie beamed at her mother. 'It certainly beats the tram! For once in our lives we're "posh"!'

The hotel manager and his staff made a gratifying fuss of the little party and as Livvie tucked into the dainty sandwiches and delicious cakes she thought that a sumptuous banquet couldn't have tasted better. Looking around happily she also thought how times were changing. Oh, there had been no word from her father and he'd not even been mentioned by anyone but here were Bessie and her parents taking tea with Maud, who was doing her very best to put Hetty and Billy at ease. Amy was chatting happily to Ernest and Selina was regaling Bessie with the details of her new home and the young maid of all work she'd employed who apparently was not yet quite up to Bessie's standard. Young Stanley was making the most of his parents' preoccupation with being polite to their daughter's employer by devouring the three cakes on his plate and the glass of lemonade provided for him, all of which Livvie knew were rare treats.

She turned to Frank, her face aglow with happiness. 'Isn't this just the most wonderful day?'

He placed his hand over hers. 'It's the happiest day of my life, Livvie, and it will be even better when we go home . . . together.'

She blushed a little, hoping she would find her first experience of lovemaking enjoyable, feeling excited by the thought that she would spend tonight in Frank's arms in her very own home. Tears of happiness sparkled on her lashes as she thought of what lay before her: a future of happiness with the man she loved. It had been a long and difficult wait, but it had been worth it and surely there couldn't be any more dark clouds on the horizon to threaten that happiness?

Chapter Thirty-Two

———◆◆◆———

'I thought we might take another day trip on Sunday, it seems ages since we went to the Isle of Man,' Frank suggested as he finished his second cup of tea.

Livvie smiled at him across the breakfast table. 'I'd like that. Where shall we go this time or will we go back to Douglas?'

'No, I thought we'd try somewhere different. Perhaps the North Wales coast. I've never been there – they say it's very pretty. They'll be stopping the day-excursion sailings soon as we're into September and the weather will be changing.'

Livvie nodded her agreement. This would be a treat and she'd never been there either. 'I've got to go into town later today; there are a few things we need that I can't purchase from the local shops. I could call into the offices of the Coast Lines and get the tickets.'

Frank got to his feet and then bent and kissed her. 'Good, it will be something to look forward to. Could you get two tickets for Sunday? I have to be off now to open up and get production started.'

Livvie too got up and followed him into the hall to see him off. He kissed her again and she watched him go down the path and into the street, tipping his hat politely to those neighbours who were already out and about. She was on friendly terms with the street and of course Frank had lived here all his life. She smiled as she closed the front door and went to clear away the breakfast dishes. The hall was now a much brighter place, she mused. All the gloomy brown paint and varnish had gone, replaced with cream paint and a pale green wallpaper sporting sprigs of white flowers. She loved her new home, which she'd made her own as well as Frank's.

Maud had called a couple of times and she'd complimented her on keeping everything so neat and tidy, remarking that marriage definitely seemed to suit her. She'd replied that she'd never been happier or more content in her life and it was true. On her last visit Maud had informed her that Selina was expecting a baby and everyone was thrilled and delighted. She'd asked Maud to convey her congratulations but had thought that she didn't want a child so soon. She'd prefer to have more time to herself with Frank but, as she'd then mused, babies usually didn't wait to be invited.

She'd intended to go on working after they were married but Frank had talked her out of it, saying she would find it difficult to go out to work and to run the house.

She'd been very reluctant at first, feeling that she would be able to cope very well. If she was totally honest with herself, she admitted that she didn't want to give up the feeling of independence that earning her own money gave her. 'I don't have to leave as early as you in the morning, Frank,' she'd pointed out. 'I'll be able to do what chores are necessary before

I leave and I'm home before you so I'll have a meal ready.'

'But then there are all the other things: the shopping, washing, ironing and cleaning,' he'd reminded her. 'You'll wear yourself out, Livvie. I don't want to come home to an exhausted wife. I want you to be happy not tired out.'

She'd pursed her lips as she'd thought about it. He was only thinking of her wellbeing, she mused, but . . . 'It won't be for ever, Frank. As soon as I find I'm . . . expecting, I'll be happy to give up work just as Mam did.'

'Your mother's case was different, Livvie. She was helping your father to get a start in life,' Frank had replied, frowning. He hadn't expected her to be so determined to continue to work and he was a little hurt. 'Livvie, if you continue working, how will that reflect on me? People will talk; they'll say I can't afford to support a wife. It's exactly what your father will think. It's a matter of . . . my pride.'

She hadn't thought about that, hadn't realised that it would diminish him in people's eyes, particularly the men he worked with, the majority of whose wives didn't go out to work no matter how hard up they were. She'd do what Frank suggested and see how it turned out. 'I . . . I didn't think about that, Frank, and you're right, it's exactly what Pa would think and maybe even remark on.'

So she'd given up her job and after a month she admitted to herself that Frank had been right and she'd done the correct thing. It was difficult enough to keep the house going and shop for meals without going out to work all day too and Frank deserved to come home to a clean and tidy house, a good supper, clean shirts and linen and the comforts of an orderly and well-run home. She still attended the suffrage meetings with Bessie and Frank always insisted he meet them to escort them home. Even though she was no longer actively involved in the civil disobedience campaign, which hadn't abated, she still held firm to her beliefs and supported their demands. Just because she was now a married woman she hadn't changed her mind and neither had Bessie.

But, yes, it would be lovely to take a day trip to Rhyl, Colwyn Bay or Llandudno for they hadn't had a honeymoon and they didn't go out a great deal. Frank worked very hard and deserved a day's leisurely sail – and she still felt a little down for last month she'd had the news that Mary had died.

Amy had called in person to tell her, she remembered as she washed the dishes in the small kitchen at the back of the house. Of course she'd known that her stepmother hadn't long left to live but she'd still been shocked when she'd opened the door to her sister that summer morning and seen the expression in Amy's eyes and that she was wearing black.

'Oh, come on in, Amy,' she'd urged, ushering her sister into the hall and then the parlour. 'It's Mary, isn't it?'

'Yes. She died yesterday morning, early, and . . . and it was a blessing really,' Amy had informed her, wiping away a tear as she sat down.

She'd nodded sadly, thinking of the last time she'd seen her stepmother. 'She'd suffered so much, hadn't she?'

Amy had nodded too. 'But she went peacefully at the end. Pa and I were with her and Nurse Slattery. She'd known Mary was . . . going and woke us both.'

'How is Pa taking it?' Livvie had asked, thinking that at least he had been there. That must have given his poor wife some comfort.

'As you'd expect. He's quiet and resigned about it. Sad of course too. He's gone to organise the funeral and after he's done that he said he'll go into the factory for a few hours, so I came to tell you. Aunt Maud has promised to help me all she can.'

'Thank you for coming. Will you let me know when it's to be?'

Amy had looked doubtful. 'Do you think you should attend?'

Livvie had thought about it. She wanted to pay her respects to Mary but she wasn't sure how her father would react to her being there. It had been no surprise that he'd said nothing to Frank about their wedding or the fact that he was now his father-in-law.

'I'll see what Frank thinks. Perhaps . . . perhaps it would be better if we just sent flowers. Mary never wanted to cause any upset or fuss and maybe we should respect that.'

'If you feel that would be best, Livvie. I know she'd understand,' Amy had replied. She wasn't looking forward to these next days, weeks or months and intended to persuade Teddy to set a date for their wedding as soon as was decently possible.

And so Livvie hadn't attended the funeral but they'd sent a lovely wreath with a black-edged card and the message 'Rest in Peace. You will be missed, Mary', signed 'Mr and Mrs Francis Hadley'.

Amy had visited Livvie regularly ever since the funeral and she'd learned that, as usual, her pa was throwing himself into work and spent little time at home. Amy and Teddy were to be married early in the February of 1913 and Amy was busying herself making plans with Maud for that.

* * *

It was after lunch when Livvie finally let herself out of the house and walked the short distance to the tram stop. She needed some new towels, tea towels and pillowcases and those she couldn't obtain in the array of grocers, greengrocers, newsagents, fishmongers and butchers that comprised the local shops. They were the sort of things you usually received as wedding gifts but of course she'd not had that kind of a wedding, and had received very few gifts. Men never seemed to notice the condition of such things as household linen, she thought with mild amusement, reflecting on the state of some of the items Frank had been using. She'd decided she'd go to either T. J. Hughes or Blackler's who offered decent quality at affordable prices.

She spent a pleasant couple of hours browsing in both shops before making her purchases and then made her way to Cooper's, the big grocery store in Church Street that stocked more exotic items than her local shop. She bought some coffee as a special treat for Frank, who liked a cup after his supper, noticing that the autumn fashions were on display in the shop windows but deciding that she would make her winter coat do for another year. Maybe she'd get something new for Amy's wedding, provided of course that she and Frank were invited. Her pa would be paying for it all so it wasn't a certainty by any means.

As it was a fine afternoon she walked up Lord Street and towards the Pier Head where she could get a tram to take her home from the terminus. It would have to pass along King Edward Street and she realised, as she boarded the green and cream painted vehicle and paid her fare, that she had time to call in on Hetty, something she did once a fortnight, and still be back in time to prepare supper.

The tram moved off and trundled onwards but after about ten minutes came to a stop. She glanced out of the window curiously. They were on the border of the Dock Estate but this wasn't a designated stop, she knew that. After a few minutes some of the other passengers started to get restless.

''Ere, mate, what's goin' on?' one man demanded of the conductor.

''Ow long are we going to be stuck 'ere for? I've to be 'ome before the kids get back from school or they'll 'ave the place destroyed!' a woman added rather irately.

'I'll go and have a word with the driver; he can see more than me,' the conductor informed them and disappeared towards the front of the vehicle.

There was some muttering amongst the passengers but Livvie sat patiently and quietly. No doubt there was some problem with the overhead trolley or maybe there had been an accident. Perhaps a cart had shed its load or the horse pulling it had bolted: it sometimes happened, blocking the road and causing hold-ups. She sighed; if they were here much longer there wouldn't be time to see Hetty.

The conductor reappeared looking grave.

'What's up then?' someone demanded. 'Has another flaming horse bolted?'

The conductor shook his head. 'Not this time. I'm sorry, folks, but there seems to have been an explosion in one of the factories on the Dock Estate. It must be serious as there are coppers, firemen and ambulances all over the place, so we won't be moving for a long time yet. If you've not far to go I suggest you'd get there quicker if you got off and walked.'

Suddenly a terrible fear gripped Livvie. 'Which factory? Do you know which factory it is?' she called to him.

'They're saying it's that big one that makes cattle feed, luv.'

'Goodwin's?' she almost shrieked.

'That's the one.'

Instantly she was on her feet, her parcels forgotten. An explosion! Oh, God! she thought in panic. Once off the tram she picked up her skirt and started to run, her heart hammering against her ribs. It must be bad if there were so many policemen, fire officers and – she could already see – ambulances, and dense black acrid smoke rising into the air. Frank! Oh, please God, don't let anything have happened to him! she prayed frantically.

The nearer she drew the more chaotic the scene appeared to be. Fire hoses were already trained on a part of the half-demolished building from which smoke poured out; police and ambulance crews and men obviously from other factories were climbing over the rubble, some shepherding dazed-looking men and lads towards the open land that bordered the extended area of the loading bay. Someone caught her arm.

'Miss! Miss, stop! You can't go any further!'

She looked up into the face of a police sergeant. 'Please, my husband is the manager here, Mr Frank Hadley. I have to go on! I have to see him, please?' she begged, tears stinging her eyes and panic clear in her voice.

'I don't think that's possible, madam. Parts of the building are unstable and could collapse and there are still men missing and I'm afraid three are . . . dead.'

Those words were like daggers being thrust into her heart.

'No! Please, don't you see I have to . . . find Frank! I . . . I have to *know*! And my pa! My pa will be here too. My father is Thomas Goodwin; it's his factory.'

He took her arm. 'Well then, we'll have to see if anyone knows anything for definite.'

Shaking and frantic with fear she let him lead her towards where three fire engines and five ambulances were positioned and a group of men, some sitting, some leaning against a wall, were being attended to by medical staff.

'Does anyone know where we can find Mr Hadley, the manager?' the sergeant shouted.

Livvie uttered a cry of pure relief as she saw the familiar figure of Frank turn towards them. 'Frank! Frank! Oh, thank God! Are you all right?'

He came over to them and she could see that his face was streaked with dirt and blood and his clothes too were covered in a black dust.

'Livvie, what in God's name are you doing here?'

She flung herself into his arms, regardless of the detriment to her clothes. 'I was on the tram! Oh, you're hurt – there's blood on your face! What happened? Where's Pa? And Billy . . . Billy Grey?'

'I'm not hurt, Livvie. It's just a graze but . . .' He led her towards one of the ambulances and she caught a glimpse of two figures on stretchers inside. The sergeant followed them.

'We don't know what happened, Livvie. I was in the office on the other side of the building when . . . when there was an almighty explosion. The whole building shook and I thought it was going to collapse on me, then I could smell smoke and there were flames too and I knew I had to get everyone out . . . It's utter chaos! I . . . I've been doing everything I can to help since . . . but there are many men who've been injured, some very badly. I think Billy is all right; he was working in the old part of the factory. It's the new part that's been damaged the worst – it took the full force.'

'And Pa? Is he all right too?' she begged.

To her dismay he shook his head. 'They've taken him to hospital, Livvie. He was . . . he was down inspecting work on the new production line when it happened.'

'Frank, how badly injured is he?' she asked fearfully. Oh, trust her pa to be down there on the factory floor of his new building instead of being in his office.

'I don't know. I'm sorry but there wasn't time for me to ask. They said they were taking him to Stanley Hospital; it's nearer than the ones in town. All you can do now, Livvie, is to go home. This is no place for you and you'll have to let Amy know somehow.'

'Come with me, Frank! Come with me and we'll go to the hospital?'

Frank shook his head. 'I can't, Livvie. Not yet at least, I'm sorry. Not until everyone has been accounted for and the injured attended to and the site is . . . secure. And I have to speak to the Chief Fire Officer. You go home and wait; I'll be back as soon as I possibly can and then . . . then we'll go to the hospital, I promise.' He could see how upset, shocked and worried she was – he was very shaken and concerned himself. It was an effort to even think straight. He turned to the sergeant, who had remained silent. 'Will you see that my wife gets back on to the main road safely, please?'

The man nodded and took Livvie's arm. 'I'll see you safely on to a tram, madam,' he urged. 'Your husband is right; this is no place for you.'

Almost in a daze she let him lead her back towards the road. How had this terrible thing happened? What could have caused such devastation and tragedy? It had been such a pleasant, ordinary early autumn day. The tickets for their Sunday trip were in her handbag and then out of the blue there had been an explosion and suddenly it had all become so . . . dark and frightening. First of all she had to get word to Amy. Her greatest relief was that Frank hadn't been hurt, but her father had, and everything he had worked for, at such a very high cost to them all, now lay in smouldering ruins.

Chapter Thirty-Three

───◆───

All the way home on the tram she tried to think more rationally and ignore the shocked, speculative conversations going on around her. Frank was safe and so he thought was Billy Grey; her main concern now was her father and getting word to her sister. She and Frank didn't have a phone at home but there was a public phone box at the bottom of the road. She'd phone Maud from there. Then she'd have to go home and just . . . wait.

Thankfully the phone box was unoccupied and as she fumbled in her purse for some pennies to put into the appropriate slot she realised her hands were still trembling. She dialled Maud's number and waited. It was Maud who answered and Livvie quickly informed her of what had happened.

'Dear God in heaven! An explosion!' Maud gasped.

'Will you tell Amy, please?' Livvie begged urgently.

'I will. Thank God Frank isn't hurt, Livvie. I think the best thing for me to do will be to send Amy to you and then perhaps it would be best if you both waited for Frank to get home. Of course if you feel you should go to the hospital right away then do so. I'll phone Stanley Hospital first, so hopefully she will have something to tell you to put your mind at ease.' Maud paused. 'I'll tell Bessie too and send her home straight away; poor Hetty will be frantic for news, I know I would be. Frank did say he thought Billy was all right?'

'Yes, he did. He was working in the old part of the building. And, Aunt Maud, thank you. I was beginning to panic.'

'Try to stay calm, Livvie. Panicking will help no one,' Maud advised firmly.

'I'll have to go, my money's running out and I've no more change. I can hear the pips.'

'Don't give up hope, Livvie. Your pa is made of stern stuff,' Maud urged and then the line went dead.

Livvie replaced the receiver, pushed open the door and went out into the street still feeling dazed and worried but a little calmer.

It was so hard to just wait, she thought as she went to the parlour window for the umpteenth time to look for Amy. She'd tried to keep herself busy by setting the table and a tea tray. If she and Amy decided to go to the hospital she would also have to think about leaving something for Frank; he was sure to be hungry and thirsty when he got home. She'd realised that she'd left her purchases on the tram but that was the least of her worries right now; she could always go to the lost property office and see if they'd been handed in when . . . when all this was over.

The daylight was fading and the street lights were being lit by the lamplighter and she was turning on the table lamp in the parlour when she heard the knock on her front door.

'Oh, Livvie! I came as quickly as I could,' Amy cried.

After hugging her sister Livvie drew her into the house. 'Did Aunt Maud phone the hospital?'

Amy nodded, taking off her hat and sitting down. Her face was white with shock. 'They wouldn't tell her much. They wouldn't even tell *me* very much. Only that his condition is serious but stable.'

'But nothing about how badly he's injured or what's wrong with him?'

Amy again shook her head.

'Shall we go there now?' Livvie urged.

Amy looked perturbed and bit her lip. 'I asked them that but apparently it's not visiting time and they emphasised that they are very strict about that, even in circumstances like this. But I told them that both you and I will definitely insist we see Pa when Frank gets home. I explained who Frank is.'

'Oh, why do they have to be so rigid with their rules and regulations!' Livvie cried exasperatedly. 'Then all we can do is wait, and hope and pray that Pa's not too bad.'

'Bessie's gone home to see what she can do to help her mother.'

Livvie nodded. Yes, Maud was right, Hetty would be frantic for news like this spread quickly by word of mouth and often became exaggerated in the telling. 'I'll make some tea – it might help to steady our nerves. Oh, I hope Frank isn't going to be much longer. It was all so terrifying down there, Amy. Rubble, dust, smoke, people injured – it was like a battlefield!'

'Shall I turn the wireless on?' Amy suggested. She did at

least feel a little better now that she was with her sister. She'd felt sick with shock when Maud had told her but her sister's presence was a comfort.

Livvie nodded and went into the kitchen to make the tea.

To their consternation no mention of the disaster was made on the wireless but no doubt it would be reported in the evening edition of the newspapers for many families in the city had been affected. However, neither of them felt they wanted to leave the house to go in search of a vendor.

'I'm sorry, Livvie. It . . . it's just the shock and coming so . . . soon after . . . Mary.'

Livvie put her arm around her. 'I know, these past weeks haven't been the easiest for you, Amy, but Aunt Maud advised us not to give up hope and that's all we can do now. Hope and pray that Pa will be all right.'

It was after eight o'clock when Frank finally arrived home, looking exhausted and haggard and still filthy dirty.

'Is everything under control?' Livvie asked as she hugged him.

'I think so. The fire brigade are still there and so are the police but not as many of them now. Everyone's accounted for and the police will inform the relatives of those injured and . . . killed and deal with any problems that might arise.'

'Oh, Frank, it's a terrible blow!'

'I know, Livvie.' He shook his head grimly. 'I don't think I'll ever forget some of the sights I've seen today. But let me get washed and changed and we'll all go to the hospital.' Frank noticed Amy for the first time. 'Did you manage to find anything out, Amy?'

'Not much. We phoned the hospital but all they'd say was

328

that he's "serious but stable" and that we couldn't see him out of visiting hours, nothing more.'

Livvie tried to be practical. 'You must be hungry, Frank. I was going to cook something but—'

'A sandwich will do. There's no time for you to cook a meal or for us to eat it. Oh, I know they're sticklers for their rules and regulations regardless of the circumstances but for once we're not going to take "no" for an answer! We've all been through too much today to have to spend the night worrying too.'

Both girls went into the kitchen while Frank went upstairs to wash off the grime and change his clothes, which reeked of smoke.

'It will be late when we get back, Amy. Do you want to stay here tonight?' Livvie offered.

She nodded. 'Yes, please. I'd prefer to do that rather than going back to that house on my own – I'm beginning to actually hate living there, Livvie – but I promised Aunt Maud I'd let her know how Pa is.'

Livvie nodded. Poplar Avenue had never been a lucky house for any of them, she thought bitterly. 'There will be a public phone at the hospital, Amy. You can telephone from there.'

They were asked to wait rather curtly by the sister on duty after they had informed her who they were and why they had come out of visiting hours. Frank ushered them to the plain wooden benches set in rows in the middle of an austere, green-tiled room which was empty apart from them. There was a strong smell of antiseptic and ether, which made Livvie wrinkle her nose in distaste. It was the first time in her life she'd ever been inside a hospital and it was a far from pleasant experience, she thought. It was only because of the seriousness of her father's injuries and of what had caused them that they were being allowed to see him, they'd been informed.

At last another sister appeared looking very officious in her stiffly starched, elaborately pleated cap, an equally stiff apron and cuffs over her dark blue dress.

'Will you come with me, please? I have to say that this is highly irregular but Doctor has agreed that you may see Mr Goodwin for a few minutes only. Doctor is still with your father.'

'May we know how badly he's been injured, Sister, please?' Frank asked.

'Dr Simms will inform you about his injuries. All I can tell you is that he has been given something for the pain and will be operated on if Dr Simms and Mr Knight – the surgeon – think it necessary,' was the brusque and unhelpful reply.

They were ushered into a small room, not a ward. The walls were part tiled, part painted white and a plain, functional light was suspended from the ceiling. Livvie gasped and she heard Amy stifle a cry as they caught sight of their father in the narrow bed. His head was bandaged, his cheeks the colour of parchment and his eyes closed. His breathing seemed laboured and there were tubes attached to one arm.

'Sir, I'm Frank Hadley. I'm Mr Goodwin's son-in-law and his factory manager. I . . . I was there when the explosion occurred and these ladies are his daughters.'

Dr Simms nodded gravely. 'A terrible occurrence and disastrous for many, so I understand, including Mr Goodwin.

I'd ask you not to distress him. I'll speak to you all before you leave.'

Amy moved to the bedside and took Thomas's hand while Livvie reached for Frank's, thinking that whatever they'd given her pa, he didn't seem to be aware they were there.

'It's Amy, Pa. How are you?' she asked quietly.

His eyes slowly opened, seeming at first not to focus but when he caught sight of Frank he struggled to speak. 'The . . . factory? Is . . . is . . . it . . . ?'

Frank drew closer to the bedside. 'Everything is under control; you're not to concern yourself. Both the police and fire service are still there and I'll be back in the morning to see what can be done,' he assured his employer.

'Pa, you've not to get distressed,' Amy pleaded for he was becoming agitated.

'All . . . all . . . gone,' Thomas murmured and there was no mistaking the note of despair in his tone.

'No, that's not true. It's not all been destroyed, only part of the new building,' Frank said firmly. 'I'll be able to keep production going in the original factory, once we've cleared up, and the men will be glad to get the orders out. Don't worry about anything; you know you can rely on me. We'll know soon enough what caused it, or so the Chief Fire Officer told me. You've got to concentrate on getting well.'

Thomas nodded slowly, closing his eyes. 'Thank you . . . Frank. Always . . . could . . . rely on you.' Suddenly he opened his eyes again. 'Is . . . is Livvie with you?'

She stepped forward and Amy relinquished his hand. Livvie took it and squeezed it gently. 'I am, Pa. Frank is right, you're not to worry about anything, just get well.'

'I'll . . . try. Can . . . rely . . . on . . . family.' His breathing became more laboured. 'You *are* still . . . family, Livvie. You and . . . Frank. Been thinking that . . . just lately, and now . . .' The words were almost a whisper.

'I think perhaps you'd better leave him now to sleep,' Dr Simms instructed. 'Sister will stay with him,' he assured them.

Reluctantly they left the room, Livvie glancing back over her shoulder, very distressed to see him so obviously in pain. She was shocked, too, that it had taken something as terrible as this for him to speak to her once more.

'What exactly is wrong with him, sir?' Frank asked of the doctor when they were once more in the corridor.

'We suspect that he has injuries to the spinal column, as well as general contusions, shock and mild concussion. From what little information I could glean from the ambulance driver, it appears he was thrown forcefully against heavy machinery by the blast. He's lucky to be alive.'

Livvie held tightly to Amy's hand. 'Will he recover, please?'

'With care, I believe so, but he will be in hospital for quite a while. He's not a young man and I'm afraid that he probably will not walk again. He will need constant care and attention.'

Frank nodded slowly. His father-in-law had indeed been lucky to survive but he now realised that if he did not have the use of his legs he would hardly be fit enough to run the factory in the future, which to a man like Thomas Goodwin would be a very unpalatable fact. 'My wife and I will make sure of that, sir. Thank you.'

The doctor nodded and shook Frank's hand, an indication that the interview was over.

Both girls were subdued and deeply distressed by the news

and so it was Frank who phoned Maud before they all left the hospital.

'What will we do now?' Amy asked rather helplessly when they'd reached home and Livvie had made a pot of tea to which Frank had added some medicinal brandy.

'We'll visit him every day of course and when he's well enough to leave hospital we'll have to make sure he's properly looked after. You heard what the doctor said, Amy, he'll need constant care for quite a while,' Livvie replied sadly, knowing it was not the way her pa had envisaged the remainder of his life. 'But the factory, Frank? What will happen? All those men depend upon Pa for their jobs.'

'I'll keep it going for him, Livvie. I'll have to discuss it all with him, but only when he's well enough. For now we have to put his health first.'

Livvie realised Frank was right. Oh, he'd been cold and heartless towards her and they'd disagreed on so many things but he was still her pa.

'Can I stay here for a few days, Livvie, please? I . . . I can't face going back to that house just yet,' Amy pleaded. She still felt very shaken and didn't want to be on her own.

'Of course you can,' Livvie assured her.

Frank passed a hand wearily over his eyes. 'It's been a long, exhausting, traumatic and tragic day.' He sighed, trying to marshal his thoughts about what the future would hold.

Livvie reached and took his hand. 'It has but there are some things to be thankful for, Frank. You're safe, Billy Grey is safe and Pa . . . survived. And even though he's going to be dependent on us, which he'll no doubt resent, we'll be a family again and that's probably the very best outcome of all.'

Frank smiled as he nodded his agreement. Yes, it seemed as if Thomas Goodwin had accepted that both he and Livvie were his family and was ready to embrace them as such.

'Aunt Maud was right; she said we shouldn't give up hope. The future will be different for all of us, but we can hope it will be better too,' Livvie added with a smile that encompassed her husband and her sister.

Chapter Thirty-Four

———◆———

Livvie and Amy visited Thomas over the next two days and were relieved to find that he was a little better each day.

'You don't seem to be sleeping as much, Pa,' Livvie commented as she sat beside the bed.

'I'm not. I told that nurse I wasn't going to take any more of the stuff they've been giving me to make me sleep. I need to start thinking what to do about the factory,' he replied testily.

Livvie raised her eyebrows as she glanced at Amy, who was sitting on the opposite side of the bed. 'Pa, they have been giving you that medicine to keep you calm and *stop* you worrying about the factory. You know Frank is taking care of everything and he'll be in this evening to set your mind at rest,' she added soothingly. It wouldn't help her pa at all if he worried himself into a state of agitation.

Thomas nodded.

'How are you feeling now, Pa?' Amy asked tentatively.

'Better, I have to admit, Amy, but I still don't seem to be able to move my legs.'

Livvie bit her lip. 'It's very early days yet, Pa. Dr Simms told us all that. For now you have to rest and let your body heal. It's all going to take some time so stop worrying, that's not going to help at all. And I hope you're eating; it's important for your recovery.'

'You've become very bossy, Livvie, since you got married,' Thomas muttered.

Livvie smiled wryly. 'Not really, Pa. I suppose I always was a bit bossy.'

Amy smiled at her but said nothing as she could see that he was already tiring.

They both waited until his eyes closed and then they rose quietly. 'Frank will be in to see you this evening, Pa,' Livvie reassured him as she bent and gently kissed his cheek.

'Do you think we should ask to see Dr Simms, seeing as how he's refusing to take the medicine?' Amy asked as they went into the corridor.

'I don't suppose it would do any harm,' Livvie replied.

They found it was not possible to see the doctor as he had just commenced his ward rounds, according to the sister. 'And I'm sure he will have very little to add. Your father is still recovering from the initial shock and concussion.'

'We were a bit worried, Sister, as Pa says he's not going to take any more medicine and he . . . well, he can be very stubborn,' Amy informed her.

Sister tutted. 'Indeed! Well, he may own a factory and be used to making important decisions but in here the decisions are made by Dr Simms and he'll have to abide by them. It's for his own good!' was the stern reply.

'She's not going to stand any nonsense out of Pa, is she?'

Livvie murmured to her sister as they walked away.

Amy nodded. 'Livvie, I think I'll go home this evening. Teddy will think I've deserted him, Aunt Maud will want to know how Pa is and I feel that I need some time there.' She hoped her pa was going to recover in time for her wedding but at this precise moment she didn't hold out much hope.

Livvie smiled at her. 'Of course and you're right. You didn't exactly come prepared for a long stay. Frank will go in this evening.'

'I'll be in to see him tomorrow, and if you want a break, I'm sure Aunt Maud would be only too happy to accompany me.'

Livvie nodded in her turn. There were things both she and Amy had to do; day-to-day life had to go on after all.

That evening Livvie persuaded Frank that it would be better if he went alone to the hospital. 'I know there are certain things he will want to discuss about the factory. There's nothing we can do to stop him worrying about it – I wish there was – but I know you won't let him get too agitated and it might indeed help to put his mind at rest if he talks to you without me or Amy being there.'

Frank agreed. 'And I'm hoping I'll be able to have a word with the doctor about your father's recovery and what it will entail for us.'

Livvie nodded. Perhaps Frank would be able to get past Sister and learn more about how her father was progressing. She had the distinct feeling that Dr Simms felt that neither she nor Amy were capable of understanding fully, which annoyed her, although it was a typical male medical attitude, she realised. There were very, very few women doctors. In fact she didn't know of any at all in Liverpool.

'You've had a pretty awful couple of days, Livvie. Stay here and take things easy. I won't be long,' Frank urged as he kissed her before he left.

She closed the front door slowly. He had had a pretty awful couple of days too, she mused. And now he had taken on the clearing up and running of the factory and for how long was anyone's guess. It might well be for ever.

Frank found his father-in-law a little better although irritable, but that he could understand. Thomas Goodwin had never been a man to sit back and let others take over and now being immobile and subject to the rules and regulations imposed upon him obviously did not sit well with him.

'I can see you are much improved from my last visit,' he greeted the older man cheerfully.

'I am and I'm not, Frank. That Sister Fletcher is a real tartar of a woman, I can tell you. But you've not come here to listen to my complaints about her.'

'No, I came to satisfy myself that you are improving and to keep you informed of what's going on.'

Thomas nodded. Despite the drowsiness and fatigue caused no doubt by the medicine that damned woman insisted he take, he was very anxious to hear what Frank had to say. He'd fretted about it – when he was awake.

'We've demolished the parts of the building that were unsafe, as instructed by the city surveyor, and the rubble is being cleared away. There are plenty of men eager to get some labouring work for a week or two. Once that's done we can think about rebuilding,' Frank informed him, although he wasn't sure about the finances for such rebuilding work. He wasn't going to voice those doubts just yet, though.

'And . . . and production?' Thomas enquired, looking anxious.

'Is going ahead as normal. Don't worry about that. The men are keen to work harder and longer to try to fulfil the new orders as well, the ones you worked so hard to obtain. It will mean of course that we'll have to pay overtime but I didn't think you'd want to risk the goodwill and possibly lose that business.'

Thomas slowly nodded. 'It's even more important now. I don't want to be seen to have failed.'

'We've not failed anyone. It was an accident, pure and simple, and we're doing everything in our power to keep things running. Things will be almost back to normal in six months. You know you can rely on me to keep my word. And should any . . . difficulties arise I'll discuss them with you, but I'm sure that's not likely.'

Again Thomas nodded, feeling more relieved now and with that relief came the onset of inevitable drowsiness, due to the opiate. 'I always could, Frank, and I'm . . . grateful.'

Seeing that his father-in-law seemed to be easier in his mind now and looked to be on the point of sleep, Frank rose. 'I'll leave you now but I'll be in regularly to keep you informed of progress and I'm sure Livvie and Amy will be in tomorrow.'

'Good . . . girls, both of them,' Thomas murmured as his eyes closed. Then he smiled to himself. 'They're good girls . . . the Goodwin Girls, Frank.'

'They are indeed,' Frank replied before he left.

When Frank sought out Sister Fletcher he was informed that Dr Simms had been called away urgently but that if he wished it would be possible to make an appointment to see him to discuss his father-in-law's progress.

'I'd like to do that, please, Sister. You see there are a great many things that depend on how much of a recovery he makes and how long it will take,' Frank informed her.

'I understand that, Mr Hadley, but at this stage I don't think Dr Simms will be able to say for certain how long it will take. A lot will depend on Mr Goodwin's attitude and co-operation,' she finished dourly.

Frank smiled at her. 'He's not a man who has been used to being inactive and he can be . . . stubborn.'

'I'm aware of that but I can assure you it's an attitude that will not be tolerated here. Everything is being done for his own good and I'd advise you to impress that upon him.'

'I'll try, Sister, I promise, but it's not going to be easy.'

'If he wants to make as full a recovery as is possible then he'd do well to heed your words,' Sister Fletcher replied firmly.

'How was he? Did you see Dr Simms?' Livvie asked when he returned home.

'They're keeping him sedated but he was of course anxious to know how things are going,' Frank replied, sitting down beside her on the sofa. 'Of course I didn't go into too much detail, that wouldn't have done any good, but I think he felt reassured. He was sleeping when I left him.'

'And what did Dr Simms say, Frank? I've been sitting here wondering what we're going to do in these next months.'

Frank took her hand and squeezed it; he could see that she was still worried. 'I didn't see him; he'd left. But I've made an appointment to see him at the end of next week. Sister Fletcher said that by then they should have more idea of how your father's progressing.'

Livvie nodded although she felt a little disappointed that they would have to wait. She was anxious and had so many things on her mind. 'Amy and Aunt Maud are going to go in tomorrow but I want to come with you, Frank, when you see the doctor.'

He kissed her cheek. 'Of course. Hopefully then we'll have some idea of what the future has in store for us all. Now, I think we both need to try to get a decent night's sleep,' he urged, getting up and drawing her to her feet.

Livvie spent the following day catching up on her household chores and shopping, for the larder was looking rather bare and Frank was getting low on clean shirts. The clothes he'd worn the day of the explosion she'd had to put in the bin; there was nothing she could do with them, they were so badly stained and still reeked of smoke.

She wasn't surprised when that afternoon both Amy and Maud called after their hospital visit but she could see that Maud was concerned.

'How did you find Pa today?' she asked, preparing to make a pot of tea.

'Much the same as yesterday, Livvie. Very drowsy,' Amy answered.

Livvie nodded. 'Frank said they are keeping him sedated – for his own good.'

'I guessed that, as he didn't have a great deal to say,' Maud added. 'I didn't expect him to look so . . . quiet or to have aged so much. But I suppose it's only to be expected.'

'Frank has an appointment with the doctor next week. Maybe by then they'll be able to tell us more,' Livvie informed them both.

Maud looked serious. 'I hope it will be good news, Livvie, but I think you should prepare yourself in case . . .'

'I've already been thinking about that, Aunt Maud. I don't know when he'll be able to go home but before he does I think there are some serious decisions that will have to be made. I can't see him ever being fit enough to run the factory again, the way he used to.'

Maud nodded as she accepted the cup of tea from Livvie. 'Well, at least they won't have to be made for some weeks yet, Livvie. I suppose everything depends on what the doctor has to say but we can't give up hope.'

Livvie glanced at Amy and saw the anxiety in her sister's eyes. Well, Maud was right. They shouldn't give up hope and it would be fruitless to worry about the future until they had heard the doctor's diagnosis.

Chapter Thirty-Five

———◆———

It seemed to Livvie that each day her father improved although he was beginning to complain about the fact that he still had no feeling in his legs, something both she and Amy tried to gloss over by saying it was early days and he shouldn't worry about it. But Thomas was worried by the fact, hoping desperately that in time movement would return.

Livvie felt both nervous and anxious as she and Frank were shown into Dr Simms's office at the end of the following week.

'We're hoping that there is more that you can tell us about Mr Goodwin's condition, Doctor,' Frank said as both he and Livvie were asked to sit down.

Dr Simms looked grave. 'He is recovering well from the shock and contusions, thanks to the rest he's been getting, and we've been doing some tests.' He paused and twisted his fountain pen between his fingers. 'I'm afraid I have to tell you that the damage to his spine is . . . irreversible.'

'You mean . . . he . . . he'll definitely never walk again?' Livvie asked fearfully.

'I'm afraid not. We suspected as much from the beginning but we had to be sure.'

'So, he'll need constant care,' Frank said grimly. 'Does he know, sir?'

Dr Simms shook his head. 'Not yet, but I'm afraid he will have to be informed of the facts.'

'He's going to find it almost impossible to bear, sir. He . . . he's always been an active man, he's worked hard all his life, and he's a very proud and self-reliant individual too,' Frank informed him sadly.

'I understand that, Mr Hadley, and it will indeed be very hard for him to come to terms with, but I'm afraid he will have to accept it. He's lucky he survived at all and that his injuries were not even worse, and that, mercifully, there is no brain damage.'

'Who . . . who will tell him?' Livvie asked timidly. She was struggling to accept what was now an undeniable fact.

'I will, Mrs Hadley, if you wish.'

They both nodded thankfully. Perhaps her father would accept the awful truth more readily from a doctor, Livvie thought.

'Thank you, sir. We'd be very grateful if you would tell him. Would it be possible to let us know when you are going to do so, so someone can be on hand . . . afterwards?' Frank asked.

The doctor nodded.

'How . . . how long will he be in here, please?' Livvie enquired, twisting her hands together in her lap.

'I should think about another five or six weeks, as long as there are no complications.' Dr Simms attempted a smile.

'You should have him home in good time for Christmas.'

They thanked him and after Frank had shaken his hand they left. Neither of them said anything on the journey home; they were both still trying to come to terms with what they now knew the future held.

'We'll have to think about what to do when he's able to come home, Livvie,' Frank said quietly as he sat beside her and handed her a glass of sherry.

'We'll need to tell Amy what the doctor said. It will affect her too, especially if he is able to go home before Christmas. Her wedding is in February, don't forget. And we'll have to think about what will happen after that.'

Frank sipped his own small brandy and nodded. She was right, but first things first. 'Maybe we should wait and see how he takes the news before we start to make any decisions. He has the right to some say in his future.'

'I can't see him taking it well at all, Frank.'

'Neither can I,' Frank agreed.

'And I'm certainly not looking forward to my first visit after they've told him,' she confided.

'I know, Livvie, but let's not get too concerned about that until we've told Amy.'

'Do you think I should telephone her in case they tell him tomorrow and she goes in unprepared?'

Frank shook his head. 'They won't tell him so soon, I'm sure. They're bound to give him a bit more time to recover. He's only just getting over the shock of the explosion.'

'Then I'll go and see her tomorrow and we can go to the hospital together,' Livvie said firmly.

* * *

So much had happened since she'd last walked up Poplar Avenue, Livvie thought to herself as she walked towards her old home. The last time she'd come here had been on Selina's wedding day. Then it had been a beautiful April day, Mary had still been alive, she and Amy had not been on speaking terms, and of course her father had been in the best of health. She shivered as the cold autumn wind buffeted her and a few more leaves from the trees fluttered to the ground.

Emily opened the door to her. 'How is the master? Oh, it was all such a terrible shock,' she asked.

Livvie managed a smile. 'As well as can be expected, Emily.'

The girl nodded. 'Bessie said to tell you that her da is getting over it and is glad he's still got a place to work and her mam said to say that she's grateful for everything you and Mr Hadley did that day.'

'Oh, I didn't do much, Emily. We just didn't want Hetty to be sick with the worry of not knowing if Billy was safe.'

'Miss Amy is in the parlour,' the girl informed her, taking Livvie's coat and hat.

'Well, what did the doctor have to say?' Amy asked tentatively as Livvie sat down opposite her.

Livvie told her briefly about their visit yesterday and Amy nodded. 'It's what we feared, Livvie, isn't it? But I'm so glad that we haven't got to tell him.'

'So am I but I know he's not going to take the news well, Amy. You know how . . . difficult he can be at the best of times and now . . . well, he's not going to be able to walk, in fact he's not going to be able to do very much for himself at all to begin with.'

'We'll have to get a nurse in for him, Livvie. Someone like

346

Nurse Slattery,' Amy suggested.

Livvie nodded. 'Of course. You certainly won't be able to cope without one and Pa would feel so utterly humiliated if either of us tried to do everything for him.'

Amy bit her lip. 'What . . . what about when I'm married, Livvie? Teddy's been looking at houses and he's seen two he thinks suitable and wants me to go and view them with him.' She hesitated. 'I don't think he'd feel very happy about living here.'

Livvie could understand that. 'And he's right, Amy. You should start married life on your own, in a home of your own, not here in a house you already feel unhappy in. But we don't have to think about that now, it's still months away. We have to get over Christmas first because there is a good chance Pa will be home for that.'

Amy looked even more dejected. 'It's not going to be a very happy time, Livvie.'

Livvie nodded but then smiled at her. 'Well, we've survived other less than joyful Christmases, Amy.' She thought fleetingly of the first Christmas after Edith had died and the one after, and then last Christmas which she'd shared happily with Hetty and her family. She had been looking forward to celebrating the feast in her own home this year but that didn't look likely now. 'We'll manage. Frank and I will spend the day here with you and Pa and I'm sure Aunt Maud and the family will call in too. Now, what we have to concentrate on is trying to give Pa as much support as we can in the next weeks and it's not going to be easy.'

'Will Frank be able to be with us after . . . after they've told Pa?' Amy asked, thinking that her brother-in-law's presence would give them both some much needed moral support.

'I don't know. I don't know when they are going to tell Pa, but at least they are going to let us know before they do.'

Amy felt that the days ahead were going to be very difficult, which would take some of the shine off viewing the houses Teddy was interested in, one of which would be her new home.

Thomas lay staring at the bare ceiling of the ward. His spirits had plummeted when he'd been told that he was paralysed and would never walk again. Oh, they'd wrapped it up in medical terms but that's what it amounted to – he was now a cripple. If he'd thought after the explosion that things had reached their nadir, when everything he'd worked for and striven to achieve had come crashing down in the ruins of the factory, he now knew he'd been very wrong. Waves of bitterness and anger washed over him. Why had this happened to him? What had he done so wrong in his life that he should be punished like this? Why had the Almighty seen fit to visit such a fate on him? Hadn't he worked hard all his life? Hadn't he lived as Christian a life as he'd been able to although he wasn't a regular church-goer? He gave employment and therefore dignity and security to countless men who might otherwise have struggled to feed their families and keep a roof over their heads. And now . . . now he who had depended on no one but himself would be totally dependent on others to see to his every need.

As he thought more deeply on this his pride was utterly crushed and he burned with humiliation. He'd be dependent on his daughters, which didn't bear thinking about. Or a nurse – a stranger and quite possibly someone like Sister Fletcher, who treated him like a fractious child. For the rest of his life he would be a useless wreck of a man with no dignity, no authority and no pride in himself. The thought was unbearable and as his anger began to drain away he felt a black cloud of despair settle over him. He'd be better off . . . dead.

He heard the door open but he closed his eyes and didn't turn his head. He had no desire to see anyone, especially Sister Fletcher, who would no doubt quote platitudes at him.

Livvie closed the door silently behind her and stood looking at her father, pity, sorrow and trepidation in her eyes. Amy was to be spared this, she thought thankfully, for at both Maud's and her insistence she'd gone to view a house with Teddy. She'd received word that they were going to break the news to her pa today. As she'd walked down the corridor Sister Fletcher had appeared and she'd asked how he'd taken it.

'Not well, I'm afraid.'

What was she to say to him now? she thought. How on earth was she going to try to comfort him?

She walked to the bedside and sat down. 'Pa, it's Livvie,' she began quietly. 'Dr Simms has told you, I know that.'

He didn't open his eyes, turn his head or speak and she bit her lip, praying for strength and that she could find the right words.

'It must be so very, very hard for you, Pa.'

'Go away, Livvie!'

Tears pricked her eyes. 'No, Pa. I'm not leaving you yet. It . . . it's been a terrible shock for us too.'

'Leave me be, Livvie! I'm no use to anyone now! I'd be better off dead!'

She was shocked. 'That's not true! You're lucky to be alive

and you're recovering. Your injuries could have been far worse; Dr Simms said so. You could have suffered brain damage! Think of how terrible that would have been!'

Still he didn't turn towards her.

'You'll be able to come home before Christmas, Pa, where you belong.'

'To what, Livvie? Life as a useless cripple!'

She drew on all her courage. 'Never that! You're our pa; we love you and want you home. When . . . when you're . . . stronger you'll be able to get around. There are bath chairs and you'll still be able to make decisions concerning the factory. You have a *life*! You can't give in to despair, Pa! You can't! For all our sakes, please try to see some hope in the future?' she pleaded.

He didn't reply and as the silence lengthened she realised that it would be useless to try further now. Perhaps when he'd had more time to think he'd at least be able to see that he'd been fortunate to an extent and that his disability didn't mean that his life was useless or over – because it wasn't.

'I'll leave you to rest now, Pa, but I'll see you tomorrow,' she said quietly, getting to her feet.

When she'd gone Thomas opened his eyes. He had no wish to see her tomorrow but he knew that wouldn't stop her. She was determined, as he had once been. In many ways she was like him, or at least the way he had been before . . . She'd shown great strength and loyalty ever since the accident; he admired and respected her for that. And even though it was obvious that she was still fond of him, the feeling of bleak depression didn't lift.

Then, slowly, her words came back to him. His injuries

could have been worse. He could have suffered brain damage and that didn't bear thinking about. He could hope for some kind of a life . . .

Despair gave way to self-pity and he felt tears stinging his eyes. And . . . and she'd said they loved him and wanted him home where he belonged. Had she really meant that? He hadn't given either her or Amy much consideration or affection, he'd even turned Livvie out of her home to fend for herself, so why did they love him? His thoughts turned to Edith. He missed her still and even more so now. He'd loved her from the day he'd first set eyes on her. She'd been more than his wife; she'd been his friend, his support too. Everything he'd worked for had been so she and his girls would have a better life. Perhaps he should have told her just how much he loved and needed her while there had been time, but that hadn't been the way things were between them. She'd known he loved her, she'd not needed to be reassured of it time upon time. She'd known how much he'd longed for a son and she'd never denied him and she'd not blamed him. And poor Mary, she'd not known much happiness in her short life. If only . . .

The tears slowly slid down his cheeks. It was too late now for regrets and he had little left to look forward to. For the first time in days he was relieved when a nurse came in to administer the sedative. He wanted to sleep. He wanted to seek oblivion from the thoughts and emotions that were tormenting him.

Chapter Thirty-Six

All the way home Livvie could not shake off her feelings of anxiety and distress. Oh, she understood that at the present moment he felt useless and bitter, but she hoped that in the days to come his spirits would rally. He couldn't just give up. That had never been his way. Had she said enough? Could she have been firmer with him? Would that have helped? Or should she have been more sympathetic, tried to coax him out of his despair? She just didn't know.

When she arrived home she made herself a cup of tea and sat at the kitchen table, staring into space and wondering vaguely how Amy was getting on. Her sister should be thrilled at the prospect of viewing what might be her new home. Livvie had been when she'd first gone to see Frank's house. Amy should be looking forward to the coming months planning furnishings and the final details of her wedding, but their father's condition overshadowed all that.

When her pa was able to leave hospital it would be Amy who would spend the most time with him and of course the nurse they would engage, just as Amy had had to do with Mary. Livvie would visit as much as she possibly could but what would happen when Amy was married and had moved into her own home, as it was obvious that she and Teddy would do? Their first responsibility would be to their respective husbands. How much time then would her pa spend alone, save for the impersonal care of a paid nurse? Many long hours, she realised, and the thought saddened and distressed her further. It was no way for him to spend the rest of his life. She thought of her mam. Mam wouldn't have wanted him to end his days like that, no matter how dictatorial, self-centred and hard-hearted he'd been in the past. But what could they do?

Slowly, very slowly, the answer to that question crept into her mind. Mam would want her to look after him. Mam wouldn't want him to be cared for by a stranger or have to spend hours alone, unable to move around freely and with no one to talk to, and she was the eldest. Wouldn't it be better if she and Frank moved into the house in Poplar Avenue to help care for him? To try to improve the quality of his day-to-day life, give him an interest in the work in progress in the factory, make him feel he was still part of a family and had a future?

But then the doubts beset her as she refilled her cup. She hated that house. It held so many painful memories: could she ever look on it as 'home' again? And what of Frank? Would it be fair to expect him to give up his own home? Would it be fair to expect him to give up the degree of independence he now had and the life they shared? And what of herself? Would she find it hard to adjust to a very different kind of life? In the short time she'd been married she'd come to love her home and her life with Frank. Her pa had always been a difficult man to live with – hadn't they clashed often enough in the past? – and he'd be worse now that he'd been deprived of his independence, his pride and self-assurance, and his life's work. Could she cope with that? She hoped too that she and Frank would have a family – would that still be possible? Would she be able to care for her father and her children? And what kind of a life would those children have as they grew up, with a bad-tempered grandfather and a mother whose nerves would be rather frayed? A situation which would no doubt result in arguments?

She tried to push all these thoughts away. They must first and foremost see if Pa would try to come to terms with what lay ahead of him. At length she got up and washed her few dishes. She was restless and disturbed in her mind and it would be hours before Frank would be home, she realised. She'd drive herself to distraction if she stayed here. She'd go and see Maud, she decided. She felt in need of someone to talk to and perhaps Amy would be back and with good news concerning the house.

'How is he, Livvie?' Bessie asked as she took Livvie's coat and hat.

'Very low in spirits, I'm afraid, Bessie. They told him this morning that he's paralysed and it's hit him hard.'

Bessie nodded. It must be a terrible thing for a man like him to have to face but he'd just have to accept it. Well, her mam always said the Lord worked in mysterious ways and maybe now Thomas Goodwin would think about how badly he'd treated his family in the past, including his poor deceased second wife. It was a sobering thought.

As Bessie showed her through to the drawing room, Maud welcomed her warmly and asked Bessie to bring some tea.

'I wondered if Amy and Teddy might be back and I . . . I, well, I didn't feel as if I could stay on my own until Frank got home.'

'I take it you've been in to see your father?' Maud deduced.

Livvie nodded. 'They told him this morning and he's devastated! I think he's very bitter about it.'

Maud looked sympathetic. 'That's only to be expected, Livvie. It must have come as a terrible blow to him – to all of you.'

Livvie bit her lip. 'He said . . . he said he'd be better off dead!'

Maud frowned. 'I hope you told him that he's very lucky to be alive? Three of his workers are not so fortunate and neither are their families.'

Livvie nodded. 'I did and I stressed that the doctor said his injuries could have been worse but I could tell he wasn't listening, that he couldn't really . . . care.'

'Give him time, Livvie. It sounds as if he's feeling very sorry for himself and I suppose that's only natural too.'

'I hope he'll try to accept it in the future but I've been wondering about how we are going to manage now? When he comes home, I mean. Of course we'll engage a good nurse – Dr Sumner should be able to help with that – and Amy will be with him too – until February. I'll come to see him as often as I can but . . . but I can't help thinking that after Amy's married he'll be alone for a lot of the time and . . . and that's upsetting me. It's not what Mam would have wanted. So, I was thinking that perhaps Frank and I should move—'

Maud nodded her understanding; she could see where Livvie's train of thought was leading, but it was a serious matter. 'Have you mentioned any of this to Frank?' she interrupted.

'No.'

'Then I think you should, Livvie. It's a very big step for you both to take. It will change your lives entirely and maybe even put a strain on your marriage.' Maud paused, choosing her words carefully. 'Now, this might sound . . . harsh, but, well, your father is no longer a young man and he has lived his life exactly as he pleased, and you have to admit that he gave little thought to either you or Amy and what you both wanted from life. Oh, I'm not judging him; that's not for me to do. But now that everything has changed I think you should think very carefully about giving up your home and your independence. Both you and Frank have your lives ahead of you; Frank has already taken on the huge responsibility of the running of the factory for him and when you have children, Livvie, you will have their futures to think of too. I agree your mother wouldn't have wanted him to end his days a lonely and probably embittered old man, but I urge you, Livvie, don't make any hasty decisions out of a sense of loyalty to Edith or duty to your father.'

'Oh, Aunt Maud, I'm even more confused now,' Livvie admitted.

'Talk to Frank. He's your husband and I know he'll share and understand your anxieties and your doubts.'

Livvie nodded. 'I will.'

Maud smiled. 'Your pa will come to terms with what life now holds for him. It will take time but eventually he will.

He'll have to,' she finished firmly. Then she decided that a change of subject was required. 'Well, I think that when Teddy and Amy get back they'll have made up their minds. Teddy wasn't all that keen on the first house but this one is much better and not too far away either. It's in Walton Park, which is a lovely road, rather like this one. It's large enough for a family without being too big. And the price is reasonable.'

Livvie smiled at her. 'It sounds ideal and Amy deserves to have something to take her mind off Pa. It's hard for her, especially when this should be a happy and exciting time.'

'She's not a child now, Livvie, and you've both had a lot to contend with recently. But don't forget what I've said. Think long and hard before you make any decisions.'

Livvie rose and kissed her on the cheek. 'I will and thank you, Aunt Maud, for . . . for, well, being here. I felt I needed someone older and wiser to talk to.'

Maud nodded, thinking that although now a grown woman it was obvious Livvie still missed her mother.

Livvie decided to give the matter more thought before she broached the subject with Frank, for she knew he was very preoccupied with keeping the factory running at full production, and she wanted time to digest Maud's advice. It was true her pa had lived his life exactly as he'd wanted to and there hadn't been much consideration given to Amy and herself. In fact the way he'd treated her after she'd been arrested and had viewed her marriage to Frank still rankled, but she also knew what her mother would have expected of her.

Over the next few days both she and Frank noticed with

concern that Thomas's mood and spirits did not lift. Frank always tried to interest him in the news of the factory and ask his opinions, although there was little response. His physical condition, however, was improving and thankfully as the week passed Livvie was relieved to notice that he seemed a little less depressed, although he didn't converse freely. During that time she'd been in a constant state of anxiety and uncertainty and had finally decided that she would have to tell Frank why for he'd remarked on it on more than one occasion.

'Frank, there's something I'd like to talk to you about,' she began tentatively after they'd returned home from the hospital that weekend. Frank had spoken at great length about how the factory was now running and she'd watched her pa's face during that time and seen the spark of interest that had come into his eyes. It was the first sign of animation she'd spotted so far and it had made her think that if they were to move into her old home, where he would feel less cut off from his old world, it might well aid her father's recovery.

Frank nodded and put his arm around her shoulders, drawing her to him. 'There's something troubling you, Livvie, and I don't think it's entirely to do with your pa's condition. There's more to it, isn't there?'

She nodded. 'It's been bothering me a great deal that when Amy is married, he'll be spending a lot of time on his own – apart from the nurse. Of course both Amy and I will visit as often as we can but . . . but it won't be the same as . . .'

'As having his family living there with him too,' he ventured. He'd been almost certain that this was what had been worrying her and he too had been giving it a deal of thought.

'How did you know?' she asked, surprised but glad that it was out in the open now.

He kissed her on the forehead. 'Because I know you, Livvie, and despite everything you care about him. You're a very caring person.'

'I keep thinking him being left alone so much is not what Mam would have wanted, but Aunt Maud said I had to remember that Pa's no longer a young man and . . . and that we have our lives ahead of us and that he hasn't given us much thought or consideration in the past.'

Frank nodded his agreement to that. 'That's very true, Livvie, but I don't think dwelling on past wrongs is the right way for us to think now.'

'She also said I . . . we might find it very difficult to adapt to a new life, a loss of our independence.'

'She's right, but if worrying and feeling guilty about your pa all the time is going to upset you so much, then life isn't going to be very happy for either of us in the long term.'

She could see his point but she was still unsure. 'But you'd have to give up everything and I don't feel as if it's fair of me to expect that.'

'So would you, Livvie,' he reminded her gently.

'Oh, I just don't know what to do for the best. I'm so confused. But today when you were talking to him I saw that he was really taking an interest for the first time and then I began to feel that . . . well, we should move in with him.'

Frank had already made his decision. He knew she would fret if they didn't and that was something he didn't want her to have to suffer. The strain would make her feel constantly guilty and miserable. 'After Christmas, Livvie, we'll move into

Poplar Avenue to be with him. It will allow Amy more time to concentrate on her wedding and give us time to adjust.'

She looked up at him, the tears stinging her eyes. 'Are you really sure that's what you want to do?'

'I am. Are you?'

She nodded slowly.

'I want my wife to be happy and you won't be unless you can help care for him. You'd always be blaming yourself for not doing what your mother would have expected of you, you know you would. And I'd suggest that it won't be for very long because the house isn't at all suitable: hopefully in time he will be able to get around in a bath chair and there are far too many stairs.' He smiled down at her, seeing the relief in her eyes. 'And I know that you are not very fond of that house.'

'I'm not,' she replied firmly.

'Then shall we sell it?' he continued 'Perhaps the money from the sale of Poplar Avenue can go towards rebuilding the factory?' When his father-in-law was out of hospital he was going to have to discuss with him the finance for rebuilding. In fact they would have to discuss many things. 'And this one too and buy something that will be more suitable for all of us?'

Livvie looked thoughtful. Although she loved this house Frank's suggestion was the solution to the dilemma. She nodded and smiled. 'Yes, I think that would be best.'

'So now, Livvie, do you feel happier and easier in your mind?'

She hugged him tightly. 'I do, and . . . thank you.'

'For what? For loving my wife and wanting her to be happy?'

'It won't be easy, Frank, not if he doesn't try to make an effort to look at the rest of his life with some optimism.'

'I know but I'm sure it will help if he knows he's going to have his family around to help care for him.'

She nodded. 'No doubt there will be rows. You know what he can be like.'

He managed a wry smile. 'Oh, I know that only too well but he needs us, Livvie, and Amy too.'

She smiled back. 'And I don't suppose that fact will please him either, but I'll tell him of our decision tomorrow. It might just make him start to look forward to going home. And I'll tell Amy too. I know she at least will be happy about it and will now be able to enjoy the time leading up to her wedding.'

Frank got to his feet and poured them both a drink. 'Here's to a new and probably very different life, Livvie. But we'll cope with whatever it brings – between us.'

She smiled at him, thinking that she was so very fortunate to have such a loving, caring and considerate husband. She couldn't wish for anyone better.

Livvie felt much calmer and more confident now, she thought as she went to the hospital the next day and was pleased to see her father half sitting up, aided by pillows.

'You look much better today, Pa,' she greeted him.

'If you say so, Livvie,' he mumbled.

'Well, they've got you sitting up, so that's an improvement.'

Thomas didn't reply. It had been frustrating to have to be hauled into a semi-upright position while pillows were piled around and behind him.

'And Frank and I have been discussing what we're going to do when you go home.'

Thomas looked away. He'd been thinking about that too and it had depressed him still further. What was there to go 'home' to?

'You'll be able to spend Christmas at home, Pa, and we'll all try to make it as festive as possible, and then . . . well, then Frank and I have decided that we'll move into Poplar Avenue – if you'd like us to, of course?' she added hastily. After all it was his home, and he should at least be consulted. 'And then later on when you no longer need a nurse and are able to get around more, we could think about looking for somewhere more suitable where we could all live – together.'

Again Thomas said nothing. Despite himself he'd been thinking of what would happen to him after Amy got married in February. Both girls would then have husbands and homes of their own; they'd have little time to spare for him. A burden to everyone. What use would his money and his business be to him now? His days would be spent in bitter solitude with only some officious nurse like Sister Fletcher for company. His despair had deepened until he'd felt crushed beneath it all. But now . . . now Livvie was saying she and Frank wouldn't let him suffer that fate. They wanted him to live with them, in a new house. He hardly dared to believe it. Slowly he nodded his agreement.

Livvie smiled, relieved that he wasn't going to be awkward. 'Frank said that we really should look for another house as there are too many stairs in Poplar Avenue. So, we're going to sell our house and after Christmas we'll start to search for one—' She was about to chatter on about their plans to keep up a sense of optimism but he interrupted her.

'I might be a cripple, Livvie, but what I don't want from either of you is . . . pity!'

She stared at him hard for a few seconds and then pursed her lips. 'Oh, you'll get no "pity" from me, I can assure you. I'm the one who needs "pitying". I'm the one who's going to have to live with the stubborn, irascible and sheer bloody-minded man that you are, Pa!'

He stared back astounded, and then slowly he began to smile. 'I'm all those things, Livvie, aren't I?'

She laughed as she nodded her agreement. For the first time since the accident she saw a glimpse of the man he'd always been: proud and determined. The father she still loved. 'It's not going to be easy for any of us, Pa, but we'll cope. We'll make a new life, I promise you that.'

He continued to smile as he nodded. He'd been wrong in the decisions he'd made concerning both her and Frank and he regretted that, but now at least he could begin to look forward. The darkness of despair was beginning to lift.

Epilogue

━━━◆━━━

1914

It was shaping up to be a long warm summer if these past weeks were anything to go by, Livvie thought as she and Violet carried the tea things out into the garden that Sunday afternoon. A mild May had turned to June and the sky was a clear azure blue and the garden drenched in sunlight. Amy and Teddy had called as they usually did every week to visit her pa, Frank, herself and baby Thomas, who was fast asleep in his pram in the shade of the elder tree. She smiled to herself as she made her way towards the little group sitting in the arbour. She loved this house; you could see the sea from one of the front bedrooms – in the far distance of course. It had been Frank's idea to move to Blundellsands further down the coast towards Southport, even though it took him longer to travel to the factory.

'It's a quiet residential area and I'm sure the air will be beneficial to your father's health,' he'd assured her when she'd voiced some doubts. Once she'd seen the house all those doubts had disappeared. It was a large modern bungalow set in lovely gardens and not far from the railway station where Frank could get the train that ran along the coast to Liverpool. She could also get a train into Southport which she knew had wonderful shops in its arcades and the air would indeed benefit her pa and he would be able to get around fairly easily in his bath chair.

'I thought we'd have tea outside, it's such a gorgeous day,' she informed her family as she set the tray down on the wrought-iron garden table.

'This weather looks set to hold,' Amy added as she helped Livvie with the cups and saucers.

'It's very pleasant to sit out here in the garden in the fresh sea air. Makes a change from being stuck in the office of the haulage yard,' Teddy remarked.

'Or in a factory,' Frank added.

'It puts me in mind of the summer we had some years ago – do you remember it, Frank? The factory was like a furnace,' Thomas said, thinking back to the summer when Mary had miscarried and Livvie had been out somewhere with Frank, he couldn't remember where. His memory wasn't as sharp these days, he mused. It hadn't been since the accident. It had been a long, slow recovery and for months he'd railed against his infirmity; he was aware that it had been a far from easy time for Livvie but she'd not complained. Of course Nurse Connors had been a very different kettle of fish but he'd come to respect her abrupt and forthright comments and in time he'd learned to accept his condition. He could get around the house and garden in the bath chair, which gave him a degree of independence. At first he'd not been happy about giving up the house in Poplar Avenue but, like Livvie, once he'd realised that this was an even better area and a more modern and – for his needs – a more manageable house, he'd resigned himself to it.

'I hope it won't get as hot as that summer, Tom. As I recall it was unbearable for everyone but especially the men,' Frank reminded him. They treated each other almost as equals these days, although he always gave the older man the respect he felt his age, position and experience deserved. The part of the factory that had been destroyed had at last been rebuilt and new and more modern machinery installed; new safety measures had also been introduced, for no one had realised before that some of the ingredients they used were combustible, which had caused the explosion. He now had a good manager and assistant manager and reliable foremen, including Billy Grey, all of whom lessened his workload, and the business was profitable. They were one of the best employers in the city, paying a fair wage, and although there was still a great deal of industrial unrest it did not seem to affect them to a great extent.

'Mother is talking about going to somewhere on the North Wales coast for two or three weeks if it gets very hot and I don't blame her,' Teddy informed them. Maud had persuaded Charles to retire last year after he'd suffered a mild stroke and Teddy now ran the business, so he and Frank had become not only business associates but friends and of course, when he'd married Amy, brothers-in-law.

'That might be something you should consider, Livvie,' said Frank. 'You could take Tom and the baby to somewhere like Rhos-on-Sea. We could rent a house and I could come over at weekends and when we shut the factory down for the week's holiday of course.'

'How would you manage by yourself?' Livvie asked, smiling.

'I managed very well, Mrs Hadley, before we were married, if you remember? And Violet will be coming in each day so I won't starve.'

'Would you like that, Pa? A few weeks in Wales by the sea?' Livvie asked.

'Maybe, but I don't see how you can push the pram and this bath chair,' he replied.

'I could come too, if you won't mind, Teddy?' Amy suggested. She and Livvie got on so well together now, she thought, and had done ever since she'd left Poplar Avenue and all its depressing memories.

'I won't mind. It would be good for you too, my love. I could come over at weekends too.'

'It would certainly do little Thomas good,' Livvie thought aloud and then sighed as a fretful wail came from the pram beneath the tree. 'Sounds as if he's awake,' she announced, getting to her feet.

The baby stared up at her with eyes the same colour as her own and waved his little fists as she picked him up. He'd be six months old in a couple of weeks and he was the pride and joy of his father and grandfather. Her own love for him knew no bounds.

'Oh, let me hold him, Livvie, please,' Amy begged and, smiling, Livvie duly passed her son over to his aunt. Selina and Henry now had two children and Amy and Teddy were expecting their first in six months' time. Emily and Bessie were married and Maggie engaged and Annie now worked for Maud, having left her previous employment. Bessie had suggested to Maud that her youngest sister take her place when she left and Maud had agreed. Maud had also persuaded Charles to help in obtaining an apprenticeship for young Stanley and Hetty had been delighted that the lad – unlike his father – would have a trade and earn a decent steady living.

'Well, seeing as we are all here together, this little lad included, I've something to tell you,' Thomas announced, producing a document from his pocket and handing it to Frank. This was the right time to make the announcement, he thought. All the years he'd hoped and longed for a son to pass his business on to were in the past; Frank was the closest thing he had to a son and a fine substitute, and he did now of course have a grandson. More than that, he was proud of both his daughters. He'd come to realise that both were intelligent women, as were the nursing staff both in the hospital and at home, for whom he had great respect.

'What's this?' Frank asked, looking bemused.

'Read it,' Thomas instructed.

Livvie looked at her father quizzically. While he could still be irascible at times he'd certainly mellowed and he was looking very pleased with himself about something now. 'What have you done, Pa?'

'I've changed the name of the business, Livvie. Something that's long overdue. It's no longer "Goodwin's Animal Feeds" . . .'

'It's "Hadley and Goodwin Ltd, Manufacturers of Animal Feeds",' Frank read out.

'Frank and Livvie, it's yours and in time will be little Thomas's. It's all been done legally.'

Frank looked up from the document, stunned. 'I don't know what to say, Tom. I . . . We never expected . . .'

Livvie got to her feet and hugged her father. 'Oh, Pa! Thank you!'

'You both deserve it,' Amy added happily. She was content with her life; she didn't begrudge Livvie and Frank the inheritance for they'd taken on the responsibility of both her father and the factory. Mayhew's Haulage would be Teddy's one day, they had a beautiful home and she wanted for nothing – not now that they too were to become a family.

'Oh, that's enough fussing, Livvie, the child is wondering what's going on,' Thomas said with mock severity although everyone could see he was pleased.

'This certainly calls for something a bit stronger than tea, Livvie,' Frank urged, still trying to come to terms with the fact that the factory now belonged to Livvie and himself.

Livvie laughed. 'I'm really not fond of champagne, as you know, but I think there's a bottle of wine in the larder, on the marble slab so it will be chilled. I'll go and get it. This is certainly a day to celebrate.'

'I'll fetch the glasses,' Amy offered, handing little Thomas to his grandfather.

The baby was instantly attracted by the sunlight shining on his grandfather's gold watch chain with its heavy fob and reached out to grasp it. His grandfather chuckled. 'Now, little Tom, you can't have everything. This will be for your Aunt Amy's little boy, something for him to remember me by.'

'Pa, it might be a girl,' Amy reminded him, smiling. 'Will she not get it?'

He considered this but then nodded. 'She will, Amy. Times are changing, I have to admit,' he conceded although he knew he probably wouldn't live to see them. Well, he thought, that might not be a bad thing. Not judging by the way events in Europe were heading.

The two girls paused before entering the house and looked back at the little family group.

'Did you ever think you would see the day when Pa would admit that times are changing, Livvie?'

Livvie smiled as she shook her head. 'No, and I never thought he'd do something like giving us his precious factory. There was a time when I thought he'd give me nothing and I wanted nothing from him either.'

'Mam would have been pleased,' Amy added a little wistfully.

'She would but I somehow think she does know,' Livvie replied, a note of sadness in her voice. Then she laughed. 'Let's get the wine and glasses for a toast before my son decides Pa's watch fob is no longer of any interest to him.' And with their arms around other's waists they went into the house.

Note on Women's Suffrage

It was as far back as 1897 when Millicent Fawcett founded the National Union of Women's Suffrage Societies in Great Britain, prompted no doubt by the fact that women in New Zealand were given the vote in 1893. It was the general consensus of male thinking at this time in this country that women could simply not understand how Parliament worked and should therefore have no say in the affairs of this establishment. Not a view that went down well with the majority of the female population, who were increasingly becoming better educated!

The movement gained in popularity and in 1903 the wife and daughters of the Manchester MP and lawyer Richard Pankhurst – Emmeline, Christabel and Sylvia – formed the Women's Social and Political Union (to become known as the 'suffragettes') with the aim of gaining the right to vote for all women. Their campaign was characterised by their slogan 'Deeds not Words' – a reference to the fact that the politicians refused even to speak to them – which actively encouraged civil disobedience. They demonstrated, chained themselves to railings, refused to pay fines and taxes and eventually resorted to arson and vandalism, incurring harsh prison sentences.

Their response to such treatment was to go on hunger strike, thus causing as much disruption for the prison authorities as possible, who in turn resorted to the painful, degrading and frankly appalling process of force-feeding, which often resulted in damage to long-term health. Two major events in their campaign occurred in 1913: the partial destruction of the home of the Prime Minister, David Lloyd George, and the death of Emily Davison, who threw herself in front of the King's horse Anmer during the Derby at Epsom and was tragically killed.

With the outbreak of the First World War in August 1914 Mrs Pankhurst suspended all suffragette activities and urged women to support the war effort, which they did to such an effective degree that when the war ended in 1918 the first Representation of the People Act was passed. This gave the right to vote to all men aged twenty-one and over and to women aged thirty and over, providing they met the stipulated, stringent property requirements or were married to a man who did – not exactly what the suffragettes had been demanding.

It was not until 2 July 1928, with the second Representation of the People Act, that women of twenty-one and over were given the right to vote with no restrictions attached.

It had been a long fight undertaken by many brave, determined and dedicated women. A hard-won battle on behalf of all the women of the United Kingdom!

Lyn Andrews
2016

**Read about the inspiration
for the novel in a Q&A with**

*Lyn
Andrews*

Q&A with Lyn Andrews

Why did you choose to set LIVERPOOL SISTERS in the early 1900s?

I chose to set the book then mainly because my inspiration for the novel was my great-aunt Rose, who was a young woman with a mind and will of her own and who was growing to maturity at that time.

How closely does the novel stick to Rose's own story?

The story does stick quite closely to what I know of Rose Gorry. My great-grandfather, William, was a self-made businessman – a wealthy coal merchant – and had a typical Victorian attitude toward his wives and daughters. My great-grandmother, Mary Farmer, died leaving four children. William married again relatively quickly as the youngest child was only two, and Mary O'Donnell, his new wife, was not much older than his two eldest daughters. She was indeed kept in the dark about their ages, something we today find it hard to believe or understand. For years I thought she must have been incredibly weak-willed and naïve, until I understood more about the attitude of Victorian men towards women.

William was horrified when Rose became a suffragette and outraged when she went to prison. He did throw her out and he later went on to throw out my grandmother too, because she wanted to marry a non-Catholic. She ignored him and married my grandfather just the same, and it was a long and happy marriage! Both my grandmother and Rose (and Anne, another daughter) were denied any share in the business when William died. This was not solely because they'd greatly displeased him, but because they were women and therefore he did not think them capable of running a business. Everything was left to his three sons. William died rather prematurely and some would say needlessly. He was kicked from one of his shire horses and he neglected the wound, which turned septic and led to blood poisoning.

What research did you do on the women's suffrage movement and the local meetings that Livvie begins attending? Did you use many real-life accounts of women who joined the cause?

There is a great deal of information now on the internet about the women's suffrage movement in all parts of the country, including many photographs which I found useful, particularly for the Liverpool Suffrage Movement. The involvement of Lady Lytton, her imprisonment under an assumed name, and the imprisonment and shocking treatment of both Selina Martin and Leslie Hall, are well documented.

The tragedy of the *Titanic* sinking occurs towards the end of the novel. What effect do you think the disaster had on the shipping industry in Liverpool and people's confidence in the increasing size of ships and their use for travel?

The sinking of the *Titanic* shocked the world but particularly devastated the ports of both Southampton and Liverpool, and of course Belfast where she was built. The horrors of the naval battles and the attacks on merchant shipping in World War I were still in the future and so for decades it would be viewed as the greatest ever maritime tragedy. It did not, however, seem to have much impact upon the shipping industries in either Liverpool or Southampton, particularly as new safety measures and laws were introduced. Mass immigration to America continued, with passengers travelling mainly with the longer-established Cunard Line, whose ships had – and still have – an enviable safety record. It was Cunard's *Carpathia* which picked up the survivors of the *Titanic*, and Cunard has never lost a ship in peacetime. People's confidence in the increasing size (and speed) of these transatlantic liners certainly didn't diminish as bigger ships were built, for it was the only way to cross the Atlantic for many years to come.

The novel ends in June 1914, a few months before the First World War begins. Why did you choose to end the story here, with the characters looking forward to the summer ahead, unaware of the events that are going to unfold?

I chose to end the story just before the outbreak of the Great War, when Olivia and Amy, and of course Thomas Goodwin himself, had achieved a degree of happiness and strengthened family bonds and were looking forward to the future. They had no knowledge of the utter carnage that lay ahead and of how that conflict would change the world they knew, so I thought it best to end the story there. In any case, I have covered the Great War in earlier novels, such as MIST OVER THE MERSEY, ANGELS OF MERCY and LIVERPOOL ANGELS.

Lyn Andrews

'An outstanding storyteller' *Woman's Weekly*

Now you can buy any of these bestselling books from your bookshop or direct from Lyn's publisher.

To order simply call this number: **01235 827 702**
Or visit our website: **www.headline.co.uk**